A DRAGONBIRD IN THE FERN

A DRAGONBIRD IN THE FERN

LAURA RUECKERT

flux
®

Mendota Heights, Minnesota

First Edition
First Printing, 2021

Book design by Jake Nordby
Cover design by Sarah Taplin
Cover images by lady-luck/Shutterstock

Flux, an imprint of North Star Editions, Inc.

Library of Congress Cataloging-in-Publication Data (pending)
978-1-63583-065-1

Flux
North Star Editions, Inc.
2297 Waters Drive
Mendota Heights, MN 55120
www.fluxnow.com

Printed in Canada

For my mom, who believed when I didn't.

Stekk llens
islands

FARNSKAG

Stundvar
River

Baaldarstad

STÄRKLAND

LOFTARIA

Caotina

AZZARIA

CHAPTER 1

My shoulders stretched the silk of my split-skirted *zintella* dress as I wrenched myself up to the highest branch that would still carry my weight. A mother dragonbird in the rainbow-colored nest above cawed and flapped her wings in an attempt to drive me away. If only one of her feathers would flutter down to me. I stilled, waiting until the long-tailed, kitten-sized bird stopped panicking. But time was running out. I'd need to get the feather straight from the nest.

The iridescent blue and green bird dove down at my face then hovered, battering me with its wings. I couldn't risk injuring her or the ritual wouldn't work. My sister had been murdered nearly three months ago, but already she was making her presence—and her anger—known. The Servants of the gods said successfully completing the ritual wouldn't drive Scilla's ghost away, but it could lessen her power . . . at least for a time.

With every day that passed, her humanity receded further. Two days ago, while paying our respects at the memorial stone, my older brother Llandro and I had both yelped from the sudden jagged scratches on our arms. A scratch was harmless for now. But we all knew the stories, knew it wouldn't remain that way. Hopefully, completing the ritual would give Father time to release Scilla from her anger, release her from this world. And keep the rest of us from permanent damage—or worse.

But only if I did my part first. I curled into the tree trunk, pressing my lips together to avoid a mouthful of feathers. As gently as possible, I brushed the dragonbird away, and she landed just out of reach.

"I won't hurt you or your babies. I promise," I muttered as she hopped frantically along a thick twig.

I didn't quite trust the branch not to splinter below me, so I circled the trunk with one arm and groped up into the overly large, prickly nest above my head, praying for the sensation of one of those long, beautiful feathers against my fingertips.

Dry grass . . . twigs . . . fluffy down. That wouldn't do. The mother bird screeched at me. One egg, then two. A silky length! My heart sang even as my arm muscles cried out. I plucked the feather from the nest and hugged the trunk with both arms, subjecting my eyes to the danger of the dragonbird's beak for only a blink. One brilliant, clean feather.

"Thank you," I whispered. Now we had a chance.

I made my way down the tree faster than I should have, skidding my palms along the bark when the dragonbird shrieked and dive-bombed me. My satchel waited at the base of the tree with the other components meant to persuade the gods to shield our family from an earthwalker's deadly rage. Scilla's ghost hadn't done much more than make her presence clear so far. But even children knew that peace wouldn't last long.

Carefully, I set the feather into the bag and trudged up the hill to the memorial field. Neat rows of stones, one for each of our ancestors, stood here, smoothed by centuries of winds off the ocean. I rounded the field to stand before the only stone that was new and sharply chiseled: my sister Scilla's. I clasped my hands, brought them to my heart, and moved them up to the sky in the Commitment to the gods. "My heart in your hands."

The collections of shells were still more or less neatly stacked on top of Scilla's memorial stone. The stack created by my little brother Zito was more of a loose pile. Despite the passage of time since we'd stood on the aft deck of the royal *scritarra* at sundown and returned Scilla to the sea, Gio, the wind god, hadn't managed to knock over our offerings to ease her spirit.

A salty breeze rose up the hill from the bay. A pod of dolphins swam, cresting two at a time. I wished I were in the water now, the waves rocking me like when Scilla and I had learned to swim as small children. The wind blew again, weakly, and the sweat from my climb began to dry. But here in the memorial field, the gentle breeze couldn't hide Scilla's presence from me. A brush against my hand, a whisper against my neck. Back and forth. Pacing, restless. We needed protection before her power and anger grew.

One by one, I removed the objects from the satchel. First, the pearl my oldest brother Llandro had wrested from the sea. That was for the god of water. Next, the cup of dirt Father had brought back from the site of Scilla's murder, for the goddess of earth. Mother had clipped the crisp yellow flowers that followed the sun with their heads for the sun goddess. Finally, I retrieved my part of the appeasement: the dragonbird feather for Gio, god of winds. Feathers from other birds were easier to come by, but Scilla would know how special the dragonbird feather was and that it was from me. I prayed it would make a difference.

I placed the objects at the base of the memorial stone, lined up in the order of power each god possessed: the pearl; the bundle of flowers; the feather, stabbed into the earth so it wouldn't blow away; the cup of dirt. I bowed my head.

Please help Scilla. Please slow the darkness engulfing her heart. Give us time to find her murderer.

As the Queen of Azzaria, Mother was busy governing, with Llandro by her side like always, learning all he could for the day when he would become King. Father's first priority was the investigation into Scilla's death, so I'd volunteered to make the offering. The rest of the family would arrive later to pray. For now, my lone requests felt so pitiful, so weak. If only someone could do more. Even the gods had limits when murder touched a person's heart.

Scilla's impatience weighed down the air around me. Her questions from beyond were shivers on my neck. Why hadn't we figured out who her killer was yet? Why hadn't we brought them to justice?

I imagined her imploring, *Do something, Jiara. Save me from an afterlife as an earthwalker.*

With one finger, I brushed back a few stray strands of my hair Gio had begun to play with. There was no time for games. Not now. Not when a murderer was on the loose.

Until now, Scilla's spirit had remained with her memorial stone on the hill. It wouldn't be long before her demand for answers grew and she invaded the town or the palace, haunting Mother and Father and Llandro and me, and someday, when Scilla had lost the remaining traces of humanity, even little Zito. Father and Llandro had stopped visiting the memorial stone with Llandro's first scratch. Perhaps they were hoping she'd forget them. They'd come to pray later today as part of the ritual, but after that . . . some people said it was better to stay away, to avoid drawing the attention of a ghost.

What must it be like for an earthwalker? Trapped in our world but separate from us, loneliness, anger, and helplessness filling their hearts until they had no choice but to lash out, hurting those they loved?

"Jiara!" called a voice from down the hill. Between the memorial field's rustling palm trees and the bustling city with its almost two hundred canals far beyond, a short, wiry boy raised both arms above his head and waved.

I stood, brushed loose blades of grass and tiny chips of bark from my *zintella* dress, and waved back. "Be nice to him, Scilla," I murmured, turning to the light tickle on my left arm. "Don't forget. He's still young."

Everyone said you couldn't reason with an earthwalker, that even trying just focused their attention further, but how could I not talk to her? She was my sister. Just because she died, it didn't mean I stopped loving her.

Zito was the surprise baby, an unexpected gift from the gods, and ten years younger than the next youngest—me at seventeen. He bounded up the steep slope as fast as he could. His grin slipped from his face, and his hands moved in the Commitment as he stared at Scilla's memorial. Out of breath, he huffed, "May you dwell in peace, Scilla." He glanced down at the treasures near the base of the stone and whispered the names of the gods. "My heart in your hands. Please help Scilla."

I nodded at him. My throat tightened as the tickle moved to my neck, but Zito turned to me as if he hadn't felt anything. "Jiara." He huffed again. "The Bone Eaters are here."

"Zito!" He wasn't supposed to use the somewhat offensive term for the Farnskagers, potential allies to the north. At least no one was around to hear the mild insult, and due to distance and lack of trade, hardly any of them spoke our language. But I shook my head because he must have heard wrong. "They aren't expected for another two weeks."

Zito held both hands over his head, shaking an imaginary staff or spear, like the Farnskagers did when they were trying to impress their enemies with a war cry. He opened his mouth and waggled his tongue in what was supposed to be an intimidating growl. Despite the sanctity of the memorial field, his bright eyes were so silly a little laugh escaped my lips.

"Mother said they read the date wrong." His face had sobered, but now his tongue was outstretched again, and I shook my head.

How could the Farnskagers read the date wrong? The trip here took two weeks by carriage. Wouldn't they be especially careful to time it correctly? Especially when the visit involved their monarch?

As eldest princess of Azzaria, Scilla had been engaged to Raffar, the Farnskager king. Paying his respects was an obligation he couldn't avoid. But he should have waited until the date specified in Mother's missive, until the Time of Tears was over for us. This was Scilla's time to dissolve her bindings to us and to move on to the afterlife. It was also our three months to mourn. Only now, toward the end, were we supposed to begin bringing ourselves back to thoughts of our normal lives, to begin thinking of how to let go. The king was here too soon.

For Zito's benefit, I tried to shake off the weight of my sorrow. I snatched at his still outstretched tongue.

"Hey!" he yelled with a laugh, stumbling backward between Scilla's and Grandfather's memorial stones.

"Where are the Farnskagers now?" I asked.

"Resting in the east wing."

I nodded. Father would have had the rooms readied immediately. But Zito had hiked up here to the memorial field for a reason. "And?"

"Mother wishes to speak with you," Zito said, his words muffled by grubby hands protecting his tongue from my fingers.

Especially with foreign guests here, as the ruling monarch, Mother would be busy. I couldn't leave her waiting. I dropped a hand to Zito's shoulder. "Come on. Let's go."

With a last glance at the memorial stone and our offerings to the gods, I followed my little brother as he scampered down the hill as fast as he could, his arms flailing in the air. My eyes turned from the crowded city and its bustling canals to the tranquil, sparkling bay. Considering the appearance of the foreign delegation, it would probably be the last calm any of us would have for weeks.

Goodbye for now, Scilla. We'll find your killer, and you'll have eternal peace.

I promise.

Queen Ginevora of Azzaria, the ruling monarch and my mother, sat at the ornate desk in her office. Her hands lay flat on the polished mahogany desktop where countless contracts had been signed and sealed. Where laws had been written. Where criminals had been condemned or pardoned.

Mother's eyelids were closed, like they always were when she meditated on difficult decisions, so I watched her for a few seconds. Her hair was still shiny black, twisted in the complicated, elegant hairstyle of a married monarch. Under one of her fanciest embroidered sapphire gowns, worn only for special occasions, her frame was strong and her heart healthy. It would be a long time before Llandro, her eldest child, would need to take control of the country.

Mother inhaled a deep breath and opened her eyes. "Jiara." Her smile for me fled far too quickly, and her gaze moved strangely, hesitantly to the floor.

"What is it, Mother?" I asked. "Is there a problem with our guests?"

She shook her head and motioned me to the desk. "Your father had someone take care of their elephant birds and had their luggage brought in. They're resting from the journey."

Resting. An image, like one out of my dreams: Raffar, the young Farnskager king, only a couple of years older than me, lying on his back in a verdant field, his eyes closed, his tattoos waiting to be traced by my fingers.

Mother clasped her hands together with a quiet *clap*, stopping my wicked thoughts. "We must talk about your future."

Nodding, I exhaled and perched on the edge of her desk like thousands of times before. My future was clear and meaningful. In a few months, when I turned eighteen and was of proper marrying age, I'd be officially engaged to Duke Marro Berdonando Riccardi from Flissina, up near the northern border. With the Loftarians, our biggest enemies, only fifty miles away from Flissina, it was important that Mother strengthen our ties to the northern people and show them how important they were for our nation. Only last week, there'd been an attack—six dead. I'd be far enough from the violence to be safe and close enough to support those affected by the contested border. Mother would deal with our enemies, and I'd make sure our people knew they hadn't been left alone.

As for Marro, my future husband, he was . . . acceptable. Whenever he visited, he had a book in his hands. He answered questions politely when I asked, but never pestered for my attention like some others who sought to ingratiate themselves with the ruling family. Mother and Father expected me to be nervous, but Marro was a good man. Even my best friend Pia said so, and she took a long time to trust people. Marro'd probably never be the type to paddle the northern rivers and lakes with me or to hike through the forest to reach our remotest villages, like I dreamed of doing. But he'd surely support me in my efforts to improve morale and gather whatever messages or worries needed to be sent to the queen.

Muffled footsteps rushed past the outside of the office, and I stowed my daydreams in the back of my mind. Instead of launching into her thoughts, Mother remained quiet, her gaze on the polished dark wood floor. Her brow furrowed, and my heart constricted. Something wasn't right.

"Did something happen to Marro?" I asked. His palace was nowhere near where the border skirmishes usually took place, but . . .

Mother raised a hand. "Marro is fine. But it seems he should not be your husband after all."

My mouth opened, as if words should come out. But what could I say? Marro was . . . pleasant. But that was all.

"I'm not going to Flissina?"

"No."

I waited for some kind of emotional reaction from within myself, but I must have used it all up on Scilla. More than anything, I'd miss the idea of hours on the water, rainbow-colored birds preening in the trees and the locals showing me their villages and homes.

Mother caught my eye and smiled at me, trust shining in her eyes. She must need me elsewhere even more than in the north. I knew my duty. And I knew my parents would never subject me to a future in agony, married to a man who'd mistreat me.

"What is it?"

"You know how dangerous the Loftarians are to our northern towns, and especially the eastern coast."

I nodded, but it still made no sense. If she spoke of Loftaria, Marro would still be the perfect choice. Unless—

No. Mother couldn't want me to marry a Loftarian. They'd been attacking us for decades. Or had she begun peace talks in secret? Was she considering giving up one of our provinces after all, as they demanded? If they had direct access to the coast, they'd leave us alone. But what would happen to the people who lived on the land we'd have to sacrifice?

And how could I survive life in Loftaria when I didn't know the language? My vocal cords were paralyzed.

Mother steepled her fingers as she watched me. "Our planned alliance with the Farnskagers was not only important for Azzaria's defense, but also for port usage, fishing, and trading. They're eager to take advantage of this season's winds."

That was understandable. It must be awful to live in a country without access to the sea.

"They need our ports, and we need their assistance should Loftaria ever launch a full-scale attack on our northern border. A strong alliance with Farnskag would be such a threat to the Loftarians that they probably wouldn't dare raise their weapons again. Not when it would mean war on three-quarters of their borders. And not after they were so soundly defeated in the last war with Farnskag."

Mother's political details tumbled through my head. Farnskagers. Loftaria. Alliance.

Farnskag.

Their king was here, in this building. Supposedly to pay his last respects to Scilla, his dead betrothed.

My heart pounded at the two-year-old image of him in my mind. The tattoos. The dark leather instead of our colorful muslins and silks. The choppy language that had earned him and his countrymen the name Bone Eaters, as if they had fish bones caught in their throats. His broad shoulders. The unexpectedly warm eyes and full mouth. The impossible look that had passed between us that one time, just before Scilla's engagement . . .

The Farnskager king still wanted an alliance. And so did Mother.

I took a deep breath and tried to slow my heart. "Do you mean—"

"Now that Scilla is . . ." She didn't say the word, and I didn't want to hear it. After swallowing, she continued, "King Raffar has suggested you be his bride."

A thrill spiraled up through my chest. I beat it down as I half-stumbled from the corner of the desk and paced the length of the room, my fists clenched and my face averted from Mother. My face, which had to be as red as hot coals.

The king belonged to Scilla. It didn't matter what kind of fantasies I'd had. What girl my age didn't lie awake at night thinking of what would never be? No. I had not wanted this. I would never dream of taking Scilla's place. I was not that kind of sister.

And besides that, King Raffar didn't speak Azzarian—Scilla had told me that. With Loftaria between us, his parents hadn't seen the sense in finding a teacher for him. Mother, on the other hand, had more foresight, so Scilla had spent years preparing for a potential allyship, studied the language, the customs. She'd met Farnskagers whenever possible, conversed with them, while I had avoided their foreign appearance and the throaty, unintelligible language I'd never be able to understand.

My back to my mother, I pushed a fist into my mouth to avoid a hysterical laugh—I had problems spelling in Azzarian.

Even Zito read faster than I did. How could I expect to learn a new language when I hadn't even mastered my own?

It didn't matter how intense his eyes were, or how his smile transformed his tattooed face into the exact opposite of scary. We couldn't marry. How would we talk to each other? Through a translator? What kind of marriage was that? And a queen needed to be able to communicate with her people. How could I survive that far from home?

My eyes sought out the door, and I longed to run from the palace and down the hill to the sea. Or to Pia, to pour out my heart to her. Or maybe to beg her to hide me.

"Jiara." Mother's voice was so heavy I turned around. She pushed herself up from her seat and walked slowly to me, like an old farmer woman carrying a basket of sorrows on her back. When she reached me, she smoothed my loose hair over my head. "I will not force you. Not even to save our country, you know that. But if you travel to Farnskag, maybe you'll be far enough to escape Scilla's wrath if your father doesn't find her killer in time. It tears me up inside to think of what she must be going through, but you're my daughter too. If you go, and if your father can't help Scilla, I'll send Zito to you before Scilla gets . . ."

Truly violent. I gulped at the thought of our family so torn apart, and at the scenes my imagination created for those left here in Azzaria.

"At least that way two of us may be safe. And with a marriage that binds Azzaria and Farnskag, so may our country."

"But how will I—"

"You won't be alone. Pia will join you."

As Scilla's *gurdetta*, a kind of lady-in-waiting and bodyguard in one, Pia had also learned Farnskag. At least some. I'd always been closer to Pia than my own *gurdettas*, who complained when I climbed trees, wandered the streets of the city, or dove into the sea. One after the other, they eventually requested another post. My previous *gurdetta* hadn't been replaced yet, but the queen's guard kept extra watch over me. Apparently, Pia would now be assigned to me. For at least two years I'd begged my parents to let her be my *gurdetta*, but I never wanted it to happen like this.

A knock echoed through the door. Mother's eyes shot to it. "That's him."

"Now?" I cried. They were supposed to be resting! "What about the Time of Tears?"

"I don't understand either. Such a lack of respect and empathy . . . maybe they don't understand how important it is for us." She shook her head. "But this alliance is too crucial for me to turn them away, no matter how much it hurts. Now that he's here, we have to be strong."

"But . . ." I needed time to think. And . . . I'd hurried straight from the memorial field. Grass stains marred my bright turquoise *zintella* dress where I'd knelt next to Scilla's memorial stone. I brushed my hand against the stains, once, twice, but they remained, as if Scilla were here in this room with me, refusing to leave. As if she'd hear me discuss an engagement with the man she had planned to marry.

"You're fine, Jiara," Mother said. "I'm sure the king won't even notice."

I shook my head because my throat was completely closed up. It was too soon. Too fast. Mother took a deep breath and indicated with her hand that I should do the same.

Her voice firm, she said, "Come in."

CHAPTER 2

The heavy, intricately carved door swung open and two guards marched in. The first was a man, his blue eyes alert, his white face dappled with black tattoos, his bald head gleaming in the sunshine through the window, and his body clad in black leather. The other was a woman, her brown skin also tattooed, with hair so short it reminded me of Zito's schoolboy cut. Her black uniform was the same as the man's. Staffs, javelins, and axes made of thick-grained, nearly black wood were affixed to their backs and waists, and knives were strapped to their thighs. I stole a glance at Mother—why had she allowed them to bring weapons into the palace?

The guards' eyes swept the room, then the man said something in Farnskag. The only word I caught was *Raffar.*

A breath later, King Raffar stepped across the threshold, his boots thudding on the wooden floor, his light brown head bowed slightly, shaved like all men from Farnskag, and his hands open before him. My heart pounded so loudly I was sure he could hear it. I forced my fists to remain at my sides and not cover the organ attempting to give me away.

Our translator, a tiny, gray-haired woman named Serenna,

hurried in behind him, and a young Farnskager man followed her. Almost simultaneously, the two translators said, "May I present His Majesty King Raffar Perssuun Daggsuun of Farnskag."

Serenna narrowed her eyes at the young man. He grinned at her, his tattooed cheeks stretching wide, his eyes glittering in amusement. King Raffar watched with a careful expression, and then he laughed, his brown eyes glowing unbelievably young and carefree for someone who had lost his parents at sixteen and was already king.

He shot a flurry of words to his translator, then strode to Mother to address her. Serenna translated: "It is an honor to meet you again, Queen Ginevora." The king placed his left hand on Mother's left shoulder, and she did the same to him. Then he leaned forward, his forehead and nose almost touching Mother's. According to Scilla, the Farnskag greeting was supposed to be an offering of hearts and minds.

Mother stood still, allowing the unusual closeness. After the king leaned back, she said, "It is an honor to receive you here again, King Raffar."

The male interpreter took over this time, translating Mother's words into choppy Farnskag.

King Raffar's eyes slid over the room, over me, then riveted on Mother again while he spoke. When he was done, Serenna said, with a little catch in her voice, "My heart bleeds for your loss and for the rest of your family. I know the heartbreak of losing loved ones. Scilla was an extraordinary woman and would have made an excellent queen of Farnskag."

I couldn't help but nod. Scilla had done everything in her

power to be exactly what Azzaria needed, and what Farnskag needed. She'd been interested in politics and language and culture. She'd been daring and analytical. And despite the fact that she'd chattered exclusively about other Azzarian men—even Marro—she'd agreed to marry Raffar. For the good of the country.

Mother bowed her head slightly, accepting the condolences, then cleared her throat. "You might remember my youngest daughter, Jiara."

Raffar turned to me. I'd forgotten the shard of stone through his earlobe, a decoration so unlike Azzarian jewelry, it made me shiver. My pulse beat a little faster as he considered me. Then he stepped close enough to grasp my left shoulder, and I raised my hand to do the same. I bent too quickly, and his forehead touched mine, warm and dry. I jerked back the appropriate distance, but not before the tattooed lines, swirls, and curves burned against my skin. This close, the king smelled like leather and earthy forest. His lips were closer to me than any boy's ever had been—I didn't dare move for fear I'd accidentally touch them—and his breath warmed my skin.

The king leaned back again, and his voice was soft as he spoke to me and held my gaze. The throatiness didn't seem so harsh when his words were quiet, more like a hush than a bark. My eyes remained on him as the interpreter translated his words: "It is an honor to see you again, Princess Jiara. Like I told your mother, I'm sorry about your sister. She was a dear woman."

I swallowed and nodded, my eyes burning and my throat feeling like it was caught in a vise. She hadn't just been a dear woman. She'd been the closest person to me in the world. A sister who'd always been there for me—to read to me, to tease me about my eagerness to explore the northern forests and riverlands, to brush the tangles from my hair when Gio's play had been particularly aggressive.

"Thank you. That's very kind," I said, and his translator echoed me.

The king tore his eyes from mine, then moved back to Mother. "About the other matter, my offer stands. Has a decision been made?"

Mother smiled to lessen the blow of our lack of definitive answer. "We will have one by tomorrow. Jiara has only just heard of the proposal now."

Raffar smiled back, his teeth white against his skin. "Of course . . . of course, you need time. Then we will see you at the banquet tonight?"

Mother agreed, and Raffar turned to leave. Abruptly, he stopped and spun back to me. "I can imagine this is difficult for you. I realize Scilla prepared herself for a life in Farnskag, and you didn't."

The king was so close to guessing my thoughts, I could only swallow.

"But it is the best for both of our countries. And I promise you," he continued, his eyes earnest. "If you agree to this marriage, I know we can make it work."

———

The table was draped in emerald-colored silk and set for

twenty with heirloom-patterned porcelain. Mother sat at the center, with King Raffar at her right, and then came my chair. Father and the rest of the family faced us from the opposite side of the table.

Mother was giving Raffar and me the opportunity to get to know each other, but what was I to ask a bald, tattooed stranger?

If Pia were here, we could have tested her translation skills. But after Scilla had given her the slip during a routine visit up the coast, and everything had gone so horribly wrong, Pia'd retreated to her family's home to mourn. Mother had sent for Pia to take over as my *gurdetta*, but she wouldn't arrive for several days. Luckily, Serenna and the king's translator were here.

"Your trip was long, I heard. Was it very uncomfortable?" I finally asked Raffar, and Serenna nodded encouragingly. I smiled briefly at her as the man behind us translated. In the pauses as we waited for the translators, Raffar's eyes remained on me, making me feel like it was the most intense conversation I'd ever had.

"Not at all. I enjoy traveling, seeing different lands," he replied. I was glad for the break from Raffar's intense gaze when he gestured out the window, where the canals of Glizerra reflected the fading light of the crimson sun sinking behind the red tiled roof of a building. "And the boats on the canals here in your capital—they're quite unique. I've never seen a city with so much water. I would like to ride in a boat like that someday."

My face flushed—at least he shared my interest in water. "I will ask Father to arrange it."

His eyebrows rose, and the tattooed lines crinkled at the corners of his eyes. He looked out the window again as he waited for the translator. "That would be excellent. Would you join me?"

When his eyes met mine again, I smiled politely. We would be quite the spectacle. Not only a member of the royal family on one of the small pleasure boats, but a foreigner too. Probably more—his guards would surely join us. But I did love outings on the water.

Our superficial, maddeningly public conversation continued. Serenna and the king's translator hovered behind us throughout the meal. I was never certain whose face to look at—Raffar's or the translator's. Every morsel of the discussion took twice as long since every sentence was uttered two times. With each slow relay of information, the vise around my chest constricted a little more.

Despite his rough appearance, Raffar seemed agreeable enough. Just like I remembered from the last time he visited Scilla, there was even something magnetic in his dark eyes. But if I agreed to our marriage, my entire existence would be like this dinner—slow conversations, eternal waits for translators. I'd constantly hope they didn't have to go to the bathroom or get sick, because then all I'd be able to do was rely on body language, and who knew if that was even the same for Azzaria and Farnskag. I'd be surrounded by tattooed men and women grunting in their throaty language.

I gestured to a plate of one of my favorite dishes with an invitation for the king to try it, and he poked it tentatively with a spoon. Octopus probably didn't even exist in his country, so far from the sea. How could I live in a country without octopus?

But then another thought wormed its way into my brain. What *did* they eat? Those huge elephant birds that pulled their carriages? I'd never tasted one. What other animals did they have in Farnskag? Surely, they had chickens and cows. Didn't they? But so far north . . . mangoes, papayas, citrus fruits could never survive. My stomach clenched. *What did they eat?* Scilla had never mentioned what they ate!

Raffar bit down on a tentacle of spicy, lemony grilled octopus . . . and grimaced, ever so slightly.

My eyes fled from his face to the window, to the nearly dark city. Nothing would be the same in Farnskag. Nothing would be familiar. I'd make a fool of myself even going to a market, requesting food by pointing like a child. I couldn't even read a sign warning me of danger. The high ceiling of the dining hall loomed overhead, threatening to drop on me. My lungs screamed for air.

My chair screeched as I shoved it backward, and I cringed. "Please excuse me."

The tall double doors boomed behind me as I hurried from the dining hall. Down the corridor, I slipped into the dim library. I rushed past the infernal books that were my enemies and eased open the balcony door. Cool evening air filled my lungs, driving away the panic that had caged them before. I crept into the shadow of the *blazzini* plants, their vines snaking up the trellis, blue star-shaped flowers releasing a light perfume into the night. The moon was a crescent in the sky, sparkling off the bay below. This evening, I wore a normal gown instead of a split skirt, so I hitched up the silky fabric and climbed down the trellis.

Once in the garden, I surrounded myself with the greenery and breathed in the sea-tanged air of home. The palace was too far to hear the waves, but I imagined them lapping at my tense shoulders as I let Azzoro, the ocean god, massage away my worries.

"Princess Jiara!"

I whirled around to see a man in uniform stride past a young mango tree. Commander Torro had worked for Father for as long as I could remember. He stopped short before me and scowled, obliterating my moment of peace.

"I just wanted a short break. It's . . . strenuous."

A flicker of understanding softened his face, then his attention darted behind me, and that softness turned stiff and sharp.

"Oh, good, you've found her." Father crunched along the gravel path behind us then crossed his arms with a low huff.

I swallowed down the groan that wanted to rise from my chest. I'd only been gone a couple of minutes. The cage around my lungs tightened again.

The commander nodded. "The princess took a little walk. I was just about to escort her back."

Father turned to me. "I understand it's not easy for you, but leaving the banquet is not appropriate, and you know it." And then to Commander Torro: "As the head of the guard, I expect you to keep watch over my children, and to inform me *before* they leave an event like this."

Commander Torro began, "I'm sure—"

Father muttered a curse he'd normally never say in my

presence. "Stop. I don't want to hear groundless reassurances. It's been less than a season since Princess Scilla was—"

As he swallowed, I shook my head to make them stop, but the words crept into my thoughts anyway. *Found dead. Days from here. Six stab wounds in her back.*

Commander Torro flinched.

Father cleared his throat as if he wanted to continue, but he fell silent instead. He was always so strong in front of the servants and the soldiers. But for one second, the horror in his eyes was plain to see, the worry over Scilla's suffering and for the family's safety. The fear that her essence was growing so twisted as to hurt her own loved ones.

My hand sneaked into his, and he gave it a squeeze.

The commander didn't utter a word in response.

He didn't have to. I'd spied on the guards enough to have pieced together the details. Scilla had been up near the northern border. Based on the size and shape of the wounds, the knife could have originated from anywhere. Her purse containing a large sum of money had lain next to her, so it hadn't been a thief.

Father raised my hand as if holding up evidence. "My family must be kept safe." His voice was so sharp it could have sliced through a turtle's shell. "The assassin is still out there. With the Farnskager delegation here, we'll need to be even more careful than normal. It's not just our family now. If anything happens to King Raffar's people, we'd gain another enemy. The queen wishes to hear answers. Do you have anything new to report?"

Father was worried about an attack on Raffar?

"Two of the agents investigating on-site arrived today. I just came from their debriefing."

"Did the man wake up yet?" I asked. A local man had been found unconscious not far from Scilla's body. Physicians had kept him alive all this time with the help of the gods and a strong meat broth in the hopes that he'd regain consciousness and be able to identify Scilla's murderer. Maybe he'd finally awoken and had been able to speak with the agents.

The commander's eyes flicked to me, apparently uncertain how much I should hear. Father normally didn't involve us children in matters of security. Llandro and I'd tried to find out as much as possible, but we were surely missing some details.

"Go ahead," Father said. "As much as I'd like to keep Princess Jiara out of it, her safety may be at stake too."

"Yes. The man is awake now, and he confirmed he saw the killer. Based on the witness's testimony, it doesn't appear that the Farnskager delegation has anything to worry about." Commander Torro hesitated. "The assassin himself was most likely from Farnskag."

I gasped. "The killer was from Farnskag? Does Mother know this?" She wanted me to *marry* one of them.

Could Raffar even be behind it? But why? Scilla's death was a detriment to Farnskag, and if I declined to marry him, Mother might refuse him all use of the ports instead of only imposing fees.

Father's grip on my hand loosened as he faced the commander. "That's a serious charge, and it could have a drastic effect on our current foreign policy. What evidence do you have?"

My hands gripped the silk of my skirt. Our current *foreign policy* was that I'd marry one of them.

"Well, first we should keep in mind that the witness is Loftarian—"

I caught my breath. The witness was Loftarian? That was news.

Father cut him off. "Yes, I remember. And normally, I'd dismiss his opinion on those grounds alone. But he emigrated an entire generation ago, and he's married to one of the Volari family up in Flissina. We've known them for years. He's trustworthy. What did he say?"

"The killer was shaved bald, so a man. And he saw the assassin's tattoos, described them to us. From the little we know they were missing the typical elements of the military."

Not military. Not one of Raffar's soldiers. My shoulders relaxed slightly. At least I wasn't surrounded by them in the palace. "So, a private person. From Farnskag," I said. "But why?"

"My agents don't have any information on the motive yet. But I have a drawing in my office with the tattoos the witness described. Our next step will be to ask King Raffar's guards for assistance. Maybe they can narrow down the search."

Father held up one finger. "We must discuss this with the queen first. I'm not sure if a direct question wouldn't come across as an accusation . . . or possibly allow them to warn the culprit if they do recognize him." Father rubbed his chin thoughtfully. "Princess Jiara and I have been missing from the dinner for too long as it is. I'll discuss it with the queen after the banquet. We'll talk again tomorrow morning."

"Of course, Your Majesty."

Father and I watched as the commander headed for his office. Scilla's killer was from Farnskag. And there was even a sketch of him, or at least of his tattoos.

"Even in the dark, I recognize that look in your eye," Father said sternly. "I want you to be careful. Stay aware of your surroundings, and report anything you see that we should know. But otherwise, I want you to let your mother and me, and the commander, handle this."

With that, Father slid his arm in mine, steering me toward the palace. As we walked, I looked up the hill. In the dark, the memorial field was black, invisible. But Scilla was surely up there, pacing. Father might want me to stay out of the investigation, but if there was the slightest chance I might be able to help, I had to do it. I pulled Father's arm, hurrying back to the banquet hall. He probably thought I was eager to get back to King Raffar, but I had another mission: to memorize the lines and swirls on every Farnskager face there. Because not every person who'd accompanied the king was in the military.

And tomorrow, no matter what, I'd get a hold of that drawing.

CHAPTER 3

By noon, I was certain Commander Torro's office was never empty. My plan to stroll in unnoticed wasn't going to work. And with every hour that passed, I forgot the details of the royal delegation's tattoos a little more. Could I draw the guard out somehow and slip in? But then I'd need an accomplice for the diversion, and Pia hadn't returned yet—if she'd even help me—and I didn't want anyone to know what I was doing. Keeping secrets in the palace was never easy, and Father wouldn't like it if he heard I'd been eavesdropping or meddling in the investigation.

Two of the cook's serving women sauntered down the hall, their heads together as if gossiping. I wasn't supposed to be here. I squeezed backward into a nook filled mostly by a huge potted plant. I'd only wanted to hide until they walked by, but of course, they stopped in front of a window down the hall to rest in the ocean's breeze.

"An earthwalker . . ." sighed the older woman. "If they don't find the assassin soon, it will be the downfall of the family. Mark my words."

"You had an earthwalker in your family once, didn't you?"

The woman made a noise of assent. "I was still a child then, just old enough for the earthwalker to stop being careful around me. At least careful in the beginning when they still have a trace of their humanity. My favorite aunt had been killed, stabbed in her sleep, and at first, we didn't know who did it. My uncle figured it out after several months, which saved the rest of us."

The younger woman sucked in a deep breath. "The rest? Was it terrible?"

"You can't imagine. The earthwalker tormented us during the entire rainy season. The adults got the worst of it, but even I was hit with a hot poker from the fire." She lifted her arm, probably to show a scar I couldn't see from here. Then she shook her head, and her voice dropped. "One day, my mother gave me a basket of papayas to take to my grandparents. I can still smell them. But when I got to their house"—she swallowed—"there was blood everywhere. The walls. The table and chairs. The floor. I remember I dropped the papayas, and they rolled through puddles of red. Even the ceiling was spattered. I found grandfather and grandmother dropped like forgotten dolls on the floor next to their bed. Their bodies . . . they were crisscrossed with deep cuts. And their eyes, so big and scared, and—"

She broke off, covering her face with her hands. Her voice was muffled as she whispered, "Blood on the floor, the walls, the ceiling. I can't stand the scent of papayas anymore. Haven't eaten one since."

The other women rubbed her back, murmuring soothing

words, then she drew her along. "Maybe you need a short walk before you go back to the kitchen."

Motionless, I watched the women go. My throat felt like someone had swabbed it with cloth. Her *favorite aunt* had done all that? Earthwalkers could be violent, everyone knew that. But Mother and Father must have managed to keep people from sharing just how bad with me. How long before Scilla turned that way?

I had to see that drawing. I left my hiding spot behind the plant and wandered down the hall again, hoping the last remaining person in the office would come out soon. I had paced back toward the commander's door again when it opened.

"Princess Jiara!" Commander Torro looked up and down the corridor. "Is there anything I can do for you? Is there a problem with our guests?" His hand went to the sword at his side. "Are you worried for your safety?"

That was it. My safety. I stood taller and assumed my most royal tone. "I need to see the drawing of the assassin's tattoos."

The commander froze, and his eyes slid toward his office. "But His Majesty said you weren't to be . . . *bothered*—"

Imitating my mother, I silently held up my hand and let my position as princess speak for me.

He swallowed.

"I would like to see the drawings now," I repeated.

"Of course, Your Highness." He bowed his head slightly and opened the door. I followed him in as if I had every right to be there.

From a desk drawer, the commander extracted a book-sized piece of parchment. He slid it across the polished wood surface to me. "Apparently, the assassin had the typical swirls and lines, but only these two pictures were memorable," he said.

Two patterns had been inked on the page. At the top, a curved leaf was depicted, its border a line thick like a twig. I placed a finger on it. "All of the guards have this leaf, but not exactly this pattern. Most have a double thin line around the leaf with short perpendicular lines between them. King Raffar also. His translator does not—the translator has a similar pattern but with thin borders and a zigzag line in between."

The commander's eyes shot to my face as if he couldn't believe the queen's youngest daughter had memorized anything so well. My years of failures in schooling had been the topic of gossip. But pictures had never been a problem for me.

"You've been paying attention," he said. "My guards have been alerted to observe, and everyone has said the same. Three other members of the party don't have this leaf symbol at all. From what we understand, the leaf is the symbol of King Raffar's clan."

I nodded and checked the second drawing: a stylized dolphin or whale with its head curled strangely into its chest. I sighed in disappointment. "Almost everyone in the king's entourage has this symbol."

The commander frowned, but he nodded. "Yes. We're waiting for Queen Ginevora to confirm we may speak with the king's head guards to see what it means."

I traced the lines of the dolphin—a good sign, usually—with my finger. So wrong on the face of a killer.

But something about it seemed somehow familiar. I swiveled the drawing back and forth, then stopped so that the "head" was pointing more upward, instead of diving downward. A burst of black and white flashed in my mind. "The flags."

Commander Torro watched me with narrowed eyes.

I pointed to the figure's short neck. "The figures on the flags attached to the Farnskager carriages. If you shorten this part and remove the eyes . . ."

"Yes, I think you could be right, Your Highness. It could be the Farnskag hybrid figure—part rock, part fern, and part wind." He tilted his head as he studied it, then frowned. "If so, it's likely that many people have this tattoo."

My gaze moved up to the leaf, which might be more promising then. "These drawings are so specific. What did the witness say—why did it take this long to get them?"

"During the attack, he was injured. When he saw what had happened, he turned to run for help, and the murderer felled him with a blow to the head. The killer must have believed the man dead. It took until a week ago for the witness to regain consciousness. As soon as my agents had the drawings, they traveled back to Glizerra."

I nodded, my heart a touch lighter than it had been before. "If the illustrations don't match any of the faces of those present, it means no one in the party was the assassin."

The commander pursed his lips. "The queen puts great trust in King Raffar and his companions, so we did not expect to find the culprit among them. But we can never be too careful. Please do not leave the palace grounds without a guard, Princess Jiara."

The next morning, I strode up the memorial hill. Now that I'd heard the serving woman's story, my heart pounded, and not from the climb. But it was still early. Scilla hadn't truly attacked yet. I could handle a few scratches.

I stood alone before her memorial stone, and no one else was in hearing distance.

"Scilla," I said. "We're getting closer."

The wind blew more strongly off the sea today, and only three neat stacks of shells remained. Sometime last night, Mother's must have fallen down. I resisted the urge to straighten up the scattered pieces. Gio wanted it so, and the Time of Tears was almost over anyway. We had to let go, even if Scilla wouldn't.

A tickle ran along my cheek. Scilla had heard me, but a tickle was harmless. She must be happy to know of our progress.

Her killer was a Farnskager. Why would someone from Farnskag do that? They needed us. Without our access to the ocean, they were cut off from trading and fishing. And they would lose Azzaria as a strong ally against Stärkland, an enemy to both of us on the western side of the continent.

At breakfast this morning, I'd asked Mother and Father about the tattoos. Father had reminded me to stay out of the investigation, but Llandro objected, saying we should know all we could if we were seriously considering the king's proposal. Mother answered softly, "I'd be more worried if she were not interested."

And then she'd given an update. The hybrid figure truly was the symbol of Farnskag. The leaf indicated the ruling clan— Raffar's clan. But King Raffar had denied that anyone in the clan could have hurt Scilla. Raffar's people stood firmly behind him in his efforts to save the country from the Stärklandish threat. A marriage between our two countries would bring them nothing but benefits.

Neither Raffar nor the guards knew anyone with a thick-bordered leaf tattoo. That they didn't believe any of their clan capable of murder wasn't surprising. If someone told me our family was responsible for killing Scilla, I wouldn't believe it either.

I touched the stone. "Scilla, they might deny it, but we're closer to finding your assassin. We've ruled out Stärkland and the Loftarians and, of course, our own people. We know it was a man, and a Farnskager at that, one from Raffar's clan."

What we needed now was someone who could investigate in Farnskag, someone who could check the tattoos of every-one who lived there. But with Raffar and the Farnskag guards so certain none of their own would harm Scilla, it would be difficult for Mother to convince them to allow Azzarian agents to investigate within their borders. It might take months. By then, the killer could hear about our plans and flee.

A flash of sharp pain seared my arm. I slapped my hand over it, gripping it for a few seconds, until the sting faded. My previously unblemished skin was torn in a thin, jagged line. I licked my finger and ran it along the bloody scratch.

Oh, Scilla.

I'd been so hopeful, but no. She was losing patience already, becoming dangerous. We didn't have months to convince Raffar to allow an investigation. We needed to go after the killer now, before Scilla got worse, before she bathed her anger in larger amounts of blood. I thought of the serving woman, as a child. What if Scilla lost control faster than we expected? What if her next victim was Zito?

It might be impossible to get our agents into Farnskag, but one person had the perfect excuse to go there: me. The eventuality made me dizzy, and I lowered myself to the grass.

As queen, no one would question me if I asked to view every member of the clan. And I'd be surrounded by Raffar's guards, protected. Despite the fact that Raffar asserted his people hadn't killed Scilla, he'd promised Mother I'd have a female guard—one who couldn't be the assassin described by the witness. And Pia would be with me too.

I dragged my fingers through the grass next to Scilla's memorial stone. Only I was in the perfect position to find her killer. Except I'd never learn the language, and I didn't understand their customs, and I would be married to someone I couldn't communicate with and—

A gust of wind blasted up the side of the hill, bringing the lightest spray of water with it. As if both Gio and Azzoro had worked together to offer me their blessings. If the gods believed me capable . . .

And I'd have Pia to support me. She was on her way back now. How I'd missed her.

I straightened my back, looked out over the sea and the city. The important thing was to protect Mother and Father and Llandro and especially Zito. And anyone else in Glizerra. I looked down at the deep scratch on my arm. It seemed Scilla was as exceptional in death as she was in life. Most earthwalkers got through the Time of Tears before their rage took over. Scilla hadn't been gone three months yet, and already she'd drawn blood.

———————

After returning from the memorial field, I met Mother in her office, where she poured lemon water at the conference table. I perched on my corner of her desk and rubbed damp palms against my silk pants.

I allowed myself no time to reconsider. "All right. I will marry King Raffar."

Mother's face lit up with a smile, and she set down the pitcher and strode across the room to embrace me. "I'm so proud of you, daughter. I know you're worried about the language, but you'll learn. You will. Just have faith in yourself. And King Raffar is a good monarch and a good person. He has promised to keep you safe, and he's even sent orders to have his own agents search for the suspect, despite not believing one of his countrymen could be guilty. If I didn't believe in him, I would never let you go away."

I forced as much of a smile to my face as I could. She stroked my hair once, then hurried to her desk. "I'll have a note sent to the king. We will make the engagement official immediately."

Immediately? We couldn't even wait until tomorrow?

I walked a marble paperweight shaped like a turtle along the edge of the desk. On the outside, I was certain I looked like the same Jiara as always. But on the inside, my entire being consisted of only one thought: *King Raffar would be my husband.* My heart hammered in my chest, pounding in time with the words. *King Raffar would be my husband.*

A foreign man I couldn't understand would share my future. He'd been engaged to Scilla, and now he'd be mine.

A tickle brushed over my cheek.

Scilla, here in the palace. Slowly, a chill crept over my neck. She'd left the memorial field. But her touch—was it approval . . . or a warning?

———

"Seventeen!" Serenna's less emphatic voice echoed King Raffar's exclamation.

Only three hours after my agreement to become Raffar's wife, we were all gathered in Mother's office. The king leaned on the conference table, his palms flat on either side of the Farnskager version of the engagement document. Mother stood calmly across from him with her copy. Father and I waited off to the side of the table, with the translators behind each of the monarchs.

Raffar garbled something else, and Serenna said, "I had always thought she was only a year younger than Scilla."

I swallowed. Scilla had been three years my senior. Marrying at seventeen was not exactly recommended in Azzaria, but it wasn't unheard of, especially in royal families.

The king stepped back from the table and crossed his arms over his chest. His eyes met mine, briefly, apologetically. Then he turned to Mother. "I cannot marry a child. In Farnskag, we do not marry before eighteen."

Iron bands squeezed my heart. After being in such a rush that he proposed during the Time of Tears, now *he* didn't want to marry *me*? A *pff* escaped my lips.

Mother ignored me, but Father frowned in my direction.

I was not a child. There was only a two-year age difference between us. He'd been crowned king at *sixteen*. Surely a marriage was of less consequence than a coronation.

But then my pulse stuttered, and my eyes sought out the floor. What if he was just saying that because—now that he'd met me—he no longer *wanted* me as his wife? Liquid fire gushed up into my cheeks. Which was stupid, because I hadn't wanted to marry him anyway.

But how erratic would Scilla become by the time I turned eighteen? Five months wasn't a long time, but every day trapped on earth would only make her more bitter, more violent. *Blood on the floor, the walls, the ceiling.* No, I couldn't allow thoughts like that to distract me now.

Raffar knew nothing about earthwalkers, which came into existence when a person was murdered and no one knew who'd done it. Mother had told me the Farnskager ghosts were gentler and less powerful. They had no earthwalkers, probably didn't even believe they existed. The Servants of the gods theorized that Azzaria had a stronger sense of justice than other countries. That served us well in life, but in death, it made for ghosts consumed by wrath at the knowledge that their lives had been stolen with no consequences for the culprit. So, when it came time to let go, to move on, they didn't. They remained here, linked to their families, their rage festering until it exploded, hurting those around them.

Mother's smooth voice intercepted the king's disappointment. "Jiara will be eighteen in five months. Would you prefer to come here again then? Of course, that is a lot of travel for you and your entourage in less than a half year. A lot of time away from your citizens, who surely need you. And Farnskag will completely miss trading for the southern continent's harvest season."

The king's translator relayed the message. As a show of goodwill, Mother could have allowed the Farnskagers to use our harbors for trade before the marriage, at no cost. But her face was as hard and smooth as porcelain. Protection against the Loftarians was too urgent for us.

Now it came down to how big the taboo was of marrying someone considered underage—and the Farnskagers' desperation.

Raffar's sharp eyes focused on me. He muttered to his translator. The interpreter handed him a slate and chalk, and a thick, black leather-bound book. "I would speak alone with Jiara."

Alone? I caught Mother's eye, and once she nodded slightly, I followed the king out of the office, down the hall, and out the palace doors to the gardens. We walked across the grounds, past the reflecting pool dotted with coral-colored water lilies. It had rained a little, and my shoes were slippery on the damp grass, but Raffar slowed when I began to fall behind. That small act of attentiveness and the heat of the afternoon sun helped melt my anger at him calling me a child.

When we were far out of hearing of the palace on the edge of a grove of shade trees, he held up an open palm. Guards from the king's and Mother's armies hovered protectively around the edges of a wide, imaginary circle, as if a glass globe had been dropped over us.

The king garbled a few sentences to me, then smiled in a way that granted his eyes a warm glow and drew out my own smile—as if he wasn't a king and I wasn't a princess. As if we'd met in town, at the market while buying fresh fruit and he'd asked me to escape the humidity of the city on a boat ride with him, or to sit under a tree to snack on some pineapple.

Raffar lowered himself to the damp grass under a shady queensflower tree, gesturing to the spot next to him. My silk *zintella* dress would get wet, but it would also cool me in this afternoon's oppressive heat. I settled next to the king while he wrote on the slate. Then, word for word, he looked them up in his book, writing each letter slowly and carefully. Finally, he passed the slate to me.

I followed the Azzarian words with my finger—it was hard enough for me to concentrate on written words anyway, but with the king breathing down my neck, it was almost impossible. Words jumped off the slate, and I squinted, pulling them back. I forced the letters of each word to swim into the right order. One or two words made no sense at all, but I wasn't with a tutor, looking to master a text or to get a good grade to impress Mother. I only needed to understand the gist. And that I did: *Are you certain you want to marry me? Or is the queen forcing you? Be truthful. I will not betray your trust.*

My hand rose to my throat, and heat flooded my cheeks. Despite how important it was to both our nations to become close allies, he was offering me a way out. My eyes met his, and he leaned in my direction, scrutinizing my face, waiting for my answer. A few days ago, I would have jumped at the chance to stay home. Even now, the teeth of temptation gnawed at me. If I said I was unsure, maybe he'd call off the wedding completely. Or I could say I wanted to wait until eighteen and have a few months to learn the language.

But it wasn't just me now and what I wanted. It wasn't even just Azzaria. It was Scilla's soul, and my family's safety.

My voice steady, I said, "Yes, I am certain I want to marry you. No one is forcing me."

I wiped away his letters and wrote my own words on the slate, hoping I had the Azzarian spelled correctly, or at least mostly correctly. I bit my lip. Maybe I should have looked the translations up for him, as he did for me, but I could only imagine the snail's pace I'd need. So I let him translate, hoping they were spelled well enough to find them in the book.

When he was done checking, his deep voice rumbled next to me, and he nodded. I had no idea what he'd said, but he smiled, and he gazed out over the canals of Glizerra. He pointed to the gleaming water, and then to both of us. I nodded because Father had arranged a tour for this evening.

Then I focused on my fingers in my lap and tried not to think about the future.

CHAPTER 4

Two hours later, the contracts had been signed, and Raffar and I were officially engaged. Both sides consented to the scandalously short time period of one week. It wouldn't give Father nearly enough time to drive the palace servants to organize a wedding befitting both houses, but considering last week's brutal attack in the north and Raffar's trade plans, it would have to do.

Surrounded by six Farnskager guards and six of Mother's, I led Raffar to the palace dock where an old-fashioned blue and red *tagarro* boat waited to take us on a tour of the canals. The driver bowed to us, his eyes wide at the sight of the tattoos and hairless heads. The female Farnskager guard entered our boat first, then the king and I, then Serenna and the king's translator, and finally one of our guards. I settled next to my betrothed on a pile of jewel-colored cushions.

Hesitance hung over our party like storm clouds over the sea. I caught Serenna's eye, and she smiled encouragingly, urging me to make conversation. Really, it was silly to have two translators, but Mother and Raffar had agreed upon it. I smiled back at Serenna. Silly or not, I was grateful for her familiar face. But my mind held no more ideas for conversation than the sky reflected on the water.

The driver pushed off with his oar, and our silent boat sloshed from the dock. We were followed immediately by another boat with a second portion of guards. I took a deep breath and leaned against the pink silk pillow at my back. It would get better. Once we were underway, I could describe what we were seeing in Glizerra.

Raffar turned and gestured over his shoulder to his translator behind him. He cleared his throat and said, "Aldar."

The translator leaned forward and smiled at me, his cheeks rounding with humor. "My name is Aldar Anzgarsuun, Your Highness," he said in Azzarian. "It will be a pleasure to translate for you when you come to our capital, Baaldarstad. And I can teach you Farnskag, if you like."

"Thank you, Aldar," I said. "I'd like that very much."

I introduced Serenna and began a running commentary of the sights we passed, with Aldar repeating in Farnskag. The driver eased us through a patch of water lilies and out of the palace's canal into the largest of Glizerra's waterways: Leaping Dolphin Canal. We floated by heavily decorated homes of wealthy traders. Farther down was the newly cobbled market square, a wide empty space in front of the impressive arcade where traders sold and distributed cinnamon, nutmeg, gold, and other treasures from the southern continent, and silk and fruit from Azzaria. The guards remained stoic throughout the ride, but Raffar was all smiles when he saw it. Soon Farnskag would claim their part in international trade, sending gems, marble, and wool south.

Next to the arcade was the park with its scarlet queens-flower trees and delicate white orchids, and beyond that, the boat builders' district. We switched to the Emerald Turtle Canal before we reached the fishery. Even so, we were lucky to be upwind today. I asked the driver to take us to the floating market, and our *tagarro* boat glided alongside houses connected by arched footbridges. This deep into the city, people hurried to the edges of the canals wherever we went, gawking with cries of "the princess" and "Bone Eaters."

I glanced back at Aldar, and he winked at me, but he didn't mention the slur to the king. "Thank you," I said. "They just don't know—"

"I understand. Not every language can sound like a baby babbling . . . words made only of As and Ls and Rs, like Azzarian, right? Alla, razalla, larralla . . ." he teased. Then his smile grew even wider. "And believe me. I have eaten your silkfish before. I know how those nearly invisible bones feel going down." Choking noises emerged from his mouth, and he clutched melodramatically at his throat.

I chuckled, and my shoulders relaxed as I waved to the citizens. At least I would have one person to speak to in Farnskag. Raffar shook his head at Aldar's gagging sounds but didn't ask for details. He raised his hand to greet our citizens, and the younger girls especially blushed and giggled in response. With an amused shrug, he dropped his hand in the water, trailing it in the current. He relaxed against the sapphire pillow behind his back and closed his eyes.

I reached over and snagged his wrist. The skin-on-skin

contact was too intimate, but I pulled his hand out of the water nonetheless.

He asked a question, probably along the lines of why I'd done that.

Before Aldar could translate, I held up one finger to ask him to wait. I slid my hand into the water—it was different if one knew what to expect. Within seconds, an emerald eel latched itself onto my middle finger. I pulled my hand out of the water, and the half-foot-long, gleaming green fish thrashed around, spraying both of us with fat drops.

Laughter burst from the king, but he didn't try to shield himself from the water. "Doesn't it hurt?"

I laughed along with him. "No. I just didn't want it to scare you. They don't have teeth. They usually swallow water slugs whole. Our fingers must look a lot like slugs to them."

He chuckled at that too, then I twisted my finger sideways. The eel let go with a slurping sound, and I released it into the water, its green form glittering just below the surface as it slinked away.

After that, the entire Farnskag party marveled as we passed under Glizerra's largest walkway over the water—Sunken Rainbow Bridge, where jewel-colored glass sparkled along the underside and reflected up from the water. Following a graceful turn by our driver, we glided through a narrow canal. An old woman with her hair in the tightest bun I'd ever seen peered out a window directly above us. When she scowled at our laughing, partly-foreign party, Raffar grinned and mumbled under his breath. After he spoke, the guards chuckled softly, and Aldar translated: "Admirable restraint, don't you think? That I didn't raise a staff over my head, proclaiming Farnskag pride?"

Raffar slugged him in the arm. Aldar rubbed it. "Uh, apparently, I wasn't supposed to translate that part."

The king's eyes flashed at me, a mild apology, and heat rose in my cheeks because his gleaming eyes made me feel exactly the same as that time in the Great Hall two years ago, the first time we'd met.

Once through the narrow canal, the river opened to the floating market. Some two hundred boats crowded the water, brimming with baskets of fruit, vegetables, dried meats and fish, bowls of thick seafood stew, sacks containing spices, clothing, straw sun hats, fabrics, carpets, pots, anything a person could desire. I directed the driver to one of the boats and bought enough dragon fruit, mango, and pineapple for our party. I instructed them to give several bowls to the guards in the second boat. The merchants also offered papayas, but they reminded me of the serving woman's story about her aunt, the earthwalker, so I shook my head, my throat suddenly dry.

The sun was low and turning red when the female guard spoke. Serenna translated: "Your Majesty, Your Highness, it's getting late. It would be safer if we returned to the palace."

King Raffar shared a nod with me, and I asked the driver to head back to the canal leading to the royal grounds.

Commander Torro waited on land as each boat glided up to one side of the dock. Before we had a chance to stand up, he said, "Your Highness, I have a few urgent questions for King Raffar's security detail."

Raffar instructed two of the guards from the second boat

to take care of the discussions and sent Aldar to translate. He asked me to stay for a few moments. Thankfully, Serenna remained with me.

With one hand, the king pushed off from the dock again, and we drifted a few feet into the canal, with the driver steering to be sure we didn't hit the other shore. As the scarlet evening sun reflected off the smooth water, Raffar gave a quiet order to the female guard, who dug in her pocket and handed him two wide metal rings.

"Now that we're engaged, I'd like to make you a gift." He flattened his palms to show two bracelets. The metal rings were silver, and the centers were shaped like those Farnskager hybrid figures with two shiny black stones that looked like eyes. They were strange figures for jewelry, but I supposed it was a way of welcoming me to Farnskag.

I leaned forward to take them, but Raffar stopped me mid-reach. "These are family heirlooms. Please consider if you really accept them. Wearing them means—deep in your heart—you choose Farnskag. All of your decisions will be for the good of the people, to help them and protect them. If you choose the Watcher, and it chooses you back, you cannot take it off again."

The Watcher? Was that the bracelet? How could a bracelet choose me? I looked to Serenna. "Did he say I *may not* take them off or I *cannot* take them off?"

Serenna spoke rapidly to the king, who repeated, "If it chooses you, you *cannot* remove them later."

"I don't underst—" I began.

Raffar held up a hand. Then he pointed to his earlobe—the one with the shard of stone through it. "Watcher of Stone has chosen me." He removed the shard from his earlobe and set it on the turquoise pillow in front of him. Then he gestured to his ear.

The stone was still there.

My eyes snapped to the pillow. Empty.

Despite the warm evening air, a chill scurried up my arms. "Take it out again," I told him.

Raffar grinned. He removed the shard—and I *saw* it. It was in his hand. Then it lay on the pillow. But when I looked back to his ear, it pierced his earlobe, and the pillow was empty again. My heart pounded. So that was *cannot take them off.* How was that possible?

"You do not know anything about our Watchers?" the king asked.

If I remembered correctly from Scilla's stories, the Farnskagers worshipped inanimate objects like rocks and lakes. But the Watcher was obviously more than an inanimate object. With a sinking feeling in my stomach, I shook my head.

He considered for a moment, then continued, his voice heavy with reverence. "The Watchers make up our world. Sky, stone, water. They are everything. They are everywhere, surrounding us, providing for us. Always watching us, occasionally protecting." He pressed a fist to his chest. "They know the depths of our hearts."

Nodding because the Watchers seemed very similar to the gods, I pointed to the bracelets. "Is this also Watcher of Stone?"

The king shook his head. "Watcher of Sky." He pointed straight up, then his arm arced slowly down until he pointed to the garden beyond the palace. "Pieces of a fallen star. Very rare."

A fallen star. But black—not how I'd imagined such a brilliant object. Matter from beyond the clouds, from beyond our world . . . my fingers itched to touch them.

"Princess Jiara, do you choose Watcher of Sky?" Raffar's eyes reflected red in the setting sun.

"What does that mean? Choosing stone or sky—which is better?" I asked.

After the translation, Raffar's features pinched, and he shook his head. "Neither is better. Either one would be a privilege."

He'd said wearing the bracelets meant I put Farnskag ahead of everything. That would include Azzaria and my family. How could I agree to that when I'd never even set foot in the country? When we weren't even married yet?

My eyes flicked to the guard and then to the king. Both tattooed, with strange haircuts and oddly tailored clothing. So different.

But people, just like Serenna and me. And they would be *my* people soon. Maybe instead of trying to put Farnskag first, I could put *my people* first. Do anything I could for their happiness and prosperity and safety. And that would include my fellow Azzarians and my future Farnskagers. That was a promise I could make.

But not being able to take the bracelets off again, for the rest of my life?

Something in those glittering black stones drew my eyes, made my skin ache to feel them. Soon, I would be the foreign object in Farnskag. These stones were in a strange place like I would be. And if Raffar wanted me to wear them, surely it would be a sign to the Farnskag people that I was doing my best to be a good queen to them, even if my command of the language was nonexistent. Wearing bracelets for the rest of my life was a small sacrifice for my future people.

"Yes," I said. "I choose Watcher of Sky."

Raffar's lips widened into a smile. He picked up the first armband. I placed my hand in his, and his warm skin—again, so intimate I had to bite my lip—brushed over mine. He smoothed the bracelet over my wrist. Then he continued with the second.

I ran my finger over the polished black stones. They felt like rocks, not like some celestial entity, not sun warm or ice cold. Just stones.

I smiled at my betrothed, sure he'd be proud of my decision. But I stopped at the sight of his tight face.

"Now, try to remove them," he said.

Oh. It wasn't done. Now, we had to see if the stones chose me.

I pulled off the first bracelet and set it on the pillow. I no longer felt the weight of it on my skin. In the waning light, I could barely see the black stones, but the metal band was easy to make out against the shiny fabric. Heat seeped into my eyes, but how silly was I, to feel sad that tiny black stones hadn't chosen me?

A deep breath escaped Raffar's chest. His grin split his face, and he nodded at my wrist. The one that felt empty.

It wasn't. I shook my head. It was impossible. I removed the bracelet again and dropped it on the pillow. But it was still on my wrist. I tried it a third time, then once more with the other bracelet . . . nothing changed.

Raffar made an *mmm* sound with his lips pressed together. "Watcher of Sky has chosen you. You are protected now." He rolled his shoulders back like a weight had been removed from them.

A surprised glint reflected in the female guard's eyes, and she inclined her head to me, like a little bow. "Congratulations, Your Highness," she said. "To be chosen by Watcher of Sky is one of the highest honors one can imagine, whether you were born Farnskager or not." Her smile suddenly seemed several degrees warmer than any time before.

"Thank you," I said as I smoothed over the stones with my finger.

Raffar nodded at me, as if he'd known all along, or maybe just hoped Watcher of Sky would choose me. He took my hand in his, warm and dry. Not too intimate. Somehow right.

CHAPTER 5

"*Laadag*," I said, echoing Serenna. *Wife* in Farnskag. As if I would remember any one of the hundred words she'd just told me ten minutes from now, let alone tomorrow.

I balanced on a pedestal, and the seamstress ran her tape measure across my back again as she triple-checked her measurements. There wouldn't be time to fix a wedding dress gone wrong. Mother had already approved the azure silk, and the glimmering white, gold, and silver threads that would form the sea creatures, the sun and the wind on my torso, and Raffar's ferns scattered over the skirt. A narrow meander tiara would top off the outfit.

My wedding outfit.

I clenched my hands, then released them, willing the relaxation to flow to the rest of my immobile body. The seamstress moved on to my arm length, and Serenna said the Farnskag word for husband.

"*Maadh*," I echoed.

Serenna said it again, holding a slate up so that I could see how it was written. I repeated, focusing beyond the slate as the chalk letters flickered against the dark background.

Mother swept into the room. Normally, she stuck to matters of national importance and left running the palace to Father, but the sparkle in her eyes made it clear her daughter's wedding was different.

A servant followed Mother to each of my closets, and together, they selected what to keep and what to donate. I'd only be bringing along a small amount of clothing. *Zintella* dresses and other Azzarian pieces would look ridiculous in Raffar's court. No, not court. The correct word was *mergaad*. Or *huusdom*? *Fangdoor*? None of those? I gritted my teeth and forced the useless thoughts away. I'd never figure out the right words anyway.

In terms of clothing, the appearance was less important than the warmth. Only in the summer was Farnskag as warm as Azzaria's cooler days.

The servant whisked away a turquoise *zintella* dress with tiny suns stitched into the sleeves. I'd worn it with Scilla the last time we'd picnicked together on the beach. I was dying to snatch it back, but there was no way I could keep everything.

I closed my eyes, and slates and letters and words danced across the inside of my eyelids. The seamstress pulled down my collar and measured my neck.

"This is how you say *my name is*," said Serenna, then followed it with garble I didn't even attempt to utter.

The seamstress tugged and measured.

After a few seconds pause, Serenna repeated herself with more force. I kept my mouth shut, pretending I was still on that blanket with Scilla, chewing juicy bites of melon and laughing about her upcoming wedding and her unusual-looking husband.

"Jiara!" Mother's sharp voice ripped me from the memory.

My eyes sprang open only to be accosted by Serenna's slate and its slippery letters. I turned to Mother.

"Serenna is working hard to prepare you . . ."

The rest of her sentence was lost on me as the servant stacked hair combs in a box, topping them off with two pearl-encrusted pieces Scilla had given me. I'd planned to wear them to her wedding. And now here I stood, being fitted for a gown to marry the man meant for her.

Heat shot up my spine and flooded my neck and head until I was certain they'd burst. "Stop!" I shouted. "Just stop! I can't do—I just *can't*!"

I tried to run from the room, but the seamstress's tape around my waist held me in place. "Ah!"

With slumped shoulders, Mother raised one hand. "Everyone, please leave the room."

Serenna and the servants scurried out, and Mother beckoned me off the pedestal and patted the sofa near the window. When I dropped next to her, her hand slid up my back, and she rubbed it like she had when I was little.

I sank lower and lower until my forehead rested on her thigh. She stroked my hair, and the blood rushing through my veins pulsed against her.

"I'm sorry the wedding has to happen so quickly," she said.

I nodded against her leg.

"I know it will be hard for you, but that's not why I'm sorry. I thought I'd have another three years with you, before you took your place in the north and I only ever saw you at special events."

A sniffle.

I angled my neck to see tears brimming in Mother's eyes. She took a deep breath. "But there is one good thing about the speed. More time to prepare means more time to worry. Even Scilla wasn't perfectly fluent in Farnskag. Even she feared getting customs wrong and embarrassing herself, or Azzaria."

My heart shriveled. I hadn't even thought of that. I was representing not only myself and my family, but our entire country. "Mother, I'm not sure you're helping."

She chuckled under her breath. "Probably not."

But she had made a good point. I'd never realized Scilla was nervous. Finally, I made myself say the words, "I don't think I'm ready to be a queen. I was never supposed to be a queen."

"Ah," Mother said, then she fell silent and petted my hair again. "Do you think Llandro is ready to take my place?"

I shook my head. Llandro had a good heart, but he was too impulsive. He didn't listen to the counselors or citizens the way Mother did, and he tended to make decisions based on his current emotions and didn't think through to the final consequences.

"All right. How about Ottario? Do you think Llandro's husband is ready to be king consort?"

I sat up. Llandro and Ottario as the ruling monarchs? They would do their best, but . . .

Mother squeezed my shoulders. "I'll let you in on a secret. No one is ready. I was not ready to be queen; your father wasn't ready to be king consort. In the first few years after my father died, we embarrassed ourselves on a weekly basis. We made wrong decisions that cost money and time and sometimes bruised our reputations. Occasionally, people even got hurt."

She brushed my hair behind my ear. "But we kept working at it. And the people saw that. They saw we were doing our best and improving. And they gave us time to grow up and grow into our new roles. Do you understand what I mean?"

"That I might feel uncomfortable now, but I'll grow into being queen?"

Mother nodded.

That might be true. But Mother and Father and Llandro and Ottario all had the opportunity to learn and make mistakes in their own country. I'd be doing it thousands of miles away. In a foreign language.

Mother pushed me up so she could see my face. "You've come a long way since you were my little dragonbird."

When I was younger, she'd called me that. While Scilla and Llandro had studied with tutors, I'd run from room to room, just like the fickle dragonbirds in their search for even brighter, more colorful brushweed flowers to build their oversized nests. It wasn't like I sought something more interesting, but I'd long since abandoned trying to explain how the jumping words and dancing letters had given me headaches.

Mother stroked my cheek. "I know you don't like to read. But you can speak Azzarian. You can learn to speak Farnskag too."

A thick clump formed in my throat. Mother pulled me close, held me tight. And I watched out the window, drinking in the view of the sea that would soon be only a memory.

CHAPTER 6

My hair gleamed black with the same shine as the dark fallen stars at my wrists. Obsidian root powder was the miraculous cause, and thanks to the sinful amount of vanilla that had been dumped in with the hair tonic to cover the foul stench, my husband-to-be wouldn't turn his nose up at me . . .

. . . in only a matter of minutes.

The palace was too large to hear the groom's party from my suite, but I'd seen the blue and green fireworks, imported from the southern continent, bursting in the sky when they'd arrived. In the Great Hall, King Raffar was asking my parents for permission to marry me, according to Azzarian tradition. He and his people would offer gifts representing each of the gods, assuming they'd taken the care to research our traditions, and Mother would agree to give me away. Any moment, someone would come fetch me.

I stood, smoothing down the ocean blue gown with palms that were too damp for the elegant bride I was supposed to be. But at least I looked the part. The best seamstresses and embroiderers in the province had worked around the clock the past week. The shimmery silk dress reminded me of a dragonbird in flight along the sparkling coast. And the combs with which Mother had fixed my hair sparkled every time I turned my head. I tried to think of the blessings she had spoken over me as she did it, and not about the fact that Scilla should be wearing this beautiful dress, and not me.

A faint knock at the door sent my heart hammering.

"Come in," I called.

Five female relatives—aunts and cousins—swarmed around me. Then a beaming face pushed to the forefront—Pia!

"You're back!" I slung my arms around her, forcing myself not to hold on too long. Like a beloved folksong, the wedding had its own beat, with each tradition and ritual coming at precisely the right time. The guests downstairs might wait for us, but Solla, the goddess of sun, was in place, and she waited for no one.

"Princess Jiara! It's so good to see you again!"

"I've missed you!" Pia's golden skin was a little tanner than I'd last seen. Since she left the palace, she'd obviously spent much time in the sun. Ignoring the urgency, Pia grabbed hold of me again, and for the first time in days, the weight on my shoulders lifted. Pia would be my lifeline. Someone from home, someone I'd known for years and who cared about me as more than just a means to an end.

"Are you excited?" she whispered in my ear.

Before I could answer, my other relatives began pulling at me, chattering about the gifts the king had brought, the beautiful gowns, the uncle who was going gray, and the cousin due to give birth any day now. At most weddings, they'd gush about how handsome the groom looked too, but the group was conspicuously silent when it came to him.

Pia's eyes met mine. "Later?" I asked.

She squeezed my shoulders. "Of course."

Hands on my arms and back tugged me down the stairs, through the corridors. Pia's eyes constantly swept the area—once a *gurdetta*, always a *gurdetta*—even if she was here as my guest and not my protector. But I'd wager all of Azzoro's kingdom that she had at least three weapons hidden somewhere within her gown.

Mother and Father stood outside the Great Hall. Mother took my hands in hers and smiled so brightly my chest hurt. Father laid his arm across my shoulders and gave me a squeeze.

"Are you ready?" he asked. His moist eyes showed such trepidation I almost thought he hoped I'd panic and change my mind.

Ready? I clenched my fists to keep from . . . laughing? Crying? Running away? I wasn't sure what I wanted to do. Instead, I did the only thing I could. I leaned into his chest for a half-hug. "Yes, Father."

Servants thrust the tall double doors open to the hall. Blue and green silks draped across the walls, and huge bouquets filled the air with a spicy floral scent. Flickering paper lanterns shaped vaguely like the ocean god Azzoro's favorite creatures dangled from the ceiling. Clusters of people stood inside, mostly Farnskagers on the right and my family on the left, and they all turned in my direction, murmuring and *oohing* over my dress.

Llandro tilted his chin to me with a wistful grin, then raised his husband's hand with his own as if to welcome me to the state of marriage. Next to Llandro, Zito jumped up and down, then threw his arms over his head, brandishing an imaginary staff. My hand low, I gestured to Zito and then to Llandro, who jerked our little brother out of the king's view. My eyes swept the room, searching for Raffar.

"The bride has arrived!" announced Mother, as if it weren't already obvious, while Father wandered around, clasping hands of our guests in his, welcoming them.

Serenna was not only acting as translator today, but as a guide through the wedding for Raffar. She led him through the throng of Farnskagers. He was not dressed in traditional garb, at least not Azzarian. Like the rest of his party, after the first day in the heat, they'd given up on their leathers and now wore gauzy black pants and tunics. Raffar's gaze was everywhere at once. The family portraits on the wall, my dress, my hair, my mother—but it seemed to come back to me more often than not. He flashed me two raised eyebrows and a sigh that hinted at being overwhelmed. I nodded my agreement. And the wedding had only just begun.

A Servant of the gods, wearing a long robe of the palest blue, motioned everyone together and called for the bride and groom to follow him. He strode through the doors and out to the gardens, where the Wedding Walk had been set up. Serenna whispered furiously from behind Raffar; he nodded.

With the guests gathered in a large circle, Raffar and I were brought to stand before a line of seashells on the grass, followed by the first of the three troughs. The crowd hushed as Mother knelt to remove my shoes and stockings. Raffar's translator Aldar did the same for him, grinning up at him over a custom that must have been foreign and strange.

"On this side of the line, you are two. On that side, one. If you are ready, you may cross the line."

It was not unheard of for one of the betrothed to get leaden feet, but without a second's hesitation, Raffar strode across the line. One deep breath—this step would change my life, and our world—and I hopped over it myself.

The Servant smiled. "A decisive beginning to your new life. And now, you may take your first steps." The Servant gestured grandly to the trough of red, yellow, and orange flower petals.

I inhaled another deep breath—I couldn't believe my wedding was really happening—then picked up the corner of my gown with one hand and held out the other. Raffar clasped it, and we took our first steps as a married couple. Into the trough we went, mashing the blossoms as hard as we could, forcing as many as possible to stick to our feet.

Ten stomps later, the guests began murmuring to each other, each trying to determine how much luck we'd have based on the number of petals that clung. We reached the second station, our feet covered with sticky flower petals, and we stepped into a trough of fine white sand. As our feet slid through it, the sand stuck to the juice of the flowers until it appeared our feet were covered in sugar. The gods were smiling on us. Next came the water trough. I hiked my gown up a little higher, and we sloshed through the cool water until the bottom was gritty with sand and petals floated on the surface.

We paused, and the tattooed king looked to me as if to check how he was doing. I smiled; he gave my fingers a light squeeze. We stepped out of the water trough onto a deep blue cloth, then settled onto the bench waiting for us. Zito and a half-dozen other younger relatives knelt around us with lacy fans in their hands. Raffar followed suit as I lifted one foot, and then the other, and the children feverishly dried them with manufactured breezes. Zito in particular waved so hard he almost fell over once, and he rubbed his palm over his forehead to wipe away a sheen of sweat. I winked at him; Gio would surely agree it was a job well done.

The Servant spoke: "Raffar and Jiara, as you have begun your journey with the gods, so too, should your marriage continue. Never forget how Solla's petals that soaked up the sun and Flisessa's sand remained with you, clinging to your feet like a second skin. Never forget how Azzoro soothed and bathed you clean. Never forget Gio's cool and drying breeze. Wherever you go in this world, the gods will be with you always."

Mother and Aldar knelt in front of us again. As Mother smoothed on my stockings and replaced my shoes, she whispered blessings, ending with, "I love you, my dragonbird. Never doubt that." My heart swelled, and only the crowd gathered around us prevented me from falling into her arms.

Next to me, Aldar quietly murmured to Raffar. It was a private moment—no translator told me the meaning—but Raffar grasped the translator's shoulder with affection.

The first half of the ceremony—the request that the gods support us—was over, and we filed back into the Great Hall for the second half: the joining of families.

Portraits of my grandmothers and grandfathers hung on the wall, flanked by other more distant relations. Scilla's portrait had been propped on a shelf above them only weeks earlier. Every time I saw her there, I forgot how to breathe. From my place on the edge of the room, I glimpsed Pia, and the way she rubbed her stomach after she looked at Scilla's picture. My eyes swept to the floor for just a second. Scilla's passing had left feelings of guilt all around, but especially with her former *gurdetta*.

The Servant motioned to me. It was my turn to speak. First, to the family already gone.

"Dear grandparents, dear family," I said. "Thank you for the lives you led before us. I ask you to welcome my husband to the family."

Serenna translated my words for Raffar. Normally the groom would say something similar, but he was silent. The Farnskagers had a different connection to their dead, it seemed.

For days, I'd pondered what I should say to my sister. Nothing seemed right. How could she accept our union when I was stealing her husband, her future? But how could I say I was sorry she'd died and wasn't here to marry him herself? Raffar might take it as an insult.

I drew in a deep breath. "Scilla, I am grateful for the time I had as your sister, and I wish it had been decades more. While you walk this earth, please keep special watch over me, and I will do my best to help you move on."

A feather-soft caress brushed my cheek. Not a scratch this time.

"Thank you," I whispered.

Mother swallowed so hard that I heard it behind me. She laid a hand on each of our backs, the sign that we'd move on to the living family members now. Raffar spoke first, and Serenna translated: "Queen Ginevora of Azzaria, I ask for your blessing in this marriage."

Normally, he should have thanked my parents for raising me and said something about them keeping me safe, but with Scilla's death so recent, I understood why he'd omitted it.

But I was still alive. "Mother, Father, thank you for bringing me up and keeping me safe all my life. We ask for your blessing today."

With beaming faces, my parents assured us they were happy with our marriage. I turned to Raffar and he to me. For a few seconds, neither of us said a word. We just stood. I studied the lines in his face, the strange hybrid figure and the leaf and the other patterns and curves. Then I looked past them to the forehead and cheekbones and chin hidden there. His eyes drank me in too, then his lips twitched upward, and a little thrill whirled through my chest.

But it still wasn't over. Keeping my mind on the lengthy ceremony was a chore. Mother and Father told stories about their marriage and gave advice. Raffar sidled closer to me, and the back of his hand brushed against mine. His eyes locked on my parents, and he nodded as he listened to their translated words of wisdom, but when his hand moved ever so slightly, I couldn't help but think he was paying as little attention as I was.

Mother laughed at something Father had said and stepped forward to kiss my cheek. "Enough from us. Congratulations, Jiara."

Father strode to me and did the same. He kissed me again,

my forehead this time, like when I was a little girl, then nodded to Raffar in an old-fashioned handover.

The king took my fingers in his. He pulled me a step forward, and I was enveloped in that leather and forest scent again. My heartbeat tripped as he—very chastely—pressed his lips to mine. We were being watched by a hall full of people, after all. But for a few seconds, those people disappeared. My lips tingled and warmth crept up my neck and into my cheeks as I imagined our next kiss, in the bedroom we would share.

A hot sting flared along the back of my neck, but I barely had time to think about it because my eardrums nearly burst with the guests' applause. We turned to the crowd, smiling, and I ran my hand along my nape to shoo away the insect that had stung me. Warm wetness made me glance at my fingertips.

Blood.

Too much blood for a simple bite. That was no insect.

Scilla.

Father saw it too and pressed a square of cloth to my hand. As surreptitiously as possible, I dabbed at the cut until the blood stopped flowing.

Oh, Scilla. What do you mean? Marrying Raffar was acceptable. Kissing him, thinking of . . . later, was not? There was nothing else I could do. And I was doing this for her, at least partially. But was I ascribing more logic to Scilla's actions than was warranted? Maybe there was no thought behind her action. Maybe it was all a coincidence.

Wine made the rounds and two hundred candles were lit, bathing the room in a soft glow. Friends and family members gave well wishes and advice, until it seemed there was one speech for every candle.

Finally, the small orchestra seated on the raised platform began to play: a cheerful hammering on the *dultimo*, the delicate plucking of the *hazetto*, the heart-stirring draw of the bow on the cello. Like waves, like waterfalls of intricate droplets of music, the sounds filled the hall.

Mother and Father led us to the dinner table. Within seconds of sitting, servers brought out shrimp and crabs and octopus and fish. I remembered Raffar's reaction to octopus the other day, but there was also pork and vegetables, rice and noodles. And then, two servants came in bearing a huge platter with what appeared to be an immense roasted bird, the size of a calf.

The crowd talked and laughed. Raffar leaned close and whispered in my ear.

I shook my head at him. "I don't understand."

He gulped his wine and chuckled, waving to where Aldar, Pia, and Serenna were chatting on the opposite side of the room. Pia and Serenna hurried over, and Raffar repeated himself. Pia shook her head, but Serenna related the name of the bird and the orange mush next to it, both typical foods from Farnskag. As soon as the words touched my ears, I forgot them. I gulped a swallow of wine myself.

As we ate, one of the translators hovered close by in case we needed more translation. But the food was delicious, the room was loud, and my mind was exhausted. When my mother's oldest aunt approached the orchestra and asked to present a song, my attempts at concentrating on our conversation died.

"Mother!" I called. If she didn't catch her before the song began . . .

The queen was deep in conversation with Llandro.

"Mother!"

As the first warbly notes drifted through the room, Mother's head snapped to the side. Her shoulders fell. One song from my great-aunt wasn't a problem. Getting her away from the stage before she sang something highly inappropriate was. Luckily, she presented an unexpectedly sweet song about a new marriage and two strangers who became each other's world. Serenna whispered lyrics in Raffar's ear. By the end, his hand rested on mine.

Mother rushed to the orchestra to beg my great-aunt to come meet us. We praised her song, and the evening was saved.

The hours dragged by. After dinner—the huge bird was juicy and delicious—Raffar and I did a customary walk around the hall to greet each of the guests. Pia hit full *gurdetta* mode, scowling at anyone who dared to crowd me. Speaking with Serenna or Aldar was slow, and the amount of wine with dinner hadn't helped. Three times, I stifled a yawn.

If this had been a standard Azzarian wedding, I would have accompanied Raffar to his home an hour ago. Normally, it would have been almost time for bed.

My palms grew damp at the thought of it. It didn't matter what normally would happen. Tonight, I would sleep here in my chambers. Raffar would remain in the east wing. His culture, too, said the final step in becoming his wife was to be brought to his home. We'd leave tomorrow morning, and we wouldn't share a bed before we reached Farnskag.

CHAPTER 7

Zito's arms were so much stronger than they appeared. He squeezed them around my waist. "Don't go, Jiara."

My throat closed up. I squeezed back, my arms circled around his thin shoulders.

It was the day after the wedding, and the entire family stood in front of the palace. Mother and Father, Llandro and Ottario, Zito. Raffar and his translator waited a few paces away, close enough to observe, but far enough that we had some privacy.

A line of Farnskager carriages waited in the drive before us. The first and third held luggage and two guards each. Raffar and I would travel with Pia and Aldar in the middle carriage. The rest of the guards held the reins of the heavy-footed elephant birds as they chuffed and twitched their useless wings.

Mother's mouth was pressed in a narrow line, the corners raised in a pitiful attempt at a smile. "Zito," she said, "I told you at breakfast. Jiara will be fine. Let the rest of us embrace her. She needs to go with her husband now."

Zito ignored her and nuzzled my stomach with his head.

Father took a deep breath and embraced me over Zito. "I'm going to miss you," he breathed. "Every day."

Tears welled in my eyes, and I tried to draw them back into my body. If Zito saw me cry, it would be even harder on him.

"You two are smashing me!" Zito giggled and wiggled against me. "I'm squished like the inside of a tortellini!"

I gulped a laugh and wiped at the moisture in my eyes. Father and I broke apart, and I leaned forward to kiss Zito's shiny hair. "I'll be back to visit you." I just didn't know when. In a year? Or two?

Zito's giggles disappeared. He launched himself at me again. "Don't go, Jiara! I already lost Scilla. Don't you leave me too!"

Everything inside me withered, and the tears I'd struggled to hold in streamed down my cheeks. I hugged him so hard, his ribs flexed inward. I had to swallow before I could speak. "Zito, I promise, I will come back and see you again. And someday, you can come visit me." I met Father's gaze. We'd have to weigh the risks. How unsafe would it be to ride through Loftaria? But how necessary would it be to escape Scilla's ghost?

Over Zito's head, I swiped at my tears and looked up to Mother to see if they'd be sufficiently hidden. She nodded, and I gestured to Llandro.

He tugged Zito away with one arm and hugged me with the other. "Good luck, little sister. You make a great sacrifice for Azzaria."

I clenched my eyes shut. I didn't want to think of it like that, like I was doomed to some horrible fate. I would be the queen of a powerful country. Together with Pia, I would find out the truth about Scilla's killer. I would get to know a new culture.

And learn a new language.

I bit my lip. *Why* had I thought about the language now, of all times? This moment wasn't the time for fear. I had to be strong for Zito. And for Raffar and his guards, who were all watching me. They couldn't see their new queen fall apart.

Llandro swallowed hard, forced a smile, and lifted a struggling Zito onto his shoulders, murmuring something about him having the best view now. Ottario brushed Llandro's cheek with his lips and said, "I'm sure we'll see each other again soon. Have a good trip, Jiara."

Mother moved forward. She cupped my cheeks in her palms. "Remember our talk. You don't have to be ready. You will learn—every day. Trust your instincts. Learn from your mistakes."

I nodded, and she pulled me into a hard embrace. "If you ever need anything, remember this," she whispered in my ear, "first and foremost, you are my daughter, little dragonbird. Not just the wife of a foreign king. You need only to get me a message."

"Thank you, Mother," I whispered back.

When she released me, I nodded to Raffar, who strode forward and offered his hand. I rested my palm lightly on his, as a monarch did in public, but he twisted his hand around and clasped my fingers. His eyebrows were raised as if he wanted to ask if I was all right. I did my best to smile.

He squeezed my hand again, and his voice rumbled in a soothing way. A breeze swept up from the sea as Gio bid me farewell and Raffar helped me into the carriage. The walls were polished dark wood and the seats were soft and covered with buttery brown leather, but they might have been the iron bars of a prison for all I cared. They were taking me from my home.

Once Raffar was seated next to me on my left, and Pia and Aldar took their places across from us, the elephant birds lurched forward. I leaned out the window, smiling as hard as my cheeks would allow, waving a cheerful goodbye.

As soon as the carriage made it around the curve, I snatched the curtain next to me and pulled it shut. Pia grasped both of my hands, and despite Raffar's and Aldar's presence, I let my tears flow.

———

An hour outside of Glizerra, past the sea salt harvesting ponds, then masses of rice fields, farmland, and fruit trees, a dozen hopping children blocked our carriage's path. I'd pushed the curtains back before we'd left the city limits and had been waving to our citizens whenever I saw them.

"Pay the toll!" a particularly fearless boy yelled, both arms outstretched as if he could block the entire road himself.

Apparently, this time, a wave would not suffice. Raffar didn't want us to disembark anywhere unplanned, but I beckoned the boy to my window. Beside me, Pia tensed. The female Farnskager guard who had been assigned to me was named Freyad, and she deftly sidestepped her elephant bird mount until she was only an arm's length away. As the boy grinned up at me, I dropped one coin for each of the children in his hand. When he whooped and scurried back to the others, the elephant bird stumbled back a fidgety step. The boy distributed the money, and the group dispersed.

Raffar shook his head at me.

"It's bad luck to refuse beggars on the way to the groom's house," I explained. "Nowadays, only children do this." Surprising that more children hadn't come out. But we'd surely see plenty before the end of the trip.

Aldar translated with Pia listening intently, nodding like she approved his translation—or was relieved to understand it—and Freyad leaned close to the window to hear the explanation too. Her elephant bird was nearly twice as tall as an average man, with a long, wiry neck and a sturdy body covered in soft, gray feathers. Its triangular head sported round, black eyes the size of plums.

Native to Farnskag and other northern regions, the elephant bird couldn't fly, but its muscular, tree-trunk-like legs allowed it to run faster and longer than any Azzarian animal. At top speed, we could probably make it the thousands of miles to Raffar's home in ten or twelve days, even considering the carriages they were towing. But we'd be traveling extra slowly, greeting citizens until we left Azzaria, making contacts as we rode through Loftaria, and finally, getting to know my new country once we reached Farnskag.

When the children had cleared the way, the carriage wheels ground the gravelly road below us and we started forward again. Freyad remained close to my window. Her cropped black hair was barely long enough to shift with her movements.

My hand rose to my intricately twisted hairstyle. Normally, my hair hung past my shoulders, almost to the middle of my back. Long hair was popular in Azzaria. Maybe it made me vain, but I'd always loved mine, black and gleaming like Mother's. I turned back to Aldar. "All women wear their hair so short in Farnskag, right?"

Aldar nodded, but seemed to reconsider. "It's tradition. Not everyone follows it, especially those who are not exclusively female. Most women do, but I suppose some might shave their heads. But long hair?" He shook his head.

I imagined myself shorn, looking like a half-grown boy, like Zito. Pia frowned sympathetically; she must have read my mind.

Don't be a baby. Without an Azzarian servant to help me, I wouldn't be able to pin it so elegantly anyway. *Gurdettas* didn't waste their time learning fancy hairstyles, and Farnskager maids wouldn't have any reason to know how. But with a childish ache in my chest, I asked anyway, "Will I be expected to cut my hair too?"

"I don't think anyone would force you to do it," he said. "Either of you." He nodded at Pia, whose eyes were suddenly pinched. She covered her mouth with her hand, and I was about to ask if she was all right when Aldar translated my question for Raffar.

My husband glanced out the window at Freyad. He said something to Aldar, and his eyes smoothed over my hair, then studied the floor of the carriage.

Aldar grinned, but instead of translating, responded to Raffar. Raffar barked a phrase back at him, and, if anything, Aldar's grin grew wider. Even Pia suppressed a smile.

"King Raffar respectfully requests you to leave your hair long. In fact, he asked if you would remove the pins that are holding it up now, and wear it loose, like you did the first time he met you."

My head snapped to my left. Raffar abandoned his study of the floor to look out his window. Apparently, the wild rhododendrons were fascinating, because he wouldn't turn his head back to Aldar or me. Warmth blossomed in my chest.

I caught the interpreter's eye, and the barely restrained amusement in his tattooed features made me bite my lip for fear I'd laugh out loud. I put on my smoothest princess expression and responded, "You may inform the king that I would be happy to leave it long."

Pia's expression relaxed again, and she smirked openly. Aldar translated, and Raffar slowly turned in my direction, his face—was it possibly slightly pink?

"However," I continued, "as long as we travel through Azzaria, I must wear it pinned. This hairstyle is a symbol of marriage, and it's important that the citizens see tangible proof of our alliance."

Raffar nodded as Aldar spoke my words.

"In Loftaria also," I added. "We may have been enemies for many years, but we share a long border. They know our customs. It is perhaps even more important to keep up appearances for them."

Amusement fled from Pia's features. She was probably thinking of the danger we'd face there, of how she'd have to protect me, how she'd try to succeed where she'd failed with Scilla. I took her hand. It wasn't her fault Scilla had sneaked away.

"I understand," said Raffar, his gaze turned casually to the window.

"Once we pass the Farnskag border, I will take it down."

Out of the corner of my eye, I couldn't see Raffar's expression. But after translating, Aldar winked at me and grinned again.

———————

So much for no unscheduled stops. By our fourth day of travel, we'd halted the carriages at least a dozen times to let Pia out. She said she needed air. But we couldn't help but overhear her retching. I tried to talk to her about it, but she avoided the topic and kept falling asleep, and when she was awake, her glance skittered from mine more every day.

After the second stop today, Pia pushed her hair back from her face and waved off Aldar's helping hand as she climbed back into the carriage. "This stomach bug's awful. Don't want you to catch it."

Her palm rubbed over her belly.

And something in her movements and her exhaustion reminded me of Mother—months before Zito was born.

"Wait!"

Raffar's head snapped up.

I grabbed Pia's hand and turned to Aldar. "Tell King Raffar we need a minute. Pia, you're coming with me." I dragged her out of the carriage and off the side of the road, into a field of sweet-smelling grass.

Pia wrapped her arms around herself. She'd always been

a formidable fighter, but suddenly, she looked very small. Standing there, I realized how little we'd been able to talk the last months. And about how not only my life had gone on.

"That's not a stomach illness, is it?"

Pia's jaw was tight. She stared at me for a moment and then shook her head as her eyes filled with water. My thoughts raced as I tried to figure out what to do next, but before I could decide, tears streamed down Pia's face. "I'm so sorry. Everything's going wrong. I was supposed to protect Scilla, but that didn't . . . now I'm supposed to be there for you, but I-I keep trying to find a way. I just *can't*."

Can't. Pia would give her life for me—not that I'd want her to. So, if she said she couldn't, it was something else. Now was not the time for tact. I lowered my voice. "Pia, are you with child?"

She started shivering but nodded. "That's why I've been away so long. From the palace, from training. First, it was just grief, and anger at myself for letting Scilla slip away. But then, once I was certain—I can't risk the baby getting hurt. And I didn't know what to do. I was trying to decide when the messenger came for me. I couldn't disobey the queen, so I came when she summoned, but then it all went so fast: the wedding, the trip. We never had the chance to talk."

I wrapped an arm around her. I wasn't there for her then. I couldn't be. But now? "How did it happen?"

"He . . . after Scilla . . . he was there for me." She smiled briefly but wiped her eyes and sniffled every few words. "He was wonderful. We'd always been fond of each other, but we never . . . of course we'd never. And then he comforted me, and then . . . we weren't thinking, and I needed to stop feeling so awful, if only for an hour."

Mother and Father hadn't gone easy on Pia for not being there when Scilla had traveled, when someone had attacked. Even I'd been furious with her. Grief had overshadowed logic. And we'd all been drowning in that grief. But with time came the realization to all of us: Scilla had her own mind and acted as she felt best. She was more than capable of giving even the best *gurdetta* the slip if she so chose. That was biggest reason they'd ordered Pia to accompany me to Farnskag. She and I were so close, I had no reason to try to escape her.

Now to the situation at hand. "Does the father know?"

She shook her head. "I wasn't certain until a few days ago. I was trying to decide what to do. I"—she swallowed—"would like to talk to him. The issues that once separated us, they aren't the same anymore. And we're not far away from his home."

I threw a glance around me while I took a deep breath. "He's from the north? He lives in the Riccardis' province?"

Slowly, she nodded.

Mother had wanted Marro and me to avoid each other— as if meeting up would make any difference—but traveling through his province didn't mean we'd actually see each other. And even if we did, I wouldn't make a fuss, and Marro wasn't the type for passionate scenes. We could handle a few awkward moments if our paths happened to cross.

"Of course. We'll head to him now," I said. I tried not to think of what the baby meant for me, for my new life in Farnskag, but my stomach churned all the same.

We returned to the carriage, and I said Pia wasn't feeling well and we needed to reroute to find a doctor. "In Flissina."

Aldar narrowed his eyes at me—did he know about my previous marriage plans? Was he misreading the situation?—but informed Raffar, and Raffar gave the order to turn around.

Three hours and one more stop to let Pia out of the carriage later, we reached Flissina. The smooth-as-glass Totti River gleamed in the setting sun. After rounding a bend in the river and passing a few tall speartrees poking up from the grassy plain, the land dropped in front of us. On the left, upon a majestic hill was the ochre manor that belonged to my former fiancé's family. Below that, the bright river bisected a wild jumble of deep red roofs on white houses.

Freyad peeked into the carriage, her eyes full of concern, but whether for Pia's "illness" or a fear that the group wouldn't be secure riding into town unplanned, I didn't know. She asked something.

"To the town center?" Aldar asked, his eyes flicking again to the Riccardis' manor.

I opened my mouth to answer when Pia said something in Farnskag. And pointed up the hill.

"The manor?" I asked.

She nodded. Swallowed.

But the more I thought of it, the less it surprised me. When Marro or others in the family visited, they always brought servants with them. Raffar and Aldar conferred quietly, with occasional glances in my direction, and we headed to the Riccardis'. Considering how they watched me, perhaps there would be some awkward moments after all.

As we lurched to a stop on the semicircular drive, a deep red sunset reflected off of five decorative pools in front of the Riccardi home. We climbed from the carriages, and the scent of spring blossoms filled the air.

A young servant strode toward us.

"Please, let me," Pia said to me.

"All right. It's late though," I said. "Can you ask them to provide shelter for us tonight?"

Pia intercepted the servant before he reached us, spoke with him, quietly at first, then more insistently. Finally, I caught the words, "Or do you want me to make a scene?"

I bit my lip to keep a very unqueenly grin from spreading across my face. As always, Pia did not hold back, did whatever it took.

The servant hustled into the house and Pia returned to my side. "I've asked the servant to prepare space for us. Tomorrow they can send a messenger to let the Seminna family know we won't be stopping after all."

"And?" I asked. What about the father?

"He'll come. He's—"

Marro bounded down the front steps, a train of several servants behind him. For once, he didn't have a book in his hand. I turned to Raffar, to present him. But Pia ran to Marro's side, grabbed him by the sleeve, and tugged him away from the others.

I coughed.

I blinked.

My former fiancé. Nice but boring, predictable Marro.

Within seconds, Marro was down on one knee, his hand raised to Pia's.

Evidently, he was not as predictable as I'd thought.

"Yes!" she cried, her face glowing with happiness.

Raffar and Aldar rumbled in their throaty language, and Aldar said, "I take it your companion is not actually ill."

I answered with a weak smile. It wouldn't do to give away their secrets. As the servants worked with Raffar's guards to bring the elephant birds to stables, Raffar grinned at me and held out his arm. "I suggest we go congratulate the happy couple."

CHAPTER 8

Pia and Marro disappeared into a sitting room, most likely for an important talk with Marro's parents, and the rest of us were led to chambers to clean up from our journey. My head was still spinning from the news, from everything I hadn't known about Pia, and Marro, for that matter. If I'd ever needed proof that I wasn't emotionally attached to Marro, I had it now. I felt two emotions at learning of their affair: embarrassment that I was once again not enough—not for Marro, but also not for my friend, who had needed someone to talk to—and relief that Raffar had asked for my hand.

Which immediately made me feel guilty, as it was only possible because Scilla was no longer here. But what would have happened if Raffar and I hadn't married? Would Marro have married me, never knowing about his child? Would Pia have stayed away, desperate not to make political waves?

An hour later, we assembled in the dining hall. The Riccardis were not expecting guests, so dinner was a hodge-podge of dried fish and fruits we brought for the road, crusty bread, ham and small game, cheeses and grilled vegetables from the manor, washed down with wine and ice-cold well water. Marro's parents had always been warm, friendly people, and they appeared to take Marro's surprise announcement in stride. His mother beamed with happiness and kept asking Pia how she felt, if she needed another cushion, if she wanted another helping.

"You could not have picked a better family," I whispered to Pia as a tray of grilled rabbit was passed around the table.

Marro sat on Pia's other side, so I couldn't see his face. I tried to remember every time he'd visited, and if I'd ever seen them share conversations, or wistful glances. All I remembered was reminding myself he was an acceptable husband, it was my duty to wed him, and it would be the best for Azzaria.

Pia bit her lip. "I know. I fear I'll wake from a dream and find them screaming that a *gurdetta* isn't good enough for their son."

She laid her head on my shoulder, and whispered softly in my ear, "Marro told me he asked his parents to dissolve the engagement weeks ago. They weren't thrilled at first, but they were going to petition the queen next week, now that the Time of Tears is over."

I swallowed. So, I wouldn't have wed Marro regardless of Pia getting pregnant or not. The clear and perfect future I'd expected had never been anything of the sort. I tried not to imagine the talk that would have swept through the palace like a brush fire. Probably not only the palace, but throughout the kingdom.

"And when Marro told them about the baby, and his father started to argue about whether I'd done it on purpose"—I clenched my teeth. It was all I could do not to skewer Marro's father with a pointed look. Or worse.—"his mother slapped him on the chest and said, 'It takes two to make a baby. You know that.'"

I rubbed her back. "Well, I'm sure they could tell Marro and I were never a good match. And they should consider themselves lucky. No man will ever be as safe as one loved and protected by you."

She gave me a hard hug, then turned to answer a question from Marro.

From across the table, Raffar watched us as Aldar whispered translations from various conversations in his ear. My new husband smiled at me, but his eyes were sad, like he knew what kind of change was coming for me. Knew it, and couldn't prevent it, any more than I could. Somehow that smile made me feel a touch less alone in what I had to do.

That evening, Pia and I lay on our backs on a fluffy bed in the guest wing, patting our full bellies. After a moment, her hand slowed, began circling, more and more gently. "I'm going to be a mother. Can you believe it?"

I tilted onto my side. "I can. I'm sure you'll be a wonderful mother. Loving, and playful."

Pia sat up on her knees and looked me in the eye. "I haven't said it to you yet, I mean, I have, but you didn't know what I meant then. I am so sorry. I wasn't thinking when it happened. Only feeling. I was drowning in misery, and Marro helped beat back that misery. I always knew you weren't interested in Marro. He was only a duty to you. But that wouldn't have prevented gossip if your engagement was canceled."

I nodded. But Mother was nothing if not an excellent strategist. "You know the queen. Marro might have come out of it looking much worse." Which made me sad too. "The way things turned out was for the best."

Except for Scilla. And except for me going to a foreign country where I didn't speak the language.

Pia leaned down to give me the best hug she could while I lay on my side. "Still. I'm so sorry. You didn't deserve any of this."

Then she lay back down beside me and fell silent. So did I, because the thought of traveling to Farnskag expanded in my head until I could think of nothing else, and the time had come for one of us to say it out loud. I hadn't noticed how she felt about Marro the last years. I hadn't been there for her when she was dealing with Scilla's passing. But I could be here for her now. I could set her free and give her the opportunity to have a happy home. And as her princess—no, I was a queen now—I couldn't let her beg. I had to be the one to make the offer.

It would be impossible to find another *gurdetta* before we continued on, and leaving Pia here would mean being all alone in Farnskag, with no one to talk to but Aldar. Maybe safety should have been my foremost concern, but Mother trusted King Raffar, and I found, deep in my heart, that I did too. What I didn't trust was how I would communicate. A picture came unbidden: myself in an austere bedroom in some cold fortress far in the north, my mind and heart graying and shriveling as I pined month after month for my family, my friend, my home.

Pia smiled lopsidedly. She swallowed.

So, despite my breaking heart, I pushed out the words that had to be said. "Pia, I release you from service to me. I'm sure you'll make a wonderful home for the baby here. Warm and full of love." My voice failed me. I cleared my throat. "And with all those books of Marro's your child is bound to be intelligent too."

She gave my shoulder a gentle shove but grinned as she did it. "Thank you, my friend," she whispered.

I took a deep breath, annoyed that I couldn't suppress a shudder. "Will you promise to write to me? Even if I don't write back often? You know how—"

Tears spilled over her cheeks. "I know you don't like to write. That's all right."

I nodded. "And you'll have to describe the wedding to me. I'm going to want all the details. About the baby too. Every adorable moment."

Her head bobbed up and down, her lips pressed together. Then I flung myself at her and hugged her as hard as I could. "If anything ever goes wrong, you know you and the baby will always have a place in Raffar's court."

She nodded against my shoulder.

I squeezed her even tighter, tried to store a piece of her in my heart for someday when I was feeling all alone. I had the sense I would need it a lot.

———

We'd been traveling for six days, and we had almost reached the Loftarian border. Six days of waving until my wrist hurt and smiling until my cheeks ached . . . and sitting until my backside was numb. Now that we didn't stop so often for Pia, I'd begged to let us walk a few times. It slowed us down, but both Raffar and Aldar seemed grateful for the change too.

It had been two days since I'd seen Pia, three days since I'd smelled the sea. And six since I'd sensed Scilla's presence.

The long bumpy ride played cruelly with my imagination. In addition to the experience of the serving woman, famous stories of vengeful earthwalkers filled my head. Murder victims might not be able to prevent their deaths, but they could seek justice themselves, punish those responsible—as long as they knew who it had been. With Scilla's wounds on her back, she apparently hadn't seen who'd done it. Her rage had already begun to turn to us.

Within a couple of years, earthwalkers grew so angry their families sometimes began dying out. Eventually, earthwalkers gave up. Perhaps they ran out of friends and family members they were linked to, or maybe they eventually soaked themselves so full of blood and death that they no longer needed revenge. My family couldn't wait. We couldn't afford to pay the price.

But it appeared the Servants of the gods were correct. Scilla must have remained in Glizerra. Over and over, I shook my head to clear it from thoughts of my sister and tried to enjoy the scenery passing by us. Each night, we'd resided in homes of Mother's most trusted friends and relatives. Now that Pia was gone, Freyad shared my chamber with me for my safety. She was generally silent, more efficient than friendly. And she always had a javelin and a knife within reach.

Just before entering Loftaria, the carriages stopped. Raffar conferred with his guards while Aldar and I stretched our legs. I circled the carriages, then waded into the waist-high plants on the side of the road to pick wild zestberries. I offered some to Aldar, and his eyes lit up when he tasted them.

"These are delicious! Sweet and bitter at the same time."

I nodded.

"Jiara," Raffar said as he trudged over the thick growth at the edge of the road.

My head jerked up. Hearing his voice say a recognizable word burrowed a little hole into my heart, even if it was only my name. He motioned me out of the brush, his eyes dark, the blade of a dagger in his hand, the handle in my direction. When I'd made it out of the bushes, Raffar offered the weapon to me then handed me a holster also.

The knife was light in my hand, but awkward. In Mother's court, the guards handled all our security. I'd never had a weapon, never been trained in their use.

After Raffar spoke, Aldar said, "I know your people think a Farnskager murdered your sister. But I cannot believe it was one of my own. We have an alliance with the Loftarians, but considering the years of bad blood between your nations, I won't trust this new alliance to protect you just yet. Freyad will not be the only one guarding you. I'll have two men posted outside your chamber each night. And I want you to have this dagger in case."

"Where?" I gestured up and down my body.

The corners of Raffar's lips quirked upward. He took the holster from my hand and bent on one knee. With a slow look up at my face, he pushed my *zintella* dress leg as high as my knee. He busied himself fastening the thick leather band around my calf, then slid the knife into the holster. With one hand, he smoothed my pant leg down. The knife was invisible.

He said something, and Aldar relayed it: "Try pulling your weapon out quickly. You'll need practice in pushing aside the cloth and extracting the knife."

I made an attempt, but only succeeded in tangling the knife in the cloth. Raffar motioned with his hand: *again*. I concentrated on the direction of the sharp point, then repeated the action . . . and almost slit the silk with the blade.

Raffar held up his palm. Then he took my hand in his. Despite his position as king, his palms were calloused. From what? Holding the reins of those massive birds? Years of practice with one of those wooden staffs? He pointed my hand to the ground and curled my fingers toward my leg. Pushing my *zintella* dress leg up with my fingertips, he skimmed my knuckles upward against my skin. When he reached the top of the knife, he straightened my fingers forward, and moved them onto the hilt of the knife at the same time.

When he met my eyes, I nodded, but he led me through the movements again. His fingers trailed an attentive line along my calf this time too. I gritted my teeth. The knife was the important thing here. My safety. Not my husband's touch.

I practiced unsheathing the knife ten more times, until Raffar was satisfied with my speed.

He dropped a hand on my shoulder and looked deeply into my eyes. They glittered as he spoke. "If anything should happen, don't be afraid to use it. I'd rather someone else get hurt than you."

I was about to nod when one of the guards called Aldar's name. His eyes darted between us, and Raffar murmured something that probably meant he should go. Raffar and I shared a quiet moment. When our inability to converse began to feel too awkward, I curled my hand to motion for him to follow me to the zestberries. His head bobbed, and he waded after me into the brush.

Snort.

I stopped short. Something was in there, past the thick brambles and tall grasses. Raffar reached for me, but he was too far away to take my hand. Before I could step toward him, the grasses rustled and a hairy snout poked out among the leafy green . . . followed by bloodshot eyes.

I stumbled back. The wild boar's canines slammed into each other, clashing loudly, aggressively. It moved forward another step, revealing its huge size—easily twice as heavy as me—and a nasty gash in its side that buzzed with flies. A sickly smell wafted across the brush.

My heart slammed against my ribs. Wild boars were dangerous, especially when injured.

"Jiara . . ." Raffar started, but the rest of his sentence was lost on me. Did he want me to turn and run? Slowly walk backward? Yell to try and drive it away?

There was no time to decide. The boar barreled forward, stopping only a couple of feet before me. It lowered its head.

Raffar crooked his fingers and waved me gently backward. Slowly, I picked up my left foot, and the boar's snort rang through the air again. In a blur, the wild animal came at me. With a throaty yell, Raffar dove over the tall grasses directly for it. I screamed for help. Raffar rolled, grunting and shouting as the razor-sharp teeth of the boar gnashed and snapped in his direction. He grappled with the animal, a knife flashing in his hand as he slashed at the boar's back and head.

A rough, tortured squeal ripped through the forest. Shouting guards raced off the road toward us.

"Matid!" called Raffar. The guard jumped onto the thrashing animal, pinning its lower limbs with his knees and ducking his head as the boar snarled and squirmed.

Raffar wrenched the boar onto its back and plunged his blade into the soft skin of the animal's underside. Blood ran from the wound, coursing into the grass, and the animal's cry echoed in my ears until its power drained and finally died out.

Two guards attempted to push me out of the way, but I held back until my husband stood. His chest heaved, and blood, dirt, and grass smeared his skin and clothing, but he didn't look injured. Finally, I allowed Freyad to take hold of my shoulders with both hands and pull me back to the carriage, her gaze and foreign words soft as she tried to soothe me.

I leaned against the carriage. Someone brought Raffar a large flask of water. He sluiced the blood from his skin and used the last bit to rinse his bloody knife. All at once, I was aware of the unaccustomed pressure on my leg: the holster with the knife Raffar had given me only moments ago. I hadn't even thought to draw it.

My face flushed hot, and I rubbed my forehead. We'd been in danger, and I hadn't even taken my weapon in my hand.

"Are you all right, Queen Jiara?" Aldar asked as he rushed to my side.

I nodded, but my throat was so rough from screaming that I didn't try to respond.

The translator's eyes were gentle as he said, "Into the carriage with you, Your Majesty. You . . . you look a bit shaky. You should sit down."

I glanced down at my trembling hands. Then I let Freyad steer me into the carriage to wait for my husband—the man who had just saved my life.

CHAPTER 9

Four days later, the skin on my face and arms began to itch from the dry air. The forests around us were lush and green, so it was not as though we were in one of the deserts of eastern Svertya. But the ocean and Azzoro's reach into the atmosphere were far behind us.

While in Azzaria, Raffar and I had occasionally walked alongside the carriage to stretch our legs. For safety, we remained inside while in Loftaria, and not only because of the potential for wild animals. Not including the feeling of being cooped up, riding in the carriage with my Farnskager companions felt surprisingly like meditation. Their gruff words rolled over me, leaving me to my own thoughts, never intruding on my mind. But my limbs ached with the desire for movement.

Outside of their famous vineyards, Loftaria was a plain country. Fields of crops followed cool, leafy forests. Unadorned wooden homes with thatched roofs clustered together to form tidy villages. The inhabitants watched us from a distance as we drove by. Their fear of the black-and-white Farnskager hybrid figure flags fluttering in the wind was palpable. The war between the two countries—fought two generations ago when the Loftarian Servant-King decided the Farnskagers had to be forced to revere the gods—had been decisively won by the Farnskagers, and it seemed no one had forgotten.

The Loftarians still followed the same gods as we did in Azzaria, but they did away with their Servant-Kings shortly after the war, instead installing governors elected by the population. The only conflicts they'd had since then were for economic reasons, like with Azzaria. At least it appeared they knew when to quit. Receptions at the Loftarian governors' manors so far had been cordial but tense. Every administrator we'd met had assured us that the attacks on northeastern Azzaria had stopped the moment they'd been informed of the wedding. Their parliament was considering requesting harbor rights in some of Azzaria's coastal towns. They'd have to pay tax, but they could spare the cost of war they'd spent for so long in trying to take over our land. Some of them even sounded relieved.

Tonight, we were at the final estate on our way through the country. The governor of the region had arranged for a banquet with musicians and dancers to entertain us. Raffar muttered that they were trying to please us in the hopes that the taxes would end up a percent lower once I reported to my mother that the trip had been uneventful.

So far, Loftarian food had been similar to cuisine in northern Azzaria. Delicious rice and noodles, pork and chicken and vegetables. But today's food was different—a dish I'd only seen at my wedding. A huge bird that'd be more than enough for the entire table of thirty. Orange mush. Boiled white roots. Beans. Corn. Some kind of green leaves.

Servers portioned out plates. My Farnskager companions

dug in, grinning from ear to ear. And that was when it hit me. Just as the food in southern Loftaria was closer to Azzaria's, the cuisine here was closer to Farnskag's. My taste buds pouted at the meals that awaited me for the rest of my life.

Raffar sat on one side of me, and Aldar leaned in on the other. He pointed to everything on my plate, one after the other, naming them in my language and his. "I know they look foreign to you. They taste different than you're used to. But you'll grow to like them." His grin was a little crooked as he continued, "I've grown to love seafood, after all."

I swallowed, but my heart warmed at his encouragement. "Thank you." The bird hadn't been bad. I'd start with that. Shivers ran across my cheek, but I brushed them away. I took a deep breath and bit off a tiny morsel.

The seasoning was different on this one. Bitter, like when you licked the pit of a nectarine. My lips burned too, as if too much pepper had been used, but I forced myself to chew.

Blazing fire exploded in my mouth, searing my tongue and gums and throat. My eyes watered, and I shot up from my chair, shoving it back until it tipped onto the floor with a bang. I opened my mouth, and the partially chewed food fell onto the plate below me. But the fire didn't go away—it blasted through my mouth until my entire face was ablaze. In the span of a second, my throat closed up. I tried to pull in air through my nose, and I coughed, coughed, coughed—clutching my throat. "My mouth! My lips! Can't breathe!"

Aldar shouted over me at the others. I wiped at my tongue with my hands, trying to rub off whatever was causing this pain, but the only thing that happened was that my palms tingled too.

"Here!" Aldar passed me his wine.

I gulped a mouthful, but it, too, burned, and I spit it out, dropping the goblet to the floor.

I was surrounded—by Raffar, Freyad, Aldar. Farnskager guards. Loftarian politicians. All demanding answers, three languages tumbling over one another. Hands on my arms and shoulders tugged me in more than one direction at once. I lost my balance and slammed sideways against the table. Pain shot through my hip, and I cried out again.

Raffar, Freyad, and the other head guard Matid shoved themselves between me and the rest, and they half-carried me from the dining hall to my chamber. They tried to lay me on the bed, but I pushed them away, jumping up as panic spurted through my blood. I couldn't be still. This fire in my body—I had to douse it, to make it stop.

Freyad and Raffar spoke tense, harsh words. Matid ran out of the room. I coughed and spit lava onto the floor as tears streamed down my face. Why wouldn't it stop? It hurt. It hurt so much.

I cowered down next to the bed, curling into a ball of fiery agony, and then I froze. The world around me disappeared. The pain was gone. I floated in blackness. In silence. I couldn't smell the dust in the room or feel the beat of my heart in my chest. There was no warmth, no cold. Nothing . . .

Except the threads leading back to Mother and Father, to Llandro, Pia, and little Zito. Threads so strong I'd never want to break them. And other threads to various relatives and to members of Mother's staff I'd known all my life. And a newborn, gossamer-thin thread to Raffar. I followed one of the threads, exhausted and venomous and dark, until I found Scilla, her face sad, but no—she was full of rage—then sadness again, her expression flashing so fast I couldn't keep up. Our eyes met, and I reached for her, to bring her home—then a wave of ice flowed over me from head to toe. Brightness and sound exploded around me. I lay in the room full of hectic activity, and foreign shouts rolled right over me. My hand hovered in midair, nothing in front of it, and every fiber of my being ached with missing my sister.

Then it all came together in my mind. The pain. The burning. The fact that *I had seen Scilla.* My mouth was fine— absolutely fine—as if nothing had ever happened. I stood, then backed up and lowered myself to the edge of the bed. "I'm all right."

Raffar shouted at Freyad, and she called back as she filled a cup with water. No one had heard me, so I raised my voice. "Aldar! Tell them I'm all right."

The translator's head whipped to me, sitting calmly on the bed, and he stared for a second.

He was right to be shocked. It made no sense, but the flames in my mouth and chest and on my palms were gone. I'd seen Scilla. I knew what that meant. But now, miraculously, I was back in this room in Loftaria.

Aldar had just barked a phrase to the others when a woman carrying a physician's bag rushed in with Matid. She squinted as she examined my mouth, but other than a patch of irritated skin on my cheek, she found nothing. Aldar didn't speak

Loftarian, but Matid did, so he translated to Farnskag, then Aldar told me in Azzarian.

"It looks like—but it can't be—the queen would be . . ." the physician said as she dropped her arms helplessly. She tossed the spoon she'd used to depress my tongue onto the bed. "Her reaction indicates bladeleaf poisoning. But that plant only grows in Stärkland."

"Western Stärkland even," Matid added.

Far from here.

Raffar broke in, his eyebrows creased with concern, "Bladeleaf is deadly. All it takes is a couple of drops to kill a person."

Another guard rushed to my chamber and whispered in Raffar's ear. As he listened, the king turned to me and stared. With two long strides, he was at my side, dropping to the floor until he knelt before me.

"What are you doing?" I grabbed his hands to draw him up, to sit next to me on the bed, but he stayed where he was, and lowered his forehead to the bracelets on my wrists.

"Watcher of Sky," Aldar whispered. "Watcher of Sky has protected you."

"What?" How could bracelets protect me?

The guard rattled off more details to Raffar, and Aldar said, "After you reacted so badly, to test your food, they gave it to some kind of animal—Matid didn't know the translation. It died immediately. It spit foam and its mouth was burned bloody. It sounds like it truly was bladeleaf."

I shook my head. I'd ingested bladeleaf and survived . . .

saved by bracelets? Raffar's forehead was still pressed to my arm, but all I could think was that I should be dead.

Unless . . .

That feeling on my cheek. Had it been Scilla? Protecting me? Warning me from taking too big a bite? But she couldn't be here. And I had been dead. I even saw Scilla. Unless it was a trick of the mind, induced by the poison.

Aldar dropped to the floor next to Raffar and waited until the king allowed him to press his forehead to the Watcher. Freyad followed suit and then Matid.

And I sat there like I was made of stone with a heart that didn't know how to beat. Like some *thing*, some object they worshipped. But it wasn't me they were worshipping. It was the bracelets. And I didn't know who should get the credit for my survival. The gods? Scilla? Stones from the sky?

His voice filled with wonder, Raffar bent his neck to look up to me with moist eyes. "The Watchers have always looked out for us. And now, they have saved the life of our queen."

——————

None of us got any sleep that night. I paced, barricaded in my room. Half the guards surrounded me, either in my room or outside the door. Half remained with Raffar, who spent the entire night in conference with the region's governor. Raffar returned to my room as the sun rose and the first light crept in through the window.

"Governor Vadek doesn't know who did it," he said, with

Aldar translating as always. "He's questioning every person who stepped foot in the manor last night—"

His grip on the club at his waist, Matid tried to interrupt him, but Raffar held up his hand. "He got down on his knees in front of me. He wept. I do not believe he or his people planned this assassination. Loftaria has tried too hard to get on Azzaria's good side now that they are our allies. Besides that, memories of the last war are still fresh in their minds. They have nothing to gain and everything to lose. By attacking us, they'd be drawn into a battle on two fronts."

"The act of one person then?" Freyad pushed herself up from a chair.

Raffar nodded. "One person, or a small group. Possibly from Stärkland, considering it was bladeleaf."

My head spun from the lack of sleep and the whirlwind of possibilities. One person, or a small group, probably also responsible for Scilla's death. Except the evidence suggested a Farnskager . . . the evidence described by a Loftarian, whom Father had deemed trustworthy. And now poison from Stärkland, a country that bordered the western edge of Azzaria, Loftaria, and Farnskag. The Stärklandish army was mighty, but they normally kept to themselves.

I raised my fingertips to my forehead, then ran them down over the skin still rough on my cheek from the blade-leaf's poison. I'd focused on Farnskag, but what if the killer were from Loftaria after all? Maybe the assassin had worn a disguise, patterns of simple charcoal to throw witnesses off. And it couldn't be too difficult to buy bladeleaf, not even with the trade barriers to Stärkland. I shook my head, wishing the movement would jostle my thoughts into place. If anything, I was further from finding the assassin than I had been before.

Raffar reached toward me, taking my hand in his. He raised his head and fixed the group with his eyes. "We leave within the hour. No one eats or drinks anything unless we brought it with us."

My eyes traveled over the guards surrounding me, taking in each pinched mouth, each hard gaze. One of the Loftarians could have slipped the poison into my food. But so could one of the Farnskager guards. No, I was no closer to finding Scilla's killer. All I knew was that they were still at work.

CHAPTER 10

The Loftarian mayor bowed and apologized a thousand times as we left, but our refusal to eat or drink anything in his manor was telling enough. The sun had just brightened in the sky as we climbed into our carriage, and by late afternoon, the elephant birds hauled us over the border into Farnskag.

Our entrance into their homeland wiped away the guards' intimidating scowls and smoothed their tense foreheads. A couple of mounted soldiers chased each other in circles around the carriage, the heavy feet of their elephant birds pounding up the dust. Raffar and Aldar laughed and leaned their heads back against the carriage walls and even called out to the others, egging them on to run faster. Relief rolled off of them in waves that soothed even my uneasy soul.

Almost immediately, Raffar called for a break. Under the shade of giant ferns, we ate a simple lunch of dried fish and fruit left over from Azzaria and drank water from a cool creek. When we were ready to leave again, Raffar asked me a question and Aldar translated. "As in Azzaria, we'll be traveling more slowly again. His Majesty would like you to meet your new country and citizens. For now, would you walk awhile with him?"

If it wouldn't be so unladylike, I would have jumped for joy. Finally, some time out of the carriage.

Raffar stood and stroked the lower half of Freyad's mount's neck. "Or would you prefer to ride an elephant bird?"

The animal's long neck bent, and the hard beak pecked at Raffar. He jerked away, but not before being pinched on the top of his shoulder. As the king rubbed the sore spot, Freyad laughed at him and pulled her steed away, cooing and murmuring at it.

Aldar's smirk joined Freyad's. "The bird's name is Cloverlily, and Freyad just told her she should be gentler with the king."

Color flooded Raffar's cheeks. He regarded me earnestly. "That wouldn't have happened with Fleetfoot—my own bird."

I nodded, doing my best to maintain an earnest expression. Those giant feathered creatures were too unpredictable anyway. "Let's just walk," I said.

Pebbles crunched under my feet as I strolled along the street, Raffar quiet at my side. The road was more or less even, but he swerved off the edge, traipsing through dandelions, running his hand over knee-high fern fronds just off the way. Most of the guards dismounted also, and many threaded fingers through high grasses and ferns like Raffar, greeting the country they hadn't seen in weeks.

My husband stopped and grinned at me, pointing to pretty purple flowers low to the ground. I leaned down to sniff at them, and a familiar lavender scent engulfed me. Maybe they were related to a plant back home.

As I straightened, my coiled hair caught on one of the larger fern fronds. Tattered plant pieces fell to the ground as Raffar helped me untangle the delicate leaves, but my complicated twist was ruined. His voice rumbled, and his eyes strayed to the unruly strands framing my face. The others walked on.

Back in Azzaria, he'd asked to see my hair down. Now, his eyes begged the same thing.

My pulse throbbing stupidly for a request so simple, I pulled the jeweled pins out, handing them one by one to Raffar. I waited for his grin, but he just stared, and his eyes were dark and intense, like that time we first met.

It had been two years ago. Scilla had been in her dressing room, preparing to be presented to the King of Farnskag for the first time. In her richly embroidered silk, she'd been beautiful, elegant, regal: the perfect Azzarian princess. If I were her, I'd have been terrified, but her hands barely shook as the servants fixed her hair and dress. I hung on to every word as she described the delegation's tattoos and shaved heads so I wouldn't be surprised.

Then Zito bounded into the room with a bloodcurdling scream, and Scilla almost tripped over a chair in shock. He roared, throwing imaginary javelins. Lost in his fantasy battle, he shrieked, stabbed, and dodged.

Little brothers. "Where's your nurse, Zito?" I asked.

"Sick!" He somersaulted three times across the floor and squealed when he hit the wall.

"I'd be sick too if I had to deal with your screeching all the time," Scilla muttered.

Zito jumped up, then crouched, ramming an invisible spear into my chest. "Rawrrr!"

"Stop making fun of them like that! It's insulting!" Scilla

yelled. She snatched a hairbrush from the servant next to her and threw it at Zito. He hopped to the side, and it bounced harmlessly off the wall.

Our little brother ran past her desk and looking glass and into her bedchamber, where he jumped on her bed, howling in a made-up, guttural language. With a yell, he hunched down and sprang off. An enormous thud made the cosmetics jars tinkle on the vanity.

One of the servants left Scilla's side to take control of Zito, but his energy knew no bounds. He dashed out from under her arm. Scilla's barely shaking hands turned into definitely shaking hands.

"Pia, Jiara, help," Scilla begged. "Please take him away from here. He's making me nervous."

Zito blabbered more throaty nonsense and stuck out his tongue.

Pia and I shared a look, then I positioned myself so that he'd be able to run by me, and Pia chased him in my direction. Just before he could curve past me, I jumped into his path and caught him under his arms.

"All right. We're leaving." I held his wrists behind his back.

"Jiara!" he yelled.

"And don't let the Farnskagers see him like that," Scilla called after us as I dragged him from the room. "We're meeting in Mother's office. Just keep him away from there."

Once out of Scilla's presence, I gave up trying to control Zito, and instead played along with him. He was quieter that way. We garbled back and forth to each other, skipping down the hall and giggling until we almost fell to the floor. He jerked

me down by my hair until I growled at him. He shoved me toward the wall, and I let myself sag against it as if he were the
mightiest soldier. I righted myself, and in return, I bumped his
back with my hip so that he stumbled to his knees, cackling
like a bellowthrush.

Muted voices drifted down the corridor, but Zito was in
no condition to meet up with Mother or Father. And especially
not foreign guests. I threw open the door to the Great Hall
and forced him inside, with me squeezing in after. I pulled the
door shut and whirled around.

Six bald men in dark tunics, their faces covered with tattoos, stood there in silence along with Mother and some of
her advisers. My heart stopped. Apparently, the Farnskager
delegation was not in Mother's office.

Zito let out a squeal, and I clapped my hand over his mouth
while I tried to straighten my posture.

Mother recovered first. "Please, excuse this interruption."

I nodded, especially to the young man standing in front
of the others. The king. Cool and confident, regardless of his
youth and the gazes resting on him, awaiting his reaction.

The king smiled at Zito and even knelt down to speak to
him. Zito had no idea what the king said, but he garbled back
as if they were having a fascinating conversation. The entire
party burst out laughing.

King Raffar rose, patted Zito's shoulder, and stepped closer
to me. Despite my hair hanging down as if it had never seen
a comb, his gaze was focused on me like no one else's ever.
His eyes held an astonished eagerness, like a man who had
desperately searched for a long-lost treasure only to turn a

corner and discover it inches from his grasp. I should have been scared by his foreign appearance and intense stare, but that *something* in his eyes made me want to come closer. His shoulders rose and fell, and he smiled.

The king said only one word—one I understood. "Scilla."

My heart imploded, and my face burned with shame. By dinnertime, he'd be Scilla's betrothed. How dare I think of her future husband like that?

Mother and Serenna and I fell over ourselves to explain the mistake.

"No, I'm—"

"—that's my younger daughter—"

"This is Princess Jiara."

King Raffar blushed and excused himself with a little shrug and eyes that did not meet mine again. "It's nice to meet you, Jiara," Serenna translated once he'd finally spoken, his attention on the window behind me.

And then Mother steered them to her office while I escaped to the flower garden with Zito. Outside of the official engagement ceremony, when I'd peered from behind Llandro, I hadn't seen Raffar again until the week before our wedding.

But months later, Scilla and I had lain on her bed and giggled about the husbands we'd wed someday. When I told her I didn't think Raffar looked so bad after all, she laughed and said he'd asked about me once. Then she tickled me and accused me of wanting him for myself. I denied it, because I didn't even know him. And what kind of a sister would do that?

Scilla laughed and reminded me of Gio, the wind god, and how he had fallen in love with Flisessa, the goddess of earth.

Eons ago, they'd had a whirlwind romance. He'd swept into her heart and her soul until their bodies had merged in a wild marriage night.

We on earth had paid the price—the worst cyclone to ever hit Azzaria's northern provinces had devastated those living there.

Nothing good could come from such passion.

I'd agreed with Scilla. She was relieved she felt only respect for Raffar, and that I felt only respect for Marro. Our marriages would be perfect, safe, and secure.

Now Raffar and I stood together on Farnskager ground. This far north, the temperature was cool—more like almost spring than early summer. The forest scent hung heavy like a mist. As Raffar accepted the final pin from my hair, my heart danced at the fire in his eyes. In a low voice, he murmured a short phrase, but Aldar was speaking to one of the guards and couldn't translate, so I didn't know what. Raffar slipped the pins into a pocket in his tunic. He reached down and plucked one of purple flowers and passed it to me. With one hand, he motioned to continue on.

———

After a half hour's walk, we climbed into the carriage and the elephant birds pulled us along at a breakneck pace. The driver pushed them to hurry. It felt like the ferns had just begun to blur, and then we slowed down again. When the dust cloud cleared, Raffar leaned out his window and muttered low, reverent-sounding words.

I looked to Aldar. Dipping his head to the window, he said, "White Mother."

I craned my neck to see around my husband. A huge rock formation stood a couple minutes' walk away. It was as tall as a five-story house and shaped like an immense haystack made of sparkling, white rock. Seven smaller haystack monoliths surrounded it.

Three guards next to the carriage dismounted and made for the rocks.

"Can I go see it?" I asked.

Aldar's gaze flicked to Raffar, who raised a hand to the shard in his ear and closed his eyes. Aldar shook his head at me, just barely, and spoke softly, "It would be best not to. We know the Azzarians do not share our belief in the Watchers. Ours is a simpler faith. A deep connection to the world around us. Just because we don't have your divine interactions and complicated rituals does not mean the Watchers are not important to us"—he pointed to his chest—"here, inside. Your presence at White Mother would be seen as ridicule."

I bowed my head. "That wasn't how I—"

"I know you don't mean it that way." Aldar's smile was weak, but understanding. "But for us, it is not just a big sparkling rock to gawk at." He whispered to Raffar, who creased his brows and nodded. The two men disembarked.

With strong hands holding back Cloverlily's reins, Freyad paraded around the carriage and stopped at the window. "*Skriin* Jiara," she said in greeting. *Skriin* was *queen*, I understood that much.

I slid over to Raffar's seat and smiled at her. She cocked her head in a questioning way. If only I had the vocabulary to ask for her thoughts. Following a brief lift of her chin, she nodded and continued circling the carriage. A few other guards remained with me while the rest headed for White Mother. When they arrived, they leaned forward in their typical greeting.

But no . . . it wasn't their normal greeting. Instead of reaching out with the left arm only, they reached out with both, and they seemed to actually touch foreheads to the rock, instead of remaining a breath away, as they did with people. It reminded me of when Raffar and the others had touched their foreheads to my bracelets. A few moments passed, and one by one, the soldiers returned to the group. The guards who had remained with me took their leave, until everyone in our party had visited the monoliths.

Everyone except me. Despite being hidden away in the carriage, I felt as if I were on a pedestal under an immense spotlight with a ringmaster blaring, "Jiara does not revere White Mother!"

When Raffar left the formation and headed toward me in the carriage again, his eyes met mine. It seemed there was a sad question in them for me. I looked to the floor and slid back to my own seat as he climbed in. He spoke, that low rumble I could almost feel in my chest. But Aldar wasn't there yet, so his words were a mystery. It was exactly how I'd expected once it was clear Pia wouldn't be coming with me.

Raffar ran a finger over the shard in his earlobe then inclined his head to the haystack monolith. A Watcher. I nodded.

The sadness didn't leave his face.

A few uncomfortable moments later, the carriage lurched

with Aldar's weight on the step. "Queen Jiara, we're less than an hour from the next village. It's time to begin meeting your new people."

CHAPTER 11

Five days later, I was certain I'd met the entire country already. We'd stopped at two or three villages each day. Our travel route must have been advertised, because representatives from other villages often came to pay their respects. I'd repeated the *gakh*, the traditional greeting, so often my neck and shoulders twinged each time I leaned forward. Everywhere we went, women and girls fingered my long hair as if it belonged to Farnskag and not to me. I'd learned the phrases *I'm happy to be here* and *So pleased to meet you* and, of course, with all of the feasts and performances in our honor, *thank you, thank you, thank you.*

And despite my attempts at being friendly, the whispers, the furtive glances I couldn't interpret, made my ears burn. Were they angry? Disgusted at my foreignness? Or merely curious?

In every village, I'd studied the facial tattoos of each bald person I'd seen. Most were adorned with the hybrid figure. Several had the leaf, but nowhere did I see the simple, thick-lined border as in the commander's drawing back home.

The carriage rattled along the bumpy dirt road past long stretches of farmland.

Aldar scooted to the edge of his seat, leaned toward the window. "Only a few minutes and we'll reach Baaldarstad."

Baaldarstad. The capital of Farnskag. Raffar's home.

The birds strained at the reins as they sniffed the air, and the guards crowed about seeing family and friends after weeks on the road. Raffar raised a hand and called out the window, and the guards on individual birds raced off. He laughed and waved, urging them on.

Eyes sparkling, Aldar said, "He gave them permission to go see their families. We have nothing to fear so close to home."

The first houses came into view. They were like in the other Farnskager villages we'd passed. Modest and rectangular, with one section for the families, and another for tools and farm animals. Most houses had steep thatched or wood-shingled roofs. The larger houses were crowned with finials at the peak above the door in the shape of a leaf, an eagle, ox horns, or a simple X. Little pens full of goats and chickens dotted the yards, along with small vegetable gardens and trees heavy with young, exotic fruits like apples and pears.

Farnskager buildings were simpler than those in Azzaria. Less decorated, lacking tiled roofs and spires. But the walls seemed thicker and more stable than our houses. They'd have to be here, in the north, where it grew so cold in the winter that it snowed.

An anticipatory chill crawled over my skin. I was going to live where it snowed. I pushed that image from my mind. The idea of such an extreme winter was too much.

As we rode into town, the houses were constructed of more cleanly cut lumber, fit expertly together. Yards grew smaller, and there was no longer any room for animals, but most everyone kept a small garden. Huge trees grew everywhere, so tall they were twice the height of Azzaria's tallest four-story buildings.

Raffar gestured out the window as we passed a stone and wood manor several times larger than the biggest house I'd seen. Unlike the other buildings, it had two stories. The roof was made of wooden shingles instead of thatch. Hybrid figures snaked along the roofline and reached all the way to the top of the house on either side. Above the door was a hybrid figure finial centered at the peak of the roofline. Red feathers had been strung onto the figure and fluttered in the wind.

Raffar gestured to it. "Our home."

But we didn't stop in front of it. The manor was surrounded by a huge park, and evergreen trees towered over the house on all sides. Probably thirty elephant birds wandered a penned-in area on the right side of the property. Would we stop there? To have servants take care of the animals that had traveled so far? As I tried to imagine myself in that home, surrounded by the pines and the carvings and the elephant birds, the carriage turned away, down the street.

"Where are we going?"

"The main square," Aldar said. "Just like with the other stops. Every Farnskager town has a square that belongs to the community, and we must greet the town first."

A short way down the road, the rumble of hundreds of voices filled the air. We turned the corner, and the carriage came to a smooth stop at the foot of the crowded square. More adults and children than could fit in the houses of the town milled around, some of them embracing the guards who had returned only moments before.

I smoothed my *zintella* dress and my too-long hair. With a smile, Raffar held out his hand. I inhaled a deep breath, took his hand, and followed him out of the carriage.

Children waved fern fronds, and the townspeople cried, "*Villku, villku!*" *Welcome*, I remembered from the other cities.

The sun filtered through the leafy trees, and birds chirped and sang overhead. I held back from squinting against the glaring rays of light so the first glimpse of their new queen wouldn't be a sour face.

The townspeople gathered closer as we stood in front of a large building as wide as the royal manor, but only one story. Even more care had been taken with the decorations here. Every inch was made of stone and polished wood—the hard one Aldar had referred to as ironfern wood. Patterns stained into the side looked like twisting vines. Intricate carvings ran the entire height at each corner and all along the roofline. At the crest of the roof, a huge hybrid figure finial looked out over the people gathered in the square. Like at the royal manor, red feathers fluttered in the breeze. The doors were propped open, and inside, there was probably enough space for most of the townspeople. Opposite the meeting place, a narrow monolith of pewter-colored stone reached high into the sky.

"Freyad!" a woman cried to my right, followed by a loud whooping noise. My guard hopped down from Cloverlily and was swept up in a tight hug from the other woman. She buried her face in Freyad's neck. They held each other close, and Freyad kissed the woman's head tenderly.

A man rushed over to us and laid a cloak around one of Raffar's shoulders—a cloak made of fur and topped with red feathers around the neck, the same red that adorned the house's figurehead. A staff-like weapon similar to the ones our guards always carried was pushed into his hands. I'd grown used to Raffar's shaved head and tattoos, but the fur and the feathers and the weapon turned him into one of the northern strangers from the stories of my childhood. I opened my mouth, forcing myself to breathe evenly and shallowly.

Aldar ripped my attention from Raffar's foreign image as he began making introductions. Where I hadn't even attempted to remember the names in the other towns, here, I'd need to learn them. But after the third jumble of letters ending with R or D, attached to a short-haired or bald person with tattoos, I gave up. Once again, I was all smiles in the middle of a blur of bright, tattooed faces and murmurs of "Welcome, Queen Jiara."

Except not everyone was smiling. Under a large tree laden with some kind of nut, three frowning men gestured angrily in my direction.

"Aldar, what's wrong there?" I whispered, inconspicuously angling my head to show where I meant. I searched the crowd for more scowling faces.

He cleared his throat. "Pay them no mind. There are always a few who don't agree with Raffar's . . . politics."

Of course. If Loftaria attacked Azzaria, Farnskag would be forced into war. For many, the price was too high for fishing and trading rights. I was a symbol of that potential for violence and loss of life.

Aldar smiled apologetically, then repeated himself: "Really, Queen Jiara, pay them no mind."

The next crowd surged forward and Aldar continued with introductions, but now that I knew they were there, the men under the nut tree were all I could think about. I smiled and nodded, murmured my *nice to meet yous*. Soon there was a fourth man under the tree, and the group grew louder. How angry were these dissidents? Was their rage enough for murder? Had one of them killed Scilla?

As with every town and village so far, I focused on the facial tattoos of the men. Those under the nut tree all wore leaves, but they were too far away for me to recognize whether there were double, thick, or thin borders.

The man who'd brought Raffar's cloak led us to woven mats on the ground at the base of the eighteen-foot-tall monolith. We sat close together, with the warmth of his arm just barely brushing mine as older people, heads of important families all over the country, spoke about good marriages and tying our two nations together. Aldar knelt behind me and tried to keep up with translations and introductions, but the names flew into and out of my head, and every speech sounded the same.

"Aldar," I whispered over my shoulder, "you don't have to work so hard."

He smiled gratefully at me, and when I shivered from the cool northern air, Aldar had someone bring a light woolen cloak.

After each spokesperson, a group from that family

performed a dance, waving spears or fern fronds. The music was so different from back home. Drums. One lonesome flute. Occasional singing. But mostly, the groups chanted and clapped. I'd been taken aback the first time I'd heard an entire group chant in the border town we'd visited on that first day in Farnskag. Now the rhythm—the intensity—vibrated in my chest, setting an urgent energy free, and my pulse throbbed in time with the beat.

Finally, Raffar stood. I leaned back and spoke over my shoulder without letting my husband out of my sight. "Aldar, please tell me everything Raffar says."

"Of course, Your Majesty."

Raffar stepped a few paces away so he could be seen by the crowd. "Fellow Farnskagers, thank you for the chants and the fern dances, for your inspirational speeches, and for the magnitude of delicious food you prepared to share for this feast. But most of all, thank you for your presence here today. Thank you for your acceptance of the union we have created."

As he spoke, Raffar's eyes had traveled over the hundreds of guests. But now, they settled on me. "Jiara Ginevoradaag of Azzaria, welcome to Baaldarstad. We married according to your traditions in Azzaria. Today, here in Baaldarstad, we marry according to mine. Today, I make a promise to you. I, Raffar Perssuun Daggsuun, promise to be a good husband for you and to take care of you always."

People all around the square whispered and leaned into their mates, and I smiled.

"Everyone! Enjoy yourselves! Celebrate with us!" With a

wide smile, Raffar raised a hand to the crowd and then came back to me and took his place by my side.

Another chant began and more poultry, sweet potatoes, beets, and bread were set before us than we could eat in three days. Aldar and the guards didn't have plates, so I held a platter out to them and waved to show they should take a portion.

The guards studied the ground below us, and Aldar said, "You and King Raffar have specially prepared wedding food today, specially spiced. It is good for . . . fertility. We cannot share."

Fertility? Heat crept into my cheeks. "Sorry," I said. If only this mistake would be the last one I'd make in Farnskag.

CHAPTER 12

The strong wedding celebration mead was going to my head. Rain sprinkled lightly, so I stood inside the meeting hall. The walls leaned, and the floor dipped, just the tiniest bit. Whew. Enough. Smiling at strange, patterned faces, I set my mead horn down. One leaf after another walked by, but never the one I sought.

Freyad had the evening off and another guard stood by me. True to his promise to my mother, Raffar had given another woman the job. She smiled brightly at me and steadied my elbow with her palm.

"Thank you," I said in Farnskag, and she uttered something that was probably praise for managing the word. She spoke again and waited on a reply. Aldar was nowhere in sight, and despair started crawling up my throat.

With a raised hand, Raffar caught my eye from across the room. He'd removed his furred cloak at some point. I waved back.

"Good night," my guard said. At least, I was fairly certain that was what those words meant. I looked around to see if Freyad was taking over, but then Raffar appeared at my side.

The Farnskager drums vibrated in my chest as he bent his head and whispered in my ear.

The desolation in my throat dug in its heels. "I don't understand," I breathed.

Raffar smiled and took my hand. He led me out of the building, onto the square. Whoops and shouts exploded behind us, and then uncontrollable laughter. I turned back to see them waving us out the door, shooing us away.

Fire shot to my face. It was time for my wedding night.

Shallow, even breaths would calm me. In. Out. I may never have been with a man before, but I wasn't some terrified innocent. Mother had explained everything to me. I knew where babies came from. The palace bred plenty of animals. I knew what would happen.

My heart stuttered anyway. When it came down to it, would I ask Raffar to wait? Until we knew each other better?

The square was only a short walk from Raffar's manor. Three guards followed us at a distance, and we strolled in silence. After dinner, I'd been in the house briefly as I'd washed up after the journey, so I remembered the heavy, intricately carved front door and the massive staircase that led to our suite.

My palm was damp as my husband ushered me up the polished wooden stairs. It was my wedding night. My slow breaths weren't so slow anymore.

A low voice from behind—the guards stood at attention at the bottom step—and then we were upstairs, alone.

We navigated the empty, dark-paneled halls of the second floor, until Raffar opened the double doors of our suite.

I preceded him into a sitting room with a small forest-green couch, a desk, and two chairs. After that came our dining room. The bathroom was on the left. Woven dark green carpets throughout, as if we were still in a forest. And at the back . . . our bedroom.

Thick candles flickered on the windowsills and, through the open doors, on the low chests at each side of the bed. The sitting room was so silent, every one of my husband's breaths was like a sigh in my ear.

The doors clicked shut behind me. Raffar walked in my direction. He took both of my hands in his and made that *mmm* noise that seemed to mean everything and nothing. Then he said . . . *beautiful.* Other words too, but the only word I recognized was *beautiful.*

Something tickled my neck.

Blood on the floor, the walls, the ceiling.

No. Scilla was not here. Mother had said she wouldn't come this far.

I disregarded the sensation and concentrated on the tattooed man before me. He moved slowly and deliberately, like he feared I'd run off if he spooked me.

The candle nearest us blew out. A quick glance showed me the windows were all shut, and I ignored the smoking candle too. *Scilla is not here. Not now.*

I swallowed. After a curious glance at the curling smoke, Raffar repeated himself. I tilted my head to get a better look at him. As attractive as ever—at some point, I'd grown used to the leather and the tattoos and shaved head—but despite the weeks we'd spent with each other, still somehow like a sculpture. Artwork that was appealing to the eye. But not a soul mate, not a person I knew deep in my heart.

Slowly, as if he were fighting with himself, Raffar's hand rose to my cheek. He stroked it with a calloused finger. The roughness scraped against my skin, but I felt it deeper. Like he was touching my neck and my backbone and the pit of my stomach. I closed my eyes and leaned into his hand.

He dipped his head until his nose and forehead almost touched mine the way the Farnskagers did, but we were so close that my back and neck didn't hurt at all. Raffar's breath held a hint of the scent of mead. He groaned and gave in to whatever had held him back, his cheek skimming along mine, his lips trailing down the side of my face and onto my neck.

His arms snaked around my back as my fingers traced the tattooed lines on his face. Warm hands tangled in my hair, and when he urged my hips closer, my core turned hot and achy. How could I have been so wrong? He was nothing like a sculpture to be admired from afar. I pressed against him in response, and any notion of wanting to wait fled. The only thing I wanted was to be with him.

Raffar stopped moving. He froze for a long moment. Had I made a mistake? My hand fell from his cheek.

Finally, he took a deep breath against my neck. He said a word I recognized: "No."

No?

With both hands, he pushed gently but firmly against my shoulders until I was two steps away. He ran a hand over his forehead and scalp, and his deep voice began rambling, rambling, rambling, and I had no idea what about. Just that it was my wedding night, and he'd said I was beautiful, and then he said, "No."

He paced to the door and back, all the while, foreign words pouring from his lips.

"Raffar," I interrupted him. I hid the hands I'd clenched into fists behind my back and shook my head, raised my shoulders to ask what was the matter.

Sensuality dropped from his frame, and his movements turned efficient as he motioned me to follow him to the bedroom, to the side of the bed. From the top drawer of a small chest, he pulled out that black leather lexicon I remembered from the palace garden in Azzaria. A book? Now? My stomach turned as his finger traveled over the words until it pointed to the translation he required. The letters swam before my eyes until I forced them to stop.

Wait.

Wait?

He wanted to wait? For what?

Then he flipped more pages and pointed again.

Eighteen.

Wait for eighteen? Wait on our wedding night? I remembered his outburst back in Mother's office, about me not being eighteen yet. It was apparently more important in Farnskag than I'd thought.

He paged back and forth, showing numerous words, until I understood more. No one in Farnskag knew I was "underage." No one but Aldar and Freyad and Matid who had been present at the negotiations and wouldn't tell. My birth date had even been removed from the marriage documents. With me so young, the marriage wouldn't exactly be invalid, but it would be frowned upon.

Raffar's eyes were open and hopeful and pleading. He waited for me to agree.

What else could I do? Waiting was the intelligent thing to do anyway. We barely knew each other. Just because I was curious and half-melted inside didn't mean I couldn't wait.

I took a deep breath and nodded. With a swallow, I attempted to squelch the tightness in my throat. It would be better anyway. To get to know each other. For me to learn more of the language. Being intimate with a man I'd never even conversed with . . . it was ridiculous, really.

He took my hand again, and we sat on the edge of the bed together. Neither of us said a word.

After a while, we both dressed for the night and lay down in the silent room. Only inches of space separated us. In the moonlight, Raffar's eyes were closed and his jaw hard. The brutal grip on my throat remained.

After a much longer while, I finally fell asleep.

I braced my feet against the floor and let the wooden posts of the chair jab into my back. For what was probably the seven-hundredth time, Aldar shook his head across the desk, and that was only counting today. He'd begun tutoring me the day after the wedding banquet. As long as I was new to Farnskag, I'd just attend events that needed a royal face, smiling and greeting. Once I'd learned the language and customs,

I could take a more active role. But the language came first, so I had sat in this chair four hours per day, every day since arriving in Baaldarstad.

That had been one week ago. Now, Aldar leaned forward in the sitting room of my suite, holding up a slate with gibberish printed on it. *Giganbaav.* My mind conjured up the image of a tree. Aldar said, "rainbow," and my heart sank again. Then he pronounced the word in a way I would never pronounce the same letters in Azzarian and waited for me to repeat it. Reading was giving me tired eyes and a headache anyway, so I ignored the letters dancing on the slate. But I said the word, over and over. *Giganbaav.* Rainbow.

I might never learn to read Farnskag, but I would learn to speak it. If I wanted to figure out who killed Scilla, I had to be able to ask questions. If only the likelihood of needing to interrogate a rainbow were higher.

Aldar corrected my pronunciation several times. He smiled when I finally had it right. Then he wiped the slate, and we repeated the process with the next word: *stul.* Chair. I wished we would stick to words that belonged together. But every day, we jumped around to all different topics.

I stretched my neck and shoulder muscles. When he held up the slate again, I recognized the next word, *gehaas*, because we'd had it every single day this week. I tried to picture what it meant, but my mind was blank, so I sounded out the letters. Aldar thinned his lips and said, "house." He repeated the word, but differently than I had said it. I slumped over the tabletop and bit my lip to force the tears down. Staying positive was harder every day. It seemed like the letters were pronounced differently for every word.

"I really appreciate you trying to teach me to read, but can we please concentrate on speaking?" With a fingertip, I scratched at the dark wood of the table before finally admitting, "I'm not good at reading. Not even in Azzarian."

He groaned, a long, soft, drawn-out sigh. "I'm failing you. And King Raffar."

Aldar blamed himself? A familiar tightness gripped my throat. "What? No, Aldar, it's always been this way. It's my weakness—"

"No, no. I am a good translator." He pounded the table softly with his fist and smiled, his teeth extra white compared to the dark ink on his face. "But I am a terrible teacher. If I weren't related to Raffar, he wouldn't have given me this position. There just isn't much call for someone who speaks Azzarian. There's hardly anyone else to teach you, and hardly anything else for me to do. Outside diplomatic circles, our countries haven't had much contact."

"I imagine that will change now that Farnskag will increase trade and fishing."

He nodded, his lips forming a smile. "Yes, someday soon, and then I'll be able to fulfill a more meaningful role." His cheeks turned a little pink. "I'm sorry. Not that teaching you isn't meaningful." He rubbed both palms on his thighs. "Of course, it is, but I, uh, I mean, until then . . . please give me another chance. I just need more time."

I opened my mouth to speak, but he went on. "I don't want to have to leave court. Please don't tell Raffar, but I don't feel comfortable in the university at Gluwfyall. It makes me sound like a child, but it's far from my family. And Raffar. We grew up together, you know."

"You did?"

He abandoned the slate on the table, and I vowed to keep him talking as long as I could.

With a nod, he said, "I even lived here in the manor part of the time. My room was right down the hall. Raffar and I were like brothers."

I smiled, imagining them terrorizing the manor staff like Zito did at home. The way they acted together also made more sense. Their behavior certainly hadn't been what I'd expected from a king and his translator.

"When Raffar's parents only had the one child, they adopted several others from throughout the province. I wasn't adopted, but my parents spent so much time in other cities, I lived here for months at a time. There were six of us kids in the royal manor. It could be chaotic at times, especially with the little ones, but at least Indgar wasn't bad. She was only two years younger and nearly impossible to beat in a footrace. But we usually managed."

I rolled my eyes, and Aldar smiled at a memory only he could see. Then he leaned forward as if sharing a secret. "But Raffar and I were the closest."

"What was he like? As a child?"

Aldar looked out the window and grinned. "Wilder than today. A little dangerous sometimes."

I followed his eyes and pictures of two boys climbing fern trees appeared in my head.

When he met my gaze again, the windows reflected off his sparkling eyes. "We had a plan. He'd be king, and I'd be the commander of the military. Together, we were going to take over the entire continent."

"The entire continent?" A disbelieving laugh burst from my mouth.

He put on an insulted face. "It would be possible."

I turned my eyes to the desktop. Boys and their plans. "Of course. I don't doubt the might of the Farnskager army."

"Now you're teasing." Slowly, his grin disintegrated. "But during that one summer, he lost his parents; the other children couldn't be raised by government advisers, so they were sent to live with families who could take care of them; Raffar started spending all his time with strategists and the Grand Council . . ."

The loneliness of a younger Aldar made me reach out and give his arm a pat. After a moment, I asked, "What made you decide against being a soldier then?"

He sighed. "My scrawny, weak body."

Aldar was as tall as Raffar and wasn't scrawny in the least. "But—"

"I didn't shoot up until I was at the university. Quite late. Too late to go back to a military career. And by then, my father was pushing me into politics, into a place on the Grand Council, so I could advise Raffar."

Pushing. Sounded like he wasn't particularly content with his father's plans.

"If you want to do something else, I'm sure Raffar—"

He stopped me with a shake of his head. "This is fine for

now. I'm close to my father. And my work is useful." He raised both eyebrows at me.

"It is," I agreed.

"Then let's continue." He picked up the slate, and my shoulders dropped.

"Could we skip the read—"

"I promise, Your Majesty. I'll make sure you learn." He scribbled a word on the slate and nodded vigorously, hope shining all over his face.

After a moment of herding the letters around, I sounded out the word in my mind: *taavad.* The tablet seemed to mock me. I had no idea what the word meant, but I remembered it too. I said it out loud. His smile unwavering, he corrected my pronunciation, repeating it once, twice, three times.

I echoed him, once, twice, three times, the pit in my stomach growing deeper with every repetition. I still didn't know what it meant.

CHAPTER 13

That day after lunch, my head buzzed and letters flashed behind my eyelids every time I blinked. When Freyad came to take me on my daily walk through town, I was so quick to jump up that I almost knocked over my chair.

"I can't come with you today," Aldar said. He explained something to Freyad, who nodded sympathetically.

My fear of being in this foreign land was growing smaller, but my stomach still clenched. If I needed urgent help and Aldar wasn't around, no one would be able to understand me.

While he spoke with Freyad, Aldar's eyes pinched together and his tone turned brittle.

"Is something wrong?" I asked.

He packed the slate and chalk in the drawer. "My father is ill. It's . . . very serious. I'm going to see him. I don't know how much time he has left."

Here he was, working patiently to teach me a language I'd probably never learn, and what he really needed was to spend time with his dying father. "I'm so sorry to hear that," I said.

He flashed a weak smile. "It's not your fault. And he's proud of my role in helping you adjust to life here in Farnskag."

We left the royal manor together, but Aldar headed the opposite way down the street from us. Usually, if we weren't already expected for an event somewhere, he asked me if there was anything special I'd like to see. In the past days, we'd toured the market and three schools and the meeting hall, where I'd searched every face I saw for the telltale tattoo. Today, Freyad looked to me, raised her shoulders in a resigned sigh, and waved her hand for me to follow. Playing nanny to a helpless girl was probably not part of her normal soldierly duties.

We strolled along the wide road and turned into a narrow alley. Like everywhere in Farnskag, the street was made of firmly packed dirt. The houses on this one were narrow but had two stories, and to the side of each, a little vegetable garden provided constant fresh food. The alley was so tight that a carriage couldn't fit, and balconies hovered over our heads. A few older people draped wet laundry on lines between balconies over the street. Like light rain, drips from the laundry sprinkled on our heads as we passed through. Freyad rubbed her short hair until it stood up even more than normal. She twisted her lips and raised her eyebrows until I laughed so loud, the people above stared down.

Freyad laid her head to the side, considering me. Then she laughed too.

A jaw dropped as one of the women recognized me. I'd given up on my silk *zintella* dresses, so it wasn't the clothing that gave me away. Today, I wore a tunic and pants made according to my specifications, which meant not quite as loose as most Farnskager women wore them. But my hair was unmistakable.

The woman gasped and called, "*Skriin* Jiara!"

The people stared as we tried to protect ourselves from the laundry rain. I could have sworn they shook the damp clothes out extra hard now. They laughed and jabbered more phrases, but I only caught my title and name.

Their tones were open and friendly. Not suspicious or angry. The image of the men beneath the nut tree upon my first arrival haunted me every day. I beamed at Freyad for bringing me here to meet normal people who were happy to see me.

I held my head higher. These people weren't acting like the dissidents, and they deserved a queen they could have confidence in. I smiled and waved up at them. "*Guuddug?*" I whispered to Freyad to be sure it meant *hello*. She nodded almost imperceptibly. "*Guuddug!*" I called. I threw my head back and smiled my brightest smile as I waved harder. "*Guuddug!*"

One of the women clapped and nodded at me. I squeezed Freyad's arm and wanted to thank her, but despite the fact that I must have said it thousands of times, the only word that came to mind was *guuddug*. But *hello* and *thank you* couldn't be the same word, could they? I inclined my head to her instead. She called out to the women in goodbye and motioned me to continue down the alley.

A man about Llandro's age trudged toward us. He stopped at one of the houses on the right to push open the door, and I had to bite my lip not to cry out. Dried blood smeared his cheek all the way up to his eye, and the skin was swollen and purple around a crisscross cut. For the briefest of seconds, the serving woman's story about her favorite aunt took over my heart. Being so far away, it was tempting to forget what was happening with my family back home. Were they all safe?

Once he'd disappeared into his house, I gestured questioningly to where he'd stood and then to my own face. "What happened?" I asked.

Freyad nodded and pointed to her forehead. "*Devsiin.*"

"*Devsiin?*" I repeated. Why *forehead* when I'd asked about his cheek?

She traced the swirls on her forehead. "*Devsiin.*"

"Oh!" The tattoo.

The tattoo! He'd just received a new tattoo. That meant someone here must give them. Who better to ask about the leaf with the thick outline than a local tattoo artist?

I mimed swirls on my cheek and then pointed to my eyes to show I wanted to see it done. Freyad squinted at me, then pointed to my eyes and to her forehead, poking as if she was applying the ink with her finger.

"Yes! Show me."

Freyad considered for a moment then nodded. "Yes." She gestured for me to follow.

My feet wanted to fly down the road. A tattoo expert!

Scilla, are you really here? Because this is our best chance yet. We were finally going to make progress in finding her killer.

———————

Freyad led me through a labyrinth of narrow alleys bordered by two-story houses, then the street opened up into the wider roads of the town center. A girl skipped from a house, a black fur cloak flowing from her head as if it were hair. She laughed and fluffed her imaginary long tresses. When I smiled at her, she giggled and waved back. An old woman hobbled out behind the girl. With a bark and a yank, the cloak flew from the girl's head. The old woman's wrinkles deepened as she frowned at me.

I turned my back on the scene and concentrated on keeping my face neutral. My new subjects needed time to get used to me and my foreign appearance. My heart wouldn't quiver like this all the time. It would get better. Surely.

Freyad and I crossed the square in front of the meeting hall. She raised her hand to greet someone on the other side: in front of the monolith stood Raffar, surrounded by three men.

My worries lifted a little as I spied my husband, but my smile died when he gestured toward the manor and shouted angry words I didn't understand.

We continued in his direction, but the violent red faces of his companions stopped me in my tracks. Raffar yelled again and threw his hand toward us and then away in a gesture for us to leave. Her face tight, Freyad gripped my arm. She tugged me away from Raffar and toward the manor.

One of Raffar's companions, an older, slightly taller and much beefier man, leaned in closer to him. He hadn't been one of the men under the tree that first night, but the other two were. This man's bellow in Raffar's face echoed across the square. If I'd learned one thing since coming to Farnskag, it was that they had a much more casual sense of royalty. In Azzaria, no one would yell at my mother or father. Here, Aldar and Freyad called the king by his given name alone, something not even Pia did with me, despite how long we'd known each other. And now this.

Raffar flinched at the shout but held his ground. Freyad was still pulling at my sleeve, but I dug in my heels. "Wait!" I wasn't leaving before I found out how bad the situation was. Would it help if they got to know me? Saw me as a person instead of some kind of travel souvenir?

Several guards ran into the square from a side street, apparently alerted by the clamor. Aldar followed them, then stopped, scanning the crowd.

"Aldar!" I called. Finally, someone who could help me understand what was going on. And whether my presence could help or harm the situation.

The translator caught my eye, but first looked to Raffar, obviously offering his support. Raffar waved him off. Aldar ran to my side, muttering to Freyad. She stopped tugging my arm.

"What's happening?"

"I'd mentioned before that not everyone is satisfied with the king's politics. Raffar wants to really open the borders. Until now, only registered Loftarians have been allowed into Farnskag, and vice versa. But he wants to increase trade, especially considering we can get goods from the southern continent more cheaply now. We can buy from the south and sell to Loftaria. We've always had an uneasy peace with them. Some feel the alliance with Azzaria will be seen as a deliberate threat."

"But we were in Loftaria. We spoke to several of their governors. That's not at all how they seemed to take it," I said.

Shaking his head, Aldar smiled down at me. "You and Raffar

fit each other well. Very optimistic. Have you forgotten the attempt on your life there?"

It felt like a slap in the face, or at least the admonishment of a naive girl. Yes, the Farnskagers were much more casual with their royalty. I wasn't stupid. But we had no proof it had been a political issue. It may have been the work of one hurt individual who had lost a relative in a border skirmish. And I hadn't forgotten the possibility that it had been one of Raffar's party or even a Stärklandish citizen in disguise.

Aldar didn't have to agree with me, but he could at least help me understand what was going on. I gestured to the argument. "What are they saying?"

"I need to get closer." He took hold of my upper arm and propelled me forward. Freyad barked at him, and he answered calmly without turning around. She skipped to catch up and scowled at the two of us.

The wind gusted across the square as we advanced a few steps, and I gathered my hair in one hand to keep it from flying in my face. "Who are those men?"

"Some of the Grand Council. They advise the king. The tall one doing the most talking is Geord."

"And this yelling . . . is that 'advising'?"

Aldar chuckled. "That is how it tends to go, yes. Past kings have followed the council's advice more closely than Raffar does. Sometimes I believe Geord thinks if he just says it loud enough, it will get through Raffar's thick skull."

I bit my lip. Such a remark would be unthinkable in Azzaria. Geord hollered again, and this time, Raffar shouted back. The sight of the tattooed men, their faces beet red with anger, made a part of me want to run back to the manor after all.

Freyad rocked on the balls of her feet as if she could barely keep herself from rushing to Raffar's side.

"Interesting . . . they're talking about the prisoner from Stärkland," Aldar said, his voice hushed.

"What? You have a prisoner from Stärkland?"

He nodded, his ear turned to the men. "Raffar says the Stärklandish queen requested help in finding lost emissaries. I have no idea who that could be. Our attempts to communicate with the prisoner have been unsuccessful." His gaze slid to me. "I should know. I've tried to help. Raffar requested a translator fluent in Stärklandish, but the man never arrived. And now . . . no. That can't be."

Aldar silently glared at his king until I prodded his arm. "Tell me."

He pursed his lips. "Despite the fact that we've never gotten any information out of the prisoner, Raffar isn't sure that it might not be a misunderstanding. He doesn't believe the Stärklandish queen wants conflict, so he's considering sending the prisoner back as a peace offering. The man hasn't even been punished."

It was too easy to envision the awful damage Farnskager staffs and clubs could do to a body. I pushed the images of battered bodies from my mind. "What is the punishment for?" Why did they even have a prisoner?

A lump in his throat bobbed. "That *man*"—he spat the word as if it was too noble a description for the prisoner—"is the only survivor of a small troop that attacked a group of our soldiers. I was there. It was awful . . . a massacre."

Aldar's forehead creased with worry, and in contrast, Raffar's features had smoothed. They were overly calm, placating. Geord kicked the dirt with his toe. His face was as tense as ever.

"He's apparently also thinking about a treaty with Stärkland," Aldar said, his voice dropping at the end as if he couldn't believe his king's words either. Geord shouted and slapped his hands together. Aldar cleared his throat. "The older generation thinks he's insane . . . and . . ."

"And?"

"I'm afraid Raffar is beginning to believe any road to peace is a good one. But not like this. Not when we'd come out in a position of weakness. We have peace with Loftaria because they know not to cross us. Despite how many of our own were killed in the ambush, he wants to believe giving back this Stärklandish prisoner will help."

Raffar and Geord shouted at each other for another several minutes. Finally, one of the council members looked in my direction and muttered something that turned his face sour.

"What did they sa—" I started.

Aldar shook his head, his eyes narrowed.

The group glared at me with gazes laced with bladeleaf. Raffar spat another word. He turned and left them standing there, mouths open.

He strode to me and offered his arm. His face was hard as stone as he escorted me back to the manor.

When we walked by the council members, I checked each

one's face. No sign of a leaf with a thick border. Raffar's arm muscles were marble under my hand. My visit to the tattoo artist would have to wait.

CHAPTER 14

A couple of days later, Aldar brought me back from an appearance at the riverfront, where the newly rebuilt dock had been opened. The body of water, regardless of how tiny, reflected the trees and the sky and felt almost like home. But the riverfront trip was like all the others—so many people wanted to see the new queen that my afternoons were booked in advance. Which meant, despite my insistent requests, we hadn't visited the tattoo artist's house yet. The only thing I could do was study each tattoo I did see. Unfortunately, without success.

Most evenings, Raffar and I ate in the main dining hall with Aldar and some visitors and advisers or influential townspeople. Tonight, after my husband shared a word with Aldar, the translator whispered with a glint in his eye, "I believe His Majesty would like a break from the constant guests. He asks if you would like to dine with him in your suite tonight."

All smiles, I turned to Raffar. "Yes! I'd love to!"

Once he heard the translation, Raffar beamed back at me. Aldar spoke to Raffar again, and then translated for me. Aldar was always good at including me in conversations that happened around me. "Raffar, thank you for visiting my father. It means a lot to him."

My husband leaned against the desk. "He's a good man. I only wish there was more I could do."

Raffar gripped Aldar's arm, their lifelong friendship an almost tangible thing in the air. Aldar shook himself. "I do too. Goodnight, Queen Jiara. Goodnight, Raffar." He left the room.

Raffar and I were alone.

It was so quiet. It was always quiet when we were alone, but when he looked at me, the lines of his face were softer than normal. As if it were a balm to be here, with only me as company.

I smiled back at him. If only I could ask him everything. About the tattoo artist, about the prisoner from Stärkland.

Raffar gestured to my chair. Once I sat, he started talking. I watched his expressions, tired, then, as he spoke and ate, more energetic. When our meal was finished, I told him about my week, in Azzarian, of course. About the walk with Freyad, about how Geord's shouting had worried me, about how seeing the river made me feel, about failing to find the right tattoo so far and my plan to visit the tattoo artist. He didn't understand, but he watched me and listened.

There was one word I remembered. "*Devsiin*," I said.

Raffar's eyes shot to mine. "*Devsiin*?" he repeated. He traced the lines on his face, then he reached out and brushed a thumb over my cheek.

All the breath left my lungs. Did he think I wanted a tattoo? I'd been around them long enough that they didn't seem alien to me anymore. The whorls and lines were fascinating, told stories even, and my fingers longed to touch Raffar's again. But that man in the alley . . . it looked painful.

I shook my head, and my eyes must have shown my panic because he smiled and shook his head too.

Raffar asked a question, but the only word I caught was *Aldar*. So, he probably wanted to know how my language lessons were progressing.

I ignored the sinking feeling in the pit of my stomach. I had learned a few phrases.

"Hello. My name is Jiara," I said in Farnskag.

A grin split his face. "Hello, Jiara. My name is Raffar," he answered—and tears pricked my eyes. Our first conversation.

To prolong it, my thoughts scrambled for something else I could say. I pointed to the rice on the table. "I like rice."

My face warmed. Such a boring sentence.

But Raffar dragged his chair closer. He pointed to the orange mush. "I like sweet potatoes." He pointed to several of the other dishes and said he liked them, but I didn't catch their names.

I couldn't make him understand the laundry rain or the smiles of the friendly children who'd allowed their curiosity to rule them as they fingered my hair, but I could let him know I was happy with my personal guard. "I like Freyad."

"Good . . ." he said and garbled a phrase I didn't get. My confusion must have been obvious. He held up a finger. "Freyad." Then he mimed throwing an object. "Freyad. Good."

When I still didn't understand, he held his hands out about four feet apart. He pretended to throw again, then clutched his chest as if he'd been hit there.

Oh. Freyad was good at throwing a weapon. A javelin based on the size Raffar had mimed. That was important apparently. Especially with how violently the Grand Council members argued.

I considered the other people I'd met. "I don't like Geord."

Raffar waved as if brushing away a fly. He hesitated, his brow wrinkled. Carefully, he said, "Geord. Not bad. Geord loud." Then he spoke several sentences, while pointing to his heart, then sliding his hand up to his mouth and out into the air. Geord let what was in his heart out his mouth. So, he was passionate?

I was probably saying it wrong, but I asked, "You like Geord?"

Raffar's eyebrows rose and fell. He laughed deeply. And he didn't answer the question, which was answer enough.

A servant came and cleared the table for us. Raffar set out a square piece of nearly black wood inlaid with golden stars and white diamonds. Then he set white stones on the diamonds and dark stones on the stars.

"*Vansvagd*," he said, pointing to the game.

He moved a black stone, then gestured to me. A game that I didn't know how to play. Well, he'd stop me if I was wrong. I pushed a white stone to an adjacent free space. He moved one of his. It went back and forth until he pushed a stone and smiled at me. There were no free spaces next to any of my stones. I was trapped.

I tried to remember the word for *again*, but couldn't, so I slid the stones back to their original places. I moved the first one randomly. Once more, we shoved the pieces around, one space at a time. Raffar commented constantly, and I realized he was teaching me words, so I repeated them. *Black* and *white*, *stone* and *board*. *Star*. *You*.

By the end of our fourth game, I'd learned the words for *I win* . . . even if I hadn't been able to say it myself.

———

Two days later, Aldar had not yet arrived for our lesson when the door to the suite banged open.

"Jiara!" The lines of Raffar's tattoos were distorted by his smile. He held out both hands, and the eager gleam in his eyes made me grasp them and follow him down the stairs.

His gruff voice flowed over me as he stopped at the kitchen to accept a bag, then he tugged me out of the house and down the road to the western side of town. His gait was quick and his hold on my hand never loosened. After about twenty minutes, we passed the last houses and reached a field bordered by people of all ages, all quietly staring into the grass. I craned my neck to see what was so captivating. Multicolored flower petals appeared to bob in the breeze, but other than that—

Raffar pointed to his eyes and then the field. When I nodded, he raised his arm to get everyone's attention. Then he dropped it. A loud clap echoed from across the field, and the sky came alive with thousands of butterflies. White, yellow, blue, and orange exploded in the air.

Children raced onto the field and began sprinkling something on the ground. Laughing infectiously, Raffar dragged me after them. He took apple slices and tiny white and larger yellow flowers from the bag and placed them in a pattern on the grass. The butterflies fluttered above us, but they flew lower and lower, heading for the field again.

With the gradual landing of the butterflies, Raffar's pattern began to make sense. The blue butterflies landed on the apples. The white ones were drawn by the yellow flowers, and the orange and yellow to the white flowers. Raffar dropped the last apple slices and stood back next to me. He raised a hand for me to wait. We held perfectly still, and the butterflies sought out the offerings. A couple even landed on Raffar and me. The sight of a delicate orange butterfly on his shoulder, so close to the rock shard in his ear, made me want to grab hold of his face and kiss it. I swallowed and turned my gaze to the field.

Mostly children, but also a few adults had created these living pictures. A smiling face made of white and blue butterflies, then one with a thick orange tongue sticking out, the wings fluttering up and down as if the tongue wiggled in anticipation of a tasty morsel.

"Jiara," Raffar's finger drew my attention back to his picture.

My breath caught.

A boat, the same shape as the *tagarro* boat we'd used to tour the canals back in Glizerra, floated in a sea of blue butterflies. As their wings opened and closed, the water lapped at the yellow and orange boat, with tiny tufts of white in the blue signifying waves.

The field, the butterflies, the forest surrounding us . . . it wasn't anything like home. But Raffar's picture was a thoughtful way of trying to make me feel *at home*.

Raffar pointed to the boat. "I like . . ." I didn't understand the last word he said, but I nodded.

"I like too," I breathed.

His hand grasped mine again, and he squeezed it. I wanted to say so much more. *I like you.* And despite not knowing the language or the customs . . . *I'm glad we're married.*

Scilla's face flashed in my mind, smothering my gratefulness and joy. I was only here because she was dead. I wasn't supposed to have Raffar as my husband.

His smile tugged a sense of acceptance over my bruised heart. Maybe I wasn't supposed to be here, but I was. I drew Raffar closer, and when I leaned into his side, he nuzzled the top of my head. We watched our boat as the breeze blew and the sun moved overhead, until finally the butterflies flew away, filling the sky with brilliant color.

The townspeople gave up their vigils at the edges of the field, wandering hand in hand or with friends back toward town. Raffar tilted his head toward the others, and I nodded. It was time to get back.

He flinched and slapped the back of his neck. "Ow!"

His palm came away bloody; it was apparently some kind of insect. I pulled his head down to see how bad the bite was.

But there was no bite. Just two deep, crossed lines that made my stomach clench and my hope wither as I thought of the servant woman as a young girl, her grandparents brutally murdered with crisscross cuts. Mother had definitely been wrong. Scilla could travel this far. My heart thudded faster than butterfly wings could beat as my gaze darted around the field, searching for the danger I knew I wouldn't be able to see. Nothing could protect me from her now.

I pressed the hem of my sleeve against Raffar's cut to stop the bleeding. His injury was far worse than the scratches Scilla had inflicted on Llandro and me so far. For once, I was glad of my weakness with the language. How was I supposed to explain Scilla's behavior? Especially when Farnskagers didn't believe in earthwalkers at all?

We'd always thought earthwalkers didn't leave Azzaria, but my heart iced over as I realized we'd never know if a ghost killed someone visiting another country. They would just disappear, and we'd assume they'd built a new life for themselves far away. No, the distance wasn't going to protect me—my breath caught because that meant Zito wouldn't be safe either, if Mother sent him to live with me.

And now Scilla was drawing Raffar into her vengeance. I couldn't allow that. I had to stop her from hurting all of us. I had to.

The next morning, a letter from Pia lay on the table in our suite. A warm glow enveloped my heart—she wrote! She was fine, less exhausted than during our trip, and she was getting along with Marro's family.

Writing back to her, sharing my life here would mean so much to me. I made three starts, but between my worries about the people who disagreed with Raffar and my unsuccessful attempts to find the tattoo artist, concentrating on letters wasn't working. At the top of the page, I drew a butterfly, and that gave me an idea. I wrote a few words, but then drew Raffar and me, surrounded by butterflies. I smiled. It wasn't a perfect letter, but Pia'd know I was thinking of her.

The evening before, I'd asked to see the tattoo artist again, but she was out of town for the day. Until I could interrogate her, I was out of ideas regarding Scilla's killer. All night I'd pondered it and come to a decision. A cut on his skin was only a tiny thing. Scilla would need more time walking the earth to strengthen her anger, to truly wield it as a deadly weapon. But that didn't mean Raffar was out of danger. Who knew what Geord was capable of? Or the Stärklandish queen, who'd said she'd sent an emissary, but the only person they'd found was the man who had attacked Aldar's party. Luckily, my translator was an excellent source of information.

"Tell me more about the prisoner from Stärkland," I said as Aldar extracted the slate from the drawer.

He *tsked*. "Your Majesty, you are only stalling your lessons."

I glared at him, overdramatically. "I am not. Or, I am, but I want to know, and I'm the queen. Where is he?"

He chuckled and bowed his head in a supremely deferential pose in response. "Of course, Your Majesty. There's a prison on the far side of town, past the square and the ironfern wood artisans' workshops. Since he's a political prisoner, the cell is in a corridor underground. Don't worry—he'll never get out. Unless Raffar releases him."

Aldar's deliberately bland expression didn't hide the fact that he still believed the king was foolish for entertaining such thoughts.

"Why do you say Raffar is too trusting?" Ever since my husband had told me Geord was not a bad person, I'd been wondering if Aldar might be correct. Maybe Raffar wasn't careful enough.

Aldar tossed the slate and the slate pencil on the table. He scratched his chin. "That he's even considering talking to them. They sent a troop of killers."

I wished I could hear Raffar's side of the argument. Aldar talked like Raffar wasn't thinking at all, and my hackles rose automatically. I held back the unfounded defense forming on my lips. "Do you speak Stärklandish?"

He stretched his arms and folded them behind his head. "It is not as good as my Azzarian, but it's not bad."

My heart sank a little. Aldar could speak, read, and write in three languages. I could barely read my own. I pushed away those thoughts. My stupid, bruised pride wasn't the important thing here. "So, you could translate for me."

Aldar's arms were in the process of coming forward from his relaxed pose, but he froze. "Has King Raffar requested that you speak to the prisoner?"

I pictured my mother, calm, sure of herself. "No, but as queen, there should be no reas—"

"This man and his people killed three of our soldiers. Eight others are still recovering from serious wounds. I will not take you to speak to him." He glared at me, and following several silent heartbeats, he tacked on, "Your Majesty."

Fire crept up my face and the back of my neck. I gave him my hardest stare. If I were in Azzaria, I'd just go myself. I'd order my way in or manage some kind of deception, like I had when I'd viewed the commander's tattoo sketches. And I would talk to the man on my own. But now, even if I found the prison, I couldn't speak enough Farnskag or Stärklandish to extract any useful information from him. I was dependent on Aldar to get anywhere.

His shoulders drooped, and he sighed in a drawn-out way. "I'm sorry, Queen Jiara. It probably sounds so disrespectful when I say that. I heard your sister was not far from the Stärklandish border when she was killed. It's understandable that you'd try to leave no stone unturned. But don't forget—she was even closer to the Loftarian border."

Mother must have given Raffar's people more information about Scilla's death than I'd thought. It was true, she'd been in the vicinity of both borders.

He continued, "I'm sure you want to find out who is responsible, but I can't imagine the prisoner knows anything about the assassin. What kind of coincidence would that be? Given the years of contention, it was most likely someone from Loftaria, trying to prevent an alliance between our two countries. Someone who was, luckily, unsuccessful. It's a good thing for Farnskag that Raffar is so stubborn." He smiled and picked up the slate.

Letters appeared, and Aldar said words, which I repeated, but try as I might, they just wouldn't stick in my head. All I could think about was how helpless I was in this country. I was like one of those fancy, rainbow-colored birds from the southern continent, repeating, but understanding nothing. Word after unknown word built up until I had to think of something else or I'd cry in front of my tutor. I pictured the map Mother had hanging in a corner of her office. Scilla had been in the upper northwest of Azzaria when she'd died. We'd all concentrated on the Loftarians, since they'd always been openly hostile. And then, on the Farnskagers, because of the witness's description.

It sounded like the Stärklandish prisoner had been arrested shortly after Scilla had died. I'd never considered it before Aldar had mentioned it, but what if Scilla's murder and the arrival of the Stärklandish scouting party were related? If it had been politically sanctioned by the Stärklandish government, the prisoner might even know details about the assassin.

She'd only been a half-day's ride from Stärkland. Close to Stärkland, close to Loftaria. An Azzarian witness of Loftarian origin. A Farnskager tattoo.

I buried my hands in my hair, trying to imagine how the puzzle pieces could fit together.

Because there was one fact no one was privy to but our family and Pia.

We'd told everyone that Scilla had been traveling on behalf of the queen, checking the health and prosperity of our western regions. But in reality, none of us knew what Scilla had been doing. She'd left without telling anyone, without servants, without soldiers or her *gurdetta*.

What if her trip really had something to do with Stärkland? What if the prisoner possessed information about it? What if my only chance to talk with him was a translator who refused to do my bidding?

CHAPTER 15

The next day was a disaster. After a tour of the hospital, where I'd consoled patients with my few Farnskag words and the *gakh* greeting until my aching back had screamed, I'd slipped away to try and find either the tattoo artist or the prison myself. Not taking into account that I couldn't read signs and wasn't even certain how I'd communicate once I got there, within an hour, I'd drawn the laughter of a dozen men by begging for help with a fire when it was only a smokehouse with the door accidentally left open. Worse—my shouts had scared the owner's dog so much it had nipped at my leg. As a souvenir, I now sported a purple bite-shaped bruise. I was lucky it hadn't been worse.

The only consolation for the horrid experience was my dinner alone with Raffar in the evening. Maybe the kitchen staff had heard of the day's ordeal, because the table held a unique sight for Baaldarstad: a fried fish on a platter. My mouth watered as I imagined which of the sea's fish it would taste like most. One bite, and I thanked the gods we weren't surrounded by townspeople in the dining hall, so no one could see my reaction. My teeth sank into what felt like an old sponge, and a thick juice leaked out, a fetid mud on my tongue.

I took a deep breath. No wonder they never ate seafood here.

Raffar had waited while I took the first bite. Before I could warn him, a morsel of fish disappeared into his mouth. Two jaw movements later, his chewing slowed dramatically. His throat jerked as he forced the mouthful down. He sucked in a large gulp of ale and looked from the fish to me as if unable to comprehend how I could adore a food so vile.

"I don't like the fish," I said. I pointed at it, keeping my fingers inches away. "That bad fish."

He coughed and sputtered, "Very bad fish." He pushed the platter away, I covered it with a napkin for good measure, and we filled ourselves with bread and potatoes and a bright salad of green leaves and juicy beets.

After dinner, we went for a stroll through the manor gardens. The sky was darkening already, but the air had that humid, herbal freshness of the early evening that made me want to stay out for hours. Unlike the carefully cultivated lawn and flowerbeds of home, the Farnskager garden was natural. Grass and bushes, shadows dancing with fireflies, stones as high as my waist clustered in small groups with curious fleshy plants growing directly on the rocks.

As we walked, Raffar pointed out different objects and said their names. *Firefly. Rock. Grass. Tree, tree, tree*—three different words—so apparently, he was telling me the kinds of trees. At least I still remembered *rock* and *grass*.

The forest that grew up to the manor loomed black ahead,

but the cloudless sky glowed a dark sapphire above us. Raffar and I sat on some old tree stumps, hewn into rough chairs. In the sky, stars twinkled into view.

"You like Farnskag?" he asked suddenly.

I fought not to break his gaze. It was too early to ask a question like that. Especially considering today's mess. Out of politeness, I nodded.

"You miss Azzaria?"

"Yes." I swallowed. "I miss . . . family." I combed my brain for the correct vocabulary. "Mother, father, brothers, sister."

I squeezed my eyes shut. Sister. My dimwitted brain. Scilla wasn't in Azzaria anymore.

A soft caress slipped over my neck. I whirled around, but nothing was behind me, and no mosquito or firefly flew away from where we sat. It must be Scilla again. Since her last act had been to hurt Raffar, I should have been scared. Instead, it felt as though a warm blanket had been nestled around my shoulders. At least someone familiar was here with me in this foreign land. Earthwalkers were unpredictable, but did I dare hope she'd be gentle from time to time, now that we'd seen each other back in Loftaria?

Raffar sighed and snatched a stick from the ground. He scratched the bark of an empty stump chair across from us with its tip. When he spoke, I only understood a few words of each sentence. ". . . sorry . . . you miss her. I know . . . I miss my mother and father."

He'd been king for three years now, and he'd only been crowned so young because both parents had died. With Scilla, it was all so fresh, like a wound that had only barely begun to scab over. What was it like for him?

To soften my words, I picked up a second twig and tapped his with mine. "How . . . they die?" I asked, inwardly cursing my lack of linguistic elegance.

His voice rumbled quickly, and though I strained, I didn't understand one word of his answer. He must have seen it in my eyes. He said clearly, "mother," then coughed until he slowly laid his head to the side.

Lung fever, probably. A slow, horrible way to die. An awful thing to watch. My heart pinched for him, and I nodded. At least it meant he'd had time to say goodbye.

Then, "Father." He rubbed his stomach, over and over, and he shook his head. I wasn't sure what it meant, but it seemed to be another illness.

His finger tapped his heart three times. "Father . . . good king. I try . . . good king . . . father."

Those no longer here left so much behind. Expectations, reputations. Scilla, with her intelligence and ambition, lived in my heart too.

His voice was low when he said, "Miss them . . . like yesterday . . . like forever."

Crickets chirped, but otherwise, the night was silent, as if we were the last people on the continent. Raffar had lost his parents, and then his adopted brothers and sisters had been sent away all at once. The responsibility for an entire country had been thrust upon him at the same time. I ran my twig along his stick until it gently nudged the back of his hand.

Like yesterday. Like forever. For me too, it felt like Scilla had only been gone a day or two, but I was beginning to forget things I shouldn't. The exact shade of her hazel eyes. The sound of her laugh. I remembered how she repeatedly brushed a finger down over her nose when she was deep in thought, but as a fact, and not as a picture. And that forgetting . . . it made everything tight inside me, like all my muscles were freezing up from holding in the sadness.

For Raffar, it must be the same, but the forgetting would be even more intense. I wished I could wipe that ache away for us. We'd both lost our families, whether due to death or distance.

But we were here; we had each other. Dropping my stick, I stood in front of him. I trailed my hand up the back of his neck, over a three-stripe tattoo to the day's stubble on his head. He watched me for a moment, then leaned forward until his forehead rested against my abdomen. The tiny bristles of hair massaged my fingers as I stroked his head.

He took a deep breath. His fist was balled as it came up the side of my hip and pressed against my waist. He turned until his cheek and ear were flush against me. A cozy fire blossomed inside me, and I wanted to curl up next to him until I forgot about missing my family and my country and not being able to speak properly.

I leaned down, craving the rough sensation of his shaved head against my lips. But before I reached him, his hand glided from my waist. He scooted back on the tree stump and cleared his throat. "Bag," he said gruffly, pointing to the sack he'd asked me to bring.

My heart slammed my ribs ten times before I could force myself to take a step backward. Mechanically, I reached inside and withdrew the lexicon. I sat back down on my wooden stool and placed the book into his hands—instead of whacking him over the head with it. His annoying obsession with my age . . . as if a couple of months really made a difference. My birthday was less than three months away.

Before opening the lexicon, he pointed to my bracelets. Then he showed me a word: *carnival.*

"Only one," he said, leaning forward to give his words weight.

Carnival? I blinked several times and looked at the word again. Not carnival. *Careful.* He was telling me to be careful and "only one."

But I had two bracelets. "Only one what?"

He considered, then leafed through the book again. Several words later, it clicked together. I was supposed to be careful because the bracelets only worked one time. Every Watcher only protected a person once. I'd "used up" my protection in Loftaria with the bladeleaf poison.

"I understand." Although . . . it might have been the gods or Scilla protecting me. The idea that inanimate objects could influence our lives still made me want to shake my head.

He pushed up my pant leg and ran a finger over the teeth marks there. "Careful."

My face burned. It wasn't as though I'd deliberately been attacked by an animal because I thought the Watcher would save me anyway.

For a few seconds, we sat in silence. He was only trying to help. Then I remembered our earlier conversation. "Your parents? No Watcher?"

"Father, no Watcher. Mother . . . yes. But . . ."

I got lost in his words again, so we used the lexicon. It turned out Watchers could only save a person from an accident or act of violence. Not from illness, which was part of nature. Raffar repeated that a Watcher could only save once.

I pointed to the shard in his earlobe. "Still work?"

His lips curved softly upward, and he shook his head. "I was . . . wild boy. Climbing trees. Even *gigantruv*. Racing elephant birds. Lucky . . . Watcher." He frowned and scratched his chin. "Don't tell. Secret."

"Secret?"

"Only Aldar knows. Aldar was with me." He pointed to my bracelets. "Don't tell."

I rubbed my forehead and fought the familiar panicky squeeze to my throat. *Don't tell what?*

With the help of the lexicon and a half hour of headache-inducing squinting and misread words, I finally comprehended. Part of the protection of the Watchers was psychological. If would-be assassins thought you were protected by a Watcher, they might not even try, under the assumption that you would survive anyway. Back in Loftaria, Raffar had sworn the guards to secrecy. Almost no one knew my protection was gone.

When I finally understood, a gentleness seeped into Raffar's eyes, and his brows rose. "You . . . good. Better . . . Farnskag."

I groaned. He was telling me my language skills were getting better, and yet, I'd barely understood the sentence he'd used to say it. But the look in his eyes . . . as if he were impressed with me.

A tiny reflection in the shard in his ear glinted in the

moonlight. If the Watchers truly had the power to protect, I was thankful they'd kept Raffar safe until I could share my life with him.

——————

For the next three days, I desperately tried to get Aldar to take me to see the Stärklandish prisoner, but to no avail. I even dragged him before Raffar, for certainly, he'd give his permission if he understood how important it was.

I didn't know what the translator had told him, but based on Raffar's easy smile when he said no, Aldar sure hadn't posed my question. Even now, the knowledge made my blood pulse in anger. But the burst of emotion must have spurred on my strategic thinking because I came up with an idea. So, when Aldar needed to visit his father again, and I had a free afternoon with Freyad, I took my chance.

"Freyad, I have to go to the prison." A first step would be to get a look at the prisoner. Azzarians often joked that all Farnskagers looked alike because of their tattoos. Maybe the people in Stärkland weren't any different. Scilla had been the same height and had a similar hair and skin color and figure to mine. If I was lucky, the prisoner would be confused and would say something that would give him away. Freyad would be with me. Assuming he spoke Farnskag, she'd understand.

She cocked her head. Apparently, I hadn't used the right words to ask about the prison. How to show it? I clamped a hand around my wrist, like a shackle. Then the same for my ankles. Then I pointed to my eyes again and out toward the square. Aldar had said it was past there.

Freyad's eyebrows rose. "*Kahngaad*?"

Now I apparently knew the word for prison. I followed when she motioned me to walk with her.

A weight lifted from my shoulders. It was that simple? Perhaps the difficult part was still yet to come—the interrogation—but at least I could catch a glimpse of the man.

Freyad led me through the town streets. A group of people weaving baskets waved and greeted, and I smiled and waved back. "*Guuddug*," I called. "*Guuddug*."

We walked on, and either I was confused or we'd taken a wrong turn compared to where the square was. There were hardly any houses here. And suddenly, we stood in front of a small building past the quiet east edge of town in the shade of two huge, swaying pine trees.

This was the prison?

Freyad rapped on the door, then nudged it open, whispering several words to me, ending with, "*Devsiin*."

Devsiin? I raised my hand to smother a laugh. When I tried to see the tattoo artist, I was distracted by angry council members. When I wanted to go to the prison, I was taken to the tattoo artist. But at least I was here now.

A woman about my mother's age perched on a high chair next to a table where a man lay on his back. His face was tattooed, but long since healed, not like the man we'd seen in the alley. His shoulder was bare, and charcoal lines had been drawn on it to mark where the newest tattoo should go. An elaborately carved bowl was half-full of black ash waiting to be cut into the man's skin, and a leather satchel lay unrolled, organized with blades of various shapes and sizes. One blade slot was empty.

"*Devsiin kahngaad*," Freyad said to me.

So *kahngaad* wasn't prison. Maybe tattoo artist? Either way, I rolled up onto my toes, eager to ask questions that might bring us progress in the search for Scilla's killer.

I waited impatiently as Freyad spoke with the woman, who gripped an intricately etched, not-yet-bloody knife in her hand.

Raffar's thumb on my chin . . . A shiver crept up my back. No. No tattoo for me.

The woman's hand stole to a pendant around her neck and her wary eyes studied me like she didn't want me present while she cut ink into the man's shoulder. Could it have something to do with their Watchers? Was tattooing an act an outsider shouldn't witness? *Sorry for disturbing you!* I thought and wished I had a way to say what I meant. But the damage had been done, and I needed answers about the leaf tattoo, so I concentrated on my original question: did someone in town have the tattoo on the commander's parchment?

Now, how to get my question across? I didn't have words or a slate or parchment. I had no other option but to draw it. If my mere presence was an issue, using her ink would probably be a major insult, so I motioned the woman out of her house. She scowled outright at me, but I was the queen, so she set down her knife. She murmured softly to her customer, then bowed her head slightly to me and said, "*Skriin* Jiara."

Once outside, I snatched a twig from the dirt below the tree. I drew the leaf with the thick border around it. Like with

Freyad, I pointed to my eyes and to the drawing, then gestured out over the town.

The woman held up her hand, shaking it as if to wipe away my thoughts. She held out a flat palm, and I gave her the twig. Then she drew three leaves. One like Raffar's and Freyad's, with the double-line border with short lines within it. One with the double border and zigzag lines like Aldar. And one with a single, very fine line—she was careful to point out how thick my line was, and that it was obviously not the same. Under each one, she scratched a picture in the dirt. Below Raffar's was a stick figure, running, holding a staff-like weapon. Under Aldar's was a slate covered in letters. The third had a house with a hybrid figurehead at the crest and an elephant bird at the side.

Then she pointed to her own eyes and to my drawing with the thick line. She shook her head and said, "No." With the twig, she drew crossed lines over it, negating it. She shook her head again and pointed to the other three. Then she nodded, gestured at Freyad and then out over the town.

If the soldiers had the tattoo like Raffar's and the scholars had tattoos like Aldar's, maybe anyone working for the king had the third version. Come to think of it, several servants in Raffar's manor had one, but not all of them.

In theory, that third version—the thin line—was closest to the drawing in the commander's office. But how addled had the witness's brain been from the attack? Could it be possible he didn't even remember it right? And the attack had taken place at night. Was it possible to concentrate on something as specific as the leaf's border during an attack in the dark? I chewed my lip as I pondered it, and the tattoo artist threw a glance back to her house. Without waiting to be excused, she exchanged a few terse words with Freyad, bowed her head ever so slightly to me, and headed for her customer.

I said thank you to her back, and again to Freyad. The tattoo artist had made it clear. No one in town—maybe no one in all of Farnskag—had the tattoo I was looking for. So, no one in town was guilty of murdering Scilla.

Or the drawing the witness had made was incorrect.

CHAPTER 16

Aldar's language lessons were crushing my heart and my mind. Every day, I fled the sitting room with strained eyes and a headache. I spent way too much time wishing Pia were here to teach me instead, even if her Farnskag wasn't perfect. But then I realized: when Raffar played *vansvagd* with me, I learned words without thinking. So, after much convincing, Aldar had agreed to try my method. He'd come up with a game.

I bounced on the balls of my feet, eager to begin a new way of learning. If I could just get rid of that infernal slate, I would learn this language. Aldar smiled coyly at me, asked if I was ready . . . and handed me a slip of parchment.

I looked down, and the letters flipped around in front of me. Like always. I swallowed and tried not to let my dismay show.

"It's a treasure hunt," said Aldar, his eyes glittering with pride. "These are all words we've learned together. If you manage to get all the way to the end, I have a surprise for you."

A surprise. I didn't care about winning some prize, at least not this time. I just didn't want to read.

"Take your time," Aldar said. "Concentrate and you'll get it."

Concentrate. I nodded. Concentrate.

I stared at the rectangle of parchment and reined in the prancing letters. I sounded it out in my head.

"Dining hall?" I asked Aldar in Farnskag.

He grinned. "See! You're learning. Maybe a game is not a bad idea after all."

I ignored the pounding already beginning behind my eyes and let out a deep breath.

"Well, go ahead. Go to the dining hall and look for the next clue."

At least I wasn't reading large amounts of text. If it was only one word per page and there weren't many pages, I would manage. The dining hall was huge, like at home in Azzaria. There was nothing on the table, and I checked every seat. Then I spotted a flash of cream color under the leg of a chair. I pulled back the chair, and a bit of folded parchment tumbled free.

Again, I gritted my teeth and stared at the letters.

"Your Majesty, would you excuse me for a few moments?" Aldar asked. "This morning, King Raffar requested that I look at a document that has arrived from Stärkland."

I stared at the letters in front of me. *Stop moving!* With a wave of my hand, Aldar backed away.

"I'll find you at one of the next stations," he said, then hurried toward Raffar's office.

There were four words with arrows between the first and second and the third and fourth. The first word was . . . GARDEN. Good, maybe the fresh air would help me focus. I left the manor.

The sun shined today, and the heat was welcome on my

face. If the air wasn't so dry and, admittedly, wonderfully apple scented, I could almost pretend I was back home.

The second word pair was BIRD and PEN, so next I'd cross the garden to the area where the elephant birds were kept. I leaned against a rough boulder topped with succulents as I forced the squirming letters of the final word to make sense. It was a number: THREE.

Three what, though? I jogged over the lawn to the pens. The birds had a huge grassy area to run in. Some of them stood quietly now, biting off long dandelion leaves. Two chased each other, their heavy feet pounding dust clouds out of the grass. One fluffed up its feathers and waved its long neck back and forth, making a deep cooing sound, probably trying to attract a mate.

But some of the birds were in smaller pens within the large area. From the left, I counted three pens. So, the next clue must be at that pen . . . which was occupied. The elephant bird rested on the ground, chewing slowly, almost sleepily. And there, just under a water-filled trough, a bit of parchment stuck out.

The trough couldn't be reached from outside the pen. I eyed the huge elephant bird. My level of appreciation for Aldar was at an all-time low.

"You won't hurt me, will you?" I asked the bird.

Its eyes closed and opened lazily, and it snapped up a beetle marching by.

Aldar might not be the world's most stellar instructor, but he wouldn't have sent me here if it was dangerous. I pushed open the wide-slatted, wooden gate and closed it behind me. With a bird of this size, there wasn't so much room for me to get around it, but I tiptoed carefully, trying not to step in its messes on the ground.

I bent to retrieve the parchment, and the elephant bird hissed behind me. The hair on the back of my neck stood on end. I looked over my shoulder.

The elephant bird was standing now, towering over me, and it spread its wings until they touched either side of the pen, increasing the bird's already formidable size threefold. It hopped from one tree-like leg to the other, opened its mouth, and hissed again.

My heart raced. It looked like it wanted to make mush out of me. I was done playing Aldar's inane game. I edged around the pen, but the bird hissed louder and snapped its long neck forward. The hard beak smacked onto the side of my head, and bright flashes burst behind my eyes. The pain wrenched a screech from my throat. My head spun—I needed to get out now.

I covered my skull with both hands, but the massive bird bumped up against me, nudging me even farther from the exit.

"Help!" I cried, craning my neck for a glimpse of a bird-keeper or gardener. In vain. I was alone.

Another hiss burst from the angry elephant bird. It stomped from one foot to the other, and its fluffy wings smacked against my face. I couldn't see, and feathers batted into my mouth and nose until I coughed. The bird slammed me again, harder this time. Then the ground was no longer under my feet, and my back hit the dirt, thrusting my breath from my lungs.

I gasped. "Help!" I yelled when I could breathe again, and then I sobbed—I didn't know how to say the word in Farnskag.

Please someone, come help me. Even if you don't understand me . . .

I curled into a little ball, and the bird knocked its hard beak against my head again. More stars flashed behind my eyes. I scrambled around in the dirt, threw a handful up at the animal, hoping to blind it long enough so that I could crawl by. It stepped back.

Then I remembered my knife. I crouched and slipped it from under my pant leg in one fluid movement. I had a fleeting, ridiculous thought that Raffar would be proud, and I said, "I don't want to hurt you, but if you—"

The bird lunged at my hand, nipping my wrist, pinching the skin so hard, it tore in a flash of fire. I had to keep the feathered monster away from me. I screamed and slashed at one of the muscular legs and met my mark. Blood trickled down to the dirt below.

Hiss!

The bird rushed me, kicking its heavy leg squarely in my chest. There was no air, and I tipped to the ground. I couldn't protect my head fast enough—the huge foot was right in front of my eyes. I pounded a fist against my chest, desperate to force myself to breathe again, and I stabbed up into the bottom of the massive, flat foot.

The bird jerked away from me. Voices. Cries. Red in my eyes.

Jerky movements of being carried. Soft, sweet-smelling clover beneath me, and I meant to open my eyes, but—*no.*

They already were open. They were open, felt scratchy, and everything was dark. "I can't see!"

Rough palms on my face, wiping, wiping.

A blurry, short-haired person came into view. "Freyad?" I sobbed.

She wiped bloody, dirt-smeared hands on her pant legs and pried the knife from my grip and shouted to the others. Matid murmured soothing words, gathered me in his arms, and rushed me to the manor. As he brought me into my suite, with Freyad close behind, I caught a glimpse of myself in the looking glass. My tunic and pants were a filthy mess of mud and dung, my hair full of clumps I didn't have to think long about to identify. Aside from the tear on my hand, a bleeding bump marred my forehead. I had scrapes and bruises everywhere, but I didn't feel like I was seriously hurt.

Matid gingerly set me onto a chair, and his eyes assessed my body for damage. With a sweeping arm, Freyad ordered the man out of the room. She helped me undress, and as she spoke, made washing movements to let me know a bath would be brought in.

I had just wrapped a robe around my filthy self when the door burst open. Raffar and Aldar stood there. Hands and arms flew, Raffar shouted at Freyad and Aldar. Both of them shouted back.

My head thundered worse than if I'd been forced to read an entire book, and I was all out of patience.

"Stop!" I yelled.

Silence fell, with only the sound of the four of us breathing heavily in the room. Then a knock. The three stared at me, so I called in Farnskag, "Come in."

Two men lugged in water to fill the tub. With a glare meant more for myself than for them, I left everyone in my sitting room and bathed as quickly as I could. I slipped into new clothes, then stopped briefly in front of some scented blocks I'd set up in honor of the gods. I clasped my hands to my heart then raised them to the sky.

"My heart in your hands." With bird legs that heavy, I was lucky to be alive. "Thank you."

I granted myself two more seconds of stillness, then returned to the sitting room where Raffar, Freyad, and Aldar were still arguing, although quieter now.

Raffar grunted a phrase at Aldar, who said, uncharacteristically formally, "The king would like to know what happened."

I nodded. I wanted to know myself. "I was playing your game." *Your stupid reading game.*

Aldar's jaw dropped, but he translated, speaking a little longer, probably to explain what the game was.

As soon as he stopped, I continued, "And the last clue I read was *Garden, Bird Pen, Three.* So, I went to the third pen."

"No," Aldar said, shaking his head emphatically. "It was the first pen. The empty one."

My language skills were pathetic, but I knew the numbers one through ten. "It said three."

Raffar barked a question, and Aldar answered. Then he asked me, "Where's the clue now?"

I fetched it from the pocket of my dirty pants, then held it out. "See. *Three.*"

Aldar examined the parchment, and his eyes sought out the floor. He covered his face with both hands so that his voice was muffled. "It is my fault, Your Majesty."

I was about to nod when he said, "I should have realized the game was too difficult. And I've done a poor job teaching you, even the numbers. That says *one*."

I snatched the paper from him, looked at it again. We'd been studying together for weeks now. I knew this word. "That's *three*." I showed it to Freyad and pointed to the word.

She held up one finger.

Humiliated, I crumpled up the page and tossed it in the corner. Then I stood there like a child, like Mother's fickle, little dragonbird, in need of yet another lecture on concentrating harder, on improving my scholarly results like Llandro and Scilla. Tears burned in my eyes. If I could have run away, I would have, but it was impossible, so I dropped into my chair and pulled my knees up to hug them. I could have been killed because I was too stupid to read the number one.

Raffar ran a hand over my damp hair. "I'm glad you're all right."

All I could do was swallow . . . until I remembered the parchment I'd seen under the trough. "I only went into the pen because I saw the next clue."

Aldar's brow wrinkled, but he translated. Everyone's soft sighs told me they were placating a childish monarch, but Freyad went down to check near the trough. She returned a few tense minutes later, with a large shard from a parchment-colored eggshell on her palm and a softness in her eyes that said she was sorry I'd been mistaken. She pelted Aldar with a crumpled ball of parchment she'd apparently also retrieved from stall number one.

"I apologize," he mumbled again, stuffing the clue from pen number one in his pocket. "It won't happen again, I promise."

Raffar's hand brushed over my face, over the cut on my forehead, which still smarted. His finger dropped to the blood-streaked knife on the table. "Freyad told me you defended yourself well. Fleetfoot's mother is injured but will still be able to care for her young."

Fleetfoot was Raffar's mount. "Her young?"

He nodded, his lips pressed tight together. "She was in the pen because she is hatching."

Not only had I almost gotten myself trampled to death, I'd injured a breeding animal that had only defended her egg.

"I'm sorry," I said, my heart breaking with every syllable. "I'm so sorry."

CHAPTER 17

Two frustrating days later, following trips to neighboring villages, I still hadn't found a person with the right leaf tattoo. I felt so useless. When Raffar opened the door to our suite that evening, his eyes were bleary.

"You all right?" I asked him.

He nodded and waved a hand, but didn't explain. Someday, I wanted him to see me as a person he could share things with. But it would time consuming for him to show me the right words now, and the droop in his shoulders said he didn't have the energy.

"Eat here today?" I asked.

He smiled tiredly. "Yes. Please."

While Raffar cleaned himself, I ran down to ask a servant to make arrangements. My broken Farnskag was embarrassing, but I wouldn't make him take over something as simple as instructions for dinner when he was so obviously exhausted.

Once our meal was over, we played a round of *vansvagd* again. Afterward, he tugged my hand to the bed. Entwining my fingers with his, he lay on his back and closed his tired eyes. I smoothed my other hand over his forehead, softening the creases between his brows. I ran a finger down one side of his face, massaging the tension there and then the other side.

". . . good . . ."

After a few minutes, I extricated my hand and switched from trailing a finger along his skin to rubbing tiny circles with both hands. I smoothed down over his head to his neck and shoulders. He sighed, and my awareness of us together on the bed heightened until it was all I could think about. Us. In bed. Together. Touching. My pulse tripped, then began to gallop.

Raffar's request to wait felt so far away. Sensibility abandoned me, and I leaned forward and kissed his forehead. He sighed and rubbed his skin against my lips. He didn't push me away, so I kissed his eyebrow. His cheek. My heart pounded now. If only he would touch me. Like an invitation, an *mmm* stole from his mouth.

My kiss found the corner of his upper lip.

He turned slowly, then all at once gripped the back of my head and crushed his lips to mine. A moan escaped me as a flare of fire shot down my chest to my abdomen. He rolled onto his side, pulling me down to him. My arms smoothed up his waist, scraping toward his shoulders. His hands kneaded my back, moving lower until he tugged my waist against him, straining through the fabric to get closer to me.

After kissing my neck, his mouth moved higher again, until he held back and looked at me. His gaze swallowed me up, and I wanted to lose myself there forever. I slid my hands up his tunic.

He stiffened. "Ah . . . no. Stop, Jiara."

I froze. He shook his head and rolled away from me, off the

bed. He strode halfway across the room and ran both hands over his face and scalp. ". . . not eighteen."

"It's all right." I shook my head. "I not afraid. I know you." I knew him enough.

"We wait," he growled. He paced away from me, taking a position at the wall next to the window, his breath still coming in gasps.

I sat on the bed, leaning back on my hands. He wanted to, at least it seemed like it. I wanted to. We were married. "Why? Why wait?" I didn't want to do anything he wasn't ready for. I just needed to understand.

Words flew from his mouth, but it was far too fast for me. "Stop!" I crawled across the bed and plucked the hated, but oh-so-necessary lexicon from his night table. His weary eyes stared at me for a moment, but he came and retrieved the book. He lowered himself to the bed, and our painfully slow conversation unfolded like a fairy tale.

Generations ago, people married early, sometimes as young as twelve or thirteen. Often their parents gave their blessings, but it wasn't a legal requirement for a marriage. Raffar's grandmother was one of them. She married an older man who promised her a good life. She was young and naive and soon worked all day for the lazy drunkard who was her husband. When she was old enough to see him for what he was, she left him, dissolving the marriage. At nineteen, she married Raffar's grandfather, who later became the king.

Raffar's grandfather changed the law. From then on, although there was no rule against intimacy between youths, marriage before eighteen was illegal. With time, the Farnskagers came to agree that people should be old enough to under-stand how their lives would change when they married and old enough to properly judge the one they were marrying.

That same argument. "But I know—"

Raffar smiled and held up his open palm and then pointed to his chest. We continued using the lexicon. "I'm happy you feel confident. I am also happy with you. When we traveled from Azzaria—do you remember the monoliths? The white ones?"

I nodded. White Mother. Where I was the only one not allowed to visit.

"White Mother is very important to us. Like her name . . . a mother, someone to give guidance, to watch over us. I prom-ised White Mother I would give you the time until you were eighteen to be certain."

There was so much I was unsure of here, but being with Raffar was not one of them. Carefully, I rested my hand on his. "Raffar, I am certain."

"Fine. Then give me the time," he said. "Let me fulfill my promise."

His promise to a rock. I slipped my hand from his then rubbed mine together. How was I supposed to understand that? Accept that?

Raffar cleared his throat. "That time I first saw you, in the hall in Glizerra . . . I'd inquired about Scilla before planning to marry her. I'd heard she was smart and proud. But also cold and aloof. And then this girl tumbled in with wild hair and eyes, and a devilish grin."

The tips of my ears burned. Zito and I had made quite an entrance that day.

Raffar's voice grew soft, but not in the way of fond reminiscence. More with self-loathing. "I wanted to grab you and marry you there and then. And to find out you were the wrong sister—and a *younger* sister at that." His fist thumped against his heart. "I am not the drunkard who married my grandmother. I will not be one who utters false promises and takes advantage of those too naive to understand."

We were already married. And I was not naive. I leaned forward and opened my mouth to attempt an explanation, but he continued. "Jiara, how can I expect my people to follow the laws set by my family if I don't have the strength myself?"

I pushed my hair back from my face and sighed. Whether anyone knew of his promise to White Mother or not, he needed to keep it—for himself, for his own self-respect. And as royalty, we had to set a good example. I shoved my hands under my thighs and rocked forward. "All right. We wait."

He leaned forward, but stilled before he was close enough to touch his lips to mine. "Two more months?"

My heart hammered in my chest, but I forced myself to nod. I would be eighteen then, and I could wait. I wouldn't try to convince him otherwise. Not if it meant so much to him.

———

After the day of the treasure hunt, language lessons were restricted to my sitting room. Not only that, everywhere I went, someone accompanied me. Usually Freyad, but sometimes

Aldar, Matid, or Raffar. But it wasn't so I'd feel more comfortable in terms of communication. No, I needed someone to protect me from myself. Was it possible to crush a person's heart without leaving a mark on the body? Every time someone came to watch over me, mine was shattered anew. Aldar and Freyad had important things to do, and yet they worried about who would look after me, save me from my own ineptitude.

When today's lesson was over, Raffar rushed into the room with Freyad right behind. Raffar paced back and forth.

"What's the matter?" I asked Aldar.

He inclined his head toward the speakers, showing me I'd have to wait while he listened, then said softly, "The head trainer for our warriors has taken ill. It is very serious. He's not expected to recover."

My fingers rose to my mouth. Raffar ran a hand over the stubble on his head, leaned against the wall.

"Raffar must appoint someone new immediately, but there are issues. Politics, experience, so much to take into account."

My husband paced by me again, muttering what sounded like the names of several candidates, none of whom were familiar to me. Freyad either nodded or shook her head at all of them. It seemed she not only was a good judge of character, but that Raffar gave her opinion much weight.

She was obviously overqualified to be my babysitter, so I asked, "How about Freyad?"

"Freyad?" Raffar repeated, as if only now noticing I was there and was, at least sort of, part of the conversation. He gestured to me and then to himself and said something to Aldar, who then responded.

Sentences flew back and forth between Raffar and Freyad like birds swooping for prey.

Aldar's eyebrows rose. "It seems you made a good suggestion. He's asking if she's interested."

Discussion continued so quickly Aldar couldn't keep up with translating. Freyad's eyes glowed with ambition, but Raffar kept gesturing to me.

No. She couldn't lose out on such an opportunity because of me. "Aldar, tell them I can go to training with Freyad. If no one else has time to guard me, I can help"—he narrowed his eyes at me—"or I'll just watch. I promise I'll stay out of the way."

Aldar translated. Another smile broke out on Freyad's face, and she took my arm, saying a sentence that contained the word *good*. Raffar's gaze traveled between the three of us, finally landing on Freyad. With a small smile, he must have congratulated her to her new position, because she almost vibrated with excitement.

After clearing up a few more details, Aldar said to me, "The soldiers are waiting now. For the first day, Freyad will need to concentrate. Matid will accompany you on your walk through town. Freyad will take you to him right away."

I nodded, eager to get out of the house and to let Freyad begin her new responsibilities. And since I still hadn't talked to the Stärklandish prisoner, I'd steer Matid toward the prison.

Aldar's lips thinned for a moment. "I hope this will not be too hard on Freyad. Raffar has always put a great deal of trust in her, but some people were not happy when someone as young as she was appointed a royal guard. And now this? Some of the soldiers are twice her age."

A hollowness opened in my stomach, but I ignored it. I had made the suggestion, but the king had the final decision. Whoever *some people* were, they'd been wrong about Freyad being too young to be a royal guard. And now she'd make a fine trainer for the warriors.

We hustled down the street, and Matid met us as planned. Except that blood dripped from a long gash on his arm. I tried to ask what had happened, but their gestures and words didn't help. It seemed like some kind of accident. The wound didn't look deadly, but it obviously needed attention. Matid and Freyad argued, and it appeared he was trying to get her to let me go with him to a physician. My cheeks burned with shame at the lengths they went to in order to be sure I'd have a babysitter. And my stomach roiled as I imagined standing by while I watched his skin being stitched up.

Freyad met my gaze, and she must have caught my queasiness, because she waved Matid off and pulled me down the street to the western edge of town. Apparently, I'd accompany her to practice today after all. I'd have to be careful. There was no way I wanted to disturb her on her first day. I was running out of ideas on finding the man with the leaf tattoo, but I'd hoped to visit the prison. It looked like that would be impossible today.

A few minutes later, we were somewhere in the vicinity of the meadow with the butterflies. Voices rose in front of us, and we came upon a cleared field littered with straw targets and lounging people of all ages.

Freyad yelled two words with a surprisingly forceful voice, considering how softly she always spoke to me. The

people—obviously soldiers by the way they jumped to attention—began sorting themselves into different groups: knives,
clubs, bows, staffs, spears, javelins, and an area with no weapons, so it must have been hand-to-hand combat. They stood
staring at her for a few minutes while she spoke. The trainees'
eyes flicked between one another and Freyad, and darted in
my direction a few times too. Freyad shouted harsh-sounding
words, and I caught my name, but the soldiers must have accepted her as trainer because they focused on their activities
after that.

There were trainees of all ages, from a couple of years
younger than me up to my parents' age. The older soldiers
instructed the younger ones. The sun bore down on my hair,
so I scooted into the shadows of a cluster of trees at the edge
of the training field and watched as Freyad had a girl prepare
javelins for throwing. She stood still until Freyad uttered a
single word. Then the girl ran a few paces, her arm blurred,
and the javelin struck the target. The rest of the soldiers be-
haved in the same way: focused and well trained. I fiddled with
the blade at my calf, drawing it over and over and sheathing
it again. Luckily no one saw me. The youngest child out there
was nimbler than I was.

A tall man with a familiar gait entered the field from the
road, and everyone stopped to watch him. Freyad looked up
from her post near the javelin-throwing target and shouted
a phrase I was proud to recognize—something about making
himself useful. The man switched directions. He headed toward
me, stopping at the hand-to-hand combat zone, which was
made up of trainees under the age of twenty.

He pivoted, and I finally glimpsed his face. It was Raffar. He must have come to lend Freyad a little support on her first day. He didn't seem to realize I was here in the dim shadows, and my lips curled into a smile. What was he like when I wasn't watching?

Raffar had a discussion with a boy about my age, who seemed to be in charge of his group. The boy nodded and both he and Raffar crouched in a battle-ready stance. The boy rushed at Raffar. With a single sweep of his hands, the boy fell to the ground, his *oof* echoing across the field.

Raffar helped him up, made a low comment and demonstrated a twist of his back and hand motions. The boy laughed. Then they flew at each other again, and this time, Raffar landed on his back. The rest of the children paired up and attempted the same moves. Dust clouds rose from all the movement. Black dirt stuck to damp skin until I could no longer tell smears from tattoos.

After a while, the oldest boy must have grown tired of being beaten, because he laughed and shouted at Raffar, but the only words I caught were *Freyad* and *good*. Raffar shook his head, but Freyad called over to him, a cocky grin on her face, "Are you scared?"

The children in Raffar's group laughed. He nodded in a mock-solemn manner and muttered. Head hanging exaggeratedly, he went to meet Freyad across from the javelin targets. He'd said she excelled with that weapon, and he shrugged like he foresaw his defeat.

The girl assisting Freyad affixed a melon-sized leaf to the center of the target with a nail. Raffar laughed and ran a hand over his head as he walked about fifty paces away. With utmost concentration, he jogged and threw his javelin. It slammed into the bottom edge of the leaf. With a satisfied dip of his head, Raffar motioned for Freyad to continue.

She nodded, her face calm and bland. I crept out from the trees. Two javelins were strapped to her back and one rested in her hand. She walked nearly twice as far away as Raffar had, and she turned to the girl who had affixed the leaf. Freyad winked, and I knew: Raffar didn't stand a chance. Moving like the wind over a field of grain, Freyad ran, whipping one javelin after the other at the target. All three speared the target, until the leaf was torn to shreds. My husband bowed slightly and clasped Freyad's shoulder. He shouted his praise so everyone could hear, and the group clapped.

Raffar pivoted as if to turn back to his hand-to-hand combat session, when he saw me. His head rolled back onto his shoulders, and he laughed out loud. Then he spread out both arms as if being bested in front of his wife couldn't be helped when it came to Freyad.

The boy who had fought with Raffar ran up to him, and my heart stopped.

He was young enough to have only few tattoos, and he was as grimy of the rest of them, but on his cheek was a leaf. And the border was thick.

My heart jumped, and the second the boy turned away from me, I pointed to him and called, "Raffar!" But then Freyad gestured to me and said something about *help*. Her voice commanding, she shouted *game* and *Queen Jiara*, and the younger trainees whooped and rushed around me, pushing me to one edge of the field.

"Raffar!" I yelled again, because this boy could be *the one*, but Raffar's eyes sparkled, and he raised his hand in a happy wave as he headed for the other side of the field with the older trainees. After that, it was a rambunctious, free-for-all type of fight with me as the prize. Every attempt to communicate on my part was a complete failure. Even if I'd been able to eke out the correct words, no one could hear me over the din.

The older soldiers were fairly gentle with the younger ones, who mainly dragged me back and forth through the field, swinging clubs and staffs to keep the others back. I kept my eye on the boy with the tattoo as best as possible. Within a short time, the older soldiers had us cornered, and a different boy on my team jabbered at me, pointing.

Up into the tree? I wanted to shake my head and give up on the soldiers' game, but the boy with the leaf tattoo was fighting with an adult down the field. He wouldn't just up and disappear, so I complied. The bark scratched at my hands as I scrambled up, while the other trainees surrounded the trunk, swinging their staffs. With my cheek pressed against the trunk of the tree, my memory whisked me back to Azzaria, to the time I'd collected the dragonbird feather to ask the gods for help with Scilla. Slowing her descent into madness had worked, hadn't it? Not including the nasty gash she'd given Raffar, anyway. *Blood on the floor, the walls, the ceiling.* As soon as this was over, I'd get a hold of that boy.

My husband stood below the tree. He put on a mock

scowl and hollered, "My wife!" like it was a battle cry. He burst through the children, taking a beating to his back and sides. In seconds, he swung up after me, his face glowing. Slightly out of breath, he said, "Good game." He kissed the top of my head. "Good queen."

We had to talk to the boy with the tattoo. "Leaf," I said, pointing to the spot on my cheek where the boy's tattoo had been. I shrugged to ask where he was.

Raffar narrowed his eyes at me, then he shook his head. He gave me a peck on the lips. "I win."

Ugh. I shoved his shoulder. "Boy. Leaf. Tattoo. *Scilla.*" I skidded down the tree, tugging on Raffar's arm to join me. The name *Scilla* must have finally gotten through to him. He followed me, shading his eyes from the sun as he searched the field.

The boy was gone. No!

"Boy. You . . ." I couldn't think of the word for *practice* or *fight.* I grunted in frustration and made motions with my hands of fighting and falling.

"Freyad!" Raffar called. When she ran to him, laughing at one of the girls chasing her, he asked a quick question. They spoke back and forth, occasionally meeting my gaze, several times shaking their heads. They clearly knew who I meant, thank the gods, but I wasn't sure they understood why. Maybe my word for *leaf* had been incorrect, otherwise, Raffar would have guessed when I'd mentioned my sister. He would have to understand how important it was.

"Gone," Freyad said to me, carefully, her eyebrows furrowed. "You and me . . . boy . . . tomorrow."

Tomorrow. Impatience boiled in me, but without a lexicon or Aldar to help, I wasn't getting anywhere. I'd look up the words for leaf and border. We'd find him. Tomorrow.

CHAPTER 18

The next morning, Raffar had already left for a meeting with the Grand Council, and I paced in front of the door while waiting for Aldar, when a hollow, rhythmic knocking echoed from the bedroom. Maybe a bird or other tiny animal had somehow gotten in and was trapped, so I followed it. Cocking my head to the left and then to the right to better locate the source, I shoved our nightstands aside to look behind them, bent to check under the bed. I found nothing.

The noise stopped.

Crash!

The sound came from the sitting room. I rushed there. No animal, no person. But the chair I usually sat in when working with Aldar rose up a few inches and dropped down with another bang. Then it wobbled back and forth, clacking on the floor, first the left legs, then the right, again and again.

It could only be Scilla.

Swallowing, I strode to the chair and tried to push it down, immobilize it, but my muscles were no match for the unearthly strength.

"Stop it, Scilla!"

The chair leg slammed right down on my foot.

"Ow!" I cried as the staccato continued.

Then the second chair vibrated back and forth, in sync with the first, and the crashing noise echoed in my head. I stepped away from the furniture and slapped my hands over my ears. "Scilla, please stop! I'm trying."

The table joined the chairs, tipping back and forth in the same creepy, hollow rhythm. With every thud, they crept across the floor, closer to me.

Crash.

Bang.

Crash.

Bang.

Hands still covering my ears, the pounding furniture backed me up against the wall. What if Scilla sent them all flying at me at once? She could break my bones, my back, my neck. The corpses of her grandparents had been discarded like dolls, the serving woman had said, and I imagined Raffar or Freyad or Aldar finding my mangled body here.

Whack! Pain shot through me as a table leg slammed onto my other foot.

I yelled, but with the wall at my back, there was no place for me to go. I slid down to a crouch, covering my head and trying to protect my feet and hands, trying to make myself as small a target as possible. "As soon as Aldar's here, we'll find the boy, Scilla. I think he's the one. You'll have your justice—I promise!"

Simultaneously, the table and chairs rose up half a foot and dropped to the floor with a *thud*.

In the silence, my gasps filled the room. It took a few moments before my quivering legs let me stand again. I inched around the table and away from the wall. Nothing happened.

Hesitantly, I ran a hand over a chair back, terrified it would move again, maybe stomp on my foot hard enough to break bones this time. But it was just a normal, inanimate piece of furniture. For the next ten minutes, I stood near the exit, half-holding my breath.

A knock sounded at the door and I jumped. But it was only Aldar finally showing up. I dragged him from the room with me. In the hall, I told him about the boy with the leaf tattoo. I'd feared he'd try to force me back into the room and through a lesson, but he said, "Of course. Come on. We'll find Freyad right away."

We had to ask six people and walk through half of Baaldarstad, but ironically, we eventually located her close to the manor, near the elephant bird pens. "Freyad!" I called when I saw her.

"Queen Jiara?" She turned to Aldar and garbled a question.

He answered, then said to me, "I told her about the boy. That he might be the one the witness saw."

Freyad pursed her lips. "The boy's name is Leonno. But a tattoo with thick lines?" Her eyes turned upward as she considered. "I don't think so."

"Leonno? That sounds Azzarian."

Freyad nodded. "It is. His grandfather was from Azzaria." She smiled to herself. "Must have been in some legal trouble. He fled the country, traveled up through Loftaria and ended up here. He always used to say he was on his way to safety beyond the mountains of Svertya, but then he met Leonno's grandmother and couldn't take another step." She chuckled. "The old man was a charmer."

So Leonno had the right tattoo and a connection to Azzaria. Not only that—an *unhappy* connection. His grandfather had probably been headed for prison. Maybe he still held a grudge. Maybe he'd put his grandson up to revenge.

"Take me to him now, please." If I was right, Scilla could rest easy. *I* could rest easy, and my entire family too.

Freyad's reminiscing eyes caught my anxious ones. "Of course. Right away. But I can't imagine how he could be involved. He's a good boy."

My guard led us on a half-hour walk out of town under towering trees, springing chipmunks, and chirping birds to where I'd seen the small houses with larger yards on the way into Baaldarstad months ago. At the first building, she raised her hand. "Leonno's family lives here."

A fence surrounded the yard, and two dogs dozed in the sun as chickens pecked around them. "Leonno!" Freyad called. "We have some questions for you!"

A woman about my mother's age peeked out of the house. "Leonno will be right back."

I nodded. I understood a word or two of most sentences by now, but luckily Aldar translated them all the same. I never knew if I'd miss crucial information without him.

The woman disappeared into the house again then strode out with a bowl in one hand while she stirred with a spoon in the other. "Queen Jiara, what a surprise! Welcome! It's nice to meet you. Hello, Freyad. How's Linnd? What do you need?"

Freyad smiled at her but didn't betray my suspicions. "Linnd's fine. A little busy with the new stable apprentices, but they'll settle in soon, like every year." She gestured to me with her chin. "Queen Jiara watched the trainees yesterday and just wanted to stop by and say hello. Leonno managed to toss Raffar down once pretty good."

Raffar. Not King Raffar.

Both women had a good laugh. I remembered my manners enough to say how impressed I was with his combat skills. Aldar translated, but seemed otherwise uninterested until a boy's voice echoed from behind the house.

"Leonno! Come out front!" his mother yelled.

The tall boy rounded the house, a stack of firewood in his arms. He tossed it in a pile near the dogs, who were so lazy, they didn't even flinch. "Freyad, did you see how I—"

Then he noticed me. His eyes widened. Mine looked for only one thing.

And my heart dove southward. His leaf tattoo was exactly like Raffar's. No thick line. I turned to Aldar and shook my head, then did the same for Freyad.

"Queen Jiara!" Leonno said, his face flushing. "It is an honor. Uh, wait . . ." His face screwed up and then he nodded to himself. "Kiss me," he said in heavily accented Azzarian, his teeth bared in amusement.

Aldar smacked him on the arm.

"Ow!"

"Leonno, what did you say?" Freyad muttered.

Aldar's lips pressed together, but Leonno smiled again

and continued. Warily, Aldar translated, "It's the only phrase grandfather taught me before he died, except—"

"Can I touch your bre—" Leonno ducked his head just before Aldar could slap him in the face this time.

Apparently, there were still limits for royalty.

Leonno's mother frowned at him, but apparently also had no idea what he was saying, since she didn't appear truly dismayed.

The juvenile phrases were the least of my worries. I rubbed my eyes. I'd seen the thick lines during training, I was certain of it. "Your tattoos—they looked different yesterday."

The boy's mother gave him a pat on the shoulder. "Filthy boys, rolling around in the dirt. No offense to King Raffar. See—" She rubbed her hand over his bald head—"I wasn't the only one to notice all those streaks of sweaty mud. I barely recognized you when you came home."

If it was possible, my heart sank even further, down into the Farnskag dirt. I had mistaken sweat and dust for the tattoo that would identify Scilla's murderer. My eyes burned. At this pace, I was never going to find her killer.

I hid my disappointment as best I could. Leonno's mother begged us to come and sit down in the shade. She offered us mugs of water and fresh green apple slices. After a round of polite conversation, the three of us wandered the road back into town.

Freyad eyed me as we walked. "You really thought Leonno might be the assassin?"

I'd concealed my feelings as long as we were with the boy's mother, but my eyes grew moist again. I nodded.

She rubbed her hands together. "I saw the drawing too, back in Glizerra. But our tattoos are not random. They have meanings. The *kahngaad* keeps her distance from people in order to hold a strong connection to the Watchers. That's how she knows which tattoos are the right ones for each person, outside of the ones that show professions or family membership, but those are specific too. I don't think anyone in Farnskag has a leaf tattoo like that. But I will keep an eye out. I promise."

Aldar chimed in, "And we'll both keep our ears open. Maybe someone will drop information that helps us figure it out."

If anything, my eyes smarted worse than before. I raised a hand to press at them before the dampness could slip out. Raffar's agents hadn't reported anything helpful lately, but now Freyad and Aldar had promised to help me. Maybe there was hope for Scilla after all. A gentle brush against my hand told me Scilla felt the same way.

———————

Aldar held up the slate. He might as well have stuck a dagger in my chest. First, I read it in Farnskag, then, taking care to make my voice not sound as hurt as I felt, I uttered the Azzarian translation: "One."

Aldar sighed. "Close, Your Majesty. It is a number. It's *four*. Let's go over all the numbers again."

He kept talking, but blood rushed in my ears, and his voice was a senseless jumble in my mind. No! I remembered that word. That was the number I'd thought was *three*, but he'd said was *one*. How was it supposed to be *four*?

The room started to spin, and a door slammed shut in the adjoining dining room. I needed a few seconds alone. "Could you please open that again?" I asked Aldar. "It was giving us such a nice breeze."

"Of course."

Aldar strode from the room, and I lowered my head to the tabletop. I inhaled and exhaled. I swallowed down years of shame. Reading had always been difficult, but how could I have this much trouble learning simple numbers? I squeezed my eyes shut and opened them again.

A crumpled piece of parchment lay on the floor, under the wardrobe in the corner. I left the table, crawling on hands and knees, reaching as far back as I could to retrieve it . . . it was the paper from Aldar's scavenger hunt, the one where I'd first proved how dangerously awful my Farnskag was. My insides twisted. As I unfolded it, I swallowed the lump in my throat and lay the slip next to the slate.

My gut cramped even worse, and my mouth felt like it had been swabbed with wool until it was bone dry. The word on the parchment . . . the word on the slate . . . it was the *same word*.

I wasn't stupid. I wasn't lazy. This word that Freyad had identified as *one*, that I had learned as *three*, Aldar now said was *four*.

He was teaching me the wrong words. Deliberately.

Aldar, who had helped me understand life in Farnskag, who had pledged to help me find Scilla's killer. Aldar . . . who now couldn't be trusted?

My heart felt ready to boil over, and I held my head in both hands, my brain scrambling to understand the situation.

What was going on? What was I supposed to do? Who could I turn to for help?

A gasp hissed from the doorway. My tutor stood, his tattoos stark against the paleness as his face drained of color, his eyes locked on the square of parchment in my hand and the slate next to it.

Hot anger threatened to wipe out rational thinking, but I needed to keep my wits about me. Why would he teach me incorrectly? Did he want to frustrate me? To drive me to leave the country? Or was he trying to steal Azzaria's respect in the eyes of the Farnskagers? What sense would that make?

Before I could decide, he flew across the room to me. If I hadn't been sitting, I would have run out the door, but within a second, he knelt at my feet, his head bowed.

"I'm so sorry, Queen Jiara. I just don't know what to do. Once you've learned Farnskag, Raffar won't need a translator anymore. He'll send me away. But my father is dying, and I can't go. I can't leave him alone when I'm the only family he has left. And I can't bear to live back at the university. It is not the life for me—"

"You've been teaching me the wrong words *on purpose*?" My stomach contracted so intensely I was afraid I'd be sick, and I gripped the tabletop.

He shook his head. "Not all of them. Sometimes."

He even admitted it! Fire rushed up my back and to my face again. After all the times I'd told him how difficult learning was for me . . . "And the reason you make me look at the spelling is because you know it confuses me."

He bit his lip. "I wasn't certain, but I had the feeling it did."

I wanted to pound him with my fists, toss him into an elephant bird pen. My hand rose to my mouth as sourness crept up my throat. I stood to fetch Raffar. Regardless of Aldar's reasons, he had abused my trust. How could I ever believe him again? How could Raffar?

Then I had another thought. Just how dangerous was Aldar? "And your scavenger hunt?"

The remaining color left his face. "A mistake! A horrible, horrible mistake. Please believe me. I only intended for you not to be able to find the last clue, to miss the prize."

He'd literally plotted against me. But at least he hadn't meant me physical harm.

Fists at my sides, I stared at him.

"I'm so sorry."

"That's it? After months of betrayal? You're sorry?" He had made me feel so inadequate, so unintelligent, so . . . no, my feelings weren't the most important thing here. "I was almost trampled to death!"

"I didn't mean that to happen!"

"I'm the queen of your country. How am I supposed to be a help to Raffar if I can't speak Farnskag? Even if you didn't care about me, you said he was like a brother to you!"

"He is." He raised his hands as if to grab hold of my legs. But he must have seen the barely controlled anger in my expression, and let them fall without touching me. "Please, I can't handle leaving my father, and my home. I can't handle leaving Raffar. Can you imagine how often I wished I were as strong as you? You go to a foreign country, and nearly everyone around finds you . . . intriguing. I'm not like that. I was always so lost.

If I had to go through that again . . . I don't know. I couldn't. I wouldn't survive."

There was a short banging on the door, then it opened and two guards entered. Their eyes snapped to Aldar, on the floor, and to me standing over him. They exchanged words with Aldar.

"They asked what's going on," Aldar said softly, his eyes pleading. "And if the queen needs help."

Through my anger and hurt, I forced myself to slow down, to see the man kneeling in front of me. He was Raffar's closest childhood friend. A person losing his father, like I had lost Scilla. And depending on whether he'd really be sent to the university, maybe even losing his home.

Deep inside, how different from Aldar was I? If it wasn't for the evidence indicating a Farnskager had killed Scilla, I never would have come this far away. I never would have left Azzaria. And why not? Because I wanted to stay home. Just like him.

I shook my head. It didn't matter how similar he was to me; his actions were inexcusable. I turned to the guards, my mouth open to ask for Raffar. But before the words hit my tongue, I had an idea. "Aldar, from this day forward, you teach me spoken Farnskag."

Aldar raised his head. Tears streaked his cheeks, and his eyebrows creased. "You're giving me another chance?"

I glared at him with the hardest queen stare I could muster. "If I ever find out you betray me or Raffar again, you will *rot* in prison."

Aldar nodded. "I won't. I promise. Thank you."

And now for the only reason I was giving him this chance.

"Tell the guards we're going on an outing. You're taking me to the prison right this minute to speak to the Stärklandish assassin."

He slumped against the wall. "Your Majesty, it could be dan—"

"Now. Or I go to Raffar."

Aldar nodded.

"And your translations will be perfect, do you understand me?"

"Yes, Your Majesty. I promise."

CHAPTER 19

The prison was all the way across town, and Gio, the wind god, and Azzoro, the water god, tussled in the sky as only brothers could, so Aldar ordered a carriage to take us there. The prison building was smaller than I'd expected for a town of this size, and I remembered that the Servants of the gods said the reason we had earthwalkers and other countries didn't was that Azzaria had a stronger sense of justice than other countries. If Baaldarstad needed so little room for prisoners, and still had a well-functioning society, what did that say about us? Could it be we in Azzaria were too strict?

Inside was only an office consisting of two desks and a rack of weapons, and six cells beyond that. An older man in one of the cells stumbled from one wall to the next, raving about just one more drink. A tattooless man in another cell covered his ears. The others were empty.

The guards on duty dropped their jaws when we entered but made no move to stop us. Aldar explained what we wanted, and a woman armed with a staff and a club led us down steep stone steps to the secure area.

Dark torches lined the rock walls. The guard lit them as we went, the glow reaching further into the dark corridor.

The first cell we passed was empty, but in the second sat a man with a scraggly beard. He covered his eyes with his hand, blinded by the sudden torchlight. His clothes were filthy, but the embroidered diamond shapes on his sleeve cuffs hinted that he'd once cared for his appearance and confirmed he was from Stärkland. No one here or at home wore embroidery like that. The guard grumbled a few words, including "*Skriin.*" So now the prisoner knew I was the queen.

I imagined how my mother could intimidate men with only a look and stiffened my back. I needed to get whatever information out of him I could.

"Your Majesty!" He stood slowly, as if his joints were stiff, and bowed. "Thank you to come."

My ears were playing tricks on me. Or Scilla's spirit was confusing me. Or what else could explain my ease in understanding his heavily accented speech?

I turned to Aldar, whose eyebrows rose. So, Aldar had heard it too. I could understand the prisoner because he knew my language.

"You speak Azzarian?" I asked the man.

"Some, Your Majesty." He brushed his hair back from his face. When he glanced at Aldar, his eyes narrowed.

The prisoner wasn't as old as I'd expected. My age. Possibly even a little younger.

He returned his gaze to me, and a sparkle touched his eyes. "The king, he let me out?"

Before I could answer, Aldar cleared his throat. "Queen

Jiara, I hate to see you waste your time with this scum. The stories the prisoner tells . . . you can't believe anything he says."

And that from Aldar. I could barely refrain from rolling my eyes. If he would have appeared nervous or fearful, I may also have told the guard to thrust him into the cell next door, certain he was trying to manipulate me again. But he leaned against the wall, bored.

"I will speak with him." If only I knew what to ask. I waved a hand and decided to begin with something simple. "Your name?"

He nodded. "Jonas."

I inclined my head, but he refused to elaborate with a family name. So, he was keeping secrets. I let it slide, for now.

"Where did you learn Azzarian?"

"I grew up . . . across border from Caotina." He spoke slowly, haltingly, as he considered the right words. "I like the spice-berries and sneak across border."

"Did you not have spiceberries in Stärkland?"

The prisoner's eyes glittered in the torchlight, and his dry lips broke into a smile. "Parents say spiceberries make sick. Sick in the head. They tear plants out of dirt. But boy gave me some once. Azzaria boy. Very good berries."

Sick in the head? How did Stärklandish people get that idea? Azzarians loved spiceberries. Unfortunately, they didn't grow in Glizerra. They needed the cooler climate of the northern provinces. A juicy combination of sweet and mildly peppery, I could imagine a daring boy venturing across the border just to snatch a few.

But Scilla had been found not far from Caotina. "How did you come to be here, in this cell?"

The prisoner's eyes flicked to Aldar and to the guard, then rushed back to me. His hands slid over knuckles crusted over with blood. For several heartbeats, he stared at me. "I came to speak with king." He pointed to Aldar. "He . . . attacked my party. Killed my companions."

Aldar attacked? He wasn't a soldier. Aldar sighed exaggeratedly as if saying he'd warned me.

"What do you know about the death of Princess Scilla?"

His lips turned up, but his eyes creased in a sad way. "Your sister, no? A smart woman. Very good woman."

I refused to let his words or his expression soften my heart. Maybe he'd heard about Raffar's marriage from the guards. Anyone could say nice things about a stranger. But the lightest caress on my cheek coaxed a shiver across my spine and a tenseness to my limbs. Scilla could be nearby, listening to the prisoner's tale.

Not that he'd divulged anything helpful but his proximity to Caotina. "What else?"

Again, he looked to Aldar, then his eyes locked on my wrist. He stared so long that I had to ignore the urge to hide my arms. "A Watcher, Your Majesty? Which one?"

I didn't answer. I was interrogating him.

He shrugged. "No matter. It is good. The Watcher keeps you safe."

Stärkland shared the same beliefs as Farnskag? Could that be? If only I had paid more attention to my tutors' details of foreign countries. "What do you mean?"

"You are safe. Not like sister. King Raffar was wise to give you Watcher."

I ran a hand over the smooth, black stones. If they'd ever protected me before, their power was used up now. Not that this boy needed to hear it.

Aldar yawned, and again I tamped down the urge to shove him into a cell. "Queen Jiara, I thi—"

I held up a hand. "Continue, Jonas."

"Yes, they protect. You don't revere the Watchers in Azzaria. But they are around you always. You should find the . . . sacred Watcher writings. I don't know the name in Azzarian." His chuckle turned into a cough. "Or Farnskag. The writings explain."

They might explain, but they would explain in Farnskag, which would be similar to having no explanation at all. Aldar's sighs and yawns grated on my nerves, and Jonas seemed hesitant to talk much while Aldar was present. Now that I knew Jonas spoke Azzarian, I would come here on my own and interrogate him without an untrustworthy man listening. All I'd have to do was to get Freyad to bring me . . . or escape my guards.

———

The entire day, Jonas's tale knocked around in my head. Not even a letter from Pia could cheer me up, not even the picture I drew for her showing me defending myself from an elephant bird with a knife.

No. I couldn't stop thinking about Jonas. Maybe I hadn't lent his words enough credence. By the evening, I paced our suite and waited for Raffar to return from a meeting with the council. I chewed on my lip as I thought of the twisted tale of the ambush, and how different it was from the "truth" Raffar knew. Most likely, Jonas had made everything up, but even so, I had to tell my husband.

The door hit the wall as it was thrust open, and my heart leaped in my chest.

"Raf—" My voice faltered. Aldar stood directly behind Raffar, with two servants behind them, their arms full of trunks.

Raffar spoke so quickly as he gathered belongings from the table next to his side of the bed and his wardrobe that all I caught was the word *leave.*

Aldar stood with hands clasped at his back and translated, "Jiara, I am sorry to have to do this so soon after your arrival, but I must travel to Gluwfyall today. It's imperative I leave immediately."

Travel? Today? I closed my eyes and tried to remember where Gluwfyall was. A couple of days east of here, if I remembered correctly, just before the mountains that formed the border to Svertya.

"The region's council there is paralyzed by constant fighting. I just found out they haven't paid the university staff in weeks, nor the registrar. Apparently the square and public buildings are in such disrepair that the citizens refuse to gather in the town's meeting hall. The sense of community is in danger." He stopped tossing things to the servants and sighed as his worried eyes met mine. "This needs my personal attention, before we face a revolt of some kind."

I nodded. A monarch had duties. He had to ensure smooth

workings in his kingdom. But shouldn't I be packing too? "And I?"

Raffar laid a gentle hand on my cheek. "I need you to stay here, to represent us at all the events planned during the next few weeks. Freyad will make sure you continue to meet people. And, you'll have plenty of time to study with Aldar."

Aldar smiled when he translated that.

My eyes flicked to the interpreter, then to the floor. But without Raffar here . . . I didn't know what to think except that since this morning, Aldar made my skin crawl. And now, Raffar wouldn't be around to listen to my suspicions.

My hand rose to take his arm, but I didn't want to cling. "Could we talk first?" I motioned to our bedroom where the lexicon was.

His eyes flicked to the chest and back to me as if calculating the time it would take to discuss anything. Then his tiny smile brimmed with apology. "I'm sorry, but it's important that I go immediately. I'm expected at the first stop along the way tonight. If you have an urgent issue, Aldar can help translate now. Don't worry, he'll keep anything you say confidential."

I couldn't mention what Jonas had said with servants listening. If I was wrong, I'd ruin Aldar's reputation—and mine. And based on my recent experiences with him, who knew if Aldar would even translate my words accurately?

I shook my head and pushed down the lonely feeling crawling up my throat. "I'll miss you."

Raffar clasped my hand. "And I you. I look forward to seeing what you've learned when we meet each other again. I'll have

Freyad and Matid bring you to meet me in Gluwfyall in a few weeks for the Lake of Light Festival."

A few weeks? I'd be alone here for a few weeks?

He strode to the bedroom and returned with a stack of books. A servant accepted them and placed them in a trunk. "After the festival, we'll return to Baaldarstad together."

Only moments later, Raffar's belongings were completely stowed. He pressed his lips to the top of my head a few seconds longer than was proper when people were watching, but no one said a word. As he left the room, the servants and Aldar followed him out.

In the hall, Raffar clasped Aldar's arm. "Give my regards to your father. And please take good care of Jiara."

As I closed the door, a vise tightened around my throat. I'd be alone—I *was* alone. And how would Aldar "take care" of me?

A fiery slap hit my face, sending me tumbling against the table. The room was empty. Tears stung my eyes, both from the pain and the realization that Scilla's violent outbursts were coming more and more often. I covered my cheeks with both hands to prevent her from striking again, but it did no good. *Smack*—another blow struck the crown of my head. My vision doubled, and I wobbled on my feet.

Earthwalkers were impossible to understand. Was she just violent? An earthwalker who'd been dead for nearly seven months now and had lost all rationality, hitting me for no reason? Was she mad at me for not finding her killer? Or because she thought my worries were inconsequential compared to hers?

"Scilla," I whispered, choosing to believe it was a

combination of the latter two reasons, as I propped myself against the table for support. "I have the right to be worried."

There was a long pause, then an invisible hand stroked over my hair.

Wetness slipped down my cheeks as I stood, all alone except maybe for a dangerous and unpredictable ghost, in the middle of this room so far from home.

CHAPTER 20

I n Azzaria, I'd had my own suite, and I'd adored the sanctuary from court life it had provided. With Raffar gone, being in my chamber felt hollow and empty. Silence weighed on my ears until I could hear each beat of my pulse.

Normally, whether we comprehended every sentence or not, Raffar and I talked. And we did understand each other, in some way. Whether it was from spoken word or smiles or gestures or with the help of the lexicon.

Now, morning meant waking up, dressing, and breakfasting alone. Every creak of settling timbers was potentially Scilla, returning to punish me for not finding out more about her murderer, not being faster. A few solitary hours after getting out of bed, I stood silently in front of the scented blocks I'd set up in honor of the gods. They didn't make me feel less alone like I'd hoped. Maybe the Farnskager way of life was influencing me. They revered no gods here, performed no rituals to keep the gods on their side. They only had Watchers, who literally watched from afar, rarely influencing life on earth, except to save a few individuals from death once in a while. It was up to the Farnskagers themselves to forge a connection to the world around them.

I imagined Mother were here. "Mother," I said, my voice rough from disuse. Then I forced myself to continue in Farnskag, with Azzarian words sprinkled in when I didn't have any idea as to the right phrase. It was good practice, and it didn't matter how many mistakes I made. "Raffar left yesterday. And now I'm . . . I don't want to act like a baby, but I feel so alone."

A caress on my hand. I tensed, waited breathlessly, because it could only be Scilla. But violence didn't come. My sister was gentle this time.

"Thank you, Scilla. I worry about Aldar." And even though I was talking to the dead, I could only make myself whisper the next part, "I don't know if I can trust him."

Scilla stroked my cheek this time, and I closed my eyes and pretended she was here and her normal, rational self.

A cheerful knock banged at the door, but it could have been a fist pounding in anger considering how I jumped. Thankfully, I'd spoken quietly. I ran from my altar and ushered Aldar in.

Tutoring was the same as always. I repeated words. Sometimes I knew the meanings, sometimes I didn't. Sometimes I suspected he'd taught me a different translation the day before. I'd carefully broached the topic with Matid and Freyad, but they hadn't understood me, and before I knew it, Matid had pulled in Aldar to translate. So I'd changed the subject. Without Raffar around, my threat for Aldar to rot in jail had little effect.

Aldar smiled encouragingly, as if nothing had ever

happened between us. "Queen Jiara, Raffar will be proud of how hard you're working."

Like every day, I nodded and wished with all my heart that my lesson would end. But today, I didn't bother trying to understand or memorize anything he taught me. I just watched his reactions for clues to his sincerity.

As soon as Freyad arrived and Aldar left the royal manor for his father's house, I headed for a room down the hall I had thus far avoided: the library. If I were at home, I'd ask a Servant of the gods if there was anything else we could do about Scilla. Maybe I could do the same thing here—but with the Watchers. But first, I had to understand them better. Jonas had suggested a book. I wanted to look at it before I spoke to him—or someone else—again.

The gut-churning scent of dusty leather assaulted me as soon as I walked in, whispering of headaches lying in wait. The library was as large as the dining hall, with a door at each end and rows upon rows of Farnskager books. Freyad sighed as I walked along the shelves, running a finger over the spines. If only Scilla or Watcher of Sky would point me in the right direction.

The longer I forced myself to concentrate on the book titles, the more I felt like I was back in the classroom with my siblings and our childhood tutors. They'd read entire pages in the time it took me to get through a single paragraph. I stopped walking and leaned my head against the books. The leather covers pressed against my skin as I tilted my forehead back and forth, but no knowledge magically entered my mind.

This was ridiculous. I needed help.

I stalked around the shelves to find Freyad at one of the windows, smiling as she looked out over the street. A woman down below struggled with the reins of an unruly elephant bird—the same woman Freyad had hugged when they'd brought me to Baaldarstad that first day weeks ago, and who I'd seen several times near the stables.

"Freyad," I said. "Who is that?" I pointed out the window.

She turned to me, the corners of her lips still raised in a smile. "Linnd." She said something else I didn't catch, except for the word *wife*.

I pointed to Linnd. "Your wife?"

She nodded absently, then turned back to the window.

"Can we open it?" I didn't wait for her answer. I shoved open the window and waved a hand outside. The woman didn't look up.

Freyad laughed at me but called, "Linnd!"

The woman yanked on the bird's reins, finally stilling it, and scanned the length of the building until she saw Freyad. The expression on her face smoothed and warmed my chest. She called up to us, and Freyad answered.

I couldn't do much, but I could say hello. "*Guuddug*, Linnd!"

The woman grinned at Freyad, then waved to me. "*Guuddug, Skriin* Jiara!"

The two women exchanged a few more phrases, then Linnd called a goodbye to both of us and tugged on the reins, dragging the reluctant animal up the street. Freyad watched until she was out of sight and asked me a question . . . possibly whether I was finished.

"No, I'm looking for a book about the Watchers." I pointed to my bracelet, then swept a hand over the books.

"Ahh," Freyad sighed. She pushed away from the window and walked along one of the shelves, her head swiveling back and forth, up and down.

As much as I would have liked to wait until she found what I sought, I gritted my teeth and forced myself to browse a different shelf. Four eyes were better than two, even if half of them belonged to me. A quarter of an hour later, I finally found something useful, even if it wasn't what I'd sought: an Azzarian-Farnskag lexicon, similar to the one Raffar kept next to the bed and had accidentally packed when he left for Gluwfyall. I wasn't looking forward to more reading, but it would definitely be helpful.

"Here." Freyad pushed a second book into my hand.

I tried to focus on the title, but the letters kept slipping around. No wonder I hadn't found it myself. "Thank you, Freyad."

". . . just a few moments," said a familiar voice from the door we'd entered. Aldar.

My stomach clenched as if I'd been caught misbehaving. Which was silly. I was the queen and had every right to be in my library. But I suddenly didn't want to see Aldar, or rather, didn't want him to see me here, among all this written word, especially not holding a lexicon. If he didn't want me to understand the language, keeping what I did understand secret seemed the right thing to do. At least for now.

I put a finger to my lips. Freyad's eyebrows wrinkled, but

she trailed after me when I grabbed her sleeve and headed for the opposite door.

Once Aldar had left the first row, we sneaked around the shelves and slipped out of the room.

Freyad shook her head at me and rolled her eyes. I shrugged. I had no way to ask her to keep the lexicon secret from Aldar, except . . . the book weighed heavy in my hand. If I had a lexicon, I could find a way. We navigated the manor's passages to the narrow staircase at the back and slipped out into the garden below.

Usually, when we went on walks, Freyad took me through the town so I could meet my people. But today, I looked up the word for water and pointed to it. She mimed a drinking motion, and I shook my head. "No, like a lake or river." I found both words and pointed to them.

She motioned for me to follow her. We walked all the way through the garden behind the manor, past the tall trees and the bushes and the stones covered in succulents. A spike-topped wooden fence surrounded the grounds, but there was an unmanned gate at the rear. Why have a fence if the gate was open? Why didn't they feel the need for more security? In Glizerra, I never left without at least two guards—not that anything had ever happened. Maybe it was more for show.

Raffar constantly went to town with no guards at all. If I hadn't proved to be such a danger to myself, I probably wouldn't have constant protection either. On the other hand, considering Scilla's death and the attempt on my life in Loftaria, maybe I would.

Freyad kicked the gate open, and we headed into a lush

span of forest. Pine trees, lacy ferns of all heights, even some of those purple flowers Raffar had given me during our journey.

Freyad ran a hand along the ferns, greeting them. "Small river," she said, pointing.

Around a copse of tall trees, we came upon a creek about three feet wide and a few inches deep. It was nothing compared to the river that emptied into the sea at Glizerra or even compared to our canals, but I crouched down and plunged both hands into the cold, clear water. I closed my eyes and tried to squelch the ache in my throat. *I've missed you, Azzoro.*

When my hands were chilled to the bone, I wiped them on my pants. A fallen log in the shade of an ironfern tree made the perfect seat, and I opened the lexicon on my lap. I looked up *Watcher*, and matched it to a word on the spine of the book Freyad had given me. Freyad said the word over and over, until I could pronounce it flawlessly. Then she told me the names of them all. Watcher of Sky, Watcher of Stone, Watcher of Water.

My guard slipped down to the ground and leaned her back against the log on which I sat. She tipped her face to the sun then squinted up at me. She pointed to the sun and said a word. I repeated it.

She did the same for the log, and one by one, named most every object around us. Like a spinning carriage wheel, she cycled through a dozen words, over and over, quizzing me until she was sure I had them.

Finally, she pointed to my bracelet. "Watcher of Sky," I said.

She beamed. "Very good, Queen Jiara."

She stood up and said we should return to the manor, but I held her back. I flipped between the pages until I knew what I wanted to say, and how to do it diplomatically. Just because Aldar gave me an odd, uncomfortable feeling didn't mean he was actually doing anything truly dangerous. And he was Raffar's cousin and oldest friend, after all.

"Please don't tell Aldar about this lexicon," I said. "I want to surprise him with my progress."

If she found my request unusual, she didn't show it. At her nod, we followed the narrow path back home.

After that first day with Freyad at the training grounds, I began accompanying her several times a week, begging her to teach me the words for everything around us. In order to see more people, I asked her to take me to more surrounding villages and towns. Everywhere we went, I studied faces, tattoos, always ready to pounce should the right tattoo come into view.

I also joined her during training. Mostly, I was a glorified assistant, handing her weapons, separating trainees into teams, and sending fighters for a couple of laps around the field when they became too hot headed. Occasionally, I joined the youngest children and tried my hand at throwing a knife, wielding a club or a staff. No one said it aloud, but weaponry skills were not my strength.

The portion of training that always earned cheers was Capture the Queen. Freyad allowed it at least once a week because it schooled strategic thinking. Whether soldiers chased me around trees or I helped to build a barricade of fallen branches, every session had me reach a point where I laughed until I thought I'd fall over.

When one of the youngest girls won her first fight with a staff, I placed my hand on her head and congratulated her for her hard work. Soon soldiers of all ages dropped to one knee before me to receive praise, and within two weeks, new recruits started showing up. Some of the eldest from Baaldarstad even began making the trek out to the training grounds, calling suggestions from the sidelines, or stepping in to help with posture or techniques to try. After a few Farnskag-style "discussions," during which Freyad's posture had been ironfern-wood strong, she'd come to an agreement with them. Outside of one man who was eventually barred from the practice field, the eldest now took direction from Freyad whenever she gave an order during training.

Shortly after I'd taken the books from the library, I stood in front of my blocks for the gods. "Thank you for providing for me here. Raffar is a good man, and a good king. And thank you for Freyad. Without her, I may not have found my place in this country. Please protect my family from Scilla, and please help me or Father find her killer so she may be freed from this world."

Freyad's knock and bright "hello" through the door broke me out of my thoughts, and I hurried with her to the front door of the manor. I had special plans today. I needed to make progress on Scilla's murder. I used the lexicon to explain I wanted to go to the prison while Aldar visited his father. Freyad scratched her short hair, but agreed to take me. Linnd, who turned out to be one of the bird masters, led an elephant bird to the two-seat carriage that would pull us there.

As we rode, Freyad tested me on the words she'd taught me lately by pointing to things and having me say their names. She corrected my pronunciation.

Suddenly, she asked, "How are you?"

My heart squeezed a little, and I swallowed. The townspeople might enjoy my appearances during military training, but outside of Raffar and Aldar, no one had ever asked.

Only, how to answer her question was a different story. Scilla had barely been around the past several days. I was luckier than I could have hoped in marrying Raffar. Despite our speech issues, we had an inherent understanding of each other. And as much as the slowness frustrated me, my Farnskager language skills were improving. Our relationship would only get better the more we could communicate.

I missed my family and Azzaria. The weather wasn't as harsh as I'd assumed—at least not now, in the summer. And I was getting used to the new cuisine. "Some good, some . . . I learn still."

Freyad patted my back. "You're doing fine. The people like you." She uttered another phrase I didn't catch, but with the lexicon, I figured it out: "You are a good support for our king."

A good support. Months ago, I'd thought I'd have a meaningful life with Marro in northern Azzaria. Despite how different everything had turned out, I was glad I could still make my life meaningful. Probably more so, considering the protection the alliance brought to Azzaria.

After a quarter of an hour, we reached the prison. The same

guard as the first time was there, and she held her torch high as she descended the steps in front of us. Again, Jonas shielded his eyes from the light, but his face was less dirt smeared, and his hair and beard had been trimmed.

"Did they allow you to bathe?" I asked, wrinkling my nose at the scent of too many unwashed bodies and no fresh air. I had never enjoyed visiting the prisons back home, and I didn't like it here.

"Queen Jiara," the prisoner said, with a voice rough from lack of use. "Yes. I wondered why." He smiled politely. "Please . . . please visit me often. Then I can keep cleaner. I see you left the translator away this time."

"He was busy. And I can understand you fine."

He chuckled, then coughed. A lung ailment? The air was chilly and damp down here. I frowned at the guard, but it wasn't her fault. Prisons were not built for comfort.

First, I'd take care of the questions most important for Raffar. "Before we can discuss doing anything for you, we need more information. You said Aldar killed your people."

He laid his head to the side as if implying I wasn't completely correct. "He did not kill. His fault they are dead."

"Explain yourself."

He walked toward the door of the cell. Ironfern wood bars kept him from reaching too far out, but I leaned back anyway.

"I say to translator that we come in peace to talk to King Raffar about treaty. He yell at his soldiers in Farnskag. Suddenly, they fire arrows at us. We don't expect it, and we shoot back, but we are too slow. All of my people dead. Only I was captured."

Chills ran across my shoulders, and my eyes slid to the

side, to the guard and to Freyad, who stood with bored expressions on their faces. They had no idea the prisoner was accusing Aldar of telling the Farnskager soldiers to fire on innocent diplomats. I'd thought Aldar incapable of killing the men himself, but he'd proven to me that he was clearly able to mislead others into making wrong—and potentially deadly—decisions. But why?

"Why do you think the translator did this?"

"Translator's Stärklandish not so good?" Jonas shook his head, and a dry, sarcastic laugh shot through the cell. "No. It makes no sense. Unless . . . there are old stories. About Watchers having favorites. Maybe he is worried Stärkland is the favorite?" He grinned a bit. "If I were a Watcher, I would favor Stärkland."

I glanced down to hide my smile. Yes, if I were a Watcher—or a god—I would choose sparkling Azzaria over the other nations also.

Still, it made no sense. If there was one thing about Aldar I believed, it was that he wanted the best for Farnskag. Or what he assumed was the best, anyway. Aldar had worried that returning the prisoner to his country would put Farnskag in a position of weakness. So, before they took Jonas prisoner, had Aldar believed that an alignment with Stärkland would elevate the other country's importance? How would killing the diplomats support Farnskag? Had Aldar assumed a preemptive strike would keep future Stärklandish troops on their own side of the border?

I stared at Jonas. No matter what I thought, there was

absolutely no proof. Should I take the word of a foreign prisoner over the king's official translator?

A heavy sigh rushed from my chest because I couldn't decide now. "And my sister Scilla—what do you know about her death?"

He shook his head. "Maybe same reason my people were killed. She came to border near Caotina to meet with me. She wanted to bring gift of peace to her betrothed."

What? Scilla had *met* Jonas and had planned to bring a present to Raffar? "A gift of peace? How?"

He gestured between himself and Freyad and the prison guard. "Peace between us . . . between our countries. Princess Scilla and I met at border. She said she would talk to King Raffar, convince him to speak with me about a treaty. I believed she had, but my letters to Farnskag went unanswered. Then I heard Princess Scilla died, shortly after our discussion."

He paced back and forth, pounding a fist into his palm. "But the idea of peace was a good one. I come here to continue discussions myself. We happened on translator and the soldiers, and he did not listen to me. I am here . . . in the dark . . . since."

The story spun in my head like a cyclone. But I still didn't know who killed Scilla. "Do you know how she died?"

His pacing stopped and he leaned against the bars. With a defeated sigh, he said, "No, but I know this—do not trust the translator."

I took a step back, ready to leave the stink and the headaches of the prison while I pondered all Jonas had said. But without evidence . . . I pivoted and surged forward again.

"This attack and the peace talks with Scilla—is there a written record?"

The prisoner's shoulders drooped. "Yes, of course. I wrote it myself, in Stärklandish, but also in Azzarian. I hope that someone—not the translator—would see it who knew one of the languages. But the translator rewrote it for the king in Farnskag."

Which meant Aldar could have changed it any way he pleased. I nodded. "I will investigate further. And I will return."

A curious smile tugged at his lips. "Thank you, Queen Jiara." His eyes dropped to my bracelets. In a perfect echo of Raffar from the other night, he said, "Keep her safe, Watchers."

I dipped my head in farewell, agreeing with his request to the Watchers. The more I learned about Aldar, the clearer it was I might need it.

CHAPTER 21

Aldar held up the slate with the number *three* spelled out on it.

Without a blink, I asked, as hopefully as possible, "One?"

He grinned good naturedly. "Great job!" An encouraging pat on my arm. "See, I told you that you would begin to remember them."

I forced a satisfied smile to form and waited for the next word. Considering all the practice with Raffar before he'd left, and with Freyad, I knew most of the words Aldar tested me on, even if reading them was a guarantee of eyestrain and a headache. But I made a point of getting at least a random third to half wrong when Aldar was around. There didn't seem to be any rhyme or reason to when he said I was correct or not. Sometimes, I had no idea what a word was and guessed. Often, I was "right."

If Raffar had been around, I would have turned Aldar in. He hadn't kept up his end of the bargain. But if it was only my word against his, would the Farnskagers believe me? Especially if my accusation was nothing more than hesitant stuttering and pointing to words in the lexicon? I'd seen them interact:

Raffar and Freyad and Matid and the others. They *liked* Aldar. They trusted him. No, I needed to keep watching him, figure out what his real goal was.

Today, Freyad and Matid were both busy. Aldar was supposed to watch over me in the afternoon, but there was research to do—research that he couldn't know about. I had to shrug off my fear of venturing out alone and keep investigating. And I had to get rid of Aldar, so I could sneak over to the royal records depository.

My tutor wiped a cloth over the slate. Before he could add a new word, I embraced the cold spot in my heart and brought up the one topic that always got to him: "How is your father?"

His eyes turned glassy, but his voice was steady when he said, "Not very good. It's hard to see him in such pain. We've been to several doctors. Raffar even asked for advice from some of the best in Farnskag. Nothing's promising. No medicine seems to help."

Aldar's sorrow seemed so earnest, but when it came to him, what was I supposed to believe? Not that it mattered. Hoping his sadness was real, I said, "Aldar, it's so important that you spend time with him now. Today even." My voice caught—I didn't have to play at being choked up. "If I had known I would lose Scilla . . ."

"But Raffar said—"

"That you needed to watch over me. I know. And Freyad and Matid are both busy at training today. But there's been a change in plans. Not sure I caught all the details—something about soldiers participating in javelin testing where

I should bestow honors to the best—what I did understand is that Freyad will be here in less than an hour. I'll just wait in my suite until she arrives. Believe me, I don't want myself in any danger. Not after the mess I got into with that elephant bird."

"You'll get there," Aldar said. "It's just a matter of practice." He sat on the edge of his seat, clearly ready to run off.

One more careful nudge should do it. "I'll be fine here. And besides, I can't handle any more tutoring today. Please, Aldar? Give me a few moments rest before Freyad comes and drags me to that dusty training field?"

He bowed his head slightly, and with a little smile, said, "All right, Queen Jiara. And thank you. I really do want to visit my father."

"Of course." I nodded and accompanied him to the exit. "I'll see you tomorrow morning."

After closing the door behind him, I rushed to the window near the desk. I could see the street in front of the manor from there. Five minutes later, he stepped out the door, and I flew from the room. The manor staff knew they were to watch out for me, so I tiptoed through the halls and toward the stairs. A servant scrubbed the floor in the entrance hall—heart pattering, I ducked back around the corner and sneaked down the rear staircase and into the fresh-cut-grass scented garden. From there, I strode past the bird pens, slowing down enough to see that Fleetfoot's mother, in pen number three, was on her feet. A weight floated from my shoulders. They might be scary animals, but it hadn't been her fault.

The records depository was in the same area as the square, just down the street from the meeting house and the monolith.

It was impossible to prevent myself from being seen, but since Raffar traveled alone all the time, I kept my head high and waved when anyone noticed me. It couldn't be common knowledge that I required a nursemaid. That would be too embarrassing for Raffar. With my long hair, being inconspicuous was impossible anyway.

The door was locked, so I pulled a rope, and a low two-tone clang sounded from within. After a few moments, a short person with soft cheeks, narrow shoulders, and a head shaved bald greeted me. I knew the registrar was a man because Aldar had spoken of him, but he was either surprisingly young to have such a position or he was *trassovi*, which was Azzarian for people whose actual gender didn't match their gender assumed at birth. The translation in Farnskag was on the tip of my tongue—I'd learned it when meeting the groundskeeper at the manor—but I just couldn't force it all the way up to my brain. I'd look it up later. For now, I smiled at the registrar, who had the same zigzag-lined leaf tattoo as Aldar. I didn't want to draw attention to what I sought, so I used my reputation as a foreigner. The more harmless I sounded, the easier it would be to get time alone with the documents. As pleasantly as possible, I said, "I hello documents water under yes?"

The registrar blinked three times. His eyebrows high, he asked if I could say it again.

I took a deep breath because I had to see my plan through, no matter how silly I appeared. Then I smiled extra nervously and said, "Sorry. Water under yes I need see?"

The man swallowed and fetched a slate and a slate pencil. "Please . . . can you write it?"

I shook my head and didn't have to fake the look of embarrassment I aimed at the floor. I pointed to my eyes and then around the room.

The registrar nodded, the crease over his nose deep. "You'd like to look around? Of course, Queen Jiara."

"Thank you," I answered with a grateful smile.

He ushered me in and, with a shrug, went back to a high desk and began writing.

I wandered the aisles. As in Mother's records depository, there were scores of wood-covered codices held together with wooden rings. Some were dark-colored woods and some light. Some gleamed from the thousands of hands that had touched them during the past decades, and others had no hint of a patina. I picked one up every now and then to get my bearings in terms of which records were kept on which shelves. Names and dates meant births, marriages, or deaths. On another shelf, names and monetary amounts indicated tax records. When I found the collection of Farnskager laws, I knew I was getting close. Then finally, a codex containing legal decisions and evidence.

I flipped through the pages until I found the last one inscribed—a theft of sweep from a local family. *Sweep?* That couldn't be. I looked again. *Sheep.* That made more sense. I paged back. Another minor crime, so back again. A loose piece of parchment rested in the codex. I didn't understand the first few words at all, and my focus hopped around, searching for a word I might recognize. At the bottom, the words were in Azzarian, just like Jonas had said. So, the document was written in two languages: Azzarian at the bottom and . . . some of the letters at the top had two dots over them. That meant it must be Stärklandish. It had to be Jonas's statement.

Slowly, I pivoted and viewed the registrar with a sidelong glance. He copied text from an extra-large slate to parchment. His eyes diligently on his work, he didn't look at me once. Turning away as casually as possible, I slipped the loose parchment under my tunic and tucked it into the waistband of my pants. Then I studied the sheet it had been stored next to. This sheet was definitely in Farnskag, and I recognized the names Aldar and Jonas, but with the words hopping like they did, I needed more time. And my lexicon.

The wooden rings holding the pages together had a small opening to allow for new pages to be added. I slid the rings around so that the openings faced the inside.

"Can I help you, Your Majesty?"

The registrar's voice was so close to the back of my neck that the codex nearly slipped from my grasp. I held it flush against my chest, both to hide what I'd been reading and to prevent pages from becoming dislodged.

He held his hands out to take the codex from me. I froze. I had to find a way to get rid of him. I had to take this page with me. So . . . I coughed . . . and coughed and coughed until I barely squeezed the word out, "Drink?"

"Yes, Your Majesty, right away!" He disappeared down a dim hallway. With a light *thud*, I dropped the codex on a table and removed the page I needed. As with the other parchment, I stuffed it in my waistband. Then, maintaining my loud, increasingly hacking cough, I turned the wooden rings back to secure the pages again and shoved the codex onto its shelf.

When the registrar rushed back with a mug of tea, I coughed even more, then drank greedily.

"Are you all right?" he asked.

I nodded. "Thank you. It was . . ." I ran a finger along one of the dustier shelves, then pointed to my throat and shrugged. "Thank you for drink."

"Shall I call someone to get you?"

I shook my head. The last thing I needed was someone to take me on a tour of the market or library or a dozen other places I'd already seen. If I returned to the manor now, I could study the documents before dinner.

The registrar accompanied me through the depository toward the door. As we passed his workstation, my eyes caught on the paper he was writing—both Raffar's and Aldar's names were listed two times.

I pointed to the sheet. "What this?"

He nodded and hesitated, obviously considering how to explain to someone with language skills as poor as mine. Then he pointed to Raffar at the top of the right column. "King."

I nodded.

"If king dies . . ." Then he slid his finger down the next names: Indgar, Gavrad, Betid, Ardeng, Anzgar.

Indgar? Anzgar? A memory scratched at my brain. I'd heard those names before. Who were they? Not that it mattered. If it was a list of names dealing with the king's death, it had to be the order of succession. I concentrated on the next word. Below Anzgar was Aldar.

Aldar was in line for the throne?

Actually, that made sense. He was Raffar's cousin, after all.

But there were two columns. I pointed to the left one where there were only three names: Raffar, Anzgar, and Aldar.

The registrar spoke slowly, "Raffar is changing it. Soon." He placed his finger on the longer column. "New." Then he pointed to the short list. "Old."

So, at the moment, Aldar was third in line for the Farnskag throne. And "soon" he would be seventh. A chill scampered down my arms.

"How?" I asked, hoping he'd understand I wondered what rule was changing.

His brow furrowed, but then he pointed to the additional names on the new list and said, "*Haamig*."

I rubbed my hands together, trying to remember the word. I'd heard it before. But every time my mind tried to grasp the meaning, it flitted away. The registrar pointed to some other text, but I only caught a few words. "He explained . . . fair . . . they are his brothers and sisters . . . they lived . . . learned. They are good people and . . . family."

Haamig and brothers and sisters. But Raffar had no siblings. I repeated the word over and over in my mind. I'd look it up as soon as I was home.

"Thank you," I said to the registrar as I left the depository.

As I walked to the royal manor, the parchments safely hidden under my tunic, my head felt light and high. I'd run an errand all by myself. I'd understood most of what the registrar had said. And I hadn't been in danger. When I saw Raffar in Gluwfyall, I'd ask him to drop the bodyguard duty. I could handle myself alone.

When I arrived at the suite, a note from Aldar was propped against the door. He would escort me to dinner in the dining hall within the hour. Some of the most powerful traders were meeting in Baaldarstad to discuss economic strategy with the southern continent. They were looking forward to meeting me, so I wouldn't have time to check the documents after all. But I slipped my lexicon from the drawer where I kept it hidden, and looked up *haamig*.

Adoption.

I slapped the lexicon closed. Now it made sense. I'd recognized the name Indgar because she was the adopted sister Aldar had mentioned.

All monarchies on the northern continent had birthright-based succession. Mother had changed Azzaria's two years ago, after Llandro had married his husband. Llandro had threatened to abdicate if the law wasn't changed, and Mother had conceded. Now Llandro's future children could inherit the throne someday. Apparently, Raffar had decided to follow my mother's example.

I pushed myself up from the table, hid the lexicon before Aldar could arrive, and paced my room. Mother had worked for years to convince our family members that it was the best for the country. And everyone had agreed: once Llandro grew older and more experienced, he would make an excellent ruler. At the time, Scilla was supposed to live in Farnskag. After Llandro, I would have been next, but with my poor language skills, no one had fought to bump me to the front of the line. And Zito had been so little.

So how did the Farnskagers see it? Did the people, especially the royalty, accept Raffar's change in plans?

Did Aldar?

CHAPTER 22

Dinner with the trade members had been a long and stiff affair, during which I'd fought to stay awake far past my normal bedtime. When I'd returned, a letter from Llandro was on my table, and I dredged the last bits of energy from my body to read it. Everyone was healthy but missed me. There was no update on finding Scilla's assassin. Loftaria hadn't attacked Azzaria since before my wedding, and the citizens were overjoyed at the newfound peace. But . . .

Scilla cut Father's hand so deeply that he almost lost three fingers. I'm talking to her more often now, in the hopes she'll shift her attention to me.

Those lines haunted me as much as Scilla herself did. There'd surely been other incidents no one had informed me of. Scilla was growing worse, so much worse. And I had no idea where else to look to identify her killer.

The next morning, when Aldar came to study, I watched him prepare the slate and the slate pencil for the day's torture.

He wrote a word I had never seen before and held it up to me. My sleep-deprived eyes drifted shut, and I pictured myself opening the window and tossing the slate as far as it would go. It would sail through the sky, be buoyed by an updraft, and then drop into an elephant bird's pen, where a heavy, three-toed foot would smash it to dust.

"Queen Jiara?"

I opened my eyes and smiled sheepishly, as if I were embarrassed to have been caught not paying attention. I was more embarrassed to realize I didn't actually care.

I *did* want to know what Raffar thought about the changes in succession, and if he was worried about his cousin's reaction. Raffar wasn't here to ask, but I could see what Aldar thought. And since my tired mind couldn't think of a delicate way to bring it up . . .

"I heard that Raffar is changing the succession to the throne."

"Wha—?" Aldar's jaw dropped. He set down the slate and ran a hand over his mouth. "Yes, that's true. Where did you—"

I didn't want him to know I'd been to the registrar. Or that I'd read. Or owned a lexicon. "I can't remember . . . maybe someone mentioned it. Or did I misunderstand again?" Playing ignorant was useful, but it was becoming tiresome.

"No. It's true. *Haamig*—adoption—is an important part of our culture here in Farnskag. Much more important than in Azzaria. It is done when parents die, but also when one family can provide special opportunities for learning or a safer place to live. Or sometimes to bind families more closely to one another. For example, if one family adopts the child of another, both families are considered related. My own father did not adopt, but Raffar's did."

His own father . . . Aldar's full name was Aldar Anzgarsuun:

Anzgar! The current line of succession was Raffar, Anzgar, Aldar. I leaned back in my chair as my mind raced to keep up the conversation, and to determine what I could safely say. "How do the people feel about changing the law?"

"Depends on the people."

"And you?" I asked, keeping my tone light and conversational. "You have a unique perspective since you're better informed about how other countries handle it."

Aldar held my gaze for a moment. Had I gone too far?

Finally, he answered, "Raffar thinks it is best for our country, and I agree with him. You might not know this, but I'm somewhere in the line for the throne too."

I raised my eyebrows in mock surprise.

"But I'll tell you a secret. I don't want to be king." He flashed a boyish grin. "The plans Raffar and I once had, they were fun because we'd do them together. I don't want sole responsibility. I've even considered abdication if it ever . . . especially now that my father is so sick. I want to have time to spend with him."

His words and voice sounded sincere, but his father was ill. Deathly ill. Which made Aldar more like second in line.

"Can you imagine if I had to run off to another city now like Raffar? To deal with some incompetent governor who doesn't keep his region in shape?" He shook his head. "No, I'm happy in Baaldarstad, assisting Raffar." He rolled the slate pencil between his fingers. "Being here for my father."

Aldar's speech made sense. Every word. If my parents were dying, I'd want to spend time with them too.

So why did I have such an uneasy feeling in my stomach? Probably because he had promised me more than once to improve his teaching only to continue changing word meanings at every chance. And of course, Jonas's story. Perhaps the worst part was the fact that he believed me when I acted so clueless and confused. He had so little faith in my intelligence; he was so certain I wouldn't catch on.

I gestured to the slate with my chin, and Aldar sat up straight again. He pronounced the word for me. I repeated it three times, forgetting it the moment it left my lips the third time. What was Aldar *really* thinking?

———————

It was Freyad's turn to watch over me the next afternoon. "Forest," she said and crooked her finger for me to follow. After a week of official visits and fruitless searches for the right tattoo, I didn't even care that she wasn't giving me a choice. A day away would be good. Fresh air, a soul bath in green.

I shook my head at myself—I was beginning to sound like the Farnskagers, wanting to be one with the world.

Forests surrounded Baaldarstad. We were never farther than a half-hour walking distance from one, so I wrinkled my brow when we beelined for the bird pen. Linnd fanned herself with a large leaf as she stood beside two thick-legged elephant birds. I told myself she was only bidding Freyad a quick goodbye. Until she held out the reins.

"No!" I hopped back a step. I was not climbing onto one of those animals.

Shaking her head, Freyad pointed to herself. She spoke extra slowly so I could understand, and she took control of her mount. "I drive. Linnd will join us. You are with me on Cloverlily."

Linnd swung herself into her saddle, and her lively bird tossed its head and danced back and forth, eager for the outing. Freyad mounted Cloverlily and pointed to the stirrup where I was to brace my foot and swing up behind her.

A downy feather floated to the ground. Cloverlily shifted her weight from one massive foot to the other, and the feather disappeared below it.

I imagined my toes disappearing under that foot, too, or even my entire foot, and shook my head.

"Are you a queen?" Linnd asked, her laughing eyes boring into me, "Or a baby?"

I glared at her. She worked with the birds. She must have heard one had almost killed me. It was natural that I wanted nothing to do with them. I should get credit for even standing this close.

Freyad made a *tsk* sound at Linnd. "She is no baby."

My face burned with shame. My entitlement to fear didn't matter. Everyone in Farnskag rode these animals, even children. Unthinkable that the queen did not.

Freyad had faith in me. I glared at her wife, then gritted my teeth. "Listen to me," I muttered to Cloverlily in Azzarian as I heaved myself up into the saddle. "Did you hear about Fleetfoot's mother? Well, I still have my knife. Be good."

The ground under me wobbled, along with the contents of my stomach. Freyad and I were high up, and the bird was not steady on its feet.

With a command I didn't understand, the two women

set the birds in motion. We left town and rode for almost an hour, out of the city limits, then past fields and a few scattered houses. Cloverlily was a surprisingly smooth runner when she got going. During the last quarter of the ride, my heart finally calmed, and I drank in the sunlight warming my neck and the herb-scented air.

The bushes turned into trees and trees turned into . . . there needed to be a separate word for trees like those that rose in front of us. Lining the narrow path, the forest giants reached hundreds of feet high, standing so tall, they seemed unreal.

"Freyad," I said, pointing to the trees. "Very big trees. Do they have a special name?"

She nodded. "*Gigantruv.*" Then she pointed to what I would have considered a tall tree back in Azzaria and said that one's name, then to a medium-sized one, and to a bush. I promptly forgot all the names but that of the mammoth tree. *Gigantruv.*

The elephant birds ducked their heads under branches when we came to a part of the forest so thick the sunlight barely made it through the leafy trees. A few moments later, the women and I dismounted and wandered over the dry, cushiony leaves and needles that covered the ground, giving bounce to each step.

I'd always considered the trees in Baaldarstad tall, but these were at least twice as high as any I'd seen there. I felt diminished, but the air was damp in my lungs, and that reminded me of home.

Plus, I'd ridden an elephant bird today.

As if she'd read my thoughts, Linnd said to me, "Freyad is right. You are not a baby, Queen Jiara. You did well."

Not that I had controlled the animal myself, but at least I hadn't run sobbing from it. Carefully, I raised a hand to Cloverlily's neck and stroked the fluffy feathers.

We traipsed along a narrow path until it ended before an immense monolith. Twice as tall as one of the row houses in Baaldarstad, it appeared as if five layers of stone had been thrust diagonally from within the earth, and had gotten stuck. The monolith was covered in two kinds of moss—spongy deep green and inch-long, feathery emerald—and whitish lichen. Saplings grew around it and even out of cracks along the surface. Thick roots trailed down the rock like the arms of an octopus.

Linnd and Freyad tied the birds to one of the smaller trees nearby. Holding hands, they stood observing the immense stone, then they reverently stepped up to it. Leaning forward, each with both of her hands on the rock, they pressed their foreheads against it.

In an instant, I was back in the carriage watching everyone greet White Mother, when Aldar told me I should stay away so they wouldn't think I was making fun of them. I took several steps backward, leaving the two women in solitude as they worshipped, or whatever it was they did. I ran my hand over a fern, like I'd seen Freyad do a dozen times. It tickled my palm.

"Queen Jiara!" Freyad called.

My head snapped up. She motioned me in her direction. "Come here. Be one."

What should I say? I didn't want to insult her.

She smiled. "Watcher of Stone doesn't hurt."

"I don't think it hurts. I—"

She huffed and motioned to me again, less patiently, so I stomped through the ferns and spiky raspberry bushes to reach her.

Linnd's eyes were closed, and her head still rested against the stone. Freyad pointed to Linnd and then to me and the monolith.

Me? But—

What if Aldar was wrong? What if my people would prefer to see me get to know their Watchers?

I nodded. "Tell me if I do it wrong," I said.

"There is no wrong," Freyad answered with a puzzled shake of her head.

This close, the monolith was no longer a simple rock. It was made of some type of granite, with sparkling alabaster veins among the gray. I picked a spot without moss or ants crawling around and leaned my palms and forehead against it. Then I closed my eyes like Linnd.

The rock was hard. I swallowed a laugh at the silliness of my thought. But it truly had appeared smoother than it was, and I shifted a bit to the side in the hope that the neighboring crags wouldn't poke my skin so much. I breathed in and out like a meditation, inhaling the damp earthiness of the forest, feeling the roughness of the stone.

No one had ever told me what kind of thoughts or prayers one was supposed to have when touching the monolith, so I let my mind wander through all my worries.

Please gods, Watchers . . . help me find Scilla's killer, and protect my family.

Inhale. Exhale. Rolling my forehead back and forth over the rock, I accepted the monolith's massage.

I'm so slow with Farnskag—if you can help me learn the language faster, I'd appreciate it.

Let things be all right with Raffar . . . and especially prevent Aldar from being a threat to him in any way.

Help me be a good queen to the people here, and not just some foreign girl who's afraid of elephant birds and doesn't like the sweet potato mush they serve at half the meals.

A crack and scraping crunch sounded above. I ripped open my eyes and stepped back, but not fast enough to avoid being pelted by a small stone, about as big as my thumb, but with rough edges, as if it had just broken off the monolith.

The two women had jumped back when they'd heard the sound, and Freyad spoke quickly, excitedly to Linnd, who beamed. Freyad pointed to the rock, which lay at my feet.

"Pick it up," she said.

Shrugging, I did as she said, rolling it with my fingertips. She skipped to Cloverlily to fetch something from a saddlebag. When she returned, a leather string dangled from her hand. She indicated I should hold it in my palm, and she wound the leather around it artfully, until the string held it tight. It wasn't particularly attractive, but maybe she wanted it as a type of necklace.

Freyad tied it together and offered it back to me. "Watcher of Stone. I think it chose you."

I stared, unable to believe what she was telling me. "But I . . ." I pointed to the bracelets I could never take off.

She nodded. "Watcher of Sky. And now, Watcher of Stone. It is good."

"But—"

She drew a similar pendant from below the neckline of her tunic. Freyad motioned hectically for me to put it on. I wanted to be a good queen to my people. This would be a sign they would like, a reason to make them trust me, something to possibly even keep me safe. So, I accepted Watcher of Stone and pulled the leather band over my head.

Freyad and Linnd bounced on the balls of their feet. "Good. Take it off again," Freyad said. She cast a sparkle-eyed glance to Linnd.

Now to see if Watcher of Stone accepted me. I removed the band from my neck and set it on a nearby stump. I didn't bother groping toward my neck with a hand. I merely looked to Freyad.

The tattoo on her cheek crinkled as a huge smile took over her face. She spoke too quickly, and I missed almost everything. I only caught, "Queen Jiara . . . good . . . two Watchers."

But why would one Watcher choose me let alone two? I wasn't even from Farnskag. "Why would a Watcher choose me?" I asked.

Linnd and Freyad met each other's gazes, then discussed something too fast for me to catch. Finally, Linnd turned to me, her hand at her chest, and spoke slowly, "We think the Watchers know what is in our hearts. They cannot be tricked by . . . false words, nor by rituals or prayers. They know who wants to serve."

"Serve?" I asked.

Freyad jumped in. "To be there for others. To not be selfish, only working for themselves or their own family." She gestured to the forest around us. ". . . to serve . . . for nature. For animals." She gestured to the three of us. "For people."

I slipped my fingers around the stone, so close to my skin it was already warming, already becoming a part of me like Watcher of Sky. It felt like the rock wanted closer contact than hanging over my shirt, so I dropped the pendant into my collar, beneath my tunic. My throat closed up at how hard I'd been trying since I had arrived and never feeling like it was enough. I still hadn't found Scilla's killer. I was so slow with the language and the customs. But the Watchers found me worthy in some way, and my heart warmed at the idea.

Freyad and Linnd patted my arms, then my back. They talked over one another, and tugged me along until I let their enthusiasm inflate my heart. I pretended this world of tattooed faces and gargantuan trees and giant birds wasn't at all foreign to me, and I skipped and danced with them under the canopy of the leaves and needles so far above.

When we returned to the royal manor, Freyad promised she wouldn't tell Raffar about my new Watcher—I'd have the pleasure of showing him myself. Then she left me at the front door and walked down the road, hand in hand with her wife. Linnd laid her head on Freyad's shoulder, at least until her unruly bird jerked her away. Their laughter trailed after me as I slid open the front door.

Only to see Aldar.

I froze, unwilling to give up my rare moment of lightheartedness for the suspicion he injected into me. Maybe I could sneak up the stairs without him noticing.

But Aldar stepped to the side, and I glimpsed the man he was talking to: Geord, who was uncharacteristically quiet. I hung back, remaining just outside the slightly open door as Aldar spoke. ". . . agree with you . . . come to the Grand Council tomorrow . . . sunset . . . agree . . . no change. The king will not . . . the throne."

What was he saying? No change? No change to the throne? Geord made motions to leave, and I slipped out the door and ran around to the back entrance of the manor.

How was I supposed to understand Aldar's words? Aldar agreed with Geord. Aldar would go to the Grand Council meeting tomorrow. No change—did that mean he didn't want the succession changed after all? That was the exact opposite of what he'd told me.

Raffar trusted Aldar. I needed to find out the truth. And if Aldar was not only betraying me, but also my husband, I needed to warn him.

CHAPTER 23

As soon as the servants had cleared away the remains of dinner, I dragged out the parchments and my lexicon and got to work. I couldn't do anything with the Stärklandish portion of the document, and my heart was still thrumming from the worry Aldar created, so I began with the simpler of the two: reading the Azzarian statement. I squeezed my eyes shut then opened them wide and forced one word after the other to make sense in my mind. When words dove around on the parchment, I gritted my teeth and reeled them back. Within a few sentences, it became clear that this was Jonas's statement of what had happened the day of the massacre.

Jonas and eight Stärklandish diplomats and guards had made the trip to Baaldarstad to continue the discussions they'd begun with Scilla concerning a peace treaty between the two countries. There was apparently a lake between both nations with three islands in it: the Stekk Ilens islands, which were contested by both parties. Although they were closer to the Stärklandish side, they were inhabited almost solely by Farnskagers. The islands hosted several monoliths sacred to both countries.

A second point of contention existed in the far south: a corner near the border to Loftaria, blessed with iron ore. It was craggy and barren and almost unsettled, but still, anyone would want to extract the iron.

Scilla had worked out a suggestion where the southern corner of land would fall to Stärkland and the islands to Farnskag. Stärkland would agree to offer preferential trade rates on the iron. Farnskag would allow Stärklandish pilgrims to pay their respects at the monoliths on the islands any time they wished. Another option would be to reverse this deal, but considering the large number of Farnskagers living on the islands, it seemed a good place to start.

I leaned back in my chair and rubbed my eyes. When had Scilla discussed all this with the Stärklandish representatives? How had she found the contacts? And when had she come up with the strategy? She must have researched, talked to Jonas and someone from Farnskag. Probably even several times. Amazing.

As my admiration for her grew, my heart shrank in my chest. Scilla had done all of that before she'd even become queen. And what had I accomplished? I growled at myself and yanked the parchment closer.

If nothing else, I would read these infernal words. Jonas went on to say that Aldar and some men surrounded them about a day's ride outside of Baaldarstad. He and Aldar had spoken, but suddenly, the Farnskagers had launched their arrows. Jonas himself would have died, but after being knocked over by an elephant bird and twisting his ankle, two of Aldar's guards grabbed his arms and tossed him over an elephant bird, which delivered him to the prison in Baaldarstad.

I dropped Jonas's statement and rested my eyes for a moment. By the time I pulled Aldar's document in Farnskag closer, my stomach began to ache, because there couldn't be a good outcome to what I'd find. Reading went so slowly, my throat closed up and I wanted to cry, but I dug in my heels. Despite the length of the document, I managed to piece the truth together. This portion of the document didn't represent Aldar's personal view of what had transpired, but the official translation of Jonas's statement.

And it was a lie. Aldar's "translation" had nothing to do with Jonas's words. Scilla was never mentioned once.

Aldar wrote that Stärklandish soldiers had stumbled upon Aldar and his guards. The leader, Jonas, had hurled insults at them, saying they were the first scouts, planning an invasion that would take place within the next months so Stärkland could seize control of the entire country. Jonas had allegedly grinned and whooped as he had tried to kill the Farnskag "animals." The document ended with the threat that it wouldn't be long now before Stärkland attacked.

I pushed the parchments to the middle of the table, raced to the bedroom and flopped onto my stomach on the bed. My head pounded. My shoulders ached. My eyes were both itchy and wet at the same time. I pressed my face into Raffar's pillow, hoping to inhale his leather and forest scent. But I'd snuggled with it too many nights since he'd departed. His scent was gone.

Either Aldar had willfully mistranslated Jonas's statement to mislead the Farnskag state, or he had willfully mistranslated it because everything Jonas wrote was a lie. But why would Jonas mention Scilla if it wasn't the truth? If it was only to get my sympathy . . . but no. He'd had no idea that I was coming. I hadn't even been engaged to Raffar when Jonas was thrown in prison. Could it have been to plant an idea in Raffar's head—the trade of islands for the iron-rich country?

And what about Raffar? He would have read the translation—only the translation. Did he expect war with Stärkland? Was that another reason he'd married me? In Azzaria, we'd thought his strongest reason was access to the sea. But what if the major goal had been military support against Stärkland?

After tracing the loops of logic in my head for a half hour, I propped myself up on both palms and thrust my tired body from the bed. I needed to hide the documents in case Aldar showed up.

———————

The next evening after dinner, I plastered a smile onto my face as I spoke my broken Farnskag with one of the servants. I pretended everything was fine and I just wanted to take a little walk in the garden.

But everything wasn't fine, not at all.

First, I'd received a letter from Pia, usually a cause for joy. She was doing fine, with the pregnancy progressing normally. She only had a month or so left to go. But her final sentences pulled tears from my eyes:

The news about your mother and Llandro reached Flissina, and I'm so sorry to hear it. The official story is that it was a terrible carriage accident. That's how the bruises and cuts have been explained. Normally, I wouldn't write something like this—I know anyone could potentially open it—but everyone in Azzaria is talking about it anyway. It was Scilla, wasn't it?

My hands shook and I lost control, flinging myself onto my bed and pounding my pillows, shouting into them. No one had told me that, not Mother or Father, not Llandro. They probably though they were protecting me from the awful truth. I cried until I fell asleep. When Aldar finally came for lessons, he must have seen something wrong in my expression. He kept class short and didn't push me like normal. Or maybe his mind was just on the Grand Council meeting later.

But Aldar's retreat didn't mean I got off lightly. As soon as he'd left the royal suite, I pulled out the book on Watchers I'd found and resigned myself to the torture of reading Farnskag. It was common knowledge that Farnskag had no earthwalkers. Could the reason be more than just our Azzarian love for justice? And could I use it to help Scilla move on?

But nothing I found was helpful. According to the book, when a person died in Farnskag, the Watchers were waiting for them in the afterlife, ready to enfold them into the one great power that is connected to and watches over the world. There didn't appear to be ties to family or friends to be severed. And Scilla had already died; without rituals, there was no way I could get the Watchers to come collect her.

I hadn't finished hiding the book in my closet when Scilla made her presence known. My back and arms ached with the map of bruises she'd created—she'd pelted books and candles and even potted ferns at me. A guard, attracted by the din, had been hit in the left cheek with a heavy vase as I'd attempted to flee the room. His horrified expression as he rubbed his injury and took in the shards on the floor had forced me to choke out an apology. What must he think of his queen now?

That evening, I pretended to wander aimlessly as I headed to the rear of the garden, giving a wave to a servant before drifting behind a copse of trees. Immediately, I slipped through the breezy park along the far edge of the property and out the front. Tonight was the Grand Council meeting Aldar had mentioned. Earlier, I'd considered informing him I planned to attend. But I'd had the sneaking suspicion the meeting would be unexpectedly postponed, so I decided to surprise him. If I just showed up, he couldn't send me away.

Aldar hadn't disclosed the location, but he had said something about the time: sunset. The only place I could imagine the council sitting together was in the meeting house. As the sun sank in the sky, turning wispy clouds into glowing orange plumes, I stood behind one of the large trees on the square and spied on the meeting hall's entrance. Within minutes, Aldar strode across the square and into the building.

A grin blossomed on my face.

I waited until several other people entered the building. When the sun dipped below the tree line, I made for the entrance. After sucking in a deep breath, I opened the door and walked in with my head held high.

The Grand Council was made up of exactly ten members. Some were lesser royalty. Some were heads of clans from other parts of the country. But there were only five at the meeting hall this evening—three men and two women. They stood in a ring around a large, polished wooden table that reflected the geometric patterns stained into the ceiling. Along with Aldar, they stared at me, their mouths slightly open. For a split second, the violent expression on Aldar's face reminded me of the men in the courtyard when they'd yelled at Raffar.

I ignored the flutter of my heart and smiled then spoke to Aldar in Azzarian. "What luck, Aldar! I thought I saw you and some of the council members. I've met traders and soldiers and townspeople. But I really need to get to know the Grand Council better. What better opportunity than one of the meetings." I left out the biggest question—why Aldar was even there. He was not a member of the council.

His fingers pressed to the tabletop, Aldar leaned back, and his mind was probably galloping after ways to reject my request, so I had to make myself seem benign. "My people should understand I'm interested in them. I realize I won't understand much more than *hello* and *goodbye*. But I want to keep up appearances. Especially with Raffar out of town."

"Your Majesty, we have so much to discuss—"

"I'm already here." I shrugged, acting oblivious to his uncertainty. "I know translating would slow things down, so don't bother today. Being here would mean a lot to me." I smiled innocently at the oldest woman then returned my attention to Aldar. "I think it would mean something to the people too."

Aldar opened his mouth, but I interrupted before he could speak, appealing to the teacher in him. "And maybe I'll learn a word. Or two. Maybe?"

His jaw tightened, but he said, "Of course, Your Majesty,"

and made a big show of introducing me. His Farnskag was slow when he said my name, and he carefully gushed about how glad he was to have me here. Then, rushing, he said, "I've been teaching her for months now. She's slow. She can barely understand a word. We can speak freely."

It was all I could do to keep the mild expression on my face and my hands from clutching at my twisting insides. There was no longer a need to wonder about his capability for betrayal, and a cold pit yawned within me. But I had to find out what was going on. Ignoring Aldar's last words, I forced a bright smile and greeted them especially slowly as if I'd understood only the introduction, "*Guuddug.*"

The words *guuddug* and *Skriin Jiara* were mumbled back to me. I also heard, "Are you sure about this?" directed at Aldar. I met each person's gaze, smiling innocently at them, as Aldar nodded. Gingerly, attempting to avoid the worst bruises on my backside, I took my seat, and wood scraped against wood as the others settled into their chairs after me.

Then there was silence. They were afraid to begin. My neck heated up. What if they refused to talk and rescheduled the meeting in secret? I might not get another opportunity to figure out if any of them could be danger to Raffar.

I turned to Aldar and asked in Azzarian, "Do you mind if I say a few words first? I've been practicing."

Aldar's jaw dropped a little, but he said, "Of course, Your Majesty." He translated for the group.

These council members would think me a fool for now, but my language skills were improving, and I'd be able to demonstrate that someday. I ignored my clammy palms and pushed on. They had to assume I was completely harmless. "Hello. Thank you. Come sunshine, yes. Lovely. Yes. Lovely. Thank you."

My face heated as I smiled at them. I prevented myself from swallowing nervously. Geord rubbed his mouth, hiding a smile, or maybe a frown. Eyes widened as the others did their best not to laugh at their queen. After a moment, they nodded in silence.

Geord was the first to speak, "When will King Raffar make his decision . . . succession?"

Aldar scanned the faces. "When he returns from Gluwfyall, I believe."

A woman swept her hand back and forth over the tabletop. "You've been talking to him for us. Will he . . . our opinion?"

Aldar leaned forward, smiling indulgently. It was as if every one of his movements existed to convince people to trust him. "When I last spoke to him, he said the council's opinion is very important. I believe so."

"And will he listen to you?" someone asked.

Aldar sat straighter. "Of course, he will. The king couldn't function without my advice."

I gasped and, covering my mouth with my hand, turned it into an exaggerated yawn. "Sorry," I muttered in Azzarian. *Raffar couldn't function?*

Aldar continued as if I hadn't spoken, "But I cannot be seen as . . . here. It would look like I'm only trying to get my father on the throne."

His father, who was dying, leaving him as the next monarch.

"What are you trying to say?" asked another member.

"What I'm saying is . . ."

I clenched my fist under the table as I missed the end of the sentence, which he uttered very quickly.

Then he said, "I have to be impartial. The king must hear the voice of the Grand Council."

Right. So, by telling Raffar he supported whatever Raffar thought was right was "being impartial?" Blood pounded in my veins. Inhale. Exhale. *Pretend you're somewhere else.* At the sea, watching the dolphins. Or in the forest, next to the big monolith.

A woman cleared her throat. "I don't think you have to worry about King Raffar believing you're trying to take his throne. He's young, one of the few chosen by a Watcher—"

One of the few? After Raffar and Freyad, I'd thought it was fairly common. The rock at my neck and the bracelets on my wrists increased in weight now that I knew they were special. I refrained from touching them. The council members shouldn't know I'd understood what they said.

"—so he'll surely live a long life."

Hmm. They didn't realize his one shot at protection had been used. As Raffar had told me, Aldar apparently had never said a word about it. But Aldar knew.

The woman continued, "And not only that, he's married. We'll . . . hear the queen is pregnant any day now."

My head shot up. Pregnant? My throat itched like it was full of briars, and my stomach sank because I wasn't supposed to appear interested in their conversation. Although, I was allowed to understand the word *Skriin*. I smiled blankly and sipped tiny breaths to calm myself.

Pregnant.

My eyes burned. Discussing our very personal, very private life, right in front of me. My fingernails cut into my skin. But things like that were normal for royalty. *Stop acting like a baby.*

The woman's eyes rested on me, then moved back to Aldar. She waved a hand. "There will be other . . . between you and the crown than your father."

Geord broke in. "This discussion has nothing to do with you or your father or Raffar's . . . children. It has to do with our traditions. Adoption is an important . . . our society, that's true. But it doesn't mean we should discard the way we have handled the throne for centuries. Farnskag has much to be proud of. Our kings and queens—the rulers chosen through our . . . traditions—have brought us this far. There is no need to throw that away."

Now I understood what Raffar meant about Geord's passion. His voice was deep and earnest. He loved his country and wanted the best for it. I only wished he agreed with Raffar on what was the best.

The council members nodded and grunted sounds of assent in Geord's direction.

He turned to Aldar. "I will send messages to the rest of the Grand Council. When the king returns, we'll face him together. He must listen to . . ."

Geord's action points signaled the end of the meeting. He and all council members but one left the room. I waited patiently as Aldar spoke with one of the men I remembered from the square on my first day. One who'd glared at me along with Geord.

The man shook his head, gritted his teeth. "Raffar is too

young. These past four years, what has he done? Married a long-haired foreigner. Tried to . . . our traditions. Your father would make a better king than Raffar. Even you, as young as you are, would make a better king. You listen to your people."

Raffar listened to his people, didn't he? Even Geord had said he'd hear out the council. But sometimes, a decision had to be made that wasn't the way things had always been done. Sometimes the best solution wasn't popular. I hated being silent, but I bit my tongue to prevent myself from shouting in my husband's defense. Until I could speak to Raffar, I had to keep Aldar in the dark.

Aldar clasped the man's upper arm. "Thank you. And you are one of the best . . . a monarch could have. I do not understand how Raffar doesn't appreciate you more. In his shoes"—he held the man's gaze, and a tiny smile crept onto his face—"I would appreciate you."

The way Aldar played the man made me want to gag.

The council member nodded. "Of course. I think . . . we have no choice but to go ahead with our plan."

Plan?

Aldar shushed the council member. Before he could turn to me, I closed my eyes as if I were dozing. My ears strained for a hint of this mysterious plan, but I didn't hear another word.

A few seconds later, Aldar's gentle hand on my tender shoulder "woke" me. "Queen Jiara."

Flinching, I faked a yawn. "Oh, I'm so sorry. How embarrassing." I stretched my arms before me.

"It has grown quite late," Aldar said, "and you worked so hard studying today."

I'd always been a peaceful person, but maybe Scilla was rubbing off on me. My hand longed to smack the false praise out of his head. "I'm sorry I dozed off. Really, it was very interesting," I said. "Raffar is right. I don't know what Geord said, but the look on his face—Geord has fire in him, doesn't he?"

The translator nodded. "Of course, Your Majesty. And now it's time to get you back to the royal manor for some rest."

CHAPTER 24

Most of the night, the council member's "plan" alternated with my fears for Scilla and my family. When I finally fell asleep, I dreamed Mother pounded on the manor door, begging to be let in. Her dress was bloodied, her hair full of burrs.

"It's Scilla. She's been killing us one by one." She grabbed hold of my tunic, her eyes wild with terror. "You and I are the only ones left."

When I woke up, my stomach turned. At the awful nightmare of course, but also because the event Pia'd sent in her last letter had finally come true. I'd dreamed in Farnskag. Of all people, in my dream, Mother had been speaking Farnskag to me. A part of my heart swelled with pride, while the other part reeled from the wrongness of it all.

By now, I'd visited all of the villages and towns within a two-day distance and found no one with the murderer's tattoo. If I were to find the killer, I'd need another lead. Before Aldar could show up, I sat down and wrote the slowest letter ever to my mother, asking how the family was and if they had any more information on Scilla's death. If they could give me new details, I could forward it to Raffar's agents and check it out myself. The serving woman's story about her aunt and the blood-smeared house wound through my mind every day. It had been so long now since Scilla had become an earthwalker. And she'd grown strong and violent. What if my loved ones were already severely injured—or worse—and I just hadn't heard about it yet?

When the letter was ready, I turned back to the other problem. If my time alone in Baaldarstad wasn't almost up, I could have sent Raffar a letter about Aldar, one hopefully not full of gibberish he couldn't decipher anyway. But my skill at letter writing didn't matter. I'd be traveling to meet Raffar tomorrow, and I'd make it to him as fast as any letter. Considering there was no concrete danger or proof of wrongdoing, the time it took for the journey would even be useful to work on formulating my suspicions.

Aldar arrived shortly afterward, and when language class was over, my head buzzed, like every day after hours of staring at the dancing letters on the slate. I needed some fresh air to clear it. I opened a window. A wagon laden with vegetables and bright summer squash towed by four elephant birds rolled by, on the way to the market. But looking outside wasn't enough. With every day Raffar had been gone, Aldar grew more lax in acting as my nursemaid. Now that several weeks had passed, he still "taught" me, but he no longer feared to leave me alone. So, I hurried down the hall and slipped out of the manor.

The warm air and caress of the fragrant summer breeze calmed me. Walking east, I passed the elephant bird pens. I'd never been to the section of forest on Baaldarstad's east side, and a servant had mentioned a pond there. A pond was a poor trade for Azzaria's ocean, but outside of the streams, it was the only solace Azzoro could offer in this part of the country.

The trees stretched to the sky before me. A narrow path trod through lacy ferns invited me deep into the forest. Insects buzzed and chirped in the underbrush, and squirrels leaped from branch to branch. Birds twittered overhead, and the sun filtered through the leaves and needles and fern tree fronds, dappling happily on the ground. Everything smelled so green and damp and alive. I sucked in a cleansing breath.

Reflected sunlight shimmered before me as the trees thinned out. The pond. I raced down the path. An insect stung my cheek as the last trees fell away, and the pond opened itself before me. It was tiny. Had it been dirt instead of water, I could probably walk across it within one minute, maybe two. But the sky's reflections were only disturbed by a few water striders inching across the surface. Small as it was, the sight began to refill my chest with peace.

Another sting, this time on my hand. Absently, I smacked at it, and my palm came away bloody, so I took the time to look at my injury. A jagged red cross. Like the other times with Scilla.

Blood on the floor, the walls, the ceiling. I stepped back, as if that would help me. "Scilla, you know I'm trying. We all are. In Azzaria and here."

In answer, a slash of fire blazed along my cheek.

"Scilla!" I raised my hand to it. This gash was deeper. My stomach rolled in on itself until it was one big knot. Scilla might have scratched me and given me bruises, but she'd never cut me this badly before. How long had it been now since she'd died? Almost eight months? Too long.

Earthwalkers didn't listen to logic, but I had to try. "You probably don't believe that we're trying to find your killer, but we are. Father still has agents working on the case. I've been—"

A hard shove at my back sent me stumbling knee-deep into the water. I whirled around. But of course, no one else was there.

"Scilla! Stop it!" I yelled. I trudged out of the pond, my shoes and pants sopping.

My eyes traveled the shoreline and the trees beyond it, but an earthwalker wasn't something you could see, wasn't something you could defend yourself against, as I knew only too well from the bruises still marring my skin. For a split second, I remembered us playing together on the beach. How could it have come this far? My big sister, now someone to be afraid of.

"I was telling you, I've been to the tattoo artist, I checked out a local boy—"

Scilla cut off my words with a slash to my other cheek, followed by one to my neck. This one was different—it burned like flames. I could barely think. Hot liquid spilled down my chest, and I forced myself to look down, to assess the damage.

My tunic was transforming into a blanket of red. Through the fiery pain, I managed a coherent thought: Scilla must have hit a main blood vessel. I tried to scream but only a wet cough erupted from my mouth. I couldn't speak. No one was there to help. Weakness stole over my body—I wouldn't be able to run for help.

The scene before me blurred, and the world tilted until my shoulder hit the muck at the edge of the pond. A thick red river flowed from me to the water's edge, washing over Watcher of Stone, which had fallen out of my neckline.

I braced my hands in the mud. With this much blood loss, I wasn't going to survive. But despite the searing pain, a grim smile stole over my face because I didn't have to. Not if the Watcher would bring me back.

Ice-cold fingers of fear gripped my heart—I was going to die—but this was no time to lose my head. I had to keep my wits about me, to use the time wisely, and to get a message across to Scilla . . . while we were both dead.

A massive weight rammed against my back, sending me down into the muck again. It was cool against my cheek, against my chest, bathed in hot blood. I flattened my hands against the mud again, pushed up, but my body was so heavy. The weight on my back held me down, held me immobile. I couldn't do anything, anything but think.

Maybe Scilla was right. I'd been so focused on Aldar and the potential danger to Raffar that I'd neglected my search for her killer. I heard her in my mind: *You are my sister. You should have done more.*

I said, "I'm sorry, Scilla," but I didn't know if it was out loud or only in my head. I had to concentrate. I had to talk to her.

After one more futile shove, my vision dimmed until there was only gray. For a second, I rested my cheek against the cool, damp mud and pretended it was the ocean, and that Azzoro cradled me in his embrace. The bird tweets disappeared, and the buzz of insects. I floated in the dark, then the threads appeared. To my family and Pia, to Raffar, and new ones to

Freyad and Linnd. They were so strong and grounding and made my heart feel grateful and full.

Scilla swooped in front of me, scowling. That same too-dark thread bound me to her, and it felt different than the others, wrong. A part of us, but also strangling.

I reached for my sister. "What can we do to help you, Scilla?"

She threw her hands over her head and screeched so loud it echoed in my skull: "Why doesn't anyone help me? Why doesn't anyone understand me?" Then her voice dropped to a whisper. "Just you, Jiara . . . so close to death, so close to me . . . but only sometimes. Sometimes even you don't care. You of all people. You're my sister—I expect more of you!" She screamed again.

"Tell me what to do! We want to help you. We're your family, and we love you. You have to remember that."

Scilla's face softened, and for an instant, she looked like her rational self. "You love me. I remember. Mother and Father, and—" She shook her head back and forth, and her voice grated, "Love is not enough! You don't know what it's like. I'm not myself like this." She clutched at her head. "I have no control. I do terrible things. I *want* terrible things. You have to find the one who did this to me!"

She lunged forward, stopped barely a breath from my face. "If you find my killer, I will do the rest."

"Scilla, you know we're—"

"FIND MY KILLER."

"We're try—"

The wildness took over her eyes again. "We're trying, we're

trying, we're trying," she mocked me. Then she floated even closer, her expression pure hatred, her hands raised to the level of my throat, and I knew I'd lost her. It was over. Blackness closed in.

In a blink, a cool, calming presence descended, a cloak like the damp forest and the cool river and the fresh night air all at once, like everyone and everything I'd ever known was gathering around me, giving me shelter. In my heart, I was certain, those were the Watchers, the ones who came to welcome me and take me beyond this world.

It felt so right. There was nowhere else I belonged. But, no! I couldn't allow it. "I'm not done in this world yet! And I have a Watcher. Please, send me ba—"

Maybe they listened. Maybe it didn't matter what I said. My body grew rigid, hardening into something without a pulse. I was a boulder, a statue. Nothing inside me moved, not my muscles, not my heart, not my lungs.

———————

A bird whistled so loudly overhead that it woke me up. The stiff, rocky sensation in my body crumbled away. The grass just before the shore of the pond pressed against my temple, the dirt damp and sticky under my cheek.

My hand flew to my neck. It was whole, healthy.

I pushed myself up to sit on the ground. A small scratch stretched over the back of my hand, but nothing severe. Blood no longer soaked the sandy shore or even my tunic.

I was alive.

My own sister had tried to kill me. No, not *tried*. She *had* killed me. I'd felt the life flow out of me, felt the deathly cold overtake my limbs. But at least I'd talked to her. Somewhere inside of all that rage my sister was still there. And she said she still understood me. At least partly.

I tugged Watcher of Stone from its place below my tunic. Twisting it made sunlight glint off the tiny crystals embedded within. I enclosed it in my palm. I could no longer deny that the Watchers had the power to save a person. Maybe they could help in other ways. I'd keep looking for Scilla's killer. And as soon as I returned to my room, I'd read more of the book on Watchers. Maybe they could help her.

I gripped the stone until its edges pinched my flesh. "Thank you, Watcher of Stone."

It was twice now that death had engulfed my heart. I probed my emotions, searching for . . . what? Instability? Did I have to fear ending up like Scilla? Out of control and vengeful, a kind of living earthwalker? No, no. I shook my head. I wouldn't end up like her, confused, forgetting who my loved ones were, punishing them for crimes they hadn't committed.

With limbs stronger than they should be for one so close to death, I heaved myself up from the ground. The birds continued singing. The tall evergreen trees swayed in the breeze.

A gentle stroke brushed across my cheek, then over my hair.

I bit my lip to keep from crying and hurried down the path to the royal manor, every rustling in the bushes a threat to my safety. What if Scilla attacked again? I wouldn't survive something like that again.

A dry branch snapped up ahead. I froze, seeking out the source, praying I'd see something tangible.

And it was tangible. But it was Aldar. I sidled behind a thick ironfern tree trunk, out of his line of sight. I dared a peek at him; he just stood there.

After everything that had happened with Scilla, I was in no condition to meet up with him, but leaving the path, going straight through the forest would not only be loud, I'd probably also lose my way. I had to wait him out.

Aldar leaned against a tree for a couple of moments. He paced several feet away. Then back, then forth. He craned his neck, peering down the path.

Waiting for someone out here? In the middle of nowhere?

I changed my mind about wanting to go to my room. I needed to see what he was up to. Within minutes, the crunch of leaves and snapping of twigs filled the air, and a man came tramping down the path. But not just any man.

He had no tattoos, and his clothes bore the same Stärklandish diamond-shaped embroidery on the sleeve cuffs as Jonas's. Why would Aldar meet someone from Stärkland? He always talked about how Raffar should avoid contact with that country.

The two men exchanged a few short words, then the Stärklandish man handed over an envelope with a black seal on it. Without a word of goodbye, the foreign man turned and stomped back out of the woods. Aldar waited a few moments, opened the letter and read it, much more slowly than he normally read. He contemplated for a few seconds, scanned the trees and bushes around him, and sauntered down the forest path.

Aldar'd had a clandestine meeting with someone from Stärkland. I needed to find out why. Which meant I needed to get a hold of that letter.

———————

Freyad was on a brief but urgent trip to one of the nearby villages, so while my tutor visited his sick father, Matid kindly obliged my request to open Aldar's office to "look for the vocabulary list I had left there." While the guard waited outside the door, I searched every drawer and cupboard, looked under furniture and in potted plants, and even checked behind the shutters on the window. Nothing.

I was taking too long as it was, so I rushed out of the room and thanked Matid for his assistance. If Aldar wasn't hiding the letter in his office, it must be in his house. The only other option would be that he'd destroyed it, but I prayed that wasn't the case. It was the first possibility of hard evidence I'd come across. If I found it, maybe I could even do something about him before I left town to meet Raffar.

I told Matid I wanted to lie down, so he dutifully dropped me off at my suite. Ten minutes later, I was on my way through Baaldarstad's streets to Aldar's house. He'd shown it to me on one of our walks, and luck was with me on two accounts. First, Aldar lived alone. And second, Farnskagers didn't lock their doors; they didn't even have locks.

The reason for that quickly became apparent. Aldar re-sided in town, in a largish house, considering he lived alone, but there were neighbors all around. And someone was always looking. The little girl next door, the grandmother on the bal-cony across the street, the teenage boy staining wood on the house two doors down. I strode past, my head high, as if I had every right to be there. When I was sure no one was looking, I sneaked onto a grassy strip between two houses across the street. From the cool shadows, I watched.

After a while, the boy finished his work on the house's fa-cade and disappeared down the street. The little girl had long since gone inside, called in by her mother. But the grandmother on the balcony above me diagonally was content to relax in the sun as she worked with some kind of vegetable, peeling and slicing, and occasionally laying her head back to rest.

Did she close her eyes? It looked like it from here. So I waited until the next time she reclined and then shot off across the street. I pushed Aldar's door open, jumped inside and shut it behind me.

For a few seconds, I stood in the dim house to catch my breath and adjust to the relative lack of light. When no one showed up to pound on the door demanding I leave the prem-ises, I went to work. Again, I checked in drawers and cupboards, under tables and chairs, only this time, it was his home. I felt like the worst kind of trespasser as I sifted through his neatly folded clothing and lifted up his mattress. A few codices were stacked on a table, but flipping through them showed me nothing.

I leaned against the wall for a bit, wishing a hint would leap out at me. Then I thought of my mother. She had countless hiding places in her office. False bottoms in drawers, nooks behind furniture just thick enough for a few sheets of parchment or a small box. My third try was a success—the second drawer in the chest next to his bed had a false bottom. When I lifted it, a large envelope with a black seal gleamed in the dim light. Finally.

I pulled it out, dropping the false bottom back into place. Before I had the chance to open the letter, scuffing sounds came from outside the door. I stuffed the letter into my undergarment beneath my tunic and scanned the room. Everything appeared as I'd found it. But there was a major problem. Besides not having locks, Farnskager houses also normally didn't have back doors. No time to think. I shoved the window on the side of the house open, heaved myself over the sill, and tumbled to the ground, rolling out like I had when Scilla and I had played as children.

For a few seconds, I crouched in the shadow of the neighbor's house, silently waiting for the door just outside my range of vision to open and whoever it was—most likely Aldar—to go into the house. When they finally did, I hustled away, my arms crossed over my chest to hold the letter in place.

From behind me, the click of a wooden door opening broke the silence.

I turned just in time to see Aldar poke his head outside, his eyes sweeping the street. When he saw me, he froze. Our eyes met, and a sudden rage blazed in his that made my heart riot in my chest. I whirled back toward the royal manor and strode down the road. Heavy stomps followed me.

The street that had been so endlessly alive with residents was now empty; even the grandmother was gone. I picked up my speed, throwing a glance back. Aldar strode toward me, and something nearly black flashed in his hand. Something nearly black? It could be anything, but my thoughts immediately flew to soldiers' training sessions, and to those impossibly hard ironfern wood clubs that could crush a skull with one blow.

I gave up on all pretense and shot off down the street, my hair flying behind me like a black Farnskager flag.

A group of giggling children herded by three adults rounded the corner, and I bounded over to them. I swallowed the dry terror in my throat and called "*Guuddug!*" as cheerfully as I could muster. Behind the children, three men carrying stacks of wood followed, and I said hello to them also, waving them to come join me.

The townspeople smiled and greeted me, and all of us together prattled on about it being a lovely day. I smiled brightly at their comments for a full minute then dared to look back at Aldar. But all I saw was his rigidly held back as he headed down the street again toward his house.

CHAPTER 25

As soon as I reached the manor, I sent a servant for Matid. With Aldar on the loose and clearly raging over what I'd done, I didn't dare stay alone.

Once in my suite, I unfolded the letter. It was in Stärklandish. The two dots over some of the letters proved it. I pounded my fists on the dining room table. I couldn't read Stärklandish!

If I had a lexicon, I *might* be able to translate it, but my head pounded at the thought of how difficult *that* would be. It was hard enough with Farnskag, and I'd actually learned to recognize many of that language's words.

What I wouldn't give for someone who could translate it for me. But the only one was Aldar.

Except . . . Jonas. Assuming he knew how to read, he could do it. The question was whether I could trust him. I knew nothing of the language, so the prisoner could tell me anything, and I'd never be able to prove him wrong.

But what other choice did I have? If I told Matid that Aldar had chased me with a nearly black something-I-hadn't-even-actually-seen, how could he take me seriously? If I said Aldar was a traitor because of this letter neither of us could read, would he believe me? Would he even understand what I meant? It wasn't like I could mime betraying the king like I used a few hand gestures to show I was ill. No, if I were to accuse Aldar, I'd need evidence and details . . . details like those that were probably contained in this letter.

Either way, I wanted a guard with me. When Matid arrived, I asked him to bring me to the prison. He stared at me for a few moments, his knitted brows distorting the tattoos on his forehead like he wanted to ask why I had so many strange requests today. But in the end, he nodded without question, and a short ride later, we descended the dank steps to the prison cells. The lone torch flickered and hissed, but the brightness was swallowed by the shadows within a foot or two. If we were going to read, we'd need more light, so I pointed to the torch and asked for a second one. One of the guards went to fetch it, and I strode over to the Stärklandish prisoner.

"Queen Jiara," said Jonas, his hopeless expression livening in surprise. "I am—"

"I'm sorry, but there is no time for pleasantries. If I show you a letter in Stärklandish, would you translate it to Azzarian for me?"

He cocked his head at me, almost like a bird, listening carefully for the sound of predators. "I can. But I am surprised. You don't ask translator to do this?"

I shook my head and unfolded the letter. When the second torch arrived and a golden glow drove the shadows back, I held the parchment closer to the cell.

"Wait"—he pointed a grubby finger through the

bars—"the . . ." He kept poking his finger toward the outer side of the letter.

"The seal?" I asked.

"Yes." He nodded repeatedly. "The seal."

I held it closer to him. With my other arm, I pulled Matid's torch lower, and the flames weaved patterns on the raised black seal.

"Hmm." He squinted at me. "This is seal of a family in south of Stärkland. They don't like the queen. They are not to be trusted."

Slowly, I bobbed my head. I turned the letter around so he could see the writing on the inside.

Jonas's eyes flew over the page. His posture straightened. "It says, 'Our first part of bargain is done. Delivery was months ago, bladeleaf, as you request—'"

"Bladeleaf!" I cried. My vision blurred, and I leaned against the bars for support. Of all the things to hear, I hadn't expected that.

Matid carefully, but firmly, pulled me away from the cell, out of Jonas's reach. "Are you all right, *Skriin* Jiara?" he asked.

For a moment, I couldn't speak. *Aldar* had requested the bladeleaf. The memory of him gesturing to each type of food on my Loftarian plate flashed in my mind. He must have sprinkled it on then. Aldar had wanted me dead. And he'd succeeded. I shivered: without Watcher of Sky, I'd be an earthwalker like Scilla.

A couple of deep breaths later, the shock began to wear off; I needed to find out more. "I'm fine," I said in Farnskag to Matid. Before I asked Jonas to continue though, I forced myself to consider if he was telling the truth. But he must have been. If he'd wanted to trick me with the bladeleaf, he would have done it at our last meeting. He'd had no certainty that I'd visit again. And it wasn't like anyone would have told him about my poisoning to begin with.

I took several deep breaths to clear my mind and gestured to Jonas and the letter. "What else?"

"Bladeleaf dangerous. Do you think someone wants to poison the Farnskag king? Or Your Majesty?"

"Keep reading," I ordered without answering him.

With a sigh, he nodded. "Yes. I read. 'When you are king—'" Jonas raised his eyebrows at me. "Who this letter belong to?"

For now, it was better to see which details he could discover without my help. "What does it say?"

He indicated I should flip it over and then back again. "Nothing. Not on outside or inside. No greeting. Also not signed by someone."

"Then please continue."

His eyebrows creased, but he must have realized I wouldn't reveal anything. "'We were unsatisfied to see you did not prevent alliance with Azzaria. But maybe it is for the best. When you are king, Farnskag army help us defeat Stärklandish queen and we take power. We hope treaty with Azzaria still binding. Maybe we need Azzaria army at our . . . disposal.' What? Someone thinks they can defeat our queen? No. That is . . ." The rest of his sentence was lost in a string of what I assumed was Stärklandish curses.

Aldar *did not prevent an alliance* with Azzaria. That meant he tried, didn't it? That meant he either killed Scilla himself or had her killed. Chills ran from my scalp down my arms. *Scilla, I hope you're paying attention*, I thought, then I said, "Jonas, please read more."

He groaned at me, squinting his eyes in an annoyed expression that made me think of my brothers. But he continued: "'As discussed, in return, we grant Farnskag the two . . . contested . . . regions Farnskag now . . . holds. We wait for good news and for date of . . . invasion.'" He looked at me again, eyes wide. Then he read the last line: "'We have gone far too long without communication. We expect your message at Meeting Place Number 2 in one month.'"

Jonas stared hard into my eyes. "Please, who is this letter to?" he begged, both hands gripping the bars in front of him.

He had helped me so much. He deserved to know. "Aldar, the translator," I said.

The prisoner let go and dropped his head in both hands, muttering in Stärklandish. I might not have understood the words, but it was a pretty good bet he was wishing his party had killed Aldar when they'd had the chance. I tended to agree. It would have been too late for Scilla, but it would have saved the rest of us.

I left the prisoner to his ramblings. My heart pounded, because now, I had enough details to bring in the royal guards. Haltingly, I explained what happened today to Matid, but he kept repeating, "Aldar is the king's cousin," and "The king places great trust in Aldar."

No matter what I said, I wasn't getting the message across. The urge to kick something almost overwhelmed me. All this wasted time! "I need Freyad," I said. She always understood me better, and the two of them would be required anyway if I was to get Aldar arrested.

Matid might not have understood how dangerous Aldar was, but he at least sensed the urgency. "I'll take you to the royal manor immediately. She should be back soon."

"Thank you." I headed for the stairs, eager to leave the dark, damp prison behind me.

"Queen Jiara!" called Jonas from his cell. We were far enough away that his face was mostly shadows. I expected him to plead with me to free him—something I didn't have time for now—but all he said was, "You must stop the translator. Please."

I nodded. "I will."

I paced my suite, wandering from one room to the next, waiting for Matid and Freyad to arrive. Finally, a half hour after being left there by Matid, there was a knock.

My hand froze on the knob. "Who's there?"

"Freyad."

I strode forward, ready to open the door, but then I remembered not only Matid trusted Aldar. "Only Freyad?"

"Freyad and Matid. That's all," came the curious sounding response.

My hand fumbled with the door, and Freyad hurried into the room, looking me up and down. "What's wrong? Matid said you visited the prisoner again, and now there's a problem with you and Aldar."

I closed the door behind them, then leaned on it while I indicated they should sit at the table with me. I wasted no time but began my story with the bladeleaf poisoning, which both had witnessed. I told them about Aldar teaching me incorrectly, about him discussing with part of the Grand Council in secret, and finally about him meeting the man in the forest and the contents of the letter. Throughout the conversation, I kept a close look on their faces to make sure they understood me. Sometimes only one of them did, then the other helped out.

When I finished, the two guards conferred so quickly, I couldn't follow them.

"You're sure it was Aldar?" Freyad asked me suddenly, her eyes searching mine.

"Yes. I'm sure."

She put a hand on my shoulder and considered for a moment. "We cannot trust the Stärklandish prisoner"—I opened my mouth to contradict her, but she continued—"but we leave for Gluwfyall to meet Raffar in the morning anyway. That's good. If there's a chance of danger to you in Baaldarstad, it's better to be far away. A scholar can give us an official translation of this letter when we arrive."

That all sounded good, but what damage might Aldar do while we were gone? "But Aldar—"

She sighed. "I may not trust the prisoner, but I trust you, Queen Jiara. If you say it was Aldar, then it was him. And this letter is definitely Stärklandish. This is no small matter—Farnskag's security is at stake. To protect the country, we have no choice but to arrest him and get to the bottom of the matter."

Matid swallowed as she said that, and his gaze sought out the floor, but he nodded as well. "There's no sense in waiting," he said with a fortifying breath as he stood up. "I'll put together a team and take him somewhere secure." He shared a last look with Freyad, then he squared his shoulders and left the royal suite.

Freyad agreed to remain in my chambers until we received the confirmation that Aldar had been apprehended. Just knowing Matid was on the way to arrest him made a massive weight evaporate from my shoulders. Finally, after all this time searching, things were going to turn out all right. For just a moment, I left Freyad in the sitting room to stand before my blocks for the gods. "My heart in your hands." And then, softly, so Freyad couldn't hear me, I whispered, "I think we've done it, Scilla. I think we've found your killer."

My stomach twisted a little at the thought that Aldar's tattoo did not match the witness's drawing. But he was clearly involved. And if he'd given someone else the task of killing my sister, we'd get the information out of him. Both Aldar and the assassin would be punished, and Scilla—and my family—would be free.

For the first time in weeks, a bright and beautiful hope blossomed in my heart.

But within an hour, Matid returned to the royal manor, and the horror on his face said it all.

"Aldar is gone."

CHAPTER 26

When the sun's rays filtered through the shutters, I jumped out of bed and nearly stumbled over Freyad, who'd had a cot brought in to be sure I was protected while I slept. I'd tossed and turned half the night, livid at myself for not acting on my suspicions earlier.

When there was a knock at the door, I nearly jumped out of my skin.

"A letter, Your Majesty."

I clambered back onto my bed and tore it open. It was from Pia! As Freyad organized her things, I devoured, slowly like always, every word from my friend.

I loved the sketch of you riding an elephant bird. I knew you'd manage there! Sorry for the short note. I don't have much time to write. I don't have much time for anything now, but the reason is the best I could imagine. Our baby is here. I'm fine and our daughter is perfect. We named her Giaah.

My jaw dropped. *Giaah* was a word in Farnskag. It meant joy.

We chose it to honor King Raffar, for supporting you when

you decided to bring me to Flissina. And to honor you. It is no coincidence that Giaah sounds a bit like Jiara.

We pray every day for Scilla and your family, and I hope with all my heart you'll visit and see our little treasure soon.

Where had the time gone? When I'd last seen Pia, her stomach had been flat. And now her daughter had been born.

In all that time, I'd made progress, but still hadn't taken Scilla's murderer into custody.

But I did know more. And we had a plan. Pressing Pia's letter to my heart, I focused on her good news, and on the fact that we were journeying to meet Raffar today. We'd increase the distance between me and my traitorous translator. And although it filled me with guilt to think it, maybe it would even take Scilla a while to find me again.

Servants carried my trunks downstairs, two carriages were filled, and Freyad, Matid, and I prepared to head north to Gluwfyall with a small guard. A few warriors who knew about Aldar remained in Baaldarstad and had been sworn to secrecy. If he were to show up, they would arrest him on sight, but quietly. Until the charges were confirmed, they didn't want to risk ruining his reputation. Especially not since he was the king's cousin.

Freyad was to ride in the carriage with me, and she embraced Linnd for the third time since we'd met in front of the manor. When the two finally parted, Linnd grunted, "Queen Jiara, you have to stop taking my wife away from me."

I bowed to Linnd, and kept my face appropriately queenly. "Please accept my apologies."

She scowled, but her eyes sparkled at me. Then she gave Freyad one last kiss. "Take her to the Lake of Nine Sisters. She'll like it."

I climbed into the carriage. When Freyad made herself comfortable across from me, I asked, "What was that about the lake?"

She waved out the window to those seeing us off and mumbled something about a little lake I might get to see while I was in Gluwfyall. I waved also, to the servants I'd come to respect, to the townspeople who had—mostly—accepted me, despite my foreignness. But I was also glad. Freyad had to leave her wife, but I was going to see my husband, and get away from the mistrust and fear Aldar had instilled in me here.

Freyad and I chatted about which design she should choose for a hair clip for Linnd for their upcoming anniversary, then she told me about the area we'd be visiting—she was obviously trying to keep my mind off my worries. I gave in and listened to her tales, imagining a lake as big as Azzaria's sea, with a horizon that stretched on forever. I tried to concentrate on the names and physical descriptions Freyad recited—important people I'd meet. Learning them now would make it easier when I met them, but instead, water sparkled in my mind. Waves rushed to shore. Whales leaped into the air, twisted and crashed down, spray exploding everywhere.

My lake fantasy was silly, but even it couldn't prevent a part of my mind from circling back to Aldar. Being absent from Baaldarstad might protect me from danger, but it also meant we could no longer keep an eye out for him. Freyad and I would tell Raffar everything as soon as we arrived, and we had the documents with us to prove it. We'd persuade Raffar to react quickly, from Gluwfyall even.

Despite the light topics Freyad continued to bring up, her tight expression showed she couldn't free her mind of Aldar either, and she eventually gave up on small talk. We sat silently in the lurching carriage, both lost in our thoughts. We could only hope we'd catch the king's dangerous cousin, and that it would be soon enough.

———————

A violent, two-day storm that toppled trees and flooded dips in the road imprisoned us in one of the towns along the way, so reaching Gluwfyall took longer than planned. I spent the hours we were trapped in guest houses poring over the book on Watchers I'd brought with me, including asking Freyad for help. And maybe, just maybe, my perpetually strained eyes were worth it. The woman who had given tattoos was called a *devsiin kahngaad*. But the word meant far more than I'd thought. A *kahngaad* was someone with a special connection to the Watchers. They lived outside of town in order to be uninterrupted in their connection to the world, and to the Watchers. We'd never consulted one about Scilla's murderer. Now we knew that Aldar was involved, but not where he was. Maybe a *kahngaad* could help. We were too far from the woman in Baaldarstad, but Freyad said there was another, a far more powerful one, not far from where we'd meet Raffar.

On our last day of travel, tree trunks and splintered branches blocked the hilly road for miles. Without clearing a path, there was no way for the carriages to pass. The guards dismounted and tied their birds to the rear carriage. Freyad and I hopped out. Not including the drivers, everyone helped drag the debris from our path as we inched forward. I'd never been so exhausted in my life, but even that couldn't prevent me from spending every second cursing the additional time before we could warn Raffar about his cousin.

We reached Gluwfyall shortly before dinner. The town was so different from Baaldarstad that it was hard to believe they were in the same country. Instead of a flat town surrounding a monolith, Gluwfyall was a half-circle on the shore of a small lake. Beyond the lake, jagged mountains rose up, separating Farnskag from Svertya. Despite its small size, the smooth expanse of water, so similar to Azzaria's sea, brought tears to my eyes. Our driver rushed through town to a large home just off the shore.

Freyad promised she'd have someone send for Raffar and would come by within a half hour. Then the guards went to their quarters as a servant led me up a wide, elegant, yet creaky stairway and down a hallway decorated with alternating leaf and tree patterns and landscape paintings. He let me in to the suite Raffar had been using since he'd arrived, and left me in peace.

Being alone, for the first time in days and far from the dangers of Baaldarstad, was like floating on the quietest canal in a *tagarro* boat. Every bit of me relaxed. My limbs tired and sore, I trudged around the small suite: a bedroom, a sitting room with a desk and a hard sofa, a washroom. A large window facing the lake. The fact that I didn't run there immediately was proof of my exhaustion.

Raffar's belongings were scattered throughout the rooms. I trailed a finger along his shaving instruments, pressed my face into one of his tunics.

It smelled much better than I did.

My skin was sweaty; my hair was tangled; and my arms, legs, and back ached so badly, I walked with a stoop like an old woman. I never wanted to see another branch again. My body begged for a bed. I sniffed my own tunic. Maybe a bath before bed.

I peeked into the bathroom again. There was a tub. I'd have to order water right away, before I fell asleep.

"Jiara!"

I spun around.

Raffar's teeth gleamed white in contrast to the tattoos on his face. My mouth curled upward at the mere sight of him. He strode to me, and his big hands grasped my shoulders. The warm heaviness drew me to him, and he pulled me to his chest.

"I missed you, wife," he said. "I know we haven't shared the manor very long, but still, I missed you."

I smiled against his chest. "I missed you too." His chest felt so good under my hands. I had the urge to—no. I forced that urge away with the practice of the past months. He wanted to wait.

Raffar's heart beat against me. His hand stroked my back, then my head, and I snuggled closer despite myself. He sighed, but like always, pushed me back. Finally, he brushed my jaw with his thumb. His eyes took on an excited glint, and he spoke so quickly, I had to laugh.

"You forget to speak slowly for me," I said.

With a short shake of his head, he grinned. "Sorry. I said, I think you will like the festival tonight."

Festival? Tonight? What Freyad and I had to say was going to crush him—how could we go to a festival? My muscles grew heavier, if that was even possible. I tugged Raffar by the hand from the washroom so I could sink onto the sofa. As he settled next to me, my eyes drifted shut, and I tried to imagine myself greeting hundreds of strangers, listening to chants and watching fern dances all evening long and pretending everything was all right.

"Wait," I said, "Freyad will come. We have something very important."

Before he could respond, a knock sounded at the door. Raffar stared at me for a second, then he opened it. He greeted Freyad with the *gakh* and whispered something that sounded like thanks for keeping me safe.

My shoulders tensed again. Aldar was Raffar's closest relative. This betrayal was going to break his heart. While Raffar and Freyad finished their greeting, I withdrew the parchments from one of my bags and sat at the table. But Freyad's expression must have given us away.

"What's wrong?" Raffar asked, looking first to Freyad and then to me. "Are you all right?"

I shook my head. "You need to know some things that happened while you were gone."

His brows creased. "What—"

With a deep breath, I told the story in chronological order. Freyad jumped in whenever the words got stuck in my head or on my tongue. How I'd noticed Aldar teaching me incorrectly, his excuse that he was trying to ensure more time in Baaldarstad, but how I'd caught him doing it just as often even after that. How I'd downplayed my knowledge of Farnskag around him. Then the discussion with Jonas and the false translations. The partial council meeting and the threat that Aldar and the other council member would "go ahead with their plan."

"Who was the other man?" he asked.

"I don't know. But he's younger than Geord. Heavyset with a wider nose." I tried to remember another specific characteristic. "A tattoo! Like a bird on the side of his face."

Raffar's jaw was made of stone, but he nodded stiffly. "All right. That sounds like Beng. But . . . not Aldar. He's my blood. We grew up together."

But I hadn't gotten to the worst part yet. I pushed the second document over to him, the letter from Stärkland. I told him how Aldar had met the foreigner and what Jonas had translated.

He rubbed his face and pulled the parchment across the table. "I know you're much better with Farnskag now, but are you sure? And this prisoner . . . we have no idea if we can tru—"

"I've ordered two translators from the university," interrupted Freyad. "They should be here within minutes."

His nod was short, his entire body tense. "I . . . it sounds terrible, but I hope you're both wrong. Aldar wouldn't do this."

My hand rubbed soothing circles over his arm. "I'm sorry,"

I said. "I liked him too. In the beginning, anyway." I imagined him joking with Raffar on the *tagarro* boat or while we were in the carriage. "He was funny. He always talked to me, gave me the feeling I wasn't alone. He even tried to keep me from making mistakes, like that time at White Mother."

"What do you mean?" he asked. "What mistake?"

Freyad squinted at me like I was the one who was confused, so I said, "He suggested I stay in the carriage so that I didn't insult anyone by gawking at White Mother."

Abruptly, Raffar turned from me to meet Freyad's eyes. Both of their jaws stiffened, then Raffar said, with barely restrained rage, "I asked him why you didn't come, and he said you didn't want to 'see the boring rock.' The guards were all talking about it, about how maybe I'd made a poor choice of wife."

My face burned and my heart stuttered. "I never said that. I may not have grown up with the Watchers, but even then, I could tell how important they are to you."

Raffar grimaced as if he were swallowing down bile. "That means he's been deceiving me—us all—for months. In little ways as well as big. I just don't understand. If he wanted to be king, why go through so much trouble? Why didn't he talk to me? Except for his years studying in Gluwfyall, we've always been close. I might have left the succession laws as they were."

There was another knock at the door, and Freyad ushered in the translators, introduced as professors from the university. One professor recited the documents written in Stärklandish, then the other took over what was in Azzarian.

With a hard swallow, Raffar gave me a short nod. The story I'd put together—all of it—was true.

My husband cleared his throat as the translators, sworn to secrecy, left the suite. "All right. We need to find him. Have two—"

"Matid and I already instructed a small team of warriors to search Baaldarstad and the surrounding area," Freyad said. "They began before we left. They'll keep it quiet until you have the chance to talk to him."

Raffar's face was like stone, but he murmured a thank you.

"And what about Jonas?" I asked. "Can you let him return to Stärkland now?"

Raffar mulled it over for a moment. "Regardless of how the prisoner said it happened, three of our soldiers were killed. I can't ignore that. Hopefully, we'll have Aldar soon, and I'll interrogate them both myself when we arrive next week." He hesitated. "No, that's too long. We must cut short our plans here." He smoothed his hand over mine. "But if all goes well, shortly after we've talked, I can send him back. Especially since it was Aldar who suggested I keep him prisoner."

We considered heading back to Baaldarstad immediately. But my guards and carriage drivers were as exhausted as I was, and Raffar said it was important to keep up appearances for at least another day or two.

There was nothing else we could do for the moment, so Freyad headed for her room. Only seconds after Raffar had closed the door behind her, another knock came.

Exhausted from the trip and the tense discussions, I

withdrew to the couch, curling as best as possible into the stiff corner.

Raffar spoke briefly with someone at the door, then slid in next to me. "That was one of the governor's aides. The festival will begin in about two hours."

The festival? After all of this?

No. For months, I'd gone to every chant, every dance, every concert, and almost every discussion at the meeting hall. Market day. Weapons training. Hospitals and schools. I'd waved, I'd let them touch my hair, I'd done the traditional *gakh* greeting. I'd smiled and smiled and smiled.

Something steely shot up from my exhausted limbs and into my back. "I can't."

"I understand how you feel, but we have to keep up appearances."

I shook my head. "No. Not today."

Raffar stared at me, his mouth slightly open. Finally, he said, as if it were obvious, "But it is the Lake of Light Festival. Most of the province will be there. Everyone will notice if you're not."

I leaned my head on the uncomfortable sofa's armrest. "I'm tired. I'm dirty. I—"

"You are beautiful."

I narrowed my eyes at him.

"It only happens once a year—"

"I can see it next year."

His jaw dropped, and panic seeped into his features. "Jiara! It's one of the most amazing—"

"Raffar! I don't want to!"

He ran a hand over his mouth. And . . . were his eyes damp?

Then he dropped from the couch and knelt on the floor in front of me. "I know I ask too much of you. And there were so many things I didn't even realize, all these months. What was going on with Aldar, how you've been watching out for me, and for our country . . . you're amazing."

My face warmed, but I didn't give in.

"A bath is already being prepared. And you can lie down for an hour before it gets dark."

"But—"

"Please, Jiara, refuse everything I ask of you the next fifty days, the next hundred even. But you will want to see this. With the way you love the water . . . I know you will. It's one of the most special events you can imagine. As if Watcher of Water itself dances for us."

Had I misunderstood his last words? The Watcher danced? Despite my exhaustion, the urge to see what he meant for myself sprouted in my soul.

Raffar took my hands in his and stared at them. He chewed on his lip and finally said, "For once, no one is asking for you to do something for Farnskag or Azzaria. Come to the festival—do it for yourself. After all that's been going on, we need some beauty in our lives."

If his eyes weren't so warm or his grip so gentle, I might have refused.

Watcher of Water dancing.

All I could say was, "All right."

CHAPTER 27

" Jiara."

Raffar's voice caressed my ears. I could listen to it all day. And he smelled so good I wanted to burrow right in. But gritty sand filled my eyes, and heavy stones weighed down my limbs. I didn't move, not even to sniff him more closely.

"Jiara, wake up. The festival."

The festival. I groaned loudly and was rewarded by Raffar's throaty laugh.

He smoothed my hair from my face and slipped his hands around mine. Then he tugged my lethargic body into a sitting position.

I slit my eyes open. "I changed my mind. I want to sleep."

"Too bad." He raised his chin at me and held out a cloak. This far north and this high up in elevation, it would be chilly in the evening. "Hurry or we'll be late."

I ignored the cloak and patted my cheeks to get the blood flowing. When that didn't work, I trudged into the washroom to throw water on my face from the basin there. And it was good I did. The looking glass showed me my hair needed brushing. Raffar never warned me; he never seemed to notice when it did.

"Jiara!"

I combed through the worst of the tangles, my hands already reaching for the cloak as I exited the washroom. We rushed from the suite and out of the house. The rear of the home opened onto a large lawn that stretched down to the shoreline. Now that the chilly air hit my cheeks, and the scent of the lake tantalized my nose, my skin began to buzz. I pulled Raffar's hand toward the water.

He grinned and asked, "Run?"

Despite my tired limbs, the water drew me. I nodded, and we jogged to the crowd waiting at the shore. My gaze flew over the mass of bodies—what if Aldar or Beng had followed us to Gluwfyall? There were so many people. He could be three paces from me and I might not notice.

As I craned my neck, citizens surged forward, all wanting to see the new queen up close. Over and over, Raffar repeated that they would get a chance for a proper greeting later. Finally, the crowd parted, allowing us to stand right next to the water. All along the lakeshore, as far as I could see, people waited, their gazes looking out over the silver-blue water.

"What kind of festival is it?" I asked. Lanterns? Boats with torches, maybe?

"Mmm," Raffar said. "Watch."

The smooth surface of the lake reflected the last light of the evening sky. Occasionally, a duck flew overhead, then one landed on the water close to us.

A flash of blue light—in the water itself, where the bird had landed.

I leaned forward, squinting to see what it was.

Raffar's hand grasped mine. Another flash a few feet to the left. Then, as if someone had lit dry grass, the lake exploded in blue light.

The entire crowd gasped and *oohed* as one. The light seemed to move in waves, randomly, lake inward on the left, lake outward on the right. When the waves met each other, it formed a ribbon of brightness, wiggling, becoming thinner. And then the waves began again somewhere else. In between the waves and ribbons were specks of light, and they moved toward each other as if seeking their own kind.

The bright blue specks and ribbons were so beautiful, so ethereal, tears sprang to my eyes as the crowd of hundreds stood, hushed in awe.

I tugged on Raffar's tunic and whispered, "What is it?"

He leaned down, and his breath tickled my ear in a way that made me wish he'd kiss it. "I don't know exactly. Some kind of tiny animal, that's what the scholars think. Every year around the end of summer, they do this. It starts slowly with patches of light—I saw them the last two nights. And then, like today, it bursts across the entire lake."

"And tomorrow?" I asked.

"By the end of tonight, it will be over. Until next year."

The swirling light captivated me in a way I'd never thought possible. In my mind, I called to Azzoro, to show him, or to thank him. Just because we weren't in Azzaria didn't mean his reach didn't extend this far.

The glorious blue glow undulated in the water. Raffar nudged me to stand in front of him. His arms encircled me, and for hours, the lake danced with light before us.

The next sensation I had was my legs being swept out from underneath me.

"What?" I asked, my eyes barely open.

I'd been sure I would stay awake all night watching the beauty in the water, but eventually, with Raffar's warm chest against my back and his arms holding me up, I must have fallen asleep.

"Time for bed," Raffar murmured.

I closed my eyes and nestled my face against his chest, and my husband carried me across the lawn to the house.

———

The next morning, my first movement confirmed it. I lived too soft a life. Every stretch of every muscle burned with the memory of bending and carrying and dragging and tossing branches. Raffar was asleep when I forced myself up and went to the window. I still wore my tunic and pants from last night. In the morning light, diaphanous mist rose from the lake. Just the sight of it made my shoulders, sore as they were, relax.

Why couldn't Baaldarstad have a lake like this?

"Was I right?" Raffar asked from bed.

I turned around. "The lights in the water last night?"

He nodded and scooted into a sitting position.

I couldn't help but smile at the gorgeous, glowing lake in my mind. "You were right."

He grinned.

"And it's only once a year?"

"Yes."

I never wanted to miss it again. "Can we come every year?"

The grin evaporated from his face. "I'd like to say yes, but it depends on the state of the country. It could be that we're needed elsewhere during the festival."

Of course. I crawled onto the bed next to him like a normal wife with a normal husband. I wanted to keep right on crawling into his arms. For a second, when our eyes met, I saw nothing but heat in them, but he blinked his desire away, and I ignored my emotions too. Between the festival and my exhaustion, we hadn't talked about the future. We were so much closer to finding Scilla's killer, but we weren't done yet. "What happens next?"

His eyes focused on something only he could see. "Freyad said once the guards find Aldar, a messenger will be sent to inform us, but now that we've changed our plans, we'll probably make it home to Baaldarstad first."

I nodded, gesturing him to go on.

"Then there will be interrogations, trials." He sighed then shook himself. "Until we leave, we're representing the monarchy. Today, we have to go on an outing planned by the governor."

Chills ran up my arms as I imagined us doing something as frivolous as sightseeing despite being so close to finding my sister's killer. I crawled under the blanket. "Isn't there anything we can do here? To help find Aldar?"

Raffar started to shrug, and I realized that he understood the importance of identifying Scilla's killer, but not the urgency. I'd avoided telling him about Azzaria's earthwalkers as long as my language skills were so poor, and if I were honest, as long as we didn't know each other well, because he might not believe me. But now he needed to hear the entire story. Haltingly, I explained about the threads to our loved ones, and the Azzarian hunger for justice. Finally, I admitted how far an earthwalker's rage could go—how Scilla had killed me in the clearing.

I lowered my eyes at Raffar's horrified expression. At first, he didn't understand, thought I must be mistaken. But he asked dozens of questions, and finally, he pulled me to him and murmured into my hair, "I'm sorry. I'm so sorry. I didn't know. How could I have known?"

I shook my head against his chest. "You couldn't. And I didn't feel comfortable explaining to Aldar about it, to get him to translate."

"Of course not. I understand." He sighed helplessly, and hugged me tighter, like he could keep Scilla away with the strength of his arms. "If I could think of anything else . . ."

I remembered the book on Watchers. "Would a *kahngaad* be able to help? Freyad said there's one somewhere around here."

Raffar straightened, leaning forward. "You're right. And she's one of Farnskag's most powerful. We could speak to her. But we can't get our hopes up too high. A *kahngaad* does their best to translate the Watchers' knowledge into a message we can understand. But their powers are limited. The Watchers don't think like we do. But still, maybe the *kahngaad* can discover some details we've missed."

Despite everything, it was still hard for me to accept the idea that the Watchers were actually here with us, so close to our lives that they saw what we were doing. But I was certainly willing to try. "Can we go today?"

Raffar nodded. "Our outing will bring us fairly close to her. I'll order the governor to make a detour."

CHAPTER 28

After a delicious breakfast of fish and some type of tiny lobster—if only the seafood in Baaldarstad tasted this good!—we both plastered on brittle, happy faces, and Raffar ushered me into a carriage for the day trip. Our visit with the *kahngaad* would have to wait for the last hours of the day. According to Raffar, twilight was when she'd have the best connection to the Watchers.

The sun was up, and the skies were cloudless. The air still had the bite of cold, and my breath formed little white puffs in front of me. Heavy cloaks kept us warm for now, but our hosts assured us it would heat up rapidly as the day went on. We'd reached the tail end of summer though, and the next weeks would see the weather cooling.

Freyad and Matid accompanied us on their elephant birds as we set out for a secret location—at least it was a secret to me. As the moments wore on and the carriage lurched up the mountainous roads, the corners of Raffar's mouth softened and turned into a real smile. Buoyed by the possibility of finding some answers from the woman who could talk to the Watchers,

I leaned my head against the edge of the window. We were doing all we could; I allowed myself to enjoy the scenery.

Finally, after an hour, we stopped at the crest of one of the foothills.

Raffar thrust open the door. "You have to see this."

I didn't even have one foot out when I gasped. The world below us had disappeared. We stood on the very top of this comparatively low mountain. Up here, cold, crisp air tickled the inside of my nose, and the leaves were beginning to turn yellow and orange. Farther to the east, jagged, rocky peaks split the countries, but below us, between this green mountain and the taller, craggy ones were nothing but clouds and fog as far as the eye could see.

"It's like the end of the world," I said.

Raffar nodded. "I've always liked coming here in the mornings. You're all alone. No one needs anything from you and the world below is blanketed in clouds, safe and perfect."

I squeezed his hand, then with the other, pointed to the fog below. "What's down there?"

He leaned forward and brushed my chin with his thumb. "*That* is the surprise. Back in the carriage with you. No peeking until we arrive."

I raised my eyebrows at him but climbed in. The elephant birds began the swaying descent through the mountain pass. As we drove, the sun burned off the fog. And when the ground finally leveled out and we rounded a corner, I saw it.

A lake. But not a small lake like the one with the lights last night. It was a sea, so huge, that were it not for the mountains on the far side, I'd have a hard time seeing the other shore. In the middle of the lake, huge pillars of stone rose up to greet the heavens. They were so tall I couldn't believe we hadn't seen them poking out through the fog.

"The Lake of Nine Sisters," Raffar said.

I inhaled a deep, damp breath and didn't bother waiting for Raffar. I threw the door open and bounded out of the carriage. With quick hops, I hurried to the pebbled shoreline.

"Nine Sisters," I repeated, and sure enough, nine tall monoliths jutted from the water.

Guards tied the elephant birds to a few of the many evergreen trees surrounding the lake. The birds picked at the grass and snapped at insects. The carriage had insulated us from the sun, but now, it pounded down. Like the others, I spread my thick cloak on the pebbles. Most of the party sat down, but Freyad and Raffar removed their shoes.

"Want to wade with us?" Raffar asked.

Water!

My shoes were off, my pants were rolled to my knees, and I was in up to my shins before they had reached the shoreline. They laughed at me, but the water on my skin was so like home that my heart swelled until it could barely fit in my chest.

With the careful way Raffar stepped over the pebbles and into the water, I almost thought his tender feet were made of the thinnest porcelain. "I know it is no ocean—"

"It's perfect," I answered.

We splashed around a little bit, then stabilized our feet in the pebbles, our heads down as we looked for colorful stones or pretty spiral shells. I showed them how to stand perfectly still until tiny minnows nibbled at our toes.

"No. No." Raffar backed out of the water. "That tickles. And . . . I don't like it."

"Baby," I sang, then winked at Freyad, who guffawed.

After a few moments, Freyad went onto the shore and sat on her cloak next to Matid.

The water was beautiful, and, after a quick question to make sure I wouldn't offend anyone, I rolled my wide pant legs higher, up to my mid thighs. If only I could swim here, but I hadn't brought a change of clothing. So, I wandered back and forth, stirring up the pebbles with my toes, imagining the press of those monoliths on my forehead. The locals probably came out here with boats sometimes just to get close to them.

Something slid along the back of my thigh, and I whirled around, my heart pounding.

But it was just a dolphin. I smiled.

Although . . . I was in a foreign land. At home, they were Azzoro's favorite pets. Could the dolphins be dangerous here?

"Do the—" I didn't know the right word, so I pointed to one—"*fish* bite?" I called.

The governor called back. "No. They usually stay away—"

The rest of his sentence was lost to water in my ears. The dolphin had nudged so hard that I went under.

I jumped up, wiping my hair from my face, blowing the water from my mouth. "I'm all right!" I waved a hand, and the others laughed on shore.

At least I had provided them with some entertainment. And the cool water was heaven in contrast to the sun on my skin. I pushed my sopping hair over my shoulder.

"Thank you, little dolphin," I said. It wasn't like I could

get any wetter. Now I had my excuse to swim. I dove under the crystal clear water, opening my eyes briefly to get a good look. Another dolphin frolicked farther away, but the first one circled me. It was slightly smaller than the dolphins near Glizerra, and its snout was longer and thinner, but something appeared stuck on it.

I came back up for air, then dove again, kicking my feet as hard as I could to catch up to it. I surfaced and the dolphin came with me, dragging with it an arm-length of net that had wound around its snout. The poor thing. It looked like it could barely get its mouth open. I cooed at the dolphin to quiet it, then pulled the twisted mesh out of a painful-looking gouge that had formed in the snout and stuffed it into my waistband so no other dolphin would get caught in it. The dolphin ducked under the surface, then burst up again, chattering as its mouth opened in what looked like a smile. I brushed against the dolphin's side with my hand.

With one strong stroke of my arms, I glided back toward the shore to where I could stand. The dolphin swam back to me, then away, then returned again, like a dog trying to convince me to play. I reached out and ran a hand along the length of its back as it circled me. If anything, these dolphins were even more playful and less fearful than those at home. The animal swam around me a second time—maybe it was enjoying this little massage.

The next circle, my hand hooked over the fin on its back, and I let it drag me a few feet through the water.

I laughed and waved to Raffar. He shook his head at my little trick, but he nodded and chuckled.

I dropped my hold on the dolphin, but it swam to me again, so I grabbed on once more.

With a swish of its tail, it dove under, pulling me with it. The water tore at me, and I couldn't even imagine how fast we were going. I opened my eyes and looked up as my lungs began to protest, but the blurred surface was farther away than I'd thought. Could I even make it up in time for a breath?

I made a whining sound and squeezed the dolphin's fin. It angled up. As soon as I broke the surface, I sucked in a huge breath.

The shore was so far away. The entire Farnskager party was standing, looking like miniature dolls, hands over their eyes to block the glare. Raffar waded into the water.

"I'm here!" I called, waving with one hand as I treaded water. "I'm fine!"

It was just going to be a long swim back to shore.

I rotated in a small circle to see where the dolphin was. Perhaps I could hitch another ride with it. But what if it took me farther into the lake? I swiveled further, and the closest monolith loomed. I was only a hundred feet from it.

I swam in that direction and pulled myself onto the base to rest before I began my journey back. Then I checked the reaction of the Farnskagers—what if I wasn't supposed to touch it? It was too far to see their facial expressions, and they always touched their monoliths, so I pressed my palms and forehead to the stone and let myself be one with the stone and the water lapping at my ankles. I thanked the gods and the Watchers that I had survived my wild ride with the dolphin. And that I'd been able to have it in the first place.

When I'd caught my breath, I dove into the water and swam at a leisurely pace back to shore. It was a long way, and as I'd discovered after the incident with the branches, my muscles had gone soft. When I arrived, breathing heavily, Raffar and Freyad waited in the water. They each grabbed one of my arms and dragged me to shore.

On land, my dripping clothes weighed as much as the monolith probably did. I let Raffar prop me up. And I couldn't keep the grin from my face. "Did you see the . . . *not fish* . . ."

"*Delfid*," Raffar supplied.

Delfid. Dolphin.

"I can't believe how fast it pulled you," Freyad said. "That could have been dangerous."

I shook my head. "I'm sorry. We were just playing, and it surprised me."

My eyes flicked to the rest of our party, some of them openmouthed. "Did I embarrass you?" I whispered to Raffar.

He shook his head. "I think they're in awe. Not many get the chance to visit one of the Nine Sisters. Or race with a dolphin."

One of the women in the party brought my cloak to me. But before she could press it around my shoulders, Freyad said, "She needs to get out of these wet clothes first."

Raffar raised his eyebrows at the thin summer clothing plastered against my body and gestured toward a tongue of forest that jutted close to the shore. His voice rough, he muttered, "Some privacy."

My guard helped me down the beach. Once out of sight of our companions, I peeled off my sopping tunic and pants and wrung them out. Freyad spread them flat on the pebbles for the sun to dry, and I wrapped myself in the cloak.

"What was it like?" Freyad asked.

"The dolphin?"

She nodded.

"Strong. Amazingly fast. A little scary. It was perfect."

After a few minutes, she pointed out over the water. "A queen who rides a dolphin has no excuse to be afraid of elephant birds."

I groaned until I laughed, and she laughed with me. I did not offer to take riding lessons.

The sun beat down, and within a half hour, my clothes were just barely damp—dry enough to put on again. Once I was dressed, we hobbled over a patch of sharp stones back to the others.

The view of the lake and the mountains beyond was magnificent, and the sight filled me with peace. Not including Scilla's murder, the gods must have blessed my life. In the months since I'd come to Farnskag, I'd come to love Raffar. I loved Freyad. I loved the towering trees and the damp air of the forests and the laundry rain the old people made from their balconies. I loved playing Capture the Queen and the looks on the soldiers' faces when I congratulated them on a job well done. If I hadn't come to Farnskag, I'd never have seen a lake explode with light. Or been pulled out to sea by a dolphin. Or felt the surface of a monolith with my forehead. And as horrible as things were with Aldar, I was doing my best for Farnskag, and I vowed to keep at it with all the strength in me.

I pulled in a deep breath of air, understanding deep in my

heart what the Farnskagers meant about being one with the world. A burst of pain zinged up from the bottom of my foot. I reached down, grasping and twisting my ankle so I could see the sole. A pointy white stone was embedded in it.

I plucked it out and was just about to toss it when Freyad said, "Stop." She wrapped her hand around mine so I couldn't accidentally drop it.

"What is it?" I asked.

"A dolphin tooth."

Scilla and I had collected ancient shark teeth on the beach as children, and Zito still kept them in a bottle in his bedroom. But they'd been black and flatter. I carefully opened my palm. This tooth was cone-shaped and white.

Freyad dragged me to Raffar and said, "Look."

I started to explain. "It's a—"

"Yours or Jiara's?" Raffar asked Freyad.

I could speak for myself. "The dolphin tooth? I stepped on it."

"It pierced her skin." Freyad said. Then she turned to me. "Not just a dolphin tooth. I believe it is Watcher of Water."

"What?" I already had Watcher of Sky and Watcher of Stone. Or they had me.

Raffar ran a hand over my damp hair and shook his head at me. "It is rare to be chosen by a second Watcher. But it is good. Put the tooth in your pocket. When we return, we can have a jeweler put a hole in it and you can wear it as a pendant."

"It's the third," I said softly. I tugged the piece of rock out from beneath my collar while Freyad beamed beside me.

His eyes snapped to mine. "Of course. You told me about your . . ."

My sister. I held my breath, hoping Scilla wouldn't see our thoughts of her as an invitation to visit. "When did it happen?"

"While you were gone. Freyad and I went into the forest to . . ." I shook my head, unable to remember the monolith's name.

Raffar uttered a long word—probably the name of the rock—then he watched me, considering. He placed both hands on my shoulders, leaned forward, and pressed his forehead to mine. He wasn't doing the *gakh*. Instead, it was like I was a monolith to be revered.

My lungs went dead and hollow.

I pushed at his chest until he was far enough away to focus on my face again. Out of the corner of my eyes, I could see that the others were staring at us. I didn't want to be treated like a big rock. "Raffar, I'm your wife."

He swallowed, and his lips formed an uncertain smile. "I . . . was just surprised. Three Watchers, and in such a short time."

He blinked over and over, and Freyad gave my upper arm a squeeze. Then she spoke in such a rush that I didn't catch most of the words. She was probably telling him about how I'd received the second one, and according to her voice, she was proud of the part she'd played.

Another stroke over my hair, and another shake of his head, and Raffar repeated himself: "Yes, it is good."

CHAPTER 29

The late afternoon sun bathed the trees in golden light as we reached the *kahngaad*'s hut several miles farther down the side of the lake. The governor's party had been sent away to take walks through the nearby wood. Raffar called a greeting through the open window.

A surprisingly young woman, maybe only a couple of years older than I was, slid open the door.

Her jaw dropped slightly. "So, the Watchers were not lying when they told me of my visitors this morning." She glared up at the sinking sun. "I was beginning to have doubts. The Watchers said nothing about them being royalty though."

Raffar bowed his head in deference. "I'm sorry to surprise you like this. We've come to ask for your help."

The *kahngaad* smirked. "None of that. You should stand tall. I am not a Watcher." Her eyes swayed to me. She smiled as if she had a secret, then she bowed her head in my direction. "Welcome, Queen Jiara."

"Thank you."

She waved at us to follow her behind her house. As in

Raffar's garden, there were several stump-like stools. She indicated we should sit.

I'd held my tongue as long as I could, but my entire body burned for answers, and I'd been waiting all day. Watchers could protect us. Maybe they could also reveal who Scilla's killer was and let us find Aldar. "My sister was murdered a few months ago. Can you help us discover who did it and where he is?"

She nodded and said, "I had heard that. I will speak to them. Please be very quiet." The woman strode to her house, where she fetched a shiny metal bowl. Then she walked to the shoreline and scooped it full of lake water. She returned to us and placed it on her lap. From a pocket, she drew a jagged rock and a tiny black stone, like one from my bracelets.

"I'm ready." She took a deep breath and closed her eyes. Tall trees in a half-circle around the yard bent gracefully back and forth as the wind across the lake picked up, and the only sound was the swishing above and the small waves crashing on the shore.

I glanced at Raffar, but he was watching the woman. She rested one hand in the water and raised the other, moving it gracefully as if tracing the swelling contours of something only she could see.

"Watcher of Water knows nothing of this crime," she murmured.

Considering where Scilla had died, that wasn't very surprising. The northwest was a dry area. The *kahngaad* groped for the polished black stone. Her other hand went straight up and pointed to the sky.

"Watcher of Sky saw it all," she said. "I will do my best to get the information you seek. Sometimes what we think of as the simplest questions are the hardest to pick out of the Watchers' knowledge." A moment later she said softly, "I see betrayal. A prison. A knife."

Her eyes squeezed more tightly closed. "Blood," she whispered. "And more blood, even since." She opened her eyes and stared at me—she knew the truth about Scilla and the earthwalkers. After a silent moment, she continued, "Back to the murder then. It's hard to see—the Watchers are not clear when it comes to appearances—but I get the feeling it was a man. A man your sister knew. One she trusted with important things."

A Farnskager man Scilla knew and trusted. How many could there be? She'd only visited a few times; she'd surely met Aldar. How many others? But the *kahngaad* hadn't said anything about the nationality yet. It still could have been someone from Loftaria or Stärkland, if all Aldar had done was arrange for it. "Was he from Farnskag?" I asked quietly, hoping my question wouldn't ruin her concentration.

Raffar watched the woman, his eyebrows knit together.

She shook her head. "I can't see. The Watchers don't see the physical differences between us. They do not understand what our clothes or hair look like." She inhaled and exhaled. "Watcher of Sky also shows me someone embracing land."

I imagined Scilla falling to the ground, a knife in her back. "The ground where my sister was found?" I asked.

"No . . ." Surprise lilted in her voice. "Elsewhere. And it is important. Keep that in mind. I have the feeling you'll need to consider it someday."

Embracing land was important? What did that even mean, and how could it have anything to do with Scilla?

Her hand rose to her forehead, and she massaged it with two fingers. "Embracing . . . grasping . . . I believe it means ownership, more than love, but it is hard to tell." The woman opened her eyes. She stared at Raffar, and slowly, a sigh escaped her lips. "Not much here . . . just . . ." The woman's back straightened. "King Raffar, I can see that you are also involved in this murder somehow."

Raffar stared sadly at the shiny black rock from the sky, cradled in her fingers.

She leaned forward in a kind of half nod. "Yes, but not directly. Not in the sense of having wanted the woman's death. Just . . . responsible . . . involved." She set the rock on her knee. "I'm sorry it is so imprecise."

If the Watchers couldn't tell the difference between one person or another, could we even ask them for help finding Aldar? "Do the Watchers see the murderer now?"

The *kahngaad* blinked several times, then she picked up the jagged rock. "Yes . . . he is outside. With another person, someone he trusts. The trees are tall and . . . I see monoliths, but I don't recognize them. Perhaps they are known in another part of Farnskag, but—"

"Could Watcher of Stone show me?" Raffar asked.

The woman's eyes flicked to the shard in Raffar's ear. She reached out the hand holding the stone. With the other, she first took my hand and placed it on hers, so it half-covered the stone. Then she did the same with Raffar's. All three of us touched the stone. My heart galloped. Any minute now, we could find out where Scilla's killer was.

"Close your eyes. I will ask where."

My eyelids slid shut. As a fuzzy picture formed, my heart lightened. It was really working. I was the forest. I saw my trees. Some were ironfern trees, some were the unbelievably tall kind Freyad had called *gigantruv*. Two figures moved among the trees. From their broad shoulders, they appeared to be men, but they were so blurred, it was impossible to see details that would make them identifiable. The focus in the vision turned to the monoliths, and the image sharpened, far clearer than the picture of the people, so short of time in this world, so transient. One gray monolith with sparkling alabaster veins came closer and closer, until my flesh hardened into granite, and I was both the ancient monolith and the girl with her palms and forehead pressed to it, her heart desperate to save her sister, her family, the world around her. The stone bored itself into my mind until I could feel the roughness against my forehead, feel its need to spring a piece of itself for the girl at its base.

"The woods!" I gasped, yanking Watcher of Stone out from under my tunic. "Near Baaldarstad. Where I got this."

"She's right," Raffar said. "I recognize it too."

The picture disappeared, and by the time I opened my eyes, Raffar was already standing up. "How certain are you that these men are there right now?"

The *kahngaad* pressed her lips together. "Time goes by differently for a Watcher than for us, so I cannot be certain. The people were there, probably yesterday or today. But whether this morning or this afternoon, or at this moment . . ." She raised her hands in defeat.

Raffar balled his fists and looked at me, his body just short of quivering with rage. "It'll take us hours to get back to Gluwfyall, so we can't head to Baaldarstad tonight. But at least it seems he's still near there. Our soldiers will find him. I'll make sure of it."

We arrived back in Gluwfyall late at night. Raffar and I had fallen asleep to the rocking of the carriage, nestled in the warmth of each other's arms. As a servant holding a candle lamp led us up the stairs, the cobwebs of sleep gradually swept from my mind. Once in our room, candles flickered on tables and windowsills, having apparently been lit in anticipation of our return.

Finding Scilla's killer was so slow, it made me want to scream sometimes. At least we knew where to look once we returned to Baaldarstad. Until then, it was more than self-ish, but I thanked the gods she hadn't been here in Gluwfyall. Hopefully, I'd gotten through to her, at least a little, and she wasn't terrorizing our family back in Glizerra.

Blood on the floor, the walls, the ceiling.

I pushed the terrible thought away. To gauge how bad she might get, I counted the weeks since Scilla had become an earthwalker.

I froze, counting the days since leaving Azzaria.

Five months had gone by since then.

After all this waiting . . . today was my birthday. Since this morning, I was eighteen years old.

I shot a quick look to Raffar, who was speaking quietly with the servant. Suddenly, it wasn't only the brisk walk up the stairs that warmed my skin.

Birthdays weren't celebrated in Farnskag like they were in Azzaria. And no one was supposed to know I hadn't turned eighteen until this day anyway. So, there would be no banquet, no gifts for the queen.

After checking with me, Raffar refused the late supper the servant had offered since we'd eaten in the carriage after meeting the *kahngaad.* Then the servant left, and we were alone.

All I could think of were the heated looks he'd given me since I'd arrived, and the careful tamping down on our feelings. I hadn't felt so conscious of us alone together since the night I'd arrived in Baaldarstad. The night he'd said he wanted to wait.

With everything going on, was it wrong of me to think of us together, to want to *be* together? Tomorrow, we'd rush to find Scilla's murderer. Did I dare steal tonight for just the two of us, to reserve one night to begin our future, instead of only looking to the tragedies in the past? Raffar flopped on his back on our bed and raised both hands to cover his eyes. He looked exhausted, but before my nerves could get the best of me, I strode to the bed.

My palms were damp, which was silly. We were married. It was a natural part of a marriage. And I wanted to. Oh, I wanted to.

I crawled across the mattress on my knees, then sat back

on my heels. This entire time, he hadn't moved. Could he have fallen asleep—

The corner of his mouth twitched.

"You're awake, aren't you?" I asked.

His eyes remained closed, but his mouth widened into a grin. "I liked knowing you were watching me. Aren't you tired?"

I straightened my shoulders, let out a sharp breath. "Today is my birthday."

Raffar's eyes popped open. "You're eighteen?"

I nodded. He sat up, the sleepiness falling from his eyes, the grin disappearing from his lips. He looked me up and down, and each stroke of his eyes made my mouth a little drier.

"It's been five months? I kept my promise to White Mother?"

"You did." I bit my lip. Knowing today was the day, brushing my hand over his felt like so much more than a caress.

"And we've had a chance to get to know each other," he breathed. His hand quivered under mine.

"Yes." I walked my fingers up his arm to his shoulder then brushed my knuckles across the stubble on his jaw.

He leaned forward, and it was as if we'd been moving under water for months, and now firm ground supported our feet again. Nothing slowed us down. Raffar plunged both hands into my hair, tangling them, drawing my face to his, making my heart pound when his lips met mine.

Everything inside me melted. I climbed onto his lap, and his mouth pressed against my neck. My lips burned as they drew across the stubble on the top of his head. But I didn't care because that burn set the rest of me on fire, and I tilted my head to kiss his ear, his jaw.

The world flipped, and I lay on my back with Raffar propped over me. I ran my hands down his shoulders and over the muscles in his back. When he pressed his body against mine, my core ached for him to be closer. I pushed up his tunic, and he sat back to remove it.

I'd seen him without his shirt before; the tattoos didn't only adorn his face. I raised a hand to trace one on his shoulder, but he distracted me by smoothing up the hem of my tunic to just above my navel.

I might have seen him without his shirt before, but he had not seen me without mine. I nodded, letting him push it up over my head, and his eyes widened at the sight of my silk undergarment, the one piece of clothing I still wore from Azzaria. I rolled to the side to let him untie it at my neck and back, and the fabric fell away.

Gently, he tugged me onto my back again, and a shuddering breath escaped his lips. "Jiara." A feather kiss to my lips. "That we can be together . . . it's so impossible, and so perfect. Sometimes it feels like a miracle."

His finger trailing from my cheek down to my collarbone and over my chest made me shiver. Then it hooked under the leather string around my neck. His head tilted to the side. "My wife. You belong to Farnskag now."

I still belonged to Azzaria, but in my heart, each country had its place. I nodded and rubbed my inner thigh against the tensed muscles of his leg. His hand stroked the side of my jawbone, and the combined stone and tooth pendant slid down my neck to lie on the bed beneath me. Now it was only Raffar and I, no countries, no Watchers, no politics. He shook his head a little bit, like he was driving away the image of the Watchers against my skin.

Then the warmth seeped back into his eyes. His lips parted, and the firm heat of his chest was on mine. Ripples of lava fanned out through my veins. I kissed him so hard, my lips pulsed, and the room spun around me. Everything external was gone, everything transformed into kisses and quick breaths and burning skin.

And I understood now why Gio and Flisessa couldn't hold themselves back, not even when they'd caused a cyclone with their love. Because Raffar and I were caught in the same whirlwind of need and heat and love. And nothing in the world could have made me stop.

———

A few hours later, in the middle of the night, the room was pitch black when fire seared my left arm. I cried out as I slapped a hand over it.

"What?" Raffar said loudly, jerking awake next to me.

Slash—another cut crossed the first one on my arm. "Stop it, Scilla!" I shouted in Azzarian.

Brightness flared, making me squint, as Raffar lit a candle on the table. "Jiara! What—" The lit candle floated from the table through the air straight for my face.

"Scilla, no!" I yelled again.

Raffar grabbed the candlestick, bracing himself against the edge of the bed. "What is this terrible magic?" he cried. The tiny flame came closer and closer to me, backing me against the headboard. Raffar struggled to pull it away, but even some-one as strong as he was could not win against an earthwalker.

My sister had killed me once already. My heart froze with fear she was here to do it again.

I shook myself—Scilla said I was the one who understood her. I had to appeal to her, pray that I'd gotten through to that rational part still left of her. I held a palm to Raffar to ask him to wait for my answer, then I continued in Azzarian. "Listen to me, Scilla! Remember how we talked? How you said I un-derstood you? I know you. You're not some monster. Even if you're angry and disappointed about what's been stolen from you, you can keep control of yourself, keep your family safe. I believe in you."

The candle stopped moving, hovering only inches from my face, so close, the warmth stung the tip of my nose. I could barely breathe. Raffar reached to snuff it between his fingers, but his hand hit an invisible barrier. The flame burned on.

I swallowed. There was something else I needed to say. Only the gods could fathom Scilla's thoughts. But I knew how I felt, how I'd felt since the day Raffar had offered his hand. "I know Raffar was supposed to be yours." For only a second, my eyes flicked to him, then they were back on the flame in front of me. "And it hurts me so much that you're gone and you never had your chance. I can understand that would make you angry. You had so many plans . . . but you have to remember that he isn't yours anymore. He's my husband now."

The flame burned higher, and I held my breath, hoping I hadn't angered her even more by saying it. But the candle didn't move.

I had to keep trying. "Scilla, I know being an earthwalker makes you confused about what's right and wrong, and your emotions must be overwhelming. I miss you so, so much. But a wicked part of me isn't only sorry about what happened, because you were right, back in Glizerra. I said Raffar looked strange and foreign, but . . . I found him attractive. And he's not foreign at all, not any more. He's careful and considerate and—Scilla, he made a *tagarro* boat for me out of butterflies, and took me to see the most beautiful lakes." Tears pricked my eyes, because for a second, I was having a normal conversation with my sister. But our situation wasn't normal at all, and she needed to understand what she could give me by sparing me, so I forced myself to keep going. "Being with him is the right thing for me. It's what I want with every last corner of my heart. Please, please don't hurt us. Don't stop us from building a future together."

I waited for my sister's reaction. Nothing happened. The candle flickered where it was, flame still high and hot so close to my face. Raffar had both hands on the candlestick again; he strained to pull it away as he stared at me with wide eyes.

Then the force holding the candle apparently vanished, and Raffar stumbled back a step. "Is it gone?" he asked.

I looked around the room, although I should have known by now that I wouldn't be able to see anything. As I was about to answer, a soft tickle brushed the back of my uninjured hand. A tear slipped down my cheek. Despite everything she'd done, she wasn't merely an earthwalker. My big sister, the real Scilla, was there too, at least for now.

"I love you, Scilla. And I promise, I haven't forgotten you."

I waited. Nothing else happened.

After a few moments of silence, Raffar repeated his question. "Is it gone?"

"I think so. We were lucky this time." I pressed a tunic he gave me against the bleeding cuts on my arm.

Raffar rubbed his hands up and down my arms as if proving to himself I was still there and in one piece. "You told me about the ghost. But—"

"It's different when you experience it. That's why I've been so desperate to find Scilla's murderer. I've been worried . . . about my family, myself, you even."

He pulled me against him, wrapped his arms around me as if he could hide me from the world. "The ghost was so strong. There was nothing I could have done."

"I know," I said, muffled against his chest. "We're doing the only thing we can. Tomorrow, we head for home . . . and we find her killer."

Fingers of ice trailed down my spine. Just because Scilla had listened to reason this time, didn't mean she would in the future. Time was running out.

Two of the guards had been sent ahead with instructions to hunt for Aldar or anyone else hanging around the monolith. On elephant birds, they could make it back before us in our slower carriages.

Now, Raffar and I were five hours from Baaldarstad, lurching along the storm-roughened road. I was determined to use as much of the trip to revel in my new husband before we arrived and chaos took over. I bit my lip, keeping my eyes trained on the trees and bushes blurring outside the window instead of imagining how my fingertips had followed the curves of his tattoos until he'd seized my wrists and kissed me senseless. My fingers itched for him. His arms, his legs, his chest. I ignored my greedy heart and slid my hands under my thighs.

Since we'd finally had our "wedding night," I tried to be the same queen everyone knew. I acted no differently than I had all along. But considering how I felt inside—all warm and relaxed and *right*—could the others tell? When the guards looked at me, could they see the joy in my eyes? How happy I was to finally have a full, real marriage? To have a love that left me grounded and dizzy and wanting?

My skills with Farnskag had improved so much, but I still had trouble when people spoke quickly or reading was required, so before we departed from Gluwfyall, Raffar had arranged for a new translator. The grandfatherly man named Greggr sat across from us in our carriage, since the other one was full of trunks. His presence was the only reason I kept my hands to myself. My cheeks warmed at the thought, and I sighed.

Raffar pulled my hand into his lap. I squeezed his fingers.

A shout echoed ahead of us, and the carriage skidded to a stop. Before we could open the door to find out what was wrong, Matid rode up to Raffar's window. "Urgent message from Baaldarstad."

Greggr and I followed Raffar out of the carriage. We stretched our legs as a guard I didn't recognize dismounted from his elephant bird. But no—those stripes on the neck seemed familiar—that was Fleetfoot, Raffar's mount.

Raffar greeted the guard as the bird rubbed its head on Raffar's shoulder. His hand absently stroked the bird's neck. His voice low, since not all of the guards knew the details, he asked, "Is Aldar in prison?"

"Your Majesty, we didn't find him at his home or in the woods. Beng either. I'm sorry. We were too late. But we have soldiers posted near the monolith and at his home and office. If he comes back, we'll get him."

Raffar frowned, and I could tell he was thinking that Aldar was too smart for that. He'd outwitted us countless other times.

The guard continued, "But that's not the reason we rode for you. A message was received last night." He handed a sheet of parchment to Raffar.

As Raffar's eyes flew over the document, the color drained from his face. Then he looked up at me, and the fear in his eyes turned my blood to ice.

"It's from Stärkland. They have declared war."

CHAPTER 30

Raffar read the short message to me. For a moment, we stood there in silence, and my stomach twisted to think of my people in danger. The soldiers, young and old, who had trained with me on the field, who'd played Capture the Queen. The guards who had accompanied me everywhere since I'd left Glizerra. But not just them. What we'd expected to happen between Azzaria and Loftaria had not come to pass. Instead, now that we were in an alliance, Azzaria would be pulled into defending Farnskag against Stärkland. And not even by the traitors Jonas had mentioned from south Stärkland. The declaration of war had come from the queen of Stärkland herself.

"The Grand Council wasn't sure how long it would take to reach you, so Geord dispatched troops to the Stundvar River at the border this morning," said the guard. "And I traveled this way to inform you."

Raffar nodded. "Good. That is as Geord and I had discussed should anything ever happen while I was away. And you brought Fleetfoot. I'll need weapons and four guards to accompany me to our army. If we leave now, we'll arrive at the border by early morning."

Leave? No! As my heart crumpled, Freyad strode forward. "I volunteer."

Raffar stopped her with a shake of his head. "You remain with Jiara."

"But—"

He didn't even look up. "That is an order. I need to know she's safe." Then he pointed to Matid and three other guards to join him. "Weapons?" he asked of them. One of them handed him a staff, a knife, and a club, and he strapped them onto his back and legs.

He strode to me and took hold of my shoulders. He opened his mouth, and nothing came out, but I knew what he meant. This was war. Finding Aldar, finding Scilla's killer, would have to wait. Regardless of the consequences.

"I understand," I said. My eyes burned like fire, but my duty was to my country now. "I'll send a message to my mother. She'll organize troops. You can be certain. Tell the Stärklandish monarch Azzaria will back us if you get the chance to negotiate."

He swallowed. "Of course."

His eyes drank me in like they'd never get the chance again, but I refused to believe it would be the last time. My heart felt like someone was wrenching it in two, and I threw myself into his arms. "Be careful."

He nuzzled the top of my head. "I will. I'm just . . . I should have been faster with the Stärklandish prisoner, shouldn't have been so blind to Aldar's deceit. Maybe it would never have come to violence."

"You can't know that. And Aldar had all of us fooled."

He sighed, and I whispered, "I love you."

"Mmm." He squeezed me so tight, I couldn't breathe. "I love you, too, Jiara. Be safe."

Then he broke free of me and swung up onto Fleetfoot. He signaled for the guards. His head high and his back straight, he didn't turn around once as they galloped off, leaving a cloud of dust in the woodsy air.

Nothing moved. It seemed like every person, every elephant bird was quiet and frozen, the only sounds the insects buzzing in the forest. But I couldn't be frozen. I had work to do.

"Freyad," I said. "We need to get to Baaldarstad immediately so I can send a request to Azzaria."

Freyad's lips were pinched together, and her eyes strayed down the road after Raffar and Matid. "Of course, Queen Jiara."

I climbed into my carriage, and Greggr followed me. Freyad and the remaining guards surrounded us on the way to town, and our driver set a brutal pace.

———

I couldn't find the official seal of Farnskag. I rummaged through the entire manor, whipping servants into a frenzy to check every nook and cranny. I found nothing. But there had to be one. To request assistance in a war, Mother would have to know the message not only came from me but was truly desired by the reigning family.

Finally, Greggr suggested I check if the registrar had an extra. We flew down the nearly empty street. Apparently, almost everyone remotely capable of fighting had left for the border. Out of breath, I yanked on the bell rope five times in quick succession. Before the door opened, Geord rushed up behind us.

"What do you need?" he asked.

The door opened, and the registrar peeked out. "Queen—"

"Do you have the seal of Farnskag?" I demanded, holding up a hand to keep Geord quiet until I'd finished with the registrar.

He blinked. "Your Farnskag is so . . . good—"

Geord's jaw dropped, then he coughed, and I would have smiled were I not in such a hurry. "Listen to me. Do you have the seal of Farnskag?" I asked again.

"Yes, of course." When he backed up, Freyad, Greggr, and I stormed into the room. The registrar raced down the hall to get the seal.

I turned my gaze to Geord. Raffar trusted him. But he'd also conducted secret talks with Aldar. By now, he realized I knew everything.

He cleared his throat. "It is not unusual for the council to meet in small groups to work on their arguments for the king."

I raised an eyebrow at him.

His back was straight, and his eyes met mine unflinchingly. "I didn't know about Aldar or Beng. I want the best for Farnskag. I won't apologize for having a different opinion than Raffar. Just because he's the king doesn't mean he's always right. I will continue to give him my opinion and continue to try to convince him to make the best decisions for our country."

What Raffar had meant, why he continued to trust the man despite their arguments, was clear now. It was just like Raffar had showed me that day. Geord's heart came through his words.

I nodded and paced the room. "I'm sending Azzaria a request for military support." Or I would if the registrar ever returned.

Geord nodded. "Thank you, Queen Jiara."

I met his gaze as I continued my pacing. "Of course."

I leaned against the wall and let my impatient foot tap, willing the registrar to hurry back. Something on the wall tickled the back of my hand. I turned; it was a bit of loose paper, a piece of a giant, detailed map of Farnskag that covered almost one entire wall. It had surely been here the last time I'd come, but I hadn't spared it a glance.

Something tucked away in my mind jumped up and waved its arms at me. Something I was supposed to remember for later.

Embracing land.

A map.

The *kahngaad.* My eyes flew over the map. What had Jonas written in his statement? That Scilla had suggested the division of two pieces of property between Farnskag and Stärkland. Three islands in a lake, in the northwest—they were easy to find on the drawing. And the second piece was a southern corner with iron ore. My eyes swept downward. As I studied the map, I realized that not only place names were listed, but people's names too.

Why would people's names be there? "Are these the names of the families who own the land?" I asked.

"More like control the land, traditionally," Freyad answered. She pointed to Baaldarstad. "See Baaldarstad and the surrounding province? It says Raffar."

I turned my attention back to the southern corner. The letters jiggled, but I finally made out Anzgar. I squeezed my eyes shut and opened them again. Then I stabbed the swaying letters with my finger. "This is Aldar's father, right?"

Freyad nodded.

Scilla had planned to trade away a lucrative portion of land owned by Aldar's family. All his anger—it wasn't just from fearing he might lose the throne someday. It was because he'd lose his family's land. Either the money or the fact that it was an heirloom.

Had Scilla known? Had Jonas?

Jonas.

A representative of the Stärklandish government was incarcerated in our prison right now. He had spoken to me before. He had wanted peace. If he still did, maybe he could help.

But first, the message to my mother. Should I ask her to send troops right away? Or merely request diplomatic assistance? I didn't want Farnskagers to die, and the same was true for Azzarians. I leaned against the registrar's high table and rubbed my forehead.

Geord sidled up next to me. His dark eyes were concerned, the skin around them etched with worry.

"Geord, you're one of the most experienced on the Grand Council."

He straightened, and his eyes widened.

"Raffar has a high opinion of you," I explained.

"Thank you, Queen Jiara."

"I can request that the Azzarian queen places political pressure on Stärkland, or I can ask her to send troops immediately."

Geord's stubble made scratching noises as he rubbed his jaw. When he stopped, he chewed on his lower lip. "Troops may mean a battle would be over more quickly. But it could potentially also result in a larger loss of life in the chaos, especially without prior coordination and the ability to communicate with one another. Raffar has always striven for peace. Surely he will try negotiations first."

My heart pounded in my throat. Geord's answer was so careful—he wasn't certain either.

The registrar bustled back into the room with wax and the royal seal.

"I will ask her to ready the troops, but to threaten Stärkland first," I said firmly.

My stomach roiled as I demanded parchment and a pen and inkwell. I took several deep breaths, but the letters kept flipping in my mind. Needing so much effort to write was madness. We didn't have that kind of time.

But . . . it didn't have to be that way. I was the queen, and I had people at my disposal.

"Greggr, I'll dictate, and you'll write."

He accepted the writing utensil and said, "Of course, Your Majesty."

Speaking slowly, I informed Mother of the threat of war. I told her we were attempting to negotiate, but asked her to send an urgent message to Stärkland, saying that she would back Farnskag if it came to an attack. Hopefully, the additional might on our side of the border would scare off the Stärklandish queen from her plans.

Once the ink was dry, the registrar melted wax for me,

and I pressed the seal of Farnskag into it. I was about to hand the letter to Freyad when I remembered something. "Azzaria is not Farnskag's only friend. Loftaria is also our ally," I said, although it felt almost like treason to me after a lifetime of deadly border skirmishes. I motioned for another sheet of parchment, and the registrar handed one over.

"Do any of you speak Loftarian?" I asked the room.

Everyone shook their heads, murmuring their dissent.

"No matter." I asked Greggr to write a similar message to Loftaria, but in Farnskag. They would have their own translators. I told him to add the line that if Farnskag fell to Stärkland, Loftaria should expect Stärklandish invaders too. Loftaria would be a simple conquest compared to Farnskag. There was no certainty that the Stärklandish army had any such plans, but inducing fear couldn't hurt.

Once the second message was also emblazoned with the royal seal, I asked Freyad, "Can you arrange for guarded messengers to travel to the Loftarian capital and to my mother?"

She snatched the letters from my hand. "Of course. I'll send the fastest teams I can find. And I'll pick you up again here in thirty minutes."

I nodded, and, along with Geord, she left the building.

I leaned against the table, and my eye fell on the map again. Jonas. There was plenty of time to check on him before Freyad returned for me. I told the registrar where I was going so my guard could find me. Then I headed for the foreign prisoner.

CHAPTER 31

The prison office was empty.

The hair on my neck stood up. Most of the guards would be on their way to the Stärklandish border. But they couldn't leave the prison completely unattended.

"Jonas of Stärkland!" I called in Azzarian from the top of the stairs.

Faint voices rose from the underground cells. "Hello! Help!" in Farnskag. "Queen Jiara!" in Azzarian.

How long had they been unguarded down there? I snatched a staff from a cabinet on the wall. The weapon under my arm, I grabbed a torch and lit it with firestone. Carefully, I eased down the stairs, and my heart stopped when I almost stepped on a figure sprawled across the last several steps. A guard, not moving. I gritted my teeth together and held my fingers in front of his mouth and nose. Nothing, but his skin was warm.

I ran back upstairs, my staff in front of me, my eyes darting everywhere at once. No one was there, so I listened intently. Was whoever had done this still around?

"Queen Jiara!" Jonas repeated. "Where guards go? Something wrong here!"

"Is anyone else down there? Other than the prisoners?" I called, ready to run in case someone came up the stairs.

"I see no one."

Jonas didn't see anyone, but it was dark down there. Still, wouldn't he have heard it if someone was walking around? Crunching on the dirt floor? I wrung my hands for a moment. It was urgent I speak with Jonas, and Freyad should be here soon anyway, so I finally sneaked back down with my torch and peeked around the corner. The cell doors were all still locked. No one stood in the hallway. I held the torch out farther into the room so that the flames illuminated the hall. There was no one.

My skin crawling in fear of whoever had killed the guard, I strode to the empty corridor in front of the cells. "How long has it been since someone was down here?" I asked in Farnskag.

Three different voices answered me, ranging from two weeks to a couple of hours. They could all still talk, so they apparently weren't dying of thirst.

"What happen to the guard? Was anyone else down here?"

A muddle of responses that all amounted to not knowing what I was talking about emanated from the cells. I stepped closer to the Stärklandish prisoner. He huddled on the dirt floor in a corner, one hand shielding his eyes against my torch's flame.

"Have you heard?" I asked. "Stärkland has declared war."

Jonas's jaw dropped, and he scrambled into a standing position. "No. No. This is not supposed to happen. We had a plan—"

"Scilla's plan? The one you mentioned in your statement?"

He nodded, then suddenly looked uncertain. "Wait. What you mean the one you mentioned? It was never discussed? I wrote it for the king."

I shook my head. "I only found the parchment a few days ago. I showed it to him, but we were out of town. The king had no chance to contact anyone in Stärkland. Before we returned, the war declaration came."

Moving stiffly, Jonas paced back and forth, rubbing his hands. "My party and I, we're missing for months. Stärkland queen must have sent requests to find out if we had arrived." He stopped and dropped to a crouch, leaning against the bars, his hands on either side of his head as it shook. "They must think King Raffar had us all killed."

"I—"

Jonas shot to his feet. "Behind you!" he yelled.

Shock stole my grip on the torch, and it plunked to the ground. I whirled around as the flame flickered in the dirt. In the now dim light, Aldar strode around a corner I hadn't noticed, tilting a staff back and forth in front of him, and my heart jumped into my throat.

He was back.

The movement of his weapon reminded me I also had one. If only I had trained with it more often, but with its length, it would be more effective than the knife strapped to my calf. I held the staff diagonally in front of me like during the practice sessions. I wasn't a skilled fighter, but I could at least use it to block his blows until Freyad came for me.

"Requests from Stärkland?" Aldar shifted to the left. "There were four of them. I managed to intercept all but the first. But that couldn't go on forever, so I finally answered the last one. I told them Raffar had all of you executed."

Aldar's eyes gleamed with pride, like he'd thought of everything. And his awful words hit me so hard I almost dropped my weapon. "But why?"

He squinted at me as if he couldn't believe I had to ask. "If Raffar is seen as incompetent, he'll be deposed. It's nothing less than he deserves . . . and it would solve all my problems."

"All your problems . . . losing the crown, losing your land."

Aldar's sudden glare could have sliced right through an ironfern tree trunk. "The land wasn't the problem. We would have been reimbursed—even for the loss of iron. Raffar is fair that way. But there are precious stones no one knows about. We can't be reimbursed for something that doesn't officially exist. I've been trading with some southern Stärklandish—"

"The south!" exclaimed Jonas. "So that's how the dissidents have been financing their fight against our queen!"

Aldar let go of the staff with one hand and held up a finger. "They said if we were willing to trade with them, they'd stop contesting possession of the Stekk Ilens islands when they came into power. It's the best thing for Farnskag."

Jonas grabbed the bars of his cell with both hands. "Those people will never come into power! The queen is too strong. They only"—he rubbed his head as he groped for the right words—"rile up some fanatics, try to convince them we should invade and take the entire western portion of Farnskag. No matter what they tell you, if the dissidents ever were successful, Stärkland would have both the islands and your land."

"Quiet!" Aldar slammed his staff against the bars, just missing Jonas's knuckles, and Jonas flinched backward.

There was no way I could overpower a man as tall and strong as Aldar. Freyad could surely do it, but I had no idea how long it would be before she arrived. No. I needed to make it out of the prison, to tell Freyad or another guard what he'd done and that he was still in Baaldarstad. I made a tiny sidestep. Maybe if I moved gradually enough, Aldar wouldn't notice me making my way toward the stairs. Jonas's eyes flicked to me, and he asked Aldar loudly, "How much money did you earn?"

He was trying to distract Aldar. Good.

"Tell me how much!" Jonas yelled, slamming his palm against the prison wall with a *whack*.

I took another step, and Aldar jabbed one end of his staff through the bars. As Jonas leaped backward, I edged a few inches farther.

"That's none of your concern. Shut up, prisoner."

"What are you going to do?" Jonas shrugged exaggeratedly. "Kill me?" He waved to the bars and made an obscene gesture.

Aldar smirked softly, dismissing him with a roll of his eyes. "I've worked so hard for this, and almost everything is in place. Once you're gone, my story will be the only story. I just had to wait until this place was nearly unguarded to tidy up the remaining mess." He turned the staff so that the sharper end faced Jonas's head. Aldar knew what he was doing; the weapon would be long enough.

I was about to make a final run for the stairs when Aldar's eyes slid to me. In the wavering light, the zigzag border on his leaf tattoo appeared to be one thick line. My breath caught, and though I knew running for help was the smart thing to do, I couldn't wait a second longer before knowing for certain. "You killed her, didn't you? Admit it," I said, my voice low and controlled.

He smiled that friendly, charming smile that had been the first other than my husband's to make me feel welcome among the Farnskagers. "We'd met on several occasions. One day, she asked my opinion on a treaty proposal. I couldn't let it happen." He wiped his brow. "I didn't let it happen."

How could he stand there so calmly? I wanted to scream, but my throat ached with the tears I held back.

"You . . ." he said, "Why did you even come to Farnskag? You were never supposed to be here. Queen Ginevora should have been so angry at the fact that Raffar wanted to propose during the mourning period that she sent him packing."

During mourning? Aldar had known about the Time of Tears?

I shook myself. Of course he had. Who else would have informed Raffar of Mother's message to come? It had obviously been simple to change the date.

Aldar sighed. "If you would have just stayed in Azzaria, you wouldn't force me to take care of you too."

"Take care of me?" I whispered as the last dredges of hope in my heart shriveled up and died.

The translator jabbed at Jonas but missed him. Then he turned to me. Aldar raised his staff, and I mirrored him. I was close to the stairs, but I'd never be able to turn and run without him striking me down. I wasn't deluded enough to think I could beat him alone in a fight.

Scilla! I shouted in my mind. It might be the last thing I would do, but I had found Scilla's killer. She needed to know.

When I didn't sense her presence, I muttered under my breath, "Scilla, did you hear that?"

Aldar shook his head and expelled a loud breath. "Crazy Azzarians . . . afraid of ghosts." With a practiced leap, he bounded forward, slamming his staff in my direction.

I thrust my weapon up to block, but his blow was so strong, my arms collapsed against my chest. Vibrations stabbed all the way to my elbows. I forced Aldar away, but he rushed me again. The staffs cracked against each other. I shoved him back once more, but I wouldn't hold out long.

"Freyad!" I yelled. "Help! Anyone!"

Jonas paced like a caged wildcat on the other side of his bars, but he couldn't do a thing to aid me. Aldar's weapon pounded in my direction again. He didn't go for my head, like I'd expected, but banged his staff against mine instead. He tilted his head to the side, his smile friendly and placating, like all those times he'd encouraged me during my lessons. My insides curled in on themselves. I took in a deep breath, ready to let out my loudest scream.

"I closed the doors upstairs," he said. "No one will hear you. And it appears you're tiring already." The *mmm* that always sounded so good coming from Raffar's lips slipped from Aldar's, and my stomach clenched again.

Slam!

My arms shuddered, but I pressed him back and shook them out. Jonas held both hands through the bars and motioned that he'd grab hold if only I could get Aldar close enough. Steeling myself, I bounded in Aldar's direction, throwing all my weight at him.

My feeble blow didn't even make him stumble. He chuckled, and furious heat shot up the back of my neck. I wanted to beat his laughter out of him. Rage boiled inside me so strong, I felt like someone else—maybe I'd become a living earthwalker after all. If I could have killed him with my stare, he would have been dead a thousand times over.

My breath caught. Me, as an earthwalker, made me think of death . . . and the Watchers. And that reminded me I still had Watcher of Water. The gods knew I was not eager to die, but no matter what Aldar did, no matter how much he hurt me, I would stay in this world. Aldar would not be rid of me, and I would make sure he was punished for his actions. Freyad would be here any moment. I just had to keep Aldar busy until she did, until she could take him captive. Scilla needed to know that Aldar had been found, and she needed to know there would be justice. I would make sure of that—no matter what it cost me now.

"You might kill us, but you think you still have a chance?" I cried, sidestepping as he made a leisurely swipe at me. "Everyone has heard the truth about you."

Aldar shook his head and expelled a *tsk* sound. "I've known Raffar all my life. Maybe a select few have been told about your 'suspicions,' but he wouldn't ruin my good reputation without speaking to me. Most likely, everyone who's heard your story will die in battle anyway."

He smacked the knuckles on my left hand so hard, needles

of pain shot up to my shoulder. When I winced, he pursed his lips. "Enough of this," he said. "I'm needed elsewhere."

He bent his legs and squared his shoulders. There was no way I'd wait for his attack. I had to make sure he didn't hurt anyone else. And he had to pay for what he'd done to my sister. "Scilla!" I screamed, running at him with all my strength. "This is for you, sister!"

Our staffs clashed, and Aldar tripped back a foot or so, but not far enough for Jonas to grasp him. A tiny grunt escaped his throat. "It's not like you can help your sister anymo . . ."

His words died off. Out of nowhere, a jagged red line etched into his skin from below his left eye to the corner of his mouth. He slapped at it, like it was a pesky mosquito.

But I knew the truth.

Egging on an earthwalker was dangerous. They were unpredictable. But she said I understood her. I could only pray she understood me, and that Aldar would remain her only target. "Again, Scilla!" I panted.

A second streak tore the right side of his face.

"Yes!" I shouted.

"What?" He turned to look behind him, and I gathered the last ounce of strength in my arms to swing the staff with all my might. He swiveled back and blocked me, but I managed to shove him a couple of steps toward Jonas's cell. Only a few inches separated him from Jonas's hands now.

Aldar braced his staff in front of his chest. His arms were strong again, and he shrugged off his uncertainty with the cuts. Like many injuries from Scilla, they were shallow and wouldn't hold him back. If only she'd kill him.

Aldar assumed a striking stance. My wobbly arms raised the staff, but it was so heavy. Blood trickling along the planes of his face, Aldar kicked at my weapon, and before I could so much as breathe, his staff came crashing down on my head.

Black and white flashes exploded behind my eyes, and I just barely heard Jonas shout, "No!"

So much pressure and pain. Shards of glass sliced down my spine, and my arms turned to mush. Aldar watched me for a second, then he carefully leaned the staff against a wall and reached behind his back. His hand reappeared with a new weapon: an ironfern wood club. From the training sessions, I knew it was the Farnskagers' preferred weapon when making a kill. I wanted to move, to crawl away, but my limbs wouldn't obey me.

"You won't succeed," I slurred, proud of myself that I managed to talk through the pain.

Aldar shrugged, and without a moment's hesitation, the club slammed down on me. A second, infinitely more terrible crunch blasted loud between my ears. Hot trails streamed from below my hair. I couldn't control my arms or legs, couldn't move even my head or neck. I leaned against the wall, sank to the floor.

Already, I could feel myself fading. I wouldn't survive Aldar's attack, but I couldn't let him out of here alive. And unless Freyad showed up right now, I only had one weapon left. My lips were thick and numb, but I managed to mumble, "Finish him, Scilla. Aldar is your killer. You can do it."

I held my breath. *Slice his neck as you once did mine, Scilla.*

A prisoner two cells down shrieked about a phantom cut on

his arm. Then Jonas cried out in pain when a red line slashed across his cheek.

I wanted to sob. What was Scilla doing?

"Focus, Scilla, please," I begged. "It's Aldar. Only Aldar."

Maybe she'd heard me, because immediately, a deep crack spread the skin from one side of Aldar's forehead to the other. Blood flowed out of it and into his eyes. His scream echoed off the walls, echoed in my slowly numbing mind.

The prison around me darkened. Had the torch gone out? My pain melted away, and it was dark and silent and still.

First, there wasn't even a speck of light, but then the familiar threads to my family and friends appeared, glowing with love in the dark. But most strongly, I saw the thread to Scilla. What had been sickly dark lightened, beginning to glow like the others.

"He killed you," I said. The lightening thread was a good sign, but it still had an oily, grimy feel to it, and she hovered in front of me, motionless. "Aldar was the one."

I expected her to explode with an earthwalker's rage, but her eyelids drooped in sadness, showing me a dejected Scilla I'd never known. "We had such a perfect idea, Jonas and I. To bring long-lasting peace. I failed. I let Aldar betray me."

"You couldn't know. Even his best friend didn't suspect."

She turned to me with a brittle smile. "I knew you understood me. I—I think I can go soon, Jiara. I think you—" Scilla shivered, and as she leaned forward, the deadly earthwalker in her took over. She scowled until I no longer recognized her face, spun around, and screamed, "Justice!" over and over, until the word was a weapon, inflicting countless deep stabs to my chest.

I ran, fell, and was suddenly swooped up by the sweet comfort of cool lake water, the beauty of twinkling stars, the silence of the grounding earth.

The Watchers.

"Not yet," I begged in a whisper, a reflex.

But a heartbeat later, I was sure they wouldn't take me against my will. Watcher of Water would not go back on its promise.

"Thank you," I said, my voice echoing in the dark. My body plunged into wetness, like I'd leaped from a cliff into a deep sapphire pool. Fluid energy rushed through me, flooding my limbs.

I ripped my eyes open. The flame of the fallen torch still burned. I blinked and blinked until the prison grew lighter. The pounding in my head receded, and I pushed myself from the floor.

It seemed only seconds had gone by here in the real world. Aldar shrieked again, and blood dripped to the floor from a new, deep gouge on his hand. Prisoners in other cells moaned and wailed in fear.

A cleansing breath as the last sensation of water on my skin faded.

Thank you, Watcher of Water.

I shook my unsteadiness away. Scilla needed her justice, and I needed to make sure Aldar was stopped. Bracing the staff horizontally in front of me, I charged Aldar as he struggled to wipe the blood from his eyes.

I struck him in the abdomen, and he stumbled backward. I thrust the weapon at him again. Two steps this time. *Whack*. Aldar's back hit the bars behind him, and Jonas's arms locked around his neck.

We had Scilla's murderer.

For a few seconds, it felt like time stopped. Like the space in the middle of the hall somehow turned blacker. Then that inky smudge swayed like waves of air on a hot day . . . into the translucent shape of a woman. Into Scilla.

"What?" growled Aldar. His eyes shot open with fear. She moved toward him, reached out a hand. It just barely brushed over his brow, but it was enough to slice another jagged cut into his flesh.

A tremble went through my arms at this version of Scilla, somehow sharper, angrier, definitely not human. Like the earthwalker from beyond, but here, in our world.

"Good. We have him, Scilla," I said. I pretended to thrust with the staff.

Aldar flinched, struggled, but Jonas held him.

For a few seconds, nothing changed, and we stood there in awe, even Aldar. Then, like watercolors melting from the page, the inky blackness drained from Scilla's form. Color returned to her sky blue dress, to her skin, to her lips, to her eyes. She didn't say a word, but that alien sharpness went away as relief seeped into her features, and affection. She looked directly at me and smiled, so beautifully, it was like a thousand loving strokes to the top of my head. My heart ached at the sight of her. Then sadness crept into her smile, but also gratefulness, understanding, and acceptance. After one last look at me, she turned to step away, her eyes taking on an eager glint. She was finally free, and she could pass to the afterlife now.

"Goodbye, Scilla."

The vision faded, faded, until I no longer felt her presence. My soul cried out at my loss, but if I managed nothing else in my life, I'd helped to save my sister. And my family.

"Queen Jiara! Where are you?"

Freyad, upstairs. A grim smile took the place of my gritted teeth. Scilla was free and now her killer would be taken into custody. Truly punished.

I turned to yell at Freyad to come help. "Down here!"

A crack sounded behind me, and a cry. Before I could see what happened, my face hit the hard-packed dirt floor.

Aldar bolted past me, up the stairs, leaving me with one final threat: "Raffar will die tomorrow."

An *oof* echoed from the stairs, then I was on my feet just in time to hear a thud and Freyad's shout. I met her halfway up.

"Are you all right? Was that Aldar?" she asked, rubbing an abrasion on her forehead, her cheek bloodied from his hand.

I nodded and caught my breath. "He admitted it. He killed Scilla. He said he'd kill Raffar."

"Kill Raffar? How?"

My heart threatened to break. Aldar couldn't kill another person I loved. "I don't know. But if we've learned one thing about him, it's that he always has a plan. We have to warn Raffar."

She gripped my sleeve. "Come with me."

I pulled back, gesturing downstairs. "Wait. We have to take

Jonas, the prisoner. He still wants peace. If anyone can convince the Stärklandish army to hold back their attack, it's him."

She considered me a moment then nodded and sprinted up the stairs for the key to free Jonas and tend to his thankfully mild injuries. Within a quarter of an hour, a new guard was posted at the prison and we'd thrown together supplies. Cloverlily and another elephant bird were saddled. With Freyad and I on one and Jonas on the other, we set off for the Stundvar River, on the border to Stärkland.

CHAPTER 32

Hours later, stiff, sore, and permeated with elephant bird stink from the all-night ride, we reached the base of a long, steep hill. The sun had risen behind us only an hour earlier, and the rumble of hundreds of voices rose before us. We were almost there. But we'd run the birds ragged to arrive so quickly, especially Cloverlily, who'd carried Freyad and me the entire time.

When the bird stumbled up the hill and almost tripped, I touched Freyad's arm from behind. "I'll walk the rest—"

"Mmm." She shook her head sharply. "Out of the question."

Cloverlily halted. The great bird stood still, listing from one side to the other. She'd ridden so hard and had nothing left in her. I patted her side.

"Go with Jonas on his mount the rest of the way," I said. The rest of the way to the battleground. The fact that I was sending Freyad into danger shredded my heart. For the first time since I'd left Pia in Flissina, I was grateful she wasn't here. Otherwise I'd have to send two dear people into danger. "You need to protect Raffar. And Jonas has to stop the Stärklandish army from attacking."

"No. King Raffar said my duty is to—"

I slid out of the saddle and onto the ground, my legs shuddering at the unaccustomed position. "Raffar is in danger! Listen to me. What if Aldar was after Linnd?"

She laid her head to the side, but didn't dismount. Her eyes narrowed. "I won't leave you defenseless."

"Cloverlily's too slow now. She can't handle any more. Please! Go protect Raffar. And Farnskag."

Still she hesitated, and the voices beyond the hill were like thunder. But there was no screaming, so hopefully, the battle hadn't yet begun. But even if it had, maybe it could be halted. Lives could be saved. I made my voice hard. "Freyad! Think of your duty! I gave you a royal order, and I'll have you thrown in prison for the rest of your life if you don't follow it."

Her forehead wrinkled. She shook her head and frowned at me. "Jiara . . . you think it's that simple? That I'm only here because it's my duty? I'm not. I *want* you safe too."

My throat constricted, and I yearned for the luxury of hiding Freyad away from the battle, along with Raffar and Matid and all the soldiers from the training field. Or a few seconds to hug her. But I swallowed, took hold of her tunic and yanked her from Cloverlily's back. At my shove, she stumbled against Jonas's bird.

I cleared my throat. "Thank you, Freyad. But I'm fine here. All the danger is that way." In the exact direction I had to send her. I flung a hand up the hill, toward the voices.

She grunted and turned her back on me, but she mounted up behind Jonas. "Find some place safe and hide," she said over her shoulder as they galloped up the hill.

Waving away the dust they'd kicked up in the air around me, I waited until they were out of sight. I brought Cloverlily to a shady grove of trees and tied her near a thick thatch of grass. She sank to the ground and snapped up some leaves. I stroked the soft plumage on her neck a few times. "You'll be fine here."

Cloverlily made a contented humming sound. I left her behind, trudging up the steep hill.

Breathing heavily, I reached the crest, and the sight iced my bones. Illuminated by the morning sun, about a quarter of a mile away stretched a huge line of people, hundreds of Farnskager soldiers with their backs to me, chanting a war cry in unison. Beyond our shouting soldiers was a shining ribbon, the Stundvar River, which served as the border between Stärkland and Farnskag. And on the other side, what was easily twice as many armed fighters. They stood like silent statues in a warrior's garden, metal armor reflecting the sunlight like mirrors, orange-and-black flags flying overhead. They looked so organized compared to our army. And formidable.

There were so many people—how was Freyad going to find Raffar in that loud, riled up crowd? One person might never manage it. She needed my help. The slaps of palms against each other echoed against the hill and hit my back as I descended. My throat pinched, and I tried to swallow down the dryness. Farnskagers were tough—with their lifetime of tattoos and battle practice, they were tougher than Azzarians, I secretly suspected—but outnumbered two to one?

At the moment, each army remained on their own side of the river. Perhaps Raffar was already negotiating. Perhaps

Jonas would make it there in time. I forced one foot in front of the other, prodded myself toward that mass of shouting, stomping bodies, and the restless army beyond it. Because it could also be that Freyad and Jonas were lost in the crowd.

I drew closer, but it was impossible to pick Raffar out of the masses, and I couldn't see Freyad or Jonas either. I was closer to the right end of the line, so I headed that way, planning to walk the entire row of soldiers until I found my husband. Maybe he could stop this whole thing if he knew about Aldar's message to the Stärklandish queen. I also had to tell him that Azzaria and Loftaria would be sending their own threats soon.

The shouting pummeled my ears and my skull until I could barely think. I asked questions, but no one could hear me, and in their battle preparation, they were so focused that I may as well have been invisible. Twice, I grabbed arms only to find strangers who stumbled back at my touch, scowling and gesturing for me to leave the area.

"King Raffar?" I shouted.

Each time, the stranger shook his head, and I walked on. Finally, I glimpsed my husband, disappearing behind a clump of bushes and accompanied by a woman I didn't recognize. Why was Raffar going away from the battlefield?

My legs shook like palm fronds in the wind, but I raced after them, following as fast as I could. What if the woman was drawing him away for Aldar?

"Raffar!" I screamed, waving, but with this many people, the Farnskager war chants were deafening, and Raffar had his back to me. He didn't turn around.

I ran on, pain pricking my side as the last few yards

disappeared under my feet. In a copse of weeping fern trees, the woman stopped and leaned against a trunk.

"Raffar!" I shouted.

My husband's eyes shot to me. "Jiara? She said you were—"

"It's a trap." My breath came in such gasps, I could barely speak. "Aldar . . . plans to kill—"

A club flew at my head, and I dove to the ground.

Beng jumped to Raffar's back and pinned one of his arms. The woman grabbed the other, yanking it up behind him at an angle that made Raffar cry out. My husband tried to shake them off, but Aldar appeared from behind a tree trunk brandishing a short knife.

The two men stared at each other. Finally, Aldar spoke: "Raffar." His eyes glimmered with tears. "I wish things could be different. You can't believe how much. But you've made it clear that you're not the right leader for Farnskag." His voice was just barely loud enough to be heard.

Thick bandages, rusty with dried blood, covered his forehead and one hand. His cheeks were still visibly marked with Scilla's anger. I pushed myself up from the ground.

"Aldar, why are you doing this?" Raffar asked, his voice cracking.

Aldar's feet stilled. His gaze softened, and his breaths seemed shallow. "You said we'd take over the continent together."

Raffar's mouth opened, but he hesitated several seconds before he finally said, "We were just children. Foolish children with foolish ideas. Farnskag has it good now. I've worked hard to give us strong allies and opportunities. Why give up our safety and prosperity? What would we gain?"

"Control. Land. Security, like we got after the war with Loftaria. If we're strong, we can gain far more opportunities than you've provided with your wife here," Aldar said, his jaw set.

"Strength? Control? What more control do we need?" Raffar's eyes were damp but angry now. "Aldar . . . all these months . . . how could you betray me? We were like brothers."

Aldar's gaze sought out the ground, then drilled into Raffar. "It was you who betrayed me first. Letting them send me off to Gluwfyall alone. You don't know what it was like. You betrayed our country and the greatness it might have achieved if we had worked together. I have to stop you from ruining everything that's good about Farnskag."

Raffar's eyes widened as Aldar drew back his throwing arm. Behind him, Beng and the woman cringed, trying to protect their heads behind Raffar's back, using my husband as a shield. I bent to draw my own knife, but Aldar kicked it from my hand, and it skidded across the dirt.

He scoffed. ". . . that you're even still here. Stupid bird was supposed to take care of you months ago."

As he advanced on Raffar, a soft breeze blew—Gio, breathing pictures of the future into my mind. If Raffar died, it would only be a matter of moments before Aldar stabbed me to death. I really didn't know how many had been told Aldar was a traitor, and hundreds could die today. Stärkland and Farnskag would be at war. Azzaria and Loftaria would be drawn in. Death would reign.

Farnskag didn't need me as queen. But it desperately needed Raffar to remain king. As Aldar thrust his arm forward, I leaped toward my husband.

When the dagger struck me, my heart stopped. A weight like a monolith bore down on my chest. I fell to the ground and looked to my torso to see the knife protruding from my body, directly over my heart. There was no breath.

The irony was a bitter herb in my mouth—that a person could be chosen by three Watchers and still be killed by a madman's blade. I'd only just begun to know my husband. I wanted to see the lights in the lake at Gluwfyall again. And walk with Freyad beneath the ironfern trees. And run and play with Pia's little girl. And despite what I'd always said, I wanted to learn to ride one of those infernal elephant birds all by myself.

Aldar's face distorted in anger and disbelief. And undeterred by my bitterness, I was grateful for one last moment of satisfaction.

You will not take my husband today.

My old translator opened his mouth. Raffar exploded, thrusting off the two traitors holding him. He dropped to the ground, bending over me. His mouth made that *mmm* sound, and it vibrated against my skin. Then he leaned back, his neck muscles straining like he was shouting. But there was no sound. He took hold of my head, lifting it, but I couldn't feel his hands on me. My skin buzzed quietly, harmlessly, while a chill seeped into my hands and feet.

Behind Raffar, Aldar bent to the ground where my knife had fallen. He picked it up.

I wanted to scream, to jump up. No! My sacrifice couldn't

be for nothing. My vision went dim like the other times I'd died. The world was quiet, dark. But this time, it was the end because the magic in my charms had already been drained.

I tried to fight the dark, but there was nothing I could grab hold of, and nothing to grab it with. There was no me. I didn't see Scilla—she had moved on—just the loving threads to Raffar and Freyad and my family. The Watchers came, comforting me, attempting to smooth my cares away.

But nothing they did could soothe my worries. I was needed in the real world. There was so much I hadn't done yet, and—

Brilliant red fire exploded from my heart and raced throughout my body. Cool water, and the energy of a windy day combined like a cleansing hurricane within me. The pain in my chest was pushed away, pushed until it shifted to my shoulder. Air wheezed like daggers into my lungs. The silence fell away, and shouts assaulted my ears. Praying I wasn't too late, I managed to cry, "Stop him!"

Like magic, a long, dark point appeared in the middle of Aldar's throat. Red blossomed there then flowed in a thick trickle down over his chest. His eyebrows moved together, and he stared at the useless knife in his hand. His eyes glazed over, and he plummeted to the ground, motionless, a javelin reaching skyward from the back of his neck. Freyad stood fifty paces behind him, shoulders heaving, teeth ground together.

In a second, Freyad and Matid and two other soldiers I recognized from Baaldarstad pounced on Beng and the woman, ramming them to the ground, jamming knees into their backs. Raffar's eyes widened when he looked back at me. "The knife . . . it was in your heart."

I looked down, and the dagger stuck out from my shoulder—not my chest. I squeezed my eyes shut, mad from the pain in my shoulder. It had pierced my heart. I knew it had. But it wasn't there now. Thank the gods.

"It moved," Raffar said. "Thank the Watchers, it moved."

Thank the Watchers? But how?

I shook my head. I didn't have the strength to tell him it couldn't have been a Watcher, that their power had all been used up.

I closed my eyes to rest. The world around me spun, and my shoulder and my throat screamed as the knife was withdrawn. Someone pressed a cloth against the wound. Water was brought to my lips, and something else, something bitter and strong. Freyad propped me up, but all I wanted to do was escape from the pain.

A foreign battle cry thundered from the far side of the river, overriding the Farnskagers' chant.

"Take care of her," Raffar said.

I opened my eyes, but he was gone.

CHAPTER 33

The shouts and claps of the war chant shook the air and vibrated in my chest. In the few moments where Raffar and I had almost died, where Aldar did die, the Farnskagers had continued their intimidation tactic. Freyad squeezed a bandage around my stinging wound and stroked my hair with her other hand. My mind buzzed dreamily like I'd had too much wine.

I was so tired . . . and the sun . . . it tumbled so beautifully through the fern fronds above. I closed my eyes to let it seep into my skin.

Another massive battle cry went up from the Stärklandish side of the river, completely drowning out the Farnskagers' chant.

I ripped my eyes open again. Raffar was gone. I'd missed something, hadn't I? My shoulder throbbed, and I wanted to close my eyes, but I grabbed Freyad's hand. "Where's Jonas? Did you tell Raffar about him?"

She winced. "No. He left too fast."

Beng and the woman were bound to a nearby tree. Matid and the others were nowhere to be seen. How long had I been out? The trees swayed more than was physically possible, and

I shook my head to clear my mind. Raffar had to be warned. "Help me up."

"You've lost a lot of blood. You're in no condition to walk."

"Then leave me. You have to take Jonas to Raffar."

She growled and gently pulled me from the ground. "Leave you. Because that worked so well the last time. Royalty," she scoffed. "A royal pain is more like it." Avoiding my sore shoulder, she gave me a hard half-hug, and her voice wavered the tiniest bit when she said: "Jiara, don't you ever make me watch you die again. Now come."

Freyad supported most of my weight as she held me in a teetering, yet standing position. After a couple of unsteady seconds, I took the cloth from her and pressed it to my shoulder myself. She steered me toward the river.

We reached the army, and Freyad commandeered a half-dozen guards I recognized from our training sessions to support me. Together, we elbowed our way through the crowd. "Move aside for Queen Jiara!" she shouted.

Far off to our right, Raffar strode alone onto a wooden bridge spanning the river.

"Let's find Jonas first," she said. "I had one of the guards keep hold of him." We headed to where Freyad had left him, only to find the soldier say he'd had to run an order down to the troops at the extreme left end and had passed Jonas on to someone else. We moved farther from the bridge.

Raffar raised a hand, and the war chant died out, bathing the plains in silence.

Across the river, the Stärklandish army parted as one, and

a stiff-backed woman wearing the armor of her soldiers strode through them and stepped onto the bridge. Behind her, the troops readied their weapons.

I took advantage of the quiet. "Jonas of Stärkland!" I yelled in Azzarian.

"Over here!" came a muffled reply.

We beelined for the sound. After pushing through another clump of Farnskager soldiers, we found Jonas, both arms wrenched behind his back by a tall, muscular soldier. Freyad signaled to the man to let him go, and Jonas shook out his arms as he hurried to us.

"There's no time to lose," I said. "To the bridge."

We hadn't yet made it to the meeting place when Jonas raised his arms and yelled toward the river, something in Stärklandish.

Raffar and the Stärklandish queen, still ten feet apart, turned to watch our approach. Before we reached them, Raffar motioned to us to stop. "Freyad, stay back with the other soldiers. No aggressive movements."

He hadn't said anything about me. With my wound, I certainly wouldn't be seen as a threat.

Freyad glared at Jonas. "You'll have to hold Queen Jiara up," she said.

Jonas didn't understand her Farnskag words, but he caught me as I slumped against him. Freyad and the other soldiers remained at the foot of the bridge. She nodded at me with teeth clenched together. Then Jonas and I joined Raffar.

I spared a glance down to the Stundvar River. The water

was low. It would be easy for the Stärklandish soldiers to rush across it and attack our army.

"What are you doing?" Raffar asked. "And who—"

There was no time for long explanations. "Two things. I informed my mother and the Loftarians. At the very least, they should send word of their support, and threatening messages to Stärkland."

He nodded. "Good. And—"

"And Jonas here is the prisoner from Stärkland. He can help."

"You brought the prisoner?" His eyes flicked between unkempt Jonas and me. "I hope you're right."

The Stärklandish queen's eyes were wide, and she leaned forward ever so slightly as she asked Jonas a question. He answered. Her shoulders drooped, and her eyes glittered.

The foreign soldiers on the other side were so close, we could see their eyes sweep from one side to the other, but they didn't change their stances.

With hands empty and outstretched, like that first time he'd walked into Mother's office requesting our betrothal, Raffar inched to the middle of the bridge. Very carefully, he said, "We do not want war."

The queen stared at him as Jonas and I followed.

"She doesn't speak Farnskag," Jonas murmured.

He scanned the crowd as if searching for a translator, but I caught his attention with a raised finger. I couldn't translate directly, but I could via Azzarian. "Jonas, you and I will make it work," I said, ignoring the wooziness in my head. "Between the two of us, we'll get messages across." I translated Raffar's words for Jonas, and he did the same for the queen.

When she reached the center, she nodded to Raffar, and then to me. Jonas handed me over to my husband and moved to the queen's side. She stretched her arm to cup his cheek and murmured to him.

"My mother," Jonas muttered, his cheeks turning a slight pink.

For a second, I closed my eyes. "He's an heir to the Stärklandish throne," I whispered in Farnskag.

"We kept the heir to the throne in our prison? For months?" Raffar rubbed his forehead. "We're lucky they didn't attack earlier."

And we were lucky Raffar had been so firm about not killing the prisoner.

As best as he could while holding me up, Raffar bowed and said how sorry he was for the horrible misunderstandings. A hot trickle seeped from my shoulder, and I gritted my teeth as I pressed the bandage against it harder. Flashing spots danced in front of my eyes. I leaned against Raffar's chest, saving my strength for speech.

Jonas and I relayed the story of Aldar's betrayal. The queen asked a question—her tone was icy—and Jonas's voice echoed it: "Where is he now?"

Raffar called to Matid, who signaled for three guards to accompany him. Moments later, they returned with Aldar's corpse. They lay it at the queen's feet. Blood covered his throat and soaked his tunic. Freyad's javelin had been removed from his neck.

Jonas gestured to Aldar's corpse as he spoke with his mother. He nodded.

"Raffar," I said, "Scilla's plan had been to offer Anzgar's lands in the south in exchange for the Stekk Ilens islands. Is it all right with you?"

He sighed. "We'd have to work out the details. But you can suggest we begin discussions."

I turned to the Stärklandish delegates. "Please tell your mother that we do not want war. We would be honored to begin the same discussions you once had with my sister. Officially now."

The corner of Jonas's mouth twitched, and he spoke with the queen. They discussed back and forth. Jonas's expression grew agitated. And all the while, that mighty army behind them looked ever readier to crush the Farnskagers. Except, we Farnskagers weren't alone.

I cleared my throat. "Jonas, both Loftaria and Azzaria are our allies. They have been informed that we may be requesting military support. I'm sure your mother would prefer to avoid war with all three countries along your entire eastern border."

A kind of hopelessness washed over Jonas's eyes when he heard that, but he translated for his mother. After a few seconds of conversation, he said, "Like King Raffar, our queen also wishes to avoid bloodshed. Since you punished the man who orchestrated the execution of our diplomatic party, she agrees to the suggestion of further talks."

For a few seconds, Raffar and the queen met each other's gazes. Raffar let his sink first, and she nodded, accepting his admission of grave error. Then she turned her back on him, like she had absolutely nothing to fear. Jonas nodded at me and followed her. She gave orders to a few of the guards at her end of the bridge. As one, the hundreds of Stärklandish soldiers turned their backs on us, too, and began to march away.

CHAPTER 34

In the three months since I'd returned Jonas to his mother, Raffar's diplomatic talks had taken him back and forth between Baaldarstad and the border to Stärkland several times. As of last week, an agreement was signed by both sides. Aldar's father had passed away the day we'd left Gluwfyall, and the remaining family members had readily agreed to give up their property—their attempt to wash the family name clean of betrayal. The three Stekk Ilens islands belonged to Farnskag, and Stärklandish pilgrims could visit them any time.

The threat of war had blown away, like storm clouds over the sea when the wind changed direction. Never had the northern continent lived in such safety.

Now, after weeks of aligning with Raffar and the other leaders, I put the finishing touches on the agenda for the first ever summit involving the leaders of Azzaria, Farnskag, Stärkland, and Loftaria. I handed it to an aide, who would make copies of it and ensure it was delivered to each country. It was amazing how much I could get done when I wasn't worrying about Scilla showing up and hurting someone, and especially without Aldar scheming to hold me back. And it was gratifying how even the most skeptical of Farnskag's citizens had begun to trust me since they'd heard about the events at the Stundvar River.

For a second, I was transported back to a time when I'd been certain I'd never come this far, to when the idea of learning Farnskag was unbelievable, to when my subjects likely considered me not very bright. I smiled, because Raffar might be advised by the Grand Council officially, but he now referred to me privately as his First Council.

"I was just given a message for you too," the aide said, as she passed me an envelope.

I steeled my back at the thought of reading, or asking the aide to read it to me. But when I opened it, my discomfort was replaced by an excited smile. Only three words were written.

"Thank you! I have to go!" I whirled around, my heart pounding as I hurried to Greggr's office, the translator's brief message clutched in my hand.

I have it.

While recovering from my injury, I'd continued studying the book on Watchers, alone in small palatable chunks, but also with Greggr. I was determined to find an explanation for my miraculous fourth survival. Eventually, I'd discovered something intriguing: a reference to a much older book—about how people change if they've been chosen by three Watchers.

I'd come to trust Greggr during my recovery, and I'd asked him to find the book. He left Baaldarstad five weeks ago, but now he was back. And he'd found it.

I reached Greggr's office slightly out of breath. Before I could raise my hand to knock, Raffar rounded the corner. As much as I wanted to talk to Greggr, Raffar had been working on something momentous for Farnskag too. "Is it done?" I asked.

He let out a contented, and exhausted sigh. "The new law of succession is signed."

I slid my arm into his. "Congratulations." Once he'd understood the extent of the opposition, he'd worked hard at convincing everyone that it was the right path for Farnskag, but he'd still been worried about whether the Grand Council would approve.

"This wasn't the way I'd imagined it, but now that Aldar and his father are gone, the council didn't have much choice."

Raffar's adopted brothers and sisters were in line for the throne. And if Raffar and I adopted someday, as was custom in Farnskag, our adopted children would be too.

My husband took hold of my hand and squeezed it. "We'll talk about that later. You received a note from Greggr?"

While I nodded, I rapped on the door with my other hand. The door *whooshed* open, as if Greggr had been hovering on the other side, just waiting for us to show up. His bright eyes said he was as eager to get to the bottom of the mystery as Raffar and I were.

He gestured for us to enter. In front of me, on a small table, lay an ancient tome, the dark-brown leather worn, the binding cracked. Greggr vibrated with excitement and greeted us with the words, "You'll never guess where I found it."

I tore my gaze from the book that could finally explain everything. "Where?"

"Loftaria." He threw his hands up. "In a private collection. It was apparently stolen from Gluwfyall during the war. The owners didn't even speak much Farnskag and had no idea what they possessed. Luckily, they were willing to part with it for a relatively low price."

If it was stolen during the war, it had happened two generations ago. For a moment, I was speechless at the thought of all the trouble and cost Greggr had gone through to find it. "Thank you. That means a lot to me."

The skin around his eyes crinkled as he smiled. Then with hands clasped together, the old man leaned forward and said with barely restrained excitement, "I read it on the way back."

I lowered myself into a chair and ran my hand over the faded, embossed lettering of the title. My throat went dry. What had Greggr found out?

Raffar moved to stand behind me, and his hands rested warm and gentle on my shoulders. "And?" he asked when my voice failed me.

"A Watcher gives a person one additional chance at life," Greggr said.

I nodded. We knew that. I'd had three. The poison, administered by Aldar while we were in Loftaria. Scilla's ghostly rage at the pond. Aldar's club crushing my skull. But I should have died a fourth time, when Aldar's blade hit my heart.

Gingerly, Greggr opened the book to a section marked with a feather then trailed a finger down the paragraphs until he reached the passage he sought. He opened his mouth . . . and gibberish came out.

My hand rose to my head, and it felt like all of my old fears about the language emerged to crash over me at once. Raffar's hands clenched my shoulders, and I turned to see his equally confused expression.

"Don't worry," Greggr said. "This book is over four centuries old. It's written in a nearly lost dialect. Probably only a handful of us can decipher it anymore."

I gestured to the page with my chin, urging him to explain.

He focused on the script beneath his finger. "Translated, it means, 'Being chosen by three Watchers is a rare occurrence indeed. Dying by injury and being brought back three times is even rarer, and it creates an unusual closeness to the Watchers.' Only two cases have been documented." He looked up, his gaze moving to Raffar. "You have heard of Grennd Orderndaag?"

"When I was younger and studied Farnskag history. She was a *kahngaad*—"

"Not exactly. We don't have a position like hers in government anymore. She lived out west nearly five hundred years ago, not far from the Stekk Ilens islands, and was responsible for ensuring that the Watchers' ideals of caring for the world around us were put into place in her region. She convinced the Farnskag king to sign a treaty with the people living in what is now northern Stärkland. She ended nearly a century of fighting. Later, she set up a transfer of grain when there was a drought."

My neck and head were hot with the pressure of comparing me to this selfless miracle worker. "But I didn't do anything like that."

"Grennd died four times in battle before the treaty was signed, protecting people, especially innocents."

I bit my lip. Dying four times and being brought back fit. But the rest sounded so much more dramatic than what I'd done.

"And the other person?" Raffar asked, oblivious to my anxiety.

"Their given name was Finnar. No family name on record."

I looked to Raffar, who shook his head to say he didn't know any details about this person.

Greggr's shoulders rose. "No one knows much about them. I assume they lived even earlier. Six, seven hundred years ago? All it says here is that they were a good person who dedicated their life to protecting animals and children, and that they also died and came back four times."

"I see the similarity, but I don't see how that really explains *why* I came back the fourth time."

Greggr clasped his hands together. "Then let me tell you the other thing these two people had in common. He flipped to another page of the book. "It says here that anyone who wore an amulet presented by either one of these people were protected in case of an accident."

Raffar leaned forward. "Protected?"

"Brought back to life. It is rumored that the amulets contained a lock of Grennd's or Finnar's hair."

"But . . . that would mean they were Watchers," I whispered.

He nodded. "Human Watchers."

"I didn't know there was such a thing," Raffar breathed.

Greggr closed the book. "No one I've talked to had ever heard of it either." He patted the faded leather cover. "But it is all in here. Being chosen by all three Watchers fundamentally changes a person deep inside, brings a nearness to death, to the realm where the Watchers exist. A person chosen by all three Watchers, and brought back by all three Watchers, *becomes* a Watcher themselves."

My head spun at the thought. I was supposed to be able to save people? How could that be when I felt exactly the same?

I smoothed a strand of hair from my face. The mere idea was preposterous . . . but if there was even the slightest possibility it might be true, I'd have to try. A disbelieving breath escaped my lips as I remembered being afraid I'd have to cut my hair when I first came to Farnskag. I'd shave it all off to give everyone I cared about lockets if there was a chance to protect them. Raffar. Freyad and Linnd. Greggr. Matid.

My family. Pia and her family.

The children who played Capture the Queen on the training field with me.

The more I considered it, the more people I wanted to protect.

But then I had a terrible thought. "These human Watchers. They weren't immortal, were they?"

"No. According to the histories, Grennd died an old woman surrounded by children and grandchildren. And Finnar seems to have died of lung fever."

So, not immortal. I exhaled in relief. The thought of continuing on forever while my loved ones left our world made my stomach cramp. But all that didn't matter if it wasn't even true. If I were a Watcher, wouldn't I *feel* different? I pushed back my chair, stood and paced to the door and back. "What you said doesn't fit for me. I haven't changed deep inside. I'm still the same Jiara."

Raffar caught me mid-pace and put his arms around me. "But you have changed. What you told me about talking to your sister. You were close to death, just like Greggr said."

"There's no way I can do all of these things Grennd did!" I cried. It was like a fairy tale. Too unbelievable. And too much pressure.

"You don't have worry about that," Raffar said. "You don't have to be anything but who you already are."

"But Grennd was this amazing woman who 'ensured the Watchers' ideals were put into place.' I'm just . . ." Just a girl who still employed a translator because she couldn't read and write well, who would probably still be wandering the halls of her mother's palace if Raffar hadn't offered to marry her.

Raffar leaned back and tilted his head to the side. "Mmm . . ." The sound tickled the pit of my stomach, like it always did when he used the Farnskager non-word. Then his arms crushed me in a hug. "Don't you see? This always thinking you should be doing more . . . it's exactly why you were chosen in the first place. There is no 'just' when it comes to describing you, Jiara."

I nuzzled against Raffar's leather tunic and shook my head at his confidence in me.

Me? A Watcher? It was unbelievable.

Greggr cleared his throat. "When it comes to the Watchers, there are few things we can truly know. But in this case, there is something you could do to test it."

All at once, I felt the pressure of the knife strapped to my leg. Greggr was right. I could test his theory, right here and now. I pushed Raffar an arm's length away, withdrew my knife, and sliced off a chunk of my hair. Greggr understood my intention immediately, jumped up, rushed out of the room, and came back with a leather string. I wound it around the hair and stood before Raffar, my heart thundering in my chest. I couldn't believe I was trying this. After all this time in Farnskag, it felt blasphemous.

But it was the only way to be certain.

"Raffar, will you accept . . . this?"

He blinked at me, once, twice. "Of course," he said, his voice hushed.

I reached up to put it around his neck. Then I held my breath as he did the final check, taking hold of the string and pulling it back over his head.

He dropped his arms to his sides.

The leather string remained around his neck.

Raffar fingered the lump of hair, his jaw dropping slightly. It couldn't be.

"Try it again," I said, although I'd seen it with my own eyes.

Raffar grinned, pulled it over his head, and gestured to it still around his neck. Then he pulled me close for another crushing hug.

"It seems we have our answer, *Skriin* Jiara," Greggr said with a soft smile. "You are a Watcher."

I shook my head, over and over. It was impossible. "But I'm just a person."

"Ah. I think you have to look at it this way. Watcher of Stone doesn't stop being a stone. Watcher of Sky is still the sky, and Watcher of Water remains water."

I started to shrug, but he went on, "Grennd and Finnar *and you* may have become Watchers, but that doesn't mean you stop being human. You are a person who was given extra chances by the Watchers—and you managed something great for our country. What happens now? You will keep living and working and sometimes succeeding, and sometimes failing. Being a Watcher doesn't make you infallible. Grennd was not successful in all her endeavors; that's well documented. And if none of us have ever heard of Finnar, perhaps they did absolutely nothing of importance?" He shrugged, then shuffled around the table to close the ancient book. "At least not on a grand scale making them worthy of note in the histories. They might very well have made a difference in many individual lives. And that is also a worthwhile thing, is it not?"

"Of course." I wasn't sure if I could accept Greggr's explanation. But either way, it still didn't answer my original question and the reason I'd sent him to find the book in the first place. It didn't explain why Grennd or Finnar or I would be saved a fourth time.

Unless . . .

A Watcher gave a person one additional chance at life.

For me, that had happened multiple times. First—Sky, second—Stone, third—Water.

I took a deep breath and dared to let myself believe that the only explanation we had was actually the correct one.

Fourth—Me.

I was the final Watcher.

My hand rose to my chest because it went against everything I'd ever believed about myself. I was the girl given up on by one tutor after the next. I was the girl who'd rather have gone swimming than study politics and history and languages, who'd been whispered about in the palace halls as the one who wouldn't amount to anything. I was the princess who would have been jilted by lesser nobility if fate hadn't intervened.

But at the same time, something bright and new, deep in my heart, told me it must be true.

I was the final Watcher.

And when Aldar threw the knife at my heart, I'd saved myself.

EPILOGUE

My old turquoise *zintella* dress stretched across my back as I bowed before Scilla's memorial stone. It had been two years since I'd worn the traditional Azzarian dress. It was tighter across the shoulders than I remembered.

The ocean still sparkled in the distance, but the air in Glizerra was warmer and more humid than my skin chose to recall. The stacks of shells we'd placed so carefully on Scilla's memorial stone had long since fallen to the grass below. I couldn't make out Llandro's pearl in the grass. The dragonbird feather and the flowers must have blown away. Only the cup with dirt from Scilla's place of death still rested at the base of the stone. A hardy tuft of grass grew up from it.

A breeze swept up the hill from the sea and whipped at my expertly twisted hair, as if Gio had grown used to me wearing it down and wouldn't tolerate the complicated married woman's hairstyle. After all this time, my heart agreed with Gio. I breathed in the wonderful, salty sea air in thanks.

Since the day Aldar had died, I hadn't felt Scilla's phantom tickle or her angry scratch. No longer doomed as an eternal earthwalker, she had moved on. In my mind, I embraced her.

Like the Watchers, she'd also done her part in saving me, and in saving countless other lives who'd have been lost during the war that never happened.

On the way south, we'd stopped to visit Pia and Marro, and little Giaah. Even at this young age, it was obvious she'd inherited her mother's tough, adventurous streak. Her chubby legs raced me around the pools in front of their manor, over and over until I couldn't run anymore. And the ignored scrapes on her knees from tripping proved nothing was going to stop her. Before I'd left, I'd given all three of them lockets with a bit of my hair inside. I hadn't told them what it was. Just Farnskag magic that would help keep them safe.

"Jiara!" Mother trudged up the hill, the brilliant crimson of her gown, and the locket I'd presented to her, shining in the sun. She paid her respects then laid her hand on my elbow. "It's time for the banquet."

We strolled down the hill. Glizerra bustled in the background behind the palace, just as it always had, with its canals glittering in the evening sun. I stored the picture in my head to enjoy it once we were traveling north again.

Mother could have sent a servant or a guard to find me. It was good to have a moment alone with her, and I stopped and squeezed her tight.

"I've missed you too," she said, embracing me with strong arms. She leaned back and brushed away a few strands of hair that Gio had managed to free. "My brave daughter."

I toed the grass and tried not to groan, remembering how I'd sobbed the day I'd left Azzaria. "I'm not brave."

She shook her head once, sharply. "Brave and smart, and

still so foolish at the same time. You have made your place in this world. You freed Scilla. You found love. Together, my two daughters have changed the world into a better place."

My cheeks warmed at the thought of my failings over the years. "If you knew how many mistakes I've made."

"Ah." She shook her head and took me by the elbow again. "But look at what you found along the way." We strolled over the lush grass. "A marriage. A language. A people."

"Maybe."

She nodded. "Ha, maybe. And how to rule. Before you left, you said you weren't ready to be queen. Are you ready now?"

I flashed a smile at her. The answer was obvious, as if I'd known it all along. As if it would never ever change.

I was. And I was not.

Mother sighed and leaned into my ear. "I'll tell you a secret. No one is ever ready."

I couldn't help but chuckle. "No. But I'm learning."

She nodded. "As am I, little dragonbird. As am I."

ACKNOWLEDGMENTS

I've wanted to write and publish a book since I was a child, and my heart is bursting at finally having the chance. But I didn't make it this far all by myself. So many people deserve my gratitude for getting to this point.

To my editor Kelsy Thompson: thank you for being a champion of my manuscript and for teasing out so many aspects that made this book better. Working with you has been amazing!

To the Flux/North Star team: a huge thank you for all you do, including Mari Kesselring for requesting my manuscript in the first place and for acquiring it, Sarah Taplin for creating a cover I can't stop staring at because I love it so much, marketing and publicity managers Emily Temple and Megan Naidl for getting the word out, and copy editor Meredith Madyda for perfecting my sentences.

I would never have made any progress without the writing community. To my spectacularly talented CPs Gabe, Caitlin, Ali, Carissa, and Mayken: thank you for reading for me, for providing your expertise, for shaping me as a writer. I might have given up on *Dragonbird* long ago if it wasn't for your encouragement; you helped make it the book it is today.

To my wonderful beta readers and expert readers: Alechia, Emma, Sam, Linnea, Mikki, Mark, Bronson, and Linh. Thank you so much for sharing your insights and wisdom, and for helping me to make this book better than it would have been without you.

Thanks to my Twitter and online writing friends for your teachings, your support, and for sharing this journey. To Meredith and Jennifer: special thanks for helping me out with my many publishing-related questions! Thanks to the Roaring 20s and 21ders groups for sharing tips and the ups and downs of publishing our debuts.

And finally, my family deserves the most gratitude. First, to my mom for instilling a love of reading, and science fiction and fantasy in me, and for her unwavering faith that I would publish a book someday. Thank you to my dad, for giving me the love of travel, elements of which are visible in this book.

To Jayden and Marcus: thank you for coping when I was in my own little world while writing, and for putting up with my "what do you think about . . ." questions. I hope you'll see this book as proof that hard work and stubbornness can help make your dreams come true.

To my husband Christian: you are the king of the country far away I crossed the globe to be with. You deserve a towering mountain of *thank yous*, for whisking away the kids to protect my writing time and for never once making me feel like I was wasting time writing in the years before my debut novel sold. I could never have done this without your love and support. I love you.

AUTHOR'S NOTE

Concentrate.
Practice more.
Try harder.

Those are all things my loved ones who have dyslexia heard over and over. The phrases were probably meant to inspire, but instead—with no additional help—they led to frustration, shame, and dreading being called on to read aloud in school.

Four years after they began learning to read and write, they were finally tested for dyslexia, finally diagnosed. At this point, they began to get what they needed: understanding and support, including special accommodations in school. I wouldn't say school life was perfect, but it definitely improved.

In *A Dragonbird in the Fern*, Jiara is never diagnosed with dyslexia, and her society doesn't understand it. She lives her entire life mistakenly believing she isn't as smart as her siblings who can read faster and spell better.

Dyslexia has many forms and can be different for each person. Some people see moving letters and others see moving words, some see rivers of white on the page, some have trouble finding the right words when they speak. Some people with dyslexia love to read, and some hate it. And these are just a few examples of differences among my loved ones and the expert readers who helped check my book for authenticity (any mistakes that slipped through are my own). What Jiara experiences may not be the same for you or someone you know.

Recent statistics say up to twenty percent of people have some symptoms of dyslexia, and if you'd like more information on it, here are a few places to start:

International Dyslexia Association
dyslexiaida.org/dyslexia-basics

The Yale Center for Dyslexia & Creativity
dyslexia.yale.edu

Dyslexia Help at the University of Michigan
dyslexiahelp.umich.edu

Understood
www.understood.org/en

Compared to how some of my older loved ones who suspect they have dyslexia were treated in past decades, we're definitely seeing progress, and it makes sense to look for help as early as possible.

There is still a long way to go. People with dyslexia tend to have certain strengths compared to non-dyslexic people, like being better at seeing the big picture, being creative, recognizing patterns, solving problems, and more. The faster dyslexic kids are recognized and helped, the quicker they can live out these and other strengths. But we need teachers trained to recognize the signs of dyslexia, we need to provide more support and understanding to those who have it, and we need to make it so that families don't have to jump through hoops to get help for their children—so that in the future, kids don't go years thinking they must just not be very smart.

ABOUT THE AUTHOR

Laura Rueckert is a card-carrying bookworm who manages projects for an international company by day. At night, fueled by European chocolate, she transforms into a writer of young adult science fiction and fantasy novels. Laura grew up in Michigan, USA, but a whirlwind romance after college brought her to Europe. Today, she lives in Germany with her husband, two kids, and one fluffy dog.

A Dragonbird in the Fern is Laura's debut novel. You can find her online on Twitter (@LauraRueckert), Instagram (laura_rueckert_writes), and at www.laurarueckert.com.